COMPELLING INFINITY

COMPELLING INFINITY (Archivist 2)
Copyright © 2021 Meghan Ciana Doidge
Published by Old Man in the CrossWalk
Productions 2021
Salt Spring Island, BC, Canada
www.oldmaninthecrosswalk.com

Library and Archives Canada

Doidge, Meghan Ciana, 1973 —
Invoking Infinity/Meghan Ciana Doidge —
PAPERBACK EDITION
Cover design by Damonza.com
Page break by Elizabeth Mackey Graphic Design
Illustration by Nicole Deal

ISBN 978-1-989571-35-4

ARCHIVIST SERIES · BOOK 2

COMPELLING INFINITY

MEGHAN CIANA DOIDGE

Published by Old Man in the CrossWalk Productions
Salt Spring Island, BC, Canada

www.madebymeghan.ca

Compelling Infinity is the second book in the Archivist series, which is set in the same universe as the Dowser, Oracle, Reconstructionist, Amplifier, and Misfits of the Adept Universe series. While it is not necessary to read all the series, **in order to avoid spoilers** the ideal reading order of the Adept Universe is as follows:

More books in the Amplifier, Archivist, and Misfits series to follow.

More information can be found at www. madebymeghan.ca/novels

For Michael
who has waded into the darkness time and time
again to gently turn me back toward the light.

A MASKED GALA. A SOLSTICE CELEBRATION WITH THE werewolves. Broken relics and doorways leading not only to other realms, other mythical and magical creatures, but to other possible futures. For me. And maybe even for Kellan.

And, well…that's all just another day at the office for me.

Though my witch disguise really wasn't going to hold up for much longer. Because even though I'd accepted my role as head curator at the magical archive of the National Museum of Ireland, and all the duties that came with being the Archivist of the Modern World, apparently I didn't like the restrictions that came along with that. Because I couldn't build the life I truly wanted—the dream unfurling in the dark chambers of my heart—on lies and half-truths.

Which meant that a moment was looming when I'd be faced with a choice that I couldn't bear to walk away from. A choice that I might be willing to lose everything else to obtain.

CHAPTER ONE

THE GALLERY HUMMED WITH ENERGY. MAGIC GENER-
ated by dozens of elaborately masked Adepts coated
the marble floors and corniced walls as I wove my way
through the tuxedo-and-ballgown-swathed crowd that
lingered along the edges of the room. The guests all appeared thoroughly entertained, watching those dancing,
nibbling on hors d'oeuvres, and discussing the artwork
and artifacts on display.

The meticulously curated exhibit.

Even if I said so myself.

Witch lights twined around the smooth marble
columns that supported the mosaic ceiling. More lights
were strung along the casings and moldings. Every surface glinted and twinkled with pinpoints of magic. To
my sight, at least.

Crystal insisted on referring to those tiny points of
magic as fae lights or fairy lights, which was slightly too
fanciful for my taste but perfectly on theme. And since
it had taken the acting head librarian over three days
to set all those pinpoints in place, each marked with an
inked personal rune, she could call them whatever she
wished.

She had also used witch lights to frame the artwork,
to curl like tendrils around the podiums, and to line the

benches set within the niches. Pine witches accessed their power through the written word—or the scribed rune in the case of this particular casting. And Crystal had invested so much of her magic into the setting and the ambience of the gala that she'd been exhausted each night that week.

I'd been doubtful at first about all the extras the librarian had decreed necessities, thinking that the art and the artifacts on display were all that would be needed to make a fundraising gala a success. But the finished effect was stunning. Breathtaking.

With Crystal's guidance, the gala was a fairy tale that had been brought to life, then filled with magic and music and laughter.

And the crab cakes were utterly delicious as well.

My silk chiffon dress brushed against my ankles as I passed a masked couple I didn't know. Dressed almost identically in shimmering shades of deep green, the pair of witches crossed onto the small dance floor that Crystal had also insisted on.

The librarian had looked resplendent in blue silk herself when I arrived. Her blond hair was curled into tight swirls pinned to her head with more pinpoints of glistening magic. She'd replaced her typical wide-framed glasses with an intricate black-lace mask that covered most of her face, leaving her ears strikingly exposed. Then she'd deliberately emphasized that effect by lining each ear with tiny diamonds.

I'd done three circuits of the room in the first hour, greeting guests and not-so-subtly directing them to the silent auction set up at the back of the gallery, just off the hall to the kitchen. The tickets to the gala had been expensive, limited to seventy-five guests, and had sold out in under a week. Though the gallery connected the nonmagical National Museum of Ireland to the offices of the magical antiquities section of that museum, Brady had informed me that the space hadn't been used or open to the public for as long as he'd worked at the archive. The Adept public specifically. The entrance was hidden from anyone nonmagical under multiple layers of masking and distraction spells. Crystal and James had reinforced all those spells over the last week.

Crystal was still standing sentry by the collection of ancient journals and letters we'd put on display for the evening. Some of the more delicate tomes were sealed under glass, with the rest set on shelves crusted in glimmering crystals. I was surprised that the librarian was still on her feet, given the time and energy she'd put into setting up the displays and everything around them.

I was more than capable of selecting and hanging the artwork or shuffling the display cases—Crystal had changed her mind three times about the 'flow,' as she called it. But delicate, precise witch magic wasn't a talent of mine. I was the complete opposite when it came to casting, tending toward the destructive end of the scale even with something as simple as a cleaning spell.

My brother, Sisu, and I had called Dublin and Wilding Manor our home for nearly two and a half months. But when it came to pretending to be a witch when I was actually a dragon in disguise, practice apparently didn't make perfect. As such, I leaned into my strengths, focusing on collecting and containing magical artifacts and creatures, while avoiding the more basic, exceedingly useful aspects of magic. So even though I might have been the head curator of magical antiquities at the National Museum of Ireland, and I might have proposed the idea of the holiday gala as a fundraiser, it was Crystal who'd put it all together and pulled it all off.

Beautifully. I felt like I was gliding through magic with every step I took.

My brown silk dress helped, cinched at the waist, then gradually flaring over my hips, with its subtle plaid patterning and sweeping boat neckline. Yes, I felt like a princess. Even if I'd had to practice walking in heeled gold sandals.

Crystal had also insisted on the event being masked and formal, because it suited her theme: Fated Mates.

I'd had no idea a gala needed a fanciful theme, other than selecting an era or a specific branch of the magical world as a focus for the artifacts and art we'd unearthed from the archive—in the most literal sense. Every magical item that had ever been collected in Ireland was housed underneath the gallery in a cavernous but completely inviting archive space—according to me, anyway—that stretched out under the offices and the entire footprint of the main museum.

"Seventeenth century, England," Crystal murmured in a hushed, reverent tone to my right as I continued toward the back of the gallery. Her American accent stood out in a room full of Irish and British intonation.

I wanted to check on the silent-auction items. Okay, fine. I was looking for more crab cakes. I was fairly certain it was the red pepper and a touch of cayenne that made them so perfectly tasty, but I needed to test at least two or three more to know for absolute certain.

Crystal settled her hand gently on the display case she was showing to a brown-haired sorcerer in a black mask and a subtly brocaded tux. "Fated mates, yes. But doomed to never wed, never see each other beyond mere glimpses years apart. But their letters..." She sighed dramatically, splaying her fingers across her chest. "Oh, their letters. I've selected a few beautiful passages..."

Crystal was a self-proclaimed romantic, and had been insistent that the Adepts of Dublin would adore dressing up and being visually beguiled. Clearly, she was right.

I'd had to get my own dress made, not just because I didn't actually own any formal wear, but because I needed pockets. Specifically, I needed a slitted pocket so I could reach the bone blade strapped to my right thigh. Not that I was planning to stab anyone—I would have hated to accidentally splatter blood on any of the collection. But we'd gone from severely tightening security for the archive after the incidents with Rook and Ayre Byrne not even two months ago, to opening fairly widely for this event. The entrances and exits were all heavily warded, of course, and each artifact, book, and piece of vellum was tagged.

Not only had I not owned any formal wear before last week, I'd never even worn any. Not once in my twenty-five years. So I was a little...out of my comfort zone. Again. Ravine had done my hair and makeup, along with her sister River's, over three hours ago back at the manor. Things were still a bit chilly with the scion of the Byrne coven, but River and I managed to be polite. When forced to do so. Mostly for the sake of her daughter, Rook, who was spending the night with Sisu and the twins at the manor.

Ravine had insisted that I borrow the simple gold mask I currently wore, a series of thread-thin strands of yellow gold that outlined my eyes and swept up over my brow. The metal mage had created it, along with the gold masks worn by her and River, which were even more intricate pieces of art. The product of years of work and additions, laced with Ravine's unique magic.

Sisu, despite vehement protests, remained at home with Rook, and with the shapeshifter twins, Lile and

Neve. Before I'd even left for the gala, the kids had already collected every pillow and cushion to be found in the manor and created a huge, comfy fort in the living room, with the TV in easy view and multiple movies queued. The twins' father, Len Murphy, had chosen to supervise the younglings, apparently not interested in dressing up or mingling with the Adepts of Dublin. Though according to Ravine, that had more to do with the fact that Gitta, the twins' mother, was currently dating someone else. At the same time she was seeing Len.

Apparently, Ravine knew who everyone with even a mote of magical power in the city was 'riding' at any particular time.

Her word, not mine.

Metal magic and that honed sense for people's entanglements were the earth witch's self-declared specialties. Since we'd met, she had continually teased me about who my first conquest among the Dublin Adept should be—and had practically pushed me into the arms of three witches and one sorcerer in the last hour.

Unfortunately, my interest was stuck on someone else. Someone entirely unsuitable. Someone who wasn't actually available.

I'd been relieved when Kellan Conall had begun limiting his hours at the estate last month, leaving the overseeing of the ongoing renovation of the upstairs bedrooms and bathrooms to his sister Gitta, and simply dropping in to build and install woodwork and cabinets as needed. Mostly when I was at work myself.

Conall Construction had multiple projects on the go, but thankfully, they had prioritized getting me a kitchen and two working bathrooms when we'd first taken occupancy. Wilding Manor was so massive, though, that it would take years to revitalize the entire estate.

Shoving thoughts of ridiculously sexy, unexplainably powerful shapeshifters out of my mind, I distracted myself by glancing around for Ravine, finding her on the dance floor in the arms of a female werewolf I didn't know. She was sheathed in layers of black chiffon—sleeveless and practically backless—with intricate Celtic-inspired bands of gold twined around her pale-skinned arms. The metal mage's sleek, dark hair slipped and shimmered around her neck and shoulders as she moved, blunt ends barely brushing her collarbone. She winked at me, but appeared to be offishly ignoring her dance partner. Or perhaps she was just allowing herself to be admired in silence.

Gitta was also on the dance floor, wearing a green sheath that was so dark it was practically black. As she spun toward me, the fairy lights brought out hues of red from the dark-brown hair that cascaded in a shiny waterfall around her shoulders. Her spiked heels added to her already impressive height, and her lively shifter magic brushed across my upper arm as she passed. She was in the arms of an imposing Nordic-looking werewolf in his midthirties—Thurston, a newcomer to the Conall pack, and her current object of interest.

Again, all according to Ravine.

An enchanted grand piano, a cello, and a harp on loan from the Byrne coven for the evening all occupied the far corner near the hall to the kitchen and bathrooms. The silent-auction items were displayed along the same wall on the opposite side of the doorway, and I was pleased to see numerous Adepts slowly making their way along the table to bid on the items I'd collected from local Adept artisans, shops, and restaurants. Putting together the auction had given me an excuse to meet other magic users who worked and lived in the city.

The current song the magical trio was playing might have been some sort of waltz, but I honestly knew nothing about music. Or dancing. Hence my having kept to the edges of the gallery all night.

I slipped, hopefully unnoticed, behind a murmured conversation between Mesa Byrne and her son, Ridge, who were discussing an oil painting by an eighteenth-century Irish sorcerer. Tiny fairies hid among the ruins of a stone tower in the expansive landscape, whose color palette was dominated by blues, greens, and golds. According to Crystal, the archive held three of the artist's works, but the landscape was the most appropriate thematically.

Though it was rare that a piece of art appealed to me, I found myself itching to take the oil painting home and hang it in my library. Crystal had great taste. Or at least her taste apparently aligned with my own.

A ruddy-haired man stood slightly apart from Mesa and Ridge, his back to the wall and an untouched glass of champagne in his hand. Dillon Garvey, Ridge's guest. According to Ravine, again and always, their relationship was new enough that the gala was the first social function they'd attended together, and the first Adept function that Dillon had ever set foot within.

Dillon, in his midthirties, was an investigator for the Garda Siochana, the national police service of Ireland. But despite his Adept heritage—his grandmother had been a necromancer affiliated with the Byrne coven—when I'd shaken his hand at the beginning of the evening, whatever magic might still simmer within Dillon Garvey's blood had felt completely dormant.

I skirted along the silent-auction display, secretly coveting at least three items—a handblown glass vase that had been donated by a pack werewolf, a spellbook donated by Mesa Byrne, and a gift basket curated by

Cove Byrne, who ran the cafe I frequented for lunch on Tuesdays, and who had also catered the gala.

I paused by my own donation—a tour of the archive and a two-hour chat with the head curator. Namely, me. Crystal had suggested it, with her, Brady, and James each offering something relevant to their own specialties as well. I'd been surprised that Crystal thought two hours of my time would be worth anything to regular Adepts. Then I'd been flummoxed when the bid had surpassed five hundred euros within thirty minutes. It was currently sitting at a bid of fifteen hundred euros.

Kellan Conall was the current top bidder.

My heart paused for a breath, then sped up for a few beats before leveling out.

I liked Kellan's handwriting. Well formed, readable, but not fancy. The thick, steady strokes indicated a firm...

What was I doing?

Who got turned on by handwriting?

Other than me, obviously.

Kellan had been bidding against Mesa Byrne and someone named Brendan Prince for the last six bids. They'd had to flip the card over.

A small plate holding three tiny crab cakes appeared under my nose. He'd approached silently. Surrounded by the energy that teemed from every surface and every one of the eighty-plus people in the room, I hadn't picked up his magic.

Kellan.

I took the plate without thinking, then actually steeled myself before turning my attention to him. I'd already caught sight of the imposing shapeshifter multiple times in the last hour, tearing my gaze away and altering my direction each time.

Kellan leaned in to read the silent-auction card. His voice was a soft purr next to my ear, his breath whispering across my exposed neck and collarbone. "Who," he murmured, "is Brendan Prince?"

His deep, playful tone did all sorts of mushy things to my insides. I met his golden-green eyes, their color vibrant and pronounced next to his light-brown skin and darker-brown hair. He wasn't wearing a mask. I forced myself to smile even though my heart had started hammering in my chest.

Because Kellan Conall might have been imposing in construction gear. Maybe even ruggedly handsome wearing a sweater and jeans. But in a tuxedo, he was devastation. Utter wanton devastation.

According to my hormones.

Even though rationally and logically, I knew he was off-limits. For multiple reasons.

Grinning, Kellan straightened to his full height, still towering over me despite my heels.

I popped a crab cake in my mouth, making appreciative noises. Even though I'd been avoiding him all evening, he'd apparently noticed how much I liked them.

His grin widened, magic sparking in his eyes as his gaze fell to my lips. And suddenly I was the one who felt utterly wanton. And exposed.

His tux looked almost plain compared to the lavish suits a few of the sorcerers and witches had bedecked themselves in. But it was perfectly tailored across his broad shoulders, tapering down to hug his hips. He'd gone with a classic white bow tie. No embellishments or jewelry.

I'd been making an effort to not stare at him all night. But I was staring now. And Kellan was staring right back.

He'd asked me a question, but I had no idea what it was.

He'd also arrived at the gala with Bethany.

The image of the two of them together flashed in my mind, somehow freeing me from his gaze. I popped a second crab cake in my mouth. As long as I was eating, I wouldn't be saying anything stupid.

I said a lot of stupid things around Kellan Conall. Most of it weird attempts at flirting that just tumbled past my lips without conscious thought.

Bethany, sheathed in gold sequins that were only a slightly darker shade than her golden cascade of hair, was an enforcer for the Conall pack and Sisu's tutor. I was also certain that she and Kellan were together, based on having seen a sexy picture of her on his phone call display. She had looked absolutely striking next to him when they'd arrived. Perhaps her elaborate outfit was the reason he'd opted for a plain tuxedo?

I glanced toward the dance floor.

Bethany had commanded that space from the moment she'd arrived. And as far as I'd seen—because yes, I'd been watching her far too closely—she hadn't doubled up on a single partner.

My gaze shifted back to Kellan.

Bethany hadn't danced with him…

Not yet, I chided myself.

Right. And now Kellan and I were staring at each other again. His golden-green eyes crinkled at the edges, amused but fixed intently to my golden-hazel gaze. I had no idea what my expression said regarding my reaction, though.

"We dropped by the manor," Kellan said smoothly, as if we hadn't just been standing in silence for long enough for me to eat two crab cakes. "On our way here."

I blinked. "My manor?"

"Sisu tried to persuade me to bring him. Then, of course, Lile and Neve had to be bribed as well."

I wasn't surprised. "They already got three movies, two flavors of ice cream, and chocolate-chip cookies from me."

Kellan huffed. "I was forced to write out IOUs before I could leave. And the house got in on it, sealing the front door."

I nodded, though I wasn't fully listening—because standing next to him, and with him looking so devastating, I suddenly felt awkward in my dress and heels. I was perfectly covered, but with my hair up, my face, neck, and shoulders felt exposed.

In a single step, Kellan could have me in his arms, trailing kisses down my—

No. No.

Nope.

I popped the third crab cake in my mouth, chewing.

Kellan raised one eyebrow questioningly.

I'd lost track of the conversation.

Again.

I was also achingly aware that I didn't have Infinity on me, as if I needed an extra layer of defense against the onslaught that was Kellan Conall. Which, rationally, was ridiculous. I'd had to leave my personal archive in my office, because Ravine had protested when I tried to figure out how to pair my outfit with a satchel or a purse, ranting about me 'ruining the lines of the dress.'

Kellan and I were doing that staring thing again.

"So…" He cleared his throat. "Have I done something? Recently, I mean." He grinned as if joking. Except I didn't think he was.

I had no idea what he was talking about.

He nodded over my head, indicating the gala. "You're avoiding me?"

I really, really was. Because he was with Bethany. I liked Bethany, but apparently my mind and body disagreed with what that meant when it came to Kellan. "I'm working."

He nodded, tension shifting through his jaw, then softening. "I was...I thought...we talked about the gala tickets, so I dropped by to pick you up, and well..."

"I'm not a guest...I've been here for two hours already. And I don't remember you saying..." I trailed off, not at all certain what information lay in the gaps between his words.

He grinned playfully. "I might not have gotten around to asking you outright. But I thought I'd been pretty clear about my interest."

I flushed, not liking being teased. I honestly...I just really couldn't figure Kellan out. It wasn't like I was ignorant about sexual relationships, but I never really flirted. Never played games.

Feeling like a childish idiot—and not liking that feeling one bit, especially while technically at work—I stepped around him, setting my empty plate on one of the servers' trays as they hustled toward the kitchen.

Kellan instantly shifted out of my way, but I caught his tight expression as I passed. The flare of his nostrils. Angry. At himself, I thought.

I cut into the hall, the kitchen opening up to my right. It was filled with servers and Cove's assistant chef, making and plating the hors d'oeuvres.

"Dusk," Kellan murmured from a few steps behind me, "I was just asking for a dance."

He didn't raise his voice. So I pretended not to hear him. A witch didn't have the hearing of a dragon. And I had been posing successfully as a witch for nearly two months.

Very successfully, in fact. After some initial... glitches.

So I continued to pretend.

Like a coward.

I was perfectly brave, even foolhardy, when facing down a death goddess or taking on the head curator position for a major archive. And completely cowardly when dealing with Kellan Conall.

He'd bid fifteen hundred euros so far for two hours with me and a tour of the archive, yet he had a picture of Bethany clothed only in a wool blanket on his phone. Why?

I was going to just have to ask him outright.

I hadn't yet because I was a coward. I didn't want to ruin...whatever was going on between us.

Yes, that was ridiculous. Shortsighted. Indulgent.

He was also a great contractor. And I valued my relationship with the pack, run by his mother.

I had lots and lots of reasons to avoid the subject. Except dragons didn't run away from difficult situations...

So it was a good thing I was posing as a witch.

Yeah, that totally justified it.

I was thoroughly pissed at myself by the time I crossed into the darkened offices of the archive, heading for my separate office. I didn't bother with the lights.

Kellan hadn't followed me.

I passed through the wards covering my office door, crossed to the desk, and retrieved my backpack from a magically sealed drawer. I pulled my personal archive out, feeling the power contained in its leather binding and rough-edged pages gently vibrate under my touch. Then I paused to gaze out the windows, holding Infinity to my chest, seeking a moment of respite.

I realized that it was possible I was socially inept.

A soft, contented hum emanated from Infinity, soothing me.

I petted the bronzed-leather, rune-etched cover as I murmured, "I'm sorry I left you for so long."

I didn't fit.

Not among the other Adepts.

And definitely not in Dublin.

That was what this feeling was all about. That was the reason for all the confusion and social awkwardness. I adored every moment I got to spend in the archive, engaged with every artifact or spellbook that passed across my desk to be assessed and catalogued. Or, in many cases, to be sold or donated to other archives or libraries.

And I absolutely loved every floor plank, every door leading to every sprawling empty room, and every blade of grass of Wilding Manor. In just a couple of months, it already felt like home for Sisu and me.

But all the relationships I was building—all the relationships I was forced to build in order to function in Dublin—were based on one fundamental lie.

I wasn't a Godfrey witch.

I was a dragon.

And it hurt. A deep, totally psychological ache that lodged in the center of my chest every time I hid my abilities, or when I was forced to share only a perfectly curated portion of my past.

I hid myself. From Ravine. From Bethany. And most definitely from Kellan. Though logically, it shouldn't have felt even worse with him.

Logically, Kellan had his own secrets. Even his own pack seemed wary of him at times, like when he'd ripped out the heart of a celestial wolf in the forest on the Conall estate that night Ayre Byrne had gone dark.

Everyone had secrets.

I just knew in my heart, in the very essence that made me, sustained me, that my secrets were the kind that destroyed trust.

And how could I care for people if they couldn't trust me? Or vice versa?

I settled at my desk, retrieving my favorite pen from my backpack, and indulged in inking my observations of the gala so far into Infinity's pages. Just enjoying watching my words as they were absorbed greedily by my archive.

This was simple. And this was on task. I was in Dublin to work and live among the Adept. Not to forge friendships.

But…the thought of not doing so made me feel empty.

I didn't see Kellan as I crossed back into the main gallery. And yes, I looked. I was completely and utterly addicted to looking for him. But apparently, I would just keep pretending that it was his unusually powerful shape-shifter magic that drew my attention. Plus the runes I swore I'd seen etched across his chest the night that Ayre Byrne had tried to unleash a death goddess on Dublin.

Bethany was spinning around on the dance floor with Owen Brady. The archive's dangerous-collections specialist threw his dark-haired head back, laughing at something the gorgeous werewolf had said. And she grinned back at him. Playfully, easily.

I hadn't even known they were friends.

A weird ache spiked in my chest. Overreacting badly, I spun away from the dance floor blindly. A sorcerer practically threw himself out of my path, as though I'd been about to barrel into him.

It was possible I'd moved too swiftly. Just for a moment.

I plastered on a smile. Earlier that night, Crystal had quite tentatively suggested that me smiling just a little more would help us reach the gala's donation goal.

The sorcerer blinked rapidly, then offered me a grin of his own. His tux was dark navy-blue with satin lapels. Silver shot through his navy tie, though dyed, not stitched. His hair was dark brown, his skin a dusky shade that made it difficult to guess at his heritage at first glance. Unusual violet eyes were highlighted by a simple dark-blue satin mask that softened his otherwise sharp features.

His grin took on a wicked edge, and he reached to shake my hand. "Dusk Godfrey, yes? Head curator. I've been trying to contrive a meeting all night." His accent was subtle, but sounded Welsh to my ears. "Well, since I came to town, actually. Brendan Prince."

I shook his hand. His grip was firm, skin smooth. He most definitely didn't do any sort of manual labor. And he was also the previously unknown third participant in the current bidding war for my silent-auction donation.

Still holding my hand, Brendan Prince stepped into my space, lowering his voice as if we were intimate acquaintances. "Fated mates. Brilliant. And the curation is top notch." He tipped his head toward the nearest display.

Even skin to skin, I couldn't get a feel for his magic. Sorcerer, definitely. But muted. Or diluted?

I removed my hand from his grasp with a slight twist.

Prince's eyes widened in surprise, which he quickly hid with a wry smile. His hair fell over his brow, brushing his sharp-edged jaw, and he swept it back with his freed hand.

I gathered I was supposed to think he was charming. But the display he'd indicated, the object that he proclaimed to so admire—a rune-marked rectangle of gold that had likely been hewn from a crown—was actually the most mundane of the items currently on display. A last-minute addition. I actually hadn't wanted to include the newly acquired relic at all, but Crystal was enamored with the tragic love story it was supposedly connected to. A tale of fated mates whose relationship was torn asunder by those who opposed their union. A tale of the so-called fae.

"I hope you're having a lovely time," I said, moving to step around the sorcerer.

Prince angled his shoulder, subtly barring my passage with another tilt of his head and another meant-to-be charming grin. "You haven't identified the century," he said. "Or the origin. It's clearly fae." His smile shifted into something that was likely supposed to read as self-deprecating, but which came off as arrogant. To me, at least.

But then, I was still on edge. Still feeling a bit smothered by my so-called secret identity.

"I'm a historian," Prince announced, still smirking. He tapped his chest, continuing as if we were actually having a conversation. "Specializing in the fae."

I sighed internally. Trying to hide my impatience.

'The fae' was a label that every Adept knew—and that most archivists rejected as a simplified and exceedingly broad classification covering beings from multiple dimensions. But the scant myths and tales of those beings—creatures who might well have walked the world at some point, but had departed it long ago—had been so popularized by speculation, so diluted of real history, that Brendan Prince might as well have announced that he was a historian specializing in the mundane world's fairy tales.

The gold relic on display was a perfect example. The rune-marked rectangle retained only the faintest magic and had even less historical importance as far as I'd been able to determine. But those who breathlessly studied the fae didn't care about verifiable facts.

And yes, I understood the irony of a creature of mythology and morality tales—namely me—drawing an arbitrary line around what was real and unreal. But I liked my history and my artifacts verifiably significant, and my mythology much less fanciful. Less sensationalized. Less diluted.

I suddenly recalled where I'd heard Brendan Prince's name even before seeing it as a bid on my silent auction. One of the books Crystal had consulted while setting up the last-minute display of the golden crown fragment had been written by a Brendan Prince.

'Research,' the librarian had called it, clutching the obviously well-read book with its creased spine and softened corners. A work of pop mythology. Of fictionalized magical history. A profitable sideline for a historian who might be lacking in other areas—such as magical prowess—but who wielded enough charisma and could turn enough beguiling phrases to woo a loyal readership.

But when Crystal had shown me the inscription inked within the pages of her copy of Prince's book—she'd apparently stood in line for over an hour to meet the author the last time he'd been in Dublin—I'd kept my opinion to myself, studiously avoiding sneering.

It only takes one believer to fuel the fantastical.
Be that believer.
– B.P. –

The downside of my practically eidetic memory—I'd now never be able to forget that cloying sentiment.

And apparently, I also wasn't getting out of the conversation Brendan Prince wanted to force upon me. Or at least I wasn't getting out with any grace.

I gave in. Holding on tightly to my unpracticed public persona, I stepped between the marbled columns, crossing toward the display case the historian had indicated. A couple of coven witches I recognized from the Cove Cafe turned at my approach, their gazes passing over me and taking in Brendan Prince.

By their reaction, I gathered they found him as intriguing as he obviously wished to be.

I just didn't see it.

Be polite. Be polite.

The gala had been my idea. Even though it had been Crystal who made it all exceedingly sparkly and intense, I was the one who'd decided that the Adepts of Dublin should take pride in their archive, and that they should get a chance to enjoy what was normally hidden in the basement behind heavy-duty wards.

Brendan Prince nodded at the witches dismissively, then gestured toward the relic on display. Constructed out of thick, age-darkened gold, the uneven square was about the size of my palm. Two of its edges were rough, as though it had been removed from a larger setting by great force. Symbols I didn't recognize and hadn't yet had a chance to study and identify were carved onto the piece's front-facing surface. A larger symbol at the center of the relic was surrounded by a rectangle of smaller runes, all swirls and curlicues.

Brady and I had found the relic last month in Galway, in a hidden niche in the basement of a Byrne witch who'd passed away. The handwritten book I'd collected alongside the crown fragment was in the middle of a pile on my desk, neglected while I focused on the gala. I might not love the idea of historians like Brendan Prince peddling ill-researched and inaccurate tales of the fae for a profit, but the unknown language in the handwritten book was definitely worth a second look.

The book had also contained a sketch of a crown that might well have been connected to the relic in the display. Interpreting the symbols, both in the book and on the relic, would give me a better sense of its history. Its real history.

The relic had barely had a chance to gather dust in the basement of the archive before Crystal had unearthed it. Not that any item ever got dusty in an archive overseen by a Pine witch. She had somehow connected the piece to an elaborate story about fated mates who had attempted to seize territory so they could build themselves a haven free from the oppression of their families. To paraphrase, anyway. Personally, I didn't find it surprising that any attempted seizing of territory would end badly. Adepts generally weren't big fans of being overrun or slaughtered, not even in the context of a mythical love connection.

Even after handling it many times, I'd sensed nothing but a slight glimmer of residual magic from the crown piece. Not even enough to identify the particular power set of the Adept who'd last worn it centuries ago, though part of that was likely due to the fact that the piece had been severed from its original form.

I scanned the card Crystal had tucked into the display case—and realized, as I should have earlier, that the story of fated mates she'd made use of was credited to a specific author. An author who happened to be currently standing just a touch too close to me.

Brendan Prince. From his *Book of the Fae, Part One*.

Part one? Ugh. He'd written multiple books on the subject? And titled them all so mundanely? I could recount having seen at least a half-dozen popular books with similar titles. Though I certainly hadn't read any of them.

"Do you know the tale of the fated mates?" Prince's tone was hushed in a way that made me think he was attempting to be beguiling. Not magically, just in an affected way. "I've been piecing it all together for...years."

Internally squirming, I nodded agreeably. I didn't usually have any issues talking with strangers. So perhaps it was talking pop mythology with strangers who professed to be experts in that pop mythology that bothered me. It was a new experience for me.

Also, it was slightly odd that he was calling my attention to a display partially based on one of his own books. Oddly self-congratulatory.

"The lovers were torn asunder," Prince continued. "Her life blood given to save him, to save their realm from invasion. I've been looking for this piece for some time." He gestured again toward the relic, stopping just short of stroking the invisible magical warding between it and him. "I was surprised to discover it's been in Dublin, for centuries perhaps? Though I understand from your librarian that it's a recent addition to the archive. Collected by your fair hand."

He grinned at me.

Apparently, 'fair hand' was supposed to be some sort of compliment. Or flattery? Except I had tanned skin and wasn't interested in flirting.

Prince's smile faltered around the edges. He returned his gaze to the display. "Most of the major archives are more...open about their collections."

That wasn't even remotely true, though I had serious doubts that Brendan Prince actually knew how many archives existed. The ones maintained by dragons, at least.

"We're implementing some new initiatives," I said stiffly.

"I've heard." He tore his gaze from the crown piece, offering me a grin that was sharp-edged now. "And actually managing to get a ticket to your gala was a most satisfying hunt in and of itself."

I caught sight of movement across the dance floor out of the corner of my eye, chastising myself inwardly for doing so even as I turned my head just enough to see him more fully. Kellan. He was watching me from the other side of the gallery, leaning casually against a marble column. His eyes narrowed. On Prince, I thought.

The so-called historian sorcerer followed my gaze but took in the dancers between us instead of spotting the predator not-too-subtly lurking across the way.

"There is comfort in believing that there is one person who is perfect for you," Prince murmured in his oddly intimate tone. "A fated mate..."

"Is there?" I said, trying to avoid sounding glib. "What if you never find them?"

"But fate is destined to bring you together. As the tales go..."

"What about fated enemies?" I asked blithely, forcing myself to look back at the historian instead of watching Kellan as he watched me. "Is that a thing?"

"Well…" Prince snorted, amused. "Logically, magic demands a balance, doesn't it? Energy can be harnessed, but only transformed. Not destroyed."

I met his violet gaze, raising an eyebrow. "So that's a yes."

He grinned at me. "I'd love to discuss it further. In a quieter venue. And…after a tour of the archive?"

"You can make arrangements with our resident historian, James Anderson."

The sorcerer sniffed dismissively. "More than a few minutes in Jim's company would bore anyone to death."

I didn't find James boring. We weren't particularly friendly, but he was articulate and thorough. He'd also been rather gleeful when I'd opened the archive up to acquisitions again, and had been traveling extensively over the last two months, returning with boxes and boxes of books.

And yes, I was exceedingly aware that I would put up with just about anything if it came with a new book.

Brendan Prince pouted playfully. "I'll just have to win the silent auction."

Bidding against Mesa Byrne? I doubted whether Kellan or Prince would get anything the formidable coven leader wanted for herself. And I just might need to wander over and assure that outcome myself. I glanced around for the elder witch, but spotted Ravine traversing the dance floor instead, alone and heading for me.

"Do you dance?" Brendan Prince asked, holding a hand out to me and clearly switching tactics.

"Not tonight," I said as politely as possible. I was more than ready to move on from the conversation. "Unfortunately, I'm working."

"Certainly your guests can spare you for a moment?"

I opened my mouth to refuse him a second time, but managed to avoid appearing rude when Ravine stepped up beside me. She tucked her shiny, dark-brown hair behind her ear and offered me a saucy grin. Then she focused her attention on Prince. A hint of witch magic curled over the intricate gold cuffs on her wrists.

"I'm available," she purred to Prince, slipping her other hand into his. "Ravine Byrne. Metal mage."

His grin, which had been souring around the edges, widened. "Brendan Prince. Historian."

"Oh, yes?" she purred. "Why don't you study me for a turn? Poor Dusk is overworked and underpaid."

"It would be my pleasure." Prince nodded to me. "I look forward to continuing our conversation."

I smiled tightly. I would need to figure out how to pawn him off on James or even Crystal.

Prince stepped away, leading Ravine toward the dance floor. The metal mage winked at me over her shoulder, letting me know that the rescue had been deliberate.

I grinned back at her, then moved on to the next display—a china dinner service for two, perfectly arranged on a small antique table. A journal was tucked into a glass case set just before the table, open to a particular entry. A thin silver bookmark that was genuine Irish metalwork was set slightly off to one side of the journal. The china was from a wedding celebration, nineteenth century. The journal entry was Crystal's evidence of the newlywed witches being destined mates, describing how they'd fallen for each other at first sight.

It was more than apparent that Crystal had been working on her own fated mates research for some time. I expected her to present me with a book proposal sooner than later.

Aisling Conall, alpha werewolf and Kellan's mother, was leaning over to read the journal. Tall with dark-red hair, she was dressed in a shimmering champagne-colored dress that fell straight to her ankles. She turned as I approached, nodding slightly. A black-feathered mask framed her bright-green eyes. "Well done, archivist."

"It's mostly Crystal's work," I said.

She snorted offishly. "Under your leadership."

I nodded, oddly uncomfortable with even offhand praise.

Aisling's gaze shifted over my shoulder, and I twisted to see Gitta as she spun past in the arms of her new…lover? Boyfriend seemed too frivolous a term to relate to a mother of two, but perhaps that was some sort of oddly ingrained perception of mine. Admittedly, anything I knew about modern relationships came from fiction, rather than experience. Dragons were rare enough that choosing a partner for life wasn't widely practiced—let alone dating. With so few of us born to each generation, the idea of waiting around for a fated mate to appear was ridiculous.

"None of your generation is ever happy with what's good for them," Aisling said. "Thereby making choices that will only lead to more unhappiness."

I had no idea what she was talking about. I had even less idea why she'd included me in the remark.

Aisling shifted her focus.

To Kellan. Who was making a beeline for us across the dance floor.

Perhaps he felt I needed rescuing from his mother? Or, given the fact that I still wasn't certain he was actually flirting with me, perhaps he was rescuing his mother from me?

Kellan got tangled up between Bethany and her dance partner, then got further tangled with Brady as he twirled his fiancee, Erin, around the room. Swathed in blue silk, including her mask, Erin Conall was Kellan and Gitta's half-sister, as well as technically their cousin. She'd inherited her height and her light-brown skin from their father, Odane, but her hair was a dark auburn.

All of them laughed as they separated from each other.

The hollow point in my chest ached again. I looked away.

Aisling Conall was watching me with a slight smile. Then she nodded, stepping from the niche toward the next display. She brushed her fingers across her son's shoulder as they passed. Kellan leaned in to kiss her cheek, causing her to chuckle and bat at him.

Then Kellan turned all his attention on me, silently holding out his hand. I stood there for far too long, hanging in the moment.

"I don't know how to dance," I said finally.

"The music will guide you."

"I just turned down someone else...I'm here to work."

"I know. I saw."

He kept his hand held out to me steadily. Inviting, not pressuring.

I was making too big a deal of it. Of all of it. I was giving the so-called lie I was currently living too much significance. I was still me. I still made the same choices, whether or not I was a dragon in a witch's guise.

A single dance wasn't a binding contract that I was signing under false pretenses.

I slipped my hand into Kellan's, and he tugged me toward him. "You are breathtaking," he murmured.

"Ravine did my hair." Even in my barely broken-in heels, he was still easily ten centimeters taller than me.

And I liked that, probably more than I should have. "And my makeup."

He snorted quietly. "It isn't your hair or makeup."

I settled my fingertips on his shoulder, barely touching. Then, pulling my magic in tightly, as if it might shield me from the onslaught that was Kellan Conall—or what I perceived as an onslaught, at least—I lifted my gaze to meet his. "Are you going to twirl me or what?" I asked teasingly.

He laughed huskily, turning my insides to mush. Again.

Warm, eager mush.

Off-limits, off-limits.

His fingers ghosted across my back, turning me into the flow of the other dancers. We raised our other lightly clasped hands to the side, his calluses a hint of roughness against my skin.

I tried to stay light on my feet, to move with Kellan rather than against him, conscious of how completely and utterly contrary it felt to most of my solo martial arts training. Only when Sisu was older would he and I train to fight in tandem.

Kellan kept his steps simple.

Thankfully.

Bethany swirled past us with yet another partner. The witch lights overhead caught in her laughing eyes, streaking her golden hair. "Kellan!" she cried. "Finally!"

Kellan frowned, seemingly chastising her.

She just laughed and spun away, surefooted.

"This…ah, is this a waltz?" I asked awkwardly.

"Your guess is as good as mine," he said. "I'm just trying to follow the tempo."

I laughed, oddly relieved that I wasn't the only ignorant one.

Kellan pulled me a touch closer.

I didn't resist. If I turned my head slightly, I'd be able to brush a kiss just under his jaw.

Oh gods, this was a bad idea.

"What do you transform into?" he murmured against my temple, moving me to the music.

"Nothing."

"You might be witch-blooded, Dusk Godfrey," he purred. "But that's not all you are. You try to hide your golden glow, but I see it between the cracks. It's the same as the trail Sisu left through the city."

He meant the night Sisu and the twins had been taken by Ayre. "That was a spell."

He hummed doubtfully. "Then why was the trail for Neve and Lile the same color as their magic?"

"I'm an archivist," I said stiffly, clinging to the truth of that title.

"I never said you weren't." He sounded amused.

Stalking me, I realized.

I tilted my head back, deliberately catching and holding his gaze. "I'm not prey. I'm not to be hunted."

"Oh…" He flashed me a smile full of all sorts of promises. "I'm not hunting."

"Bethany," I blurted. Then I found myself blinking at him like an idiot instead of explaining my abrupt change of subject.

"Bethany?" he asked in a low growl when I didn't continue, eyes narrowing. "What did my mother say to you?"

I shook my head. "No. Nothing like that. Aisling just said something about our generation never being happy with what's good for us…"

He grumbled.

I had started this conversation. I wasn't a coward. No matter how oddly I behaved around Kellan.

I would just keep reminding myself of that.

"The picture on your phone," I said. Then I added for clarity, "The picture of Bethany..."

The music faded, then stopped somewhat abruptly.

The other dancers parted, clapping and chatting quietly.

Magically amplified, Crystal's bright voice emanated from the back of the room. "The silent auction closes in ten minutes. Make sure to get your final bids in!"

I stepped out of Kellan's arms, clapping softly. "Excuse me."

"Dusk," he murmured, snagging my elbow, "the picture...it's just a remnant..."

I shook my head at him, already forced to smile at a gray-haired witch in a silver mask that matched her dress perfectly. She had deliberately caught my eye as I'd turned.

"Ms. Godfrey," she asked, her accent pure British, "I have a question about the sixteenth-century vase you've accredited to the Byrne coven..." She gestured toward the nearest display. "I believe it was actually cast and painted by a Dunkirk ancestor of mine."

"Of course," I said, stepping away from Kellan.

His hand fell from my elbow, his fingers momentarily tangling through mine as our arms stretched apart.

Just a remnant, he'd said...

I squeezed his fingers, just slightly, as if my body was acting of its own accord. Making promises I rationally couldn't keep.

But not wanting to let go.

It was after midnight, early into Saturday morning, before I crossed through the intricate wrought-iron gate that separated the estate of Wilding Manor from the rest of Dublin. One moment, I was dashing from the taxi through a light but chilly mist, through a courtyard tucked between Georgian apartment buildings. The next, I was crossing through heavy-duty boundary warding. Though the mist continued beyond the gate, I slowed to luxuriate in the magic embedded into every stone, every blade of grass, and every gnome-trimmed hedge of my home. Points of light winked awake along the edge of the path, as if Wilding Manor was coaxing me toward the main house. The lights faded as I passed.

The gala had been rife with magic. Energy had emanated from every guest, over and above Crystal's fairy lights and the individually warded relics on display. But Wilding Manor was different. It was literally anchored to a deep, somnolent well of power, rooted in that natural magic by at least one—and most likely two—ancient walnut trees. One of those trees had been converted into the carved front door, and the second was now my desk in the library.

I shouldn't have been surprised by the estate's slowly awakening magic, since the property had been claimed by a guardian dragon at least four centuries ago.

My step faltered as a small piece of a puzzle I'd been subconsciously ruminating on for months clicked into place. The former guardian of Northern Europe, Jiaotu-who-was, had somehow claimed a massive piece of property, and the power that underlaid that claim, in the middle of the territory of the current guardian of Western Europe, Suanmi. An estate that Jiaotu, Sisu's father and the guardian of Northern Europe, had then bequeathed to me. For life.

What bit of personal history would lead one guardian to claim a portion of another's territory? And why get me involved in that history way after the fact?

At the time, it had certainly felt as though Suanmi had somehow manipulated the four other guardians into agreeing to have me represent them in Dublin, though I was too young—in dragon terms, anyway—to undertake such a task.

Which was probably evidenced by the rather terrible job I was doing of the undercover portion of my mission.

The mist was chilly. I let that push me the rest of the way to the house, even as I continued to muse on the dynamics between the guardians, and what portion of those dynamics the current Jiaotu had inherited when he'd taken on the mantle of the guardian of Northern Europe.

If Suanmi's goal was to reclaim the property, why would she need to use me?

That might be a mystery I would never solve—unless I just outright asked the fire breather herself. Though, honestly, I wasn't sure I could handle knowing a guardian's secrets. And if I was being doubly honest, Suanmi scared the hell out of me.

I shook off the tired ramblings of my own mind, focusing on getting to the house and into bed as quickly as possible.

Most of the windows of the manor were dark, except for a soft glow from the lower-left living room windows and a pinpoint of light within the central tower.

A shadow detached from the upper window, stepping deeper within the tower. A moment later, the light winked out.

A candle. Snuffed out by Morgan, the so-called death goddess I'd installed in the tower just shy of two months ago.

At the silent auction, I had bid on and won a book that I thought the former-necromancer-turned-possible-divinity might like—a first-edition, early-twentieth-century romance featuring two witches from rival covens. But I would wait until morning to give it to Morgan. Conversations with the death goddess were something I needed to be well rested to navigate. Plus, no matter how well warded the tower was, I didn't like opening the door with guests in the house.

Even with Wilding Manor to back me, I knew Morgan could do a lot of damage in mere moments if she ever slipped by me. Though oddly, I liked having a death goddess tucked away in the tower. There was something...right about it. As if the estate needed her energy for balance.

Or maybe that was just justification on my part, and it was actually the two notebooks I'd already filled with transcripts of our conversations that kept me truly content with being Morgan's keeper. I had sent both notebooks to Zeke to help me fact-check them, though I hadn't seen my adopted great-great-uncle and would-be fiance since his unannounced visit just before I found myself hunting down Ayre Byrne. I knew he was waiting for an invitation to return. Just like I knew I didn't want to encourage him any further than I already had.

The light over the front door brightened when I was a few steps away from the main entrance, and the right side of the massive carved walnut door opened for me without prompting. I'd had all the nonmagical electrical outlets and lights in the manor rewired and updated, but the house had no issues controlling them magically.

I crossed into the welcoming warmth of the grand central great room, immediately crossing into the darkened temporary cloakroom to shuck off my borrowed ankle-length raincoat. I'd gotten it from Ravine, though I was fairly certain it belonged to Mesa. I didn't own a jacket that was long enough to protect my new silk dress from the mist.

Sporadic lights brightened just a touch as the house followed my progress. I retrieved Infinity from my backpack, and my personal archive hummed sleepily, just as happy to be in my hand again as I was to be holding it.

I crossed the central great room to hover in the doorway of the living room, my footsteps muffled despite the fact I was crossing marble floors in heels—the sound suppressed by the house, not by me. I wasn't that talented. The living room appeared to have been completely upended, sheets and blankets draped haphazardly across cushion-walled forts. Little bodies were curled around the pillows tucked within.

Sisu radiated power that I could feel even meters away, as he usually did when sleeping deeply. All the magic I held so tightly to me while awake most likely fell away when I succumbed to sleep as well.

Just another reason to keep my distance from Kellan.

Not that I needed to add anything to that ever-lengthening list. The top item—the fact that I was a dragon and he was a shapeshifter—was already insurmountable.

Sisu was tucked between Lile and Neve, sprawled on top of what appeared to be three thick layers of blankets. Neve on his right made barely a dent in the covers.

Lile on his left lay with her long, slim arms flung out over her head.

The embers in the fireplace were low. Len Murphy, the twins' father, was sprawled out over one half of the sectional couch. His arm hung off the edge loosely, the TV remote fallen just out of his reach. The sectional had been stripped of its cushions, but apparently the tall, brown-haired werewolf didn't need cushioning to sleep.

Rook popped her head up from a pile of pillows around a sleeping bag set closer to the fireplace. Her dark-brown hair was mussed, her golden-tanned skin kissed by the low firelight. She tucked something behind her back guiltily, then saw me and grinned widely.

I smiled back, but my expression faltered as she sat up, cross-legged, and shifted the item she'd been hiding into her lap. A black book.

Emotional echoes rippled through me. Residual panic from trying to save Rook from the spelled book that had almost killed the ten-year-old witch. I forced myself to hold onto my smile, reminding myself that I recognized the tome Rook had been reading by the embers of the fire, even though she was supposed to be sleeping. It was an Irish mythology text—a series of parables—that I'd found when sourcing romance novels for the death goddess in the tower. It was completely mundane in origin.

The echoes of terror that had gripped my heart eased.

"Do you want some warm milk?" I asked in a whisper. "Or tea?"

She nodded vigorously.

"Let me wash my face and get into pajamas. I'll meet you in the kitchen."

"I'll come with." She untangled her long, slim legs from the sleeping bag and padded over to me barefoot, heedless of how chilly the marble floor would get away from the reach of the fire. Heating the manor, along with the equally important goal of insulating it, was an on-going, long-term project. Even with the west wing still shut up tightly most days, my first gas bill after Conall Construction had begun installing central heating had been outrageous. Of course, I'd never had to pay any bill of any sort in my entire life, so I didn't have much perspective.

I pointed at Rook's feet. "Socks."

She spun back, snatching up her discarded wool socks and somehow managing to wrestle them on without putting down the book.

As I watched her, I couldn't help but wonder again about the long-term effects of her having been exposed to extreme magical conditions—specifically, being piloted around by a spelled book and forced to wield malignant magic. Such effects were different for everyone in those sorts of situations, depending on the inherent magic of the Adept. And the fact that Rook's own magic had been exceedingly immature at the time was another unknown quantity in her recovery.

The same might hold true for the twins, actually. They'd been forced into their wolf forms by Ayre Byrne at far too young an age. I glanced at Neve and Lile still sound asleep in the pillow fort. The twins' shifter magic was already reading as atypical, like their uncle Kellan. To my magic-sensitive eyes, at least.

Rook was growing fast, even with my only having known her the last couple of months. She came up to my shoulder now. I touched her on her own shoulder lightly as we crossed back through the dim great room toward the stairs.

"The theme of the gala was about the fae, right?" she asked quietly. "There are some stories about fairy-like creatures in this book."

"The theme was fated mates, specifically. There were some fae- or fairy-themed displays. But that's a broad classification of creatures in the magical world."

"Can I...can I make a list of questions to ask you?" Rook blinked up at me, tentative. "For research?"

"For one of your stories?"

She bobbed her head, casting her gaze down to the stairs we were currently traversing to the second-floor bedrooms. "Yes."

"Any question," I said. "Any time."

She smiled, head still bowed.

Rook wrote short stories, though she'd never shared any with me. Or Bethany. And yes, I'd asked the werewolf tutor. My curiosity over Rook's selective shyness was acute enough to force me to risk a personal question.

All of us were watching Rook closely after the incident with the spelled book. I had no doubt that probably had something to do with her reserving something just for herself.

"Maybe...we could add some chocolate to the milk?" The young witch asked, brushing her fingers against the flared skirt of my dress almost reverently.

"Yes. As long as we have some."

We crossed through the upper hall and into my darkened bedroom. The house obliged by increasing the lighting softly for Rook, though the little bit of moon-light that was managing to filter through the clouds would have been enough for me.

She instantly climbed up on my bed and tapped the lamp on the bedside table. Obligingly, the house brightened that particular light further. Not at all thrown by

this display of sentience, Rook leaned up against the pillows that lined the heavy headboard of the four-poster
bed, propped her book against her knees, and opened it.

I set Infinity on top of the bureau, grabbed my
pajamas, and headed into the newly renovated en suite
bathroom, leaving the door open. I avoided having my
personal archive near water. Though it was magically
protected from it—not to mention fire, spells, and so
forth—getting wet made Infinity cranky. I had learned
that the hard way while collecting water imps from a
pond outside my mother's estate. They'd been covered in
green face cream at the time as well, which I'd borrowed
from Mistress Brightshire, the estate's head brownie, to
entice the imps.

I quashed the wash of grief that even the thought
of my mother evoked these days. She was still off on a
collection and likely had no idea that she'd been gone
for over a year now.

After the collection and relocation of the water
imps, Infinity had outright refused to absorb anything
unless it was dry and at least gently wiped clean. At the
time, I had assumed that water somehow disturbed my
personal archive's magic. But on reflection and almost
two years after the incident, I now had the distinct impression that Infinity's reaction had been an actual sulk.

Because Infinity did react to things. Not like a
human, of course. But those reactions and the archive's
magical sentience had been growing with every bit of
magic or knowledge that Infinity absorbed. Even more
so after I'd tried to form a connection between the internet and the archive, triggering a massive power outage
in Oslo. Then, before having a chance to figure out what
kind of long-term effects that might have caused, I had
spent a chunk of time coaxing my archive to absorb

dozens of books shelved in the magically robust library of the guardian nexus.

"I'll read you one of the stories I found when we have our hot chocolate," Rook called from the bedroom. Her tone was firm. Not that I would have even thought of dissuading her.

"Lovely."

Tugging the delicate gold mask I'd worn all night out of my pocket and setting it on the light-gray marble counter, I swapped the dress for my floral-print pajama pants and a long-sleeved T-shirt, carefully placing the dress on the padded hanger I'd left on the bathroom door.

"I have questions about a few of the stories," Rook repeated, as if worried I wasn't going to follow through with my first promise. "And fated mates in general."

"I'm happy to discuss it."

I could hear her flipping through pages, and found myself smiling as I imagined her bent over her crossed legs, with her face practically pressed to the borrowed book.

I turned to the counter. The marble tops were original to the house. Before she'd quit the renovation project, River Byrne had insisted on the double flush-mounted sinks, so the marble had to be pieced together. It had been done so expertly that I assumed magic was involved, especially since Ridge had an affinity for stone. The extra marble for the counter and the flooring had been sourced from other currently unused bathrooms in the manor, but the iridescent brown tile in the walk-in shower was new. The Conalls had rotated the en suite's claw-foot tub to make room for the glass-encased shower stall.

I set my sheathed bone blade on the counter beside the mask. Wearing the weapon over my floral-print pajama pants while in the house, and about to make some hot chocolate with a baby witch for company, was overkill. Even for me.

Then, standing at the sink before the mirror, I started the search for the pins Ravine had used to tame my wild mane for the evening. The updo was nowhere near as pristine as it had been, though it had held through the gala. But when the last of the guests were gone, James and I had sent Crystal home with Brady and Erin. The librarian was so exhausted, I would have sworn she'd been napping while still upright. So that left only the historian and me to lock away the more valuable artifacts in the basement, then pile the extras on Crystal's desk before heading home ourselves. The rest of the organizing and tidying would happen over the following week, which had been shortened by the upcoming holidays.

The back of my updo had come partly undone on the last trip down the archive stairs. Now, after dashing through the misty evening, it was all sagging slightly to one side, even through all the layers of metal-based magic that backed Ravine's pretty pins and clips.

I carefully collected each of those, placing them into a small box to be returned to Ravine, along with the mask and raincoat I'd borrowed. I owed the metal mage a thank-you gift as well. I would have to dig through my treasure box from Jiaotu and try to find something innocuous enough that I could persuade her to accept it. A gold coin or ring, perhaps. Or even better, a hairpin for her collection.

"Sisu says we're all getting trained tomorrow," Rook called from the bedroom, "in self-defense."

I laughed quietly. Well, that was going to be a surprise to whatever trainer showed up later that morning. It was usually an apprentice of Branson, the guardian dragons' sword master. Thankfully the twins' and Rook's magical senses weren't attuned enough to see through the glamour the trainers had been wearing when other Adepts were on the property. Though Len would probably stick around as well. And at least one Byrne witch would drop by to pick up Rook. Hopefully not her grandmother.

I honestly didn't think I was fooling the coven leader in the least.

That sharp pain pinged through my chest again. From all the continual lying.

"Dusk?" Rook called from the bedroom. "That's okay, right?"

"Yes, of course." My voice sounded weird, stiff. I tried again. "I'll train with you too. It'll be fun."

"Yeah. Sisu says that Bethany has been going too soft on the twins."

I shook my head at my reflection. Sisu could be a tyrant, but it came from the best intentions. Even the son of a demigod couldn't see his best friends kidnapped and magically forced into assuming their wolf forms by a black witch, then just have all that roll off him. He was only five, after all, even if he sometimes hid it well.

Rook appeared in the bathroom doorway, peering at me in the mirror shyly. "Do you need help?"

I kneeled down in answer. The bathroom brightened further as Rook padded quietly toward me, then started searching my hair for the last few accessories.

She placed a jeweled pin that still sparkled with Ravine's blue witch magic into the small container on the counter, murmuring, "That one tickles. A little."

"Your skin or your senses?" I asked deliberately casually. Rook's power remained almost dormant, to my own senses at least.

She hummed quietly to herself, searching through my wild mane. I thought she might not answer at all, but she finally said, "No…more like my brain."

I couldn't stop the smile that swamped my face. It was totally arrogant of me, but I was bothered by still not knowing exactly how the spelled book had grabbed hold of Rook so fast and deep. "A feeling?" I said. "Like an emotion? Or more like a picture?"

Rook ran her fingers through my unbound hair, searching for any hidden pins. She crinkled her nose. "Like…a bit of happiness."

Rook was an empath.

Not an earth witch.

A rare and valuable Adept. Just the presence of an empath in a coven or a pack could lend the members a calm unity.

I had already guessed at that, in the aftermath of the book seizing her, as a possible explanation for how easily it had happened.

"What?" Rook asked, looking at me in the mirror. Her eyes narrowed suspiciously.

"Nothing."

She turned to touch the dress hanging by the door. "You looked so beautiful. Did you dance?"

"I was working. But yes, one dance."

Rook grinned. "With Kellan Conall?" she asked in a singsong voice.

I gave her a look, straightening and quickly running a brush through my even-more-unruly-than-usual hair.

"Because he dropped by looking for you," she added.

"I heard you all blackmailed him."

Her grin widened. "We totally did."

I chuckled. Kellan had been pulled away by Aisling immediately following the close of the silent auction.

"And what about Auntie Ravine? Did she dance?"

"Pretty much the entire time." Ravine had, in fact, danced with Brendan Prince for the remainder of the evening. Then they'd left together after the auction closed.

Rook nodded, suddenly sober. "There's a bunch of stories in that book about, like, tragic love stories. Or people being in love with someone they shouldn't love."

"That's pervasive in a lot of mythology. Especially stories of mundane origin."

"Why?"

I shrugged. "Makes for interesting reading, I guess."

"So it's not just...the patriarchy?"

I blinked at her, then grinned.

She scowled. "I hear things. I know things."

"It's a big topic for the early-morning hours," I said, grabbing my sheathed blade, then touching her shoulder and gently herding her out into my room. I suddenly wasn't as tired as I thought I was, invigorated by the estate's magic, perhaps. Or just by simple companionship. "And, if I'm honest, it's not something that I've had cause to wonder much about myself. In my world, prejudice is more pervasive than sexism."

"All that chasing and claiming," Rook continued matter-of-factly. "And men superior to women in strength and morals...that's not true."

I paused by my bureau thoughtfully, setting my blade next to Infinity and then laying my hand on my personal archive. "A lot of mythology is written by nonmagicals in an attempt to explain magical events and magical people that they've witnessed. Or at least that they've heard stories about. And yes, it's somewhat similar to how history is written by the winners. And

45

those so-called winners are often male, unless you look closely."

Rook grabbed the mythology book off my bed, preceding me to the bedroom door. "The story I like best isn't like that at all, though. And…" She glanced at me shyly. "You can find me better stuff to read, right?"

I scooped up Infinity. "Anytime. And always."

"But hot chocolate first."

"Priorities are very important."

Still clutching the book to her chest, the youngest Byrne witch laughed quietly, then got lost in her own thoughts as we wandered down to the kitchen together.

That pervasive pain was gone. The one that kept shooting through my chest. At home, surrounded by the comfort of the manor, and with Rook, I felt content.

I felt like myself for the very first time that day. After having pretended to be someone else for too long.

Empath, not witch. I should have figured it out sooner, just based on my own need to protect her. I had actually asked River about Rook's magic, only to have her brush me off.

But then, most covens knew how to hide a treasure in their midst.

CHAPTER TWO

THE NEXT MORNING, FEELING LEN AND THE KIDS ALready congregated in the kitchen even though the sun was barely up, I tumbled out of bed still blurry eyed. I splashed water on my face, noting my eyes were still outlined with the remnants of last night's makeup. Then I ran a brush through my hair, desperately trying to contain it in a ponytail that was destined to fail. Pulling an oversized thick wool sweater on over a tank top and drawstring pants, I grabbed Infinity.

Remembering that I'd left the book I'd won from the silent auction for Morgan in my backpack, I had to detour before heading to the central tower. Though I usually preferred to not visit the death goddess while there were guests in the manor, I also knew ignoring her for long enough to get through breakfast and a training session was a bad idea. And also…well, I wouldn't want to be left alone, even surrounded by books, for longer than a day myself.

At the top of the central stone tower, I opened the thick wooden door and slipped inside, barely stirring the wards that encased the doorway, lined the walls, and wove across the high ceiling.

After the slow process of discovering how that sort of magic worked for me and establishing the wards, I'd found that I could add a touch of my power each time I passed through, thus reinforcing the boundary that kept Morgan from draining the life force of everyone in the house and slaughtering us in our sleep. Though the death goddess incarnate might try to turn us into mindless followers first, of course. But after living with Morgan for almost two months, I had no doubt she was fully aware that even if she were powerful enough to kill Sisu and me if she had the upper hand, she'd never be able to enslave us.

Morgan, draped in a dark-red velvet cloak that pooled prettily around her bare feet, stood staring out the eastern window, watching the last blush of the sunrise. The death goddess's dark hair was brushed back from her pale face, exposing the sharp lines of cheeks and jaw. Her lips were almost the exact shade of her cloak. The tips of her fingers and toes were blackened as always, as though she'd trailed them in a pool of utter darkness at one point and it hadn't ever washed off.

She ignored me as I entered.

The fact that I came and went as I pleased had bothered her at first. But as her strength had returned and she'd settled in, claiming more and more of the tower for herself, Morgan always seemed to sense my arrival and know select bits of what had occurred in the house between our visits. Perhaps Wilding Manor fed her its own impressions, as it did for me. And on top of that, she was no doubt exceedingly skilled at bluffing based on what she could spy from her four windows.

"Do you think it will snow?" she asked. Her English had always seemed unaccented to my ear, though she'd stolen knowledge of that language from an Irish witch. I wasn't certain what that said about my own accent. I'd been raised at my mother's estate, which had been anchored just outside Manchester for the bulk of my life, but my tutors and trainers came from a variety of backgrounds and influences.

"I'm not sure." I crossed to the window, which was large enough that I could stand near the death goddess without getting too close. "I've never been in Dublin in late December." I actually hadn't ever been in Dublin at all, but I always carefully curated the information I gave to Morgan, even in seemingly casual conversation.

Jiaotu had called her 'old one' when he'd asked to be introduced, and that alone informed me that I was no match for Morgan intellectually. Not even remotely. So I tried to not play any of her games.

"The infant wolves and the tiny witch were all chattering about the upcoming Christmas celebrations last night." She sighed dramatically. "Endlessly. But my sweet boy explained the significance of the solstice to them quite well."

She meant Sisu. I knew that her inferring she had been able to listen in on the conversation within the house the previous night was an attempt to intimidate me, to undermine me. Likely just her first attempt of that morning. We played that particular game at the beginning, and often at the end, of each of our conversations.

It was far more likely that Morgan had simply picked up snippets of conversation through the windows. Still, I knew it was possible that her inherent sense for detecting life—and death—reached through the wards to let her feel anyone in the house or on the property. She'd inferred as much about the gnome who watched over the estate, and who Sisu and I still hadn't formally met. But no one entered the tower without the master house key. A key I'd begun asking Infinity to carry, since I couldn't ward the desk drawer that doubled as a safe against my brother, Sisu. Not yet, anyway.

Even at five years old, his strength and speed almost matched mine. And though his magic was unfocused, it was robust. He was, after all, the child of a demigod.

I was very careful to not parent Sisu. That wasn't my role, and I wanted a brother, not a child. I valued our sibling relationship, even if it meant dragging him with me for things that he might still be too young to experience. Selfish of me, perhaps. But visiting Morgan was too much of a temptation, so I'd laid down firm rules, then had preemptively thwarted my brother's inherent ability to turn those rules to his advantage.

Skillfully circumventing rules was a trait we both shared, so I just had to figure out how I would have done something to get around Mom, and then block that same avenue for Sisu. I was only partially successful, though, because I wasn't the child of a demigod. And as I'd only recently discovered, Sisu's great-great-grandmother had also worn the mantle of Jiaotu. So he had a triple dose of guardian magic running through his veins, whereas I only had the much thinner connection to Bixi, the guardian of North Africa who occasionally chose to look like Cleopatra in her human form.

I was utterly certain that given the chance, Morgan would use Sisu against me the moment the opportunity arose. So any visitation between the two was overseen by me. I knew that denying Sisu access to her outright would only exacerbate the situation.

She huffed as if reading my thoughts, then spoke imperiously. "What offering have you brought your goddess today?"

I gave her a look.

She blanked her expression, but not before I saw the smirk.

Always testing me.

"I have brought you, Morgan, a book. A gift. Not a tribute."

She huffed again, the dark-red cloak that was a manifestation of her power tightening around her as her fingers flicked impatiently.

I set the book on the deep windowsill, deliberately displaying it in the soft light slowly creeping into the room. The light-brown leather-bound volume was embossed with tiny golden stars and radiating lines, surrounding and emanating from the image of a full moon set into the cover. A fancy wrapping for a first edition of an early twentieth-century romance, likely only sold to select readers, dual autographed and not mass produced.

Morgan reached for the book with her blackened fingers, but then stopped herself, not wanting to appear too eager. "A spellbook?"

A whisper of residual witch magic emanated from the book, likely due to the signatures on the front page, but not in any amount that could be harnessed and corrupted. Just enough to make the book a gift rather than just another paperback for Morgan to read obsessively, then toss back into the dark-wood antique trunk that the house had unearthed for her.

"It's a personal memoir. A love story between two witches, early twentieth century. They met under the full moon whenever they could."

"You've read it, then," Morgan said dourly. "Taken it for your own."

"No. I'm merely quoting the synopsis that was put together for the silent auction. I bid on the book and won it. For you."

Morgan blinked, as she did whenever she needed to absorb something new, such as a word or a concept. I never offered clarification unless she asked.

She didn't ask often.

The death goddess brushed her fingers along the spine of the book but didn't pick it up. "Witches," she murmured. Then she grinned at me, suddenly full of wicked intent. A thin sliver of silver ringed her otherwise black eyes. A hint of her divine origins—or, more accurately, her divine rebirth. "Full-moon rituals are very powerful, Dusk. Especially those fueled with lust."

I smiled, quietly amused. Every now and then, Morgan made a halfhearted attempt to flirt with me. And then she predictably ruined it.

"If the witches are so prim as to not want to sully their souls, then multiple little deaths will do."

"As opposed to a blood sacrifice?" I asked mockingly.

Morgan shrugged as if indifferent. But she finally gave in and snatched up the book, spinning away from the window toward her chair. Or her throne, rather, given the layers of power with which she'd cloaked the antique that Sisu had selected for her. The golden brocade and carved frame of the chair had darkened with that magic, that claiming.

Instead of a bed, Morgan had placed a newly acquired black suede divan against the wall farthest from the door, then piled it with black raw-silk pillows of various sizes. I'd never seen her use it. I wasn't certain she needed sleep, just as I wasn't yet certain whether she was even alive in the traditional sense.

Morgan sprawled across her throne chair as I crossed to investigate a new addition to her decor. A second orchid had joined the one already in the north-facing window. A tiny copper watering pot was tucked next to it. The orchids were wild looking, almost deadly in appearance. The larger-leafed plant bore three mottled purple-and-white blooms, each the size of my palm. The leaves of the second plant were more plentiful and spiked with long stems of smaller, darker flowers that looked like...well, like little winged fairies or tiny, tiny pixies.

I leaned in, sensing the gnome's magic on the plants, then breathing in their scent.

"Chocolate," Morgan said smugly, already reading the book.

It smelled like vanilla to me, but I didn't say so.

"Shall we have tea later?" I asked, stepping toward the door.

"Have questions, do you?" She sniffed.

"Sisu would like to visit."

She looked up sharply, eyes narrowing as if trying to discern my truth. "The littlest one is always welcome. Bring some of that lemon pudding you've been making."

The gnome had gifted me with a basket of Meyer lemons the previous week, and I had been trying to figure out what to make with them. "I'm not happy with the recipe yet."

"No matter. The tea will cover any imperfections."

Morgan didn't need to eat, didn't need any sort of sustenance other than magic. Death magic, specifically. She was currently sustained by the trickle of energy she pulled from the house and property, a boundary within which numerous creatures, and more than likely a few humans, had once made homes and died. Still, she seemed to enjoy the experience of eating anyway. I had no idea what her system did with what she consumed. She didn't have access to a bathroom.

I turned away, opening the door.

"Dusk," the death goddess purred behind me.

I could feel the sharpness of her gaze and the power backing it. I glanced back at her over my shoulder, keeping my expression neutral.

She was curled up in her throne chair, peering at me over the edge of her book. Her long fingers were so pale they looked like bone. Or perhaps claws, ready to rend the leather and paper into tiny pieces. "You are always welcome to stay. I promise all the pleasure you can stand."

"So you can feed from my 'little deaths'?" I asked archly.

Her smile grew behind the cover of the book, her pupils darkening and widening, silvered edges glinting. "You won't even notice."

"No."

She twisted in her chair dismissively. "Have it your way, but I'm a better choice than your brutish shifter. He won't let you cage him."

She meant Kellan. She'd seen him in his massive warrior form and had been more than impressed when he'd withstood the full brunt of her power, then had actually pushed farther into it to rescue Sisu. Not that Morgan would ever admit to being impressed.

"You're not caged." I needed to remind her of that fact at least once a week. "You had a choice."

She pointedly ignored me.

A tall, brown-haired werewolf in jeans and a printed T-shirt turned from the stove toward the four eager fledglings perched on stools at the far side of the kitchen island—two six-year-old werewolves, a ten-year-old witch, and a five-year-old dragon in disguise, all in pajamas. Len Murphy flipped a single large pancake in a frying pan, once, twice. Then, with an extra spiral, he dropped the pancake on the plate my brother was holding out across the counter.

Sisu laughed, delighted. No magic needed to impress him. Excepting the innate dexterity that most shapeshifters possessed, of course.

The manor's kitchen had been renovated in contemporary style but with a lot of classical touches—or so I had been informed by River—so that it wouldn't look too out of place compared to the rest of the house. It was filled with stainless steel appliances, including a built-in coffee machine I had no idea how to use, and a built-in steamer that I wanted to use for dim sum. Frozen, of course. The dark oak cabinets, crowns, and baseboards were all Kellan's work. A breakfast nook with a custom-built table and bench seating was set into the corner by the windows. The floors were light-gray marble tile, the walls painted plain white and still needing art.

Between the kitchen, the heating and electrical upgrades, the furniture for the living room, and the two bathrooms upstairs, I had already gone through almost every cent from the sale of two rounds of items from Jiaotu's treasure chest.

"Me next!" Neve cried around a mouthful of heavily buttered pancake. Lile was mowing through her own syrup-swamped pancake with serious intent. The Conall twins might have had the same golden-green eyes as their uncle Kellan, but they were most definitely individuals, in both looks and temperament. They were also devoted to Sisu, and he to them—with an intensity that was sweet and a little unsettling.

Rook was eating at a more sedate pace, but her focus was still trained on Len as he poured batter into the hot pan again. The werewolf was certainly playing with fire by doling out pancakes one at a time. I wouldn't have been surprised if breakfast ended in a brawl. Still, one pancake at a time meant that Sisu, Neve, and Lile couldn't get into an endless debate about which one was bigger. The previous afternoon, they'd found a kitchen scale I hadn't known we owned and insisted on weighing the chocolate chip cookies I'd baked as a bribe for staying at home during the gala, doing so until they found three that matched. With each and every cookie they ate.

"Good morning," I said, crossing to the island and pouring myself a glass of orange juice from the pitcher sitting at the nearest corner. I didn't normally drink juice, but I knew better than to turn down anything the gnome contributed to any meal.

"Dusk! You're up early." Len's accent was American—Californian, according to Ravine. "You got in late enough, I thought you might sleep in."

"We've got training," Sisu said around a mouthful of pancake. He'd crammed an entire quarter into his mouth.

I considered chastising him, but I'd decided a long time ago that I didn't want everything Sisu heard from me to be a correction of some sort.

"How was the party, Dusk?" Neve asked. "You all looked so beautiful."

"Who else was there?" Lile asked on top of her sister.

"Did you dance?" Neve added.

Sisu scoffed. "Dance? Who would guard all the artifacts?"

Neve huffed. "That's Uncle Owen's job."

"He's not really our uncle," Lile added brightly. "Technically. Not until he marries our aunt Erin."

"I have lots of uncles," Sisu declared, puffing out his chest.

I met Len's amused gaze. "Apparently, I don't actually have to answer any of the questions."

"Nope," he said, grinning as he slid a perfectly golden pancake onto an empty plate, then pushed it toward me.

"Dad!" Neve cried. "No double flip? It won't be as tasty."

"Sorry, baby girl." Len placed the frying pan back on the stove and poured another round of batter into it. "Dusk looks hungry."

As one, all four of the fledglings pivoted on their stools to eye me critically. I took a sip of my orange juice, then made a grab for the butter and the maple syrup.

"That's okay, then," Lile said with an assessing tilt of her head. She pushed a bowl full of sliced strawberries and bananas toward me. "No whipped cream..." She lowered her voice, eyeing her father's broad back. "Because we got in trouble last night. For squabbling."

She shot a look at Neve, who grimaced but didn't dispute the charges.

"With the practice swords," Rook added.

The other three looked at the young witch, expressions of utter betrayal etched across their faces.

Rook's lips twitched. She ate another carefully cubed bite of pancake. "Neve broke one."

"What?" the shorter twin cried. "Not on purpose."

"Over Sisu's head."

Len's shoulders were shaking. He flipped the half-cooked pancake without turning around, covering his amusement.

I looked at Sisu questioningly.

He shrugged. "Didn't hurt."

The three other fledglings dissolved into peals of laughter. Sisu glowered at them, but the laughter grew.

A wide grin swamped my brother's face as he joined in, leaning so far off his stool as he guffawed that I was surprised he didn't topple back.

The magic embedded into every bit of the house stretched around us. The newly marble-tiled floor creaked in response. Len stiffened warily, but then deposited the fresh pancake on the final empty plate without comment.

"Our turn," Lile declared, hopping down, grabbing her stool, and hustling around the island to set it in front of the stove.

Sisu and Neve followed without their stools. Their chins barely cleared the countertop.

"Me first." Lile picked up a large spoon, stretching to reach as she hovered it over the remaining batter. Len had just been pouring freely from the bowl. "Shapes or dots?"

"Faces!" Neve demanded.

Lile nodded obligingly, climbing up to kneel on the stool.

Len watched them out of the corner of his eye as he piled sliced fruit on his pancake, then topped it with a swirl of syrup. An intense but hushed discussion sparked between the three by the stove. Apparently, Lile's smiley faces were lopsided.

Len leaned his hip against the counter, eating with his plate in one hand and his fork in the other. Dragon in disguise or not, I'd probably spill all over myself if I tried to eat standing with my plate also suspended.

Rook wandered over to join the trio, issuing quiet corrections but not taking over.

"So…" Len said casually. "How was the gala?"

"As long as everyone who bid collects their items, we more than doubled our fundraising goal."

"Yeah, the tickets were a pretty hot commodity."

"I'm...we could have found someone else to stay with the kids," I said, lying just a little. The list of people I trusted with Sisu was exceedingly short, though that was mostly out of concern for their safety, not his. Sisu's respect was hard earned, and without it, he wasn't going to listen to...well, anyone. And I knew that Len had earned himself a spot on that list because he was Neve and Lile's father. Sisu adored the twins and would never want to hurt them. Not deliberately, at least.

"Not interested," Len grunted, spooning more fruit onto his empty plate. "And Gitta had other plans." His gaze flicked to the kids, who were embroiled in trying to flip their face-shaped pancakes and getting batter everywhere. "You know how the Conalls can be, once their minds are made up."

I didn't, really. But I could make a very educated guess. Stubborn, resistant to compromise, taciturn, and possibly prone to an intense focus that verged on obsession.

Well, that was my take on Kellan, at least.

But since most of those characteristics could just as easily be applied to me, I really couldn't cast aspersions.

Gitta, scion of the pack and set to become alpha after her mother stepped down, was more diplomatic. And the Conalls were also fiercely loyal.

"I don't know them well," I said quietly.

"Let's just say there are multiple reasons Gitta asked if the kids could sleep here. Behind the protection of your boundary wards."

Because the last time Sisu and the twins had a sleepover, at Gitta's with Len looking after them, they'd been kidnapped.

"That's...that wasn't your fault."

Len grunted doubtfully. "I've been back in Dublin for almost two years now, and I still can't prove myself," he muttered, flicking his gaze to his daughters. Along with Sisu, they were just eating tiny dots of barely cooked batter straight from the frying pan now. "I might have been blind going in, but my eyes are wide open now."

I wasn't aware that Len had left Dublin for any period of time. I also had no idea what he'd been blind to. Ravine's gossip about the Conalls was all surface-level intrigue at best. And I'd never broached the subject of Kellan's uber-powerful shifter magic with her, or its clear connection to the magic of the twins, because…well, I didn't want my own unusual magic to become a topic of conversation. And I was fairly certain the Conalls already knew that Sisu and I weren't full witches. Witch-blooded, perhaps—as Kellan had called me. But definitely with something else mixed in.

With that thought, I glanced at Lile and Neve, who obviously wielded—or at least would wield some day—the same power as their uncle, given the golden-green color of their immature magic. Gitta's own magic read as bright green, typical for a werewolf, as did Len's.

Len had said he'd been blind going in—

The estate magic pinged, as though a pebble had just been dropped into the well of power that fueled it. It sent gentle ripples outward from the direction of the gate.

Then I felt the dragon striding for the house along the front path, as if he'd just been deposited within the boundaries of the estate. Not a guardian, though. They held their power so tightly that they could pass for human, as long as you didn't look too closely or have instincts acutely honed for self-preservation.

Apparently, that ping was what a portal felt like when it opened within the boundary of Wilding Manor.

A rather quiet reaction to what felt like a monsoon of power, to me at least.

"The trainer's here!" Sisu crowed, jumping backward off the stool and running out of the kitchen with a mangled pancake in hand. Neve and Lile shrieked in delight, causing their father to wince slightly. Then they barreled after Sisu.

Rook shook her head at their childish antics, carefully removed the hot pan from the stove, and turned off the gas element. Then she retrieved the book of local mythology she'd been reading last night from the counter and sauntered after the trio.

She picked up her pace the moment she stepped through the open doorway, though.

"I'm happy to pay whatever extra fee the trainer charges you, Dusk." Len had his mobile phone in hand, texting.

I blinked, momentarily thrown.

"To add the girls to the training session today," he added, clarifying. "It was just supposed to be an hour for you and Sisu, right?"

It was usually a couple of hours, or more. "Thank you, but the trainer and I trade services," I said, lying but trying to make it sound convincing. I mean, technically it was true, if the trainer ever needed the services of an archivist, they could ask me. But the chances of that were slim. Assistants to the sword master of the guardians were usually pulled from the warrior subset of dragons, and warriors weren't big on anything that required much research.

Yes, that was snobbish of me, but it was still true. I didn't assist in cleaning up demon summonings or other-dimensional invasions, and warriors didn't collect books or record history.

"That works too," Len said, tucking his phone in his back pocket. "Let me know." He was an electrician, working mostly for Conall Construction but running his own separate business as well.

I nodded, fairly certain I'd be able to just let the subject drop.

Together, we entered the great room just in time to see Sisu pull open the door and reveal a tall, dark-haired male dressed in black training leathers waiting at the threshold. His features hinted at an Asian heritage, and he had the hilt of a huge golden broadsword hovering over his shoulder. He was a couple of years younger than me, and I'd seen him in passing, but we'd never spoken.

Len stiffened, instinctively reacting to the predator on the doorstep. And he wasn't wrong.

The dark-haired dragon cast a narrow-eyed gaze across the fledglings arrayed before him. Rook stood a step behind the other three crowding the door.

Len started to surge forward, but I placed a hand on his shoulder, holding him back lightly. He looked at me questioningly.

"Sisu isn't good with meeting new people," I murmured for his ears only. "Let's give him a moment?"

"Sisu…Godfrey?" The dark-haired dragon pinned his gaze to my brother, who looked almost painfully tiny standing before the warrior. The dragon's hesitation over the last name was obvious to me, but hopefully not to Len.

Sisu nodded, then lined up shoulder to shoulder with Neve and Lile, waving Rook forward. The young witch didn't appear inclined to move closer. The twin werewolves stared up at the warrior. He was easily as tall as their uncle Kellan, so slightly taller than Len, though not quite as broad through the shoulders.

"These are my friends," Sisu said, his tone determined. "Neve and Lile Conall. And Rook Byrne. I sent a letter to the sword master last night."

The dragon nodded, taking in the twins and Rook. "And the sword master sent me. I am Drake." And with that pronouncement, he pulled the golden broadsword, knelt down just over the threshold, and laid the thick blade across his bent knee. "I will make sure no black witch ever lays hands on you again."

"You will protect us?" Neve asked, confused.

"No." Drake looked at each of the fledglings in turn, his expression deeply serious. "I will teach you to protect yourselves."

"Yes," Lile said. "That's better. Everyone else is afraid of us getting hurt."

Rook took a single step closer. "So they coddle us."

"I will not coddle you," Drake declared. "Shall we make a pact?"

The fledglings nodded in unison.

My heart was beating like mad. I couldn't quite figure out what I was feeling. An overwhelming rush of emotion, but of gratitude as well. Sisu had messaged Branson the sword master about Lile, Neve, and Rook. And Branson had sent Drake. Dragons rarely got involved in Adept business—other than to swoop in when everything else was almost lost, of course.

"Place your hand on my blade," Drake commanded. "And promise to work your hardest, to be fierce and focused. And I will teach you more than just how to break a physical hold. I will teach you how to use your magic so the black witch can't get hold of you in the first place. But it takes concentration. And practice. Do you pledge yourselves to that effort?"

The young trio surged forward, placing their hands on Drake's golden sword.

"A pledge?" Len growled under his breath in warning. "Dusk?"

"Not magically binding," I whispered back. "Drake would never, ever do anything to harm them. He just wants them to believe in themselves."

Rook finally stepped forward as well, placing her hand nearer the tip of the golden weapon. "What if…what if we don't have much magic…or strength?"

Drake cast his gaze over the young witch. She was clutching her book to her chest in one hand.

My breath caught in my throat, painfully conscious that Drake could crush her confidence with the slightest of sneers.

"You are enough, Rook Byrne," he pronounced. "It may be harder for you. But with training, you will always be enough."

She swallowed and nodded.

I ignored the rush of emotion that flushed through me once more at her display of quiet bravery. Len was already completely on edge, one step away from thrusting himself into a situation that was already perfectly under control—that had to be a shapeshifter trait, because Kellan and Brady were constantly doing the same thing. I needed to appear calm, outwardly at least.

The dark-haired dragon cast his gaze across all the fledglings. "You so swear."

"We swear!" they cried in unison.

No magic shifted at the pledge. Drake wasn't binding the children in any way. He was simply lending them the strength of conviction and focus.

He straightened, sheathing his sword with an unnecessary flourish. And while in motion, the blade thrummed with power. So much so that I had no doubt it could cut through just about anything Drake intended it to cut. Then he looked over the heads of his pupils and pinned his gaze to me.

"Dusk Godfrey," I said, raising my voice to carry across the cavernous room.

He nodded. "I know your Auntie Pearl. And your cousin Jade." His gaze fell to Sisu. He opened his mouth to say something else, then snapped it closed.

"We are well met, Drake," I said formally. "Welcome to Wilding Manor."

Drake took a full step inside, the children scattering around him. A wide grin swamped the dark-haired dragon's face as he took in the great room and its soaring cathedral ceiling. The house responded to his presence, to all the power he held barely contained, like a gigantic invisible cat. It was practically purring.

Drake laughed in response. "Are we working in the rain?"

"Nope," Sisu said. "We have a sparring room!"

My brother took off with the twins at his heels, racing back through the great room, then cutting right into the back hall. The sparring room was to the right again, just beyond the entrance to the library on the left.

Drake called out after them, "Get your mats out and remove your socks. We will start with a meditation."

Rook, blinking shyly at yet another dragon in disguise, followed the younger fledglings more slowly.

Drake strode toward us, already reaching to shake Len's hand.

Len started, but he thrust out his own hand in response. Adepts rarely touched, especially strangers. But the two shook. "Len Murphy. Neve and Lile's father."

Drake masked his surprise quickly enough that it was doubtful that Len would have picked it up. Neve and Lile's magic wouldn't have read as typical shape-shifter magic to him, or as specifically werewolf. But Len's did.

"Drake. I'm the…one of Branson's apprentices."

He was much more than that, actually. Drake was the ward of Suanmi and apprentice to Chi Wen the far seer, guardian of Asia. One day in the near future, Drake would accept the mantle of far seer himself. He was a fledgling guardian. The only one that I knew of, officially—though Sisu might be the next in line.

"You read the letter before…Branson." I almost called him the sword master, as had Drake before me.

Drake grinned easily. "I did."

That made more sense. Drake had read Sisu's letter and taken the opportunity to meet us. Perhaps because Sisu was Jiaotu's son? Or because Drake knew the Godfrey witches?

Not a question I could ask in front of Len.

"Do you mind if we watch the training session?" Len asked.

"Even better if you participate," Drake said. "We'll warm up and then practice getting out of holds today, physical and magical."

Len nodded.

"But the fledglings seem to think you're coddling them, so you have to promise to actually participate. Fully."

Tension shifted across Len's jaw.

Werewolves were accustomed to a very specific hierarchy. And Drake was younger by at least twelve years.

"We want them to feel confident," I said to Len gently.

"We want them to never have to—" Len bit off his retort. Then he shifted his shoulders, nodded stiffly, and headed for the sparring room.

Drake watched him for a moment, then turned his gaze back to me. His dark-brown eyes were warm, playful.

I offered him my hand, and he enveloped it in his own, much larger and warmer than mine. He held me for a moment, looking into my eyes. No magic shifted between us, but I could feel the tight hum of his robust power.

Drake was a fledgling dragon in age only. He read as powerful as any other adult dragon. More so, even.

I didn't ask what he was looking for from me, or within me. He was the apprentice to the far seer, after all. He would tell me if I needed to know.

"You have a freaking amazing house, Dusk," he said, grinning suddenly.

The moment broke. He released my hand.

"I do."

"A gift from Jiaotu."

"It comes with my role in the world of the Adept," I said stiffly.

Drake chuckled. "Yeah, I've been briefed. At length. It's just…I know Warner Jiaotuson." He watched me closely as he added, "The sentinel to the wielder of the instruments of assassination."

I'd heard of Warner, who was the son of Jiao-tu-who-was and was also somehow connected to the Godfrey witches. But I had no idea what the instruments of assassination were, so that was definitely something I needed to investigate. But I most certainly didn't know Drake well enough to admit to any ignorance.

"And?" I asked, my tone frosty. I wasn't liking the direction of the conversation. Or the reasons Drake might have thrust himself into our lives.

"Warner might be interested to know he has a brother in magic."

"Why wouldn't he know already?"

"He was only awoken a few years ago."

A few years? I blinked, instantly intrigued. As always.

Jiaotu had mentioned that although Warner had technically been born before him, he was the younger. But I hadn't realized that he'd been missing from the present timeline for quite so long.

Drake's grin widened, and he leaned closer. "I've never met an archivist before, but I've heard stories."

"Of course you have." It was difficult to not grin back at Drake when he was smiling. His energy was infectious. I completely understood why the house had instantly responded to him.

"You're a collector. Of books and artifacts. And magical creatures."

"I am."

"Including the powerful being you've caged in your central tower."

He could feel the death goddess, could he? Two or three years younger than me, and his senses rivaled mine. Not surprising given his actual position.

"Housed," I said smoothly. "I would never keep a sentient being against their will."

Drake raised his eyebrows. "That's going to be a hard promise to keep, archivist."

"We'll see."

He nodded, suddenly serious again. "I won't mention Sisu to Warner, or the other way around, if you don't wish…" He paused deliberately.

Waiting for me to counter him, perhaps?

I didn't.

I also didn't offer any explanation for my caution. Sisu was just getting settled at Wilding Manor and still missing Mom. Warner sounded like a potentially confusing complication. For now.

Drake nodded stiffly. "Fine. Though I would prefer to not lie to my friend. And I know I would have…I would give anything to have a brother, if only in magic."

He dropped my hand and strode away before I could respond.

I hated lying as well.

I hated lying with every cell in my body. Every drop of my power.

But there was nothing I could do about it.

Drake stayed just over two hours, promising to try to come back the following Saturday. I was fairly certain he lived in the guardian nexus full-time, so judging time in the world was likely a little difficult for him. I offered to send him a message that morning as a reminder, understanding that his presence would be contingent on no demon invasion or dimensional incursion requiring his attention, of course.

I didn't mention those possibilities in mixed company. If Drake couldn't make it, I'd take over training the fledglings, or the sword master would send another apprentice. Though I had no doubt that Sisu would complain heartily.

Drake had taught the fledglings a meditation and later showed them how to apply its breathing technique to help focus their inherent magic, using it to shield them from magical attack. He demonstrated on me using a push of his own power. It was slightly unfair, since my shielding was practically coded into my genetics, but Neve, Lile, and Rook didn't know that.

River dropped by for Rook only a few minutes after Drake departed, not bothering to step inside the house. My heart still ached a little at the stiffness of our conversation. River had loved Wilding Manor when she'd first laid eyes on it, but she'd handed the ongoing renovation project over to Ridge after the incident with Ayre. Her loyalty to her aunt had been twisted, even tainted, when Ayre went dark, and that incident still felt like a wedge driven between us.

After a series of text messages that seemed to quietly infuriate Len, he asked if he could leave Neve and Lile with me a little longer, then took off. To speak with Gitta, I thought, being more than a little nosy.

Deciding that Sisu and the twins probably needed to burn off still more energy, I set my own research aside—transcribing the last conversation I'd had with Morgan about the origins of so-called deities—and went in search of the trio to take them for a walk and to check on the imp eggs in the greenhouse.

I found Sisu, Neve, and Lile in my brother's bedroom, their heads bowed over a project that appeared to involve shredding T-shirts and braiding the resulting strands.

"If it smells like us," Neve said as I hovered in the doorway, "then the creature will bond to us when it hatches."

I stepped farther into the bedroom, noting that the bed was still stripped of its covers and pillows. After Len had rallied the fledglings to clean up the living room, that bedding had apparently been thrown in the corner instead of Sisu actually remaking his bed properly.

"Try for fit," Lile urged. She held one of the long braids, holding it loosely between splayed fingers and curling it in on itself to make a bowl shape.

Sisu gently set a golden egg just slightly larger than an average chicken egg in the makeshift bowl, holding it in place. The last time we'd visited the nexus with Sisu's demigod father, Jiaotu had plucked up the egg from atop a stack of books in the library, narrowed his eyes at it in assessment, then casually shrugged and given it to his son. Though it was seamed through the middle and magically sealed, I had no idea what the egg might contain. Sisu had been carrying it with him ever since.

"Too big," Sisu said. "It should be a snug fit for when I carry it in my backpack."

Lile grunted in agreement.

"Hey," I said quietly.

The twins squeaked, but Sisu just blinked up at me, smiling.

"How many T-shirts did you ruin?" I asked, desperately trying to not be completely delighted by their project. I mean, hatching the egg was a terrible idea, of course, but it was unlikely that a little nest made of shredded T-shirts was going to be the trigger that did it. Assuming there was even anything in the egg to hatch in the first place.

Still, with my luck, it contained a rare fire-breathing salamander that would quickly outgrow our pond. Or a miniature cockatrice that would stalk the gnome and devour all the estate's apples right before they were ready to harvest.

"Just three," Sisu said, though the twins exchanged a nervous glance.

"Mine already had a rip in it," Neve said.

"Auntie Erin taught us how to make T-shirt yarn last weekend."

"Rook said it was stupid," Sisu glowered. "That the egg was just a decoration."

"But we know," Lile said.

"We can feel it," Neve added.

With that pronouncement, all three of them cupped their hands around the golden egg, tilting their heads thoughtfully to the sides. A hushed silence fell. I swore I could feel the house listening as well.

I really didn't need the house getting involved. I wasn't even a quarter of the way through renovations. I didn't need a manticore rampaging around, gouging the hardwood floors and getting its spiked tail caught in the railings. Or any other creature that might have been incubating in the egg for that matter.

Kellan would lose his mind if any of the woodwork took damage.

And there I went, involving Kellan in thoughts that had nothing to do with him. Again.

"I thought you might like to go visit the gnome—" I started to say.

The trio were on their feet, racing out of the room and down the stairs before I even finished the sentence.

I followed at a slower pace, finding them all chattering away in the cloakroom while shoving their feet into rain boots. Sisu's black boots looked a little plain next to Lile's and Neve's, in purple and bright green. And I had to ignore a moment of disconcertion, a feeling like I might not be paying enough attention to Sisu's needs and wants on a creative level. Then I remembered he'd picked out the boots himself because he liked the buckled strap on the side. He'd been pestering me for a dagger that he could sheath there ever since.

All three turned to me expectantly, grinning.

"First, we'll take a lap around the property," I said, pulling on my own boots and rain jacket.

Neve nodded sagely. "To check the perimeter."

"And repair any holes in the boundary wards," Sisu said.

"We understand," Lile added.

I laughed. "That too."

CHAPTER THREE

MONDAY MORNING WAS CHILLY ENOUGH THAT EVEN with a thick merino wool scarf twined around my neck and my recently acquired knee-length dark-brown wool coat, I had to hustle on the way to work to keep the chill from invading my bones.

Okay, fine. The real reason for the hustle was that I'd left the manor late, taking longer than necessary to make my lunch and not departing until long after Bethany had Sisu, Neve, and Lile already cracking open their geography books in the space just off the library that she'd converted into a classroom.

I had taken the extra time because I'd hoped Kellan would make an appearance. He hadn't. Gitta had dropped in with the twins, then rushed off right after the plumbers working on the upstairs bathrooms had shown up. More Conall wolves.

Owen Brady fell into step with me about fifteen minutes from the archive. I had complained right from the beginning about the dark-haired werewolf trailing me to and from work, but had only managed to get him to agree to at least walk alongside me, rather than just ghosting my footsteps.

Even after almost two months, I still wasn't certain if the Conall pack was guarding me or simply keeping a constant eye on me.

"Thought I'd missed you," Brady said, his chin tucked into a cabled, cream-colored scarf, and his hands stuffed into the pockets of his navy wool coat. His accent was Irish, but tempered by the years of education abroad it had taken to obtain his certification to oversee dangerous collections. "Circled back."

"I can make it to work on my own," I said stiffly, feeling stupid for being late. And knowing it was because of the way Kellan had slipped his fingers through mine at the end of our dance, as if he hadn't wanted to let me go when I'd stepped away.

"So you've said, on repeat," Brady groused. He'd let his beard grow in for the winter, but still kept it neatly trimmed.

I sighed, giving in before I even got around to pressing the issue. I hated repeating myself. Well, more than three times, at least. Obviously, some repetition was beneficial when it came to absorbing new information.

"Erin loved the gala," Brady said, matching my stride perfectly. "First time we'd danced…" He laughed quietly. "Like that, at least."

I cast a look his way, but he just grinned to himself and didn't elaborate. Another pet peeve of mine—oblique comments. Though I understood that particular affectation was overused among the Adepts of Dublin, because the city was such a closed ecosystem. According to Ravine, at least.

The werewolves and witches of Dublin had been mostly raised together, so they never felt the need to elaborate. On anything. But that left me unable to gather information without asking questions—and if I asked questions, I opened myself up to personal inquiries as well. And then I had to lie or seriously edit my answers.

It was frustrating.

It was also possible I was just in a snit. I hadn't slept well for the two nights since the gala. Something was bothering me, chafing me. Like an itch I couldn't scratch, or a bruise that I couldn't figure out how I'd gotten.

I'd missed something. Or was in the process of missing something.

"You are coming to the pack's solstice celebration, right?" Brady asked, sounding tentative. That was understandable, given that I'd just abruptly dropped the conversation.

"Of course. I've never seen or even read about one."

Brady chuckled quietly again. "Not everything has to be experienced as if it's an anthropological event, Dusk. Sometimes it's just about dancing under the moon and…enjoying letting go."

I didn't let go, though. I'd never really felt the need. And I certainly couldn't let go of everything I held so tightly while in the company of the pack or any other guests.

A thought occurred to me. "But the kids are invited, right?"

Brady huffed. "It isn't an orgy."

I flushed. "I didn't mean…"

"Don't get me wrong. The solstice is revered, and lots of us worship in our own way. Lots." He hit that second 'lots' hard, side-eyeing me. "But there are plenty of mostly hidden spaces for…such things."

"I'm not a prude."

"If you dance, I'm sure you'll get offers." He flashed a grin at me. "But the kids do their own thing up at the house."

"I thought the main party was at the pack house?"

"The bonfire will be on the beach."

I blinked. I'd only been to the main pack house once—the Conall manor, on the family's forested estate, which I'd seen only while being chased through the night-shrouded woods by celestial wolves. I didn't remember a beach or even sensing the sea nearby. But then, I was easily distracted, and the discovery of mysterious runes and an amulet that had turned out to house the remains of a death goddess incarnate had taken priority.

"The woods on the far back side of the property lead to some wicked cliffs," Brady said. "Great for diving. And farther south, there's a couple of small swimming coves, as well as an actual sandy beach. A bonfire on the beach has less chance of getting out of control."

I murmured agreement. Fire and magic really didn't mix. Or rather, they sometimes mixed too well, but being near water was a natural dampener.

Still in perfect step, Brady and I rounded the side of the main museum building, heading to the hidden, plain steel door that led into the offices of the magical archive.

Brady's step hitched. He raised his chin, sampling the air just a moment before I felt a tingle of power from the vicinity of a light-gray molded-concrete bench set within a tiny area of greenery not far from the main doors. On sunny days, Crystal and I often ate our lunches on the bench, chatting about what we were currently reading.

I let Brady continue forward, crossing behind him to pause by the empty bench. The faint presence I'd picked up dissipated in the two steps it took me to close the space. A hint of magic so, so familiar, yet not robust enough for me to identify. As if it had been deliberately withdrawn. To get my attention?

I scanned the side of the building, then overhead. The chill air nipped at my nose and cheeks, but I was unable to pick up whatever had twigged my senses. I turned to find Brady watching me, his hand on the handle of the steel door. His normally brown eyes were tinted with the green of his shifter magic.

"What did you scent?" I asked.

He shook his head slightly. "Someone passed through into the archive in the last few minutes. A sorcerer, maybe, but not James."

I leaned down to place my hand on the concrete bench. I could have sworn that someone had just been sitting on it. Or...standing on it? Visually cloaked perhaps. And not a sorcerer.

Brady raised one eyebrow questioningly.

It was my turn to shake my head, stuffing my chilled hand back in my pocket.

He opened the door to the archive, and warmth greeted us as we hustled inside to the main offices.

On the far side of the main room, the door to my office was standing open, though I usually closed it in the evenings and for the weekend. I could feel someone waiting within, though I couldn't sense who it was through the wards, which I'd personally reinforced. But since James and Crystal were standing to the left of the entrance by the historian's desk in the corner, it was an easy guess that it was a stranger.

Guests could pass through my office wards by invitation from myself or any of my employees. Up to that very moment, that option had seemed only practical. But it now felt invasive, and annoying.

Apparently, the walk to work hadn't eased my snit.

"Sorry." Crystal grimaced, twisting her hands together as she followed my gaze to my office. She was dressed in a bright-blue floral-print dress over navy-blue tights and thick-heeled green shoes. "He just got here. It wasn't part of our...agreement, but he asked to talk to you before I grabbed the items he's requested. He has a book he wants to donate to the archive. To you, personally."

Brady growled something under his breath, stalking forward through the four separate open office spaces that made up the main room of the archive as he stripped off his outerwear. He tossed his jacket and scarf on his desk at the apex of the back hall, though his gaze was still fixed on my office.

"Who?" I asked, unbuttoning my coat and loosening my scarf.

"Brendan Prince," James sneered, flicking a look Crystal's way. His accent indicated a British upbringing, but like most of the archive employees, it was layered and nuanced—not atypical for anyone who'd studied and worked all over the world. He wore his usual ill-fitting navy-blue suit, layered with all the protection spells typical for a sorcerer. After almost two months of working with the sandy-haired historian, I realized that what he wore or how he presented himself wasn't a big priority for him.

Crystal hissed under her breath. "I know you don't like him, Jim. But his money is perfectly good. Enough to help finance the dig you're trying to get Dusk to okay."

I narrowed my eyes as I glanced between my two employees. The historian didn't oversee digs, which were under my and Brady's purview.

"It's not a dig," James said sourly.

I decided to focus the conversation back to the issue at hand—namely, my office being invaded early on a Monday morning when I was finally hoping to devote myself to something other than the gala. "I thought Mesa Byrne won the silent auction?" I didn't add that I also assumed I'd get a say in the scheduling of the auction item in question—the tour of the archive and a two-hour chat with me.

"Prince matched her two thousand," Crystal explained, sounding a little pained. "I didn't agree to your participation, though. And I said a tour without you wasn't an option, thinking that might dissuade him. It didn't. He's just interested in studying some artifacts and texts."

James waved a piece of partially rolled parchment, still sneering. "He was waiting at the door with a list of over twenty titles."

Crystal snatched the list from him. "I already said I'd take care of it, even though community relations is usually your job." Stepping toward me, the blond-haired witch lowered her voice. "It's not an unprecedented request, Dusk. I made a judgement call."

I nodded, trying to be gracious even though I wasn't at all feeling like it. I was the head curator. I couldn't just hole up petting and cooing over new acquisitions every day, no matter how much I wanted to.

Crystal smiled, relieved. "If you give me a few minutes to get the first few items, I'll stack them on Ayre's...on the free desk." She gestured to the empty desk to the right of the entrance.

I hadn't filled Ayre's position yet. And I wasn't in any rush to do so.

"Keeping him working away from your office will ensure that you don't have to talk with Prince for too long," Crystal added.

"Fine."

She started to turn away, then hesitated. Her gaze flicked over my shoulder, and she opened her mouth to speak. Then she didn't.

I followed that gaze. Brady had taken up sentry position in the open door to my office, leaning against the doorjamb. He was partially over the threshold and right in the middle of the wards, which couldn't be all that comfortable. "Something wrong?" I asked the librarian.

She pursed her lips for a moment, already shaking her head. "Just a sense...that you...made an impression on Brendan Prince."

I raised an eyebrow, not fully understanding the nuance underlying Crystal's observation. I thought I'd been rather cool, even offish, when I'd met Prince at the gala. Though apparently not enough to dissuade the sorcerer from inviting himself into my office. "An impression?" I asked.

Crystal sighed, laughing. "You did look amazing. That gold mask of Ravine's...and your golden eyes..." She trailed off uncomfortably. "I mean...Prince works out of the archive housed in the National Museum Cardiff, in Wales. I haven't dug into his list of requests yet." She lightly tapped the rolled parchment she was holding in the open palm of her other hand. "But even at first glance, he could have had the head curator at Cardiff request most of these items. Even the crown piece. Because even though you and Brady just found it, it's not significant." She shrugged one shoulder.

"He's in town," I said. "Maybe he wants to look over the items before making a formal request. Archive to archive."

Crystal hummed noncommittally. Then she hustled off toward the back hall that led to the stairs down to the archives in the basement.

I tugged off my backpack, then my coat, folding it over my arm and putting my backpack on again.

"I don't like it," James muttered quietly. "Showing up here with a cheque, writing his list on old parchment." He sniffed dismissively. "He's a poseur. An obnoxious, arrogant poseur. Always has been."

I eyed the historian, who I still didn't know well. He was older than me by a decade and mostly kept to himself. "Will giving him access to the items he requested cause any harm?"

James huffed, unbuttoning his suit jacket and throwing himself into his desk chair. "Only to anyone who reads his work and is somehow suckered into even considering that his theories might hold any value or validity."

I stifled a smile. "I understand."

He grimaced. "I'm not jealous. I'm appalled at his popularity."

Over three-quarters of the books housed in the archive's library had been compiled by or written by historians. The texts might not hold magic themselves, or even teach the reader how to manifest and channel their specific powers. But taken as a whole, they were invaluable.

James had three books partially written himself and grants from two other archives supporting his research. He spent a chunk of time every few months in the London and Berlin archives. Before working in Dublin, I'd had no idea that historians competed for resources or maintained rivalries among themselves.

James shook his head, presumably at my lack of response. Then he started sorting through the few books, the single notebook, and the loose papers strewn across his desk. "It's fine. Crystal and Brady can handle him. And I'll happily take a chunk of his money."

I smirked at him. When I'd said I understood him, I definitely did. Before being appointed as the head curator for the magical archives of Ireland, I'd been continually frustrated that every archivist I knew held far more exciting positions than I did. More exciting than what I'd assumed was a nothing title—Archivist of the Modern World.

Okay, fine. Not frustrated. Unlike James, I had been jealous.

Except as it turned out, Archivist of the Modern World hadn't been just a title meant to keep me distracted and placated. But it had taken me almost two years to figure that out.

"Get me that proposal," I said over my shoulder as I crossed toward my office.

"It's not a dig," James muttered under his breath. Then presumably thinking I couldn't hear him, he raised his voice. "It isn't ready yet."

I nodded, but was already focused on the deeply glowering werewolf standing sentry at my door. Brady appeared to be trying to decide what level of punishment to mete out on Brendan Prince, but he stepped away as I drew near, leaning back against the wall by the door with his arms folded instead. I had no idea if he was more pissed at the interloping sorcerer, or at Crystal for agreeing to the unscheduled trespass of the archive offices.

Werewolves liked everything to be orderly.

I did as well, always. I was just slightly more flexible than Brady. But then, unlike the werewolf, I hadn't almost died the last time one of the archive's employees—namely, Ayre Byrne—allowed an unknown entity access to the offices and the staff. Six years ago, Celeste Cameron, the previous head curator, had died after being attacked by a soul sucker posing as a mummified pharaoh.

I gave my security specialist a quelling look before I crossed through the wards that invisibly sealed the doorway. I didn't need backup in my own office. Brady's glower only deepened. I would have sworn that his magic rooted him even more firmly in position. Werewolf magic didn't work that way as far as I knew—at least not when a werewolf wasn't on their claimed territory. So I wrote it off as an impression of Brady's ridiculously stubborn nature rather than an actual manifestation of power.

The dark-haired man in the guest chair set before my large oak desk at the far side of the office swiveled at my entrance. He was dressed in a blue suit that was obviously bespoke, as was the navy-blue shirt underneath and the even darker-blue tie. His legs were crossed, displaying argyle-printed socks and shiny black-leather shoes.

Even with my limited understanding of fashion, it was obvious that Brendan Prince didn't finance his wardrobe with grant money. Or at least he didn't have any need to do so.

I hung my coat and scarf on the rack I'd set just inside the door, then crossed toward my desk. The oak bookshelves lining the two side walls were still mostly bare. Even with Crystal organizing the gala, I hadn't acquired many personal work artifacts since I'd rehoused most of Celeste Cameron's collection in the main archive.

Brendan Prince's jaw-length hair fell forward from his sharp-featured face as he rose. As he had the night before, he swept it back from his high brow, then offered me his hand, grinning widely.

Even surrounded by wards of my own construction, I couldn't get a solid read on the sorcerer's magic.
Again. He was either highly skilled at masking his
power, or it wasn't at all potent. It was likely the former.
My sense for magic was acute.

I took his hand, and he leaned in, forcing eye contact. "I'm pleased to see you again, Dusk Godfrey," he
said, something teasing in his tone.

"You went out of your way to make that possible,
Mr. Prince," I said, trying to sound professional, but
possibly erring on the side of icily cool.

Maybe I wasn't as flexible as I'd proclaimed myself
to be, even if only in my own head. Especially not in
sight of the pile of books on the corner of my desk, each
waiting patiently for me to gobble up their pages. Like
the dragon I was, guarding my ever-increasing hoard.

A smile ghosted over my face at the thought. I released Prince's hand, crossing around the desk.

"The prospect of uncovering the treasures the archive holds was worth far more effort," he said smoothly.
"Writing a cheque seems inconsequential when faced
with…" He gestured toward my desk as he took his seat
again.

No, not my desk.

Me.

I chafed internally at the suggestion that my time
could be bought, but kept the reaction to myself as I slid
my backpack into a warded desk drawer. Infinity was
still tucked within it. Prince followed my movements
with a flick of his violet eyes. But the longer the silence
stretched, the more forced his pleasant expression
became.

I sat, folding my hands on the desk.

He brightened his smile, tilting his head toward the
pile of books perched a little precariously on the corner

of my desk. "Some intriguing titles," he murmured. "I've only read two. Am I right to assume that a few of these were also recently uncovered along with the fae crown piece?"

"The connection is circumstantial," I said, chafing even more at him continuing to blithely name the relic as a so-called fae piece despite the lack of evidence. "These books simply held enough residual magic to draw my attention." And yes, I knew that Crystal had intimated that fanciful connection in the gala display write-up, but it would have been nice if the historian sitting across from me could prove he was more than just a peddler of fae tales for profit.

When Brady and I had first collected the piece in Galway, the werewolf had called me a snob—and he was totally correct. Not that I was fussed enough about the title to do anything about it.

The research I was rather desperate to dive back into, on death goddesses and death magic, was tidily shelved to my left. I had five new books waiting for me—two unearthed from the archive, two on loan from the Dunkirk witches in London, and one from Zeke. If not for Brendan Prince, I would have already been working on the first, absorbing the text into Infinity and making notes as I read.

Prince's grin sharpened. "Well, hopefully I have something to offer that might be just as intriguing as your recent finds." He pulled a book bound in red fabric with a thick black spine from the leather satchel he'd slung over the back of the chair, offering it to me. Unlike the sorcerer's other clothing, the satchel was well worn. Not shabby, but not as glossy as everything else he wore.

The title was embossed in dark-red foil on the cover, as were the edges of the pages. *A Book of the Fae*. His own book.

"Limited edition," Prince all but purred. "And autographed, of course." He set the book down, flipping it open to the inscription in question.

I dropped my gaze, my eyesight sharp enough that I could read it even across the desk.

He had signed the inset title page, dominated by an etching that was rather heavy on the flourishes. It was a door surrounded by runes or symbols I didn't recognize.

Dusk. May you discover many unexplored doorways and find many new worlds at your feet.—Prince

The inscription was oddly intimate for two people who'd barely met. And the sense that I'd missed something important or had forgotten something itched again at the back of my mind. Was it the symbols? They looked familiar…

Prince was staring at me expectantly.

"Thank you for the donation," I said smoothly. "We have copies of your work in the archive. Crystal referenced them a few times while setting up the gala." His magic was still dim, with no hint of anything even remotely nefarious about it. His grin was still fixed. Maybe it was his unusual violet eyes.

Was I that shallow? Or was it Crystal's suggestion that I'd made an impression on Brendan Prince, when all I ever really wanted was to just do my job and go mostly unnoticed?

"Of course you do," he said with a shrug. "But this is for your personal library, Dusk." He leaned forward, smiling as if sharing an intimate secret with me. "And though you might not have had the time to fill your office shelves, I imagine your personal library is…large. And varied. Yes?"

Not entirely certain if he was trying to flirt and was just terrible at it—or if he somehow hadn't yet noticed that I wasn't receptive—I dropped my gaze to the etched titled page again.

Something about those runes around the doorway were definitely familiar...

I tugged the book closer, noting as Prince settled back in his chair with a smug grin and his legs crossed, flicking a nonexistent piece of lint from his knee.

I flipped to the first chapter, quickly scanning the text.

"Ah, yes. The tale we spoke of on Saturday night," he said. "The fated mates torn asunder? A devoted lord of the fae willing to risk all to achieve the life his lady desired. They fled the constraints of their parentage and heritage, only to be cruelly separated. She murdered so he could survive..."

"And her crown was broken in pieces by the blow that took her life," I said, interrupting him. I knew the tale he was peddling—the tale that he'd brushed off and added some flourishes to, including the lovers being fae, and was now selling. Passing off fanciful embellishment as fact. No verifiable sources or references of the sort James was spending years accumulating. All the research he'd done to write the three books he was currently working on.

To any real historian, the lovers of Prince's tale were most likely a minor footnote in the history of the Adept, with some sort of Celtic roots. James agreed with me, as did Brady. Spending more time translating the runes on the crown piece would let me know for certain.

That said, James, Brady, and I had disagreed quietly in the lead-up to the gala, so as to not upset Crystal.

And it wasn't that I didn't believe in the fae as a concept. It was simply a term so broad as to be meaningless, covering too many beings, too many possible dimensions. And all those dimensions were effectively unknown to the Adepts of the world because the guardian dragons had long kept their unnamed denizens from expanding into our own dimension, sealing any and all doorways and portals to those realms as fast as they appeared.

The fae were similar in that way to elves or even demons. But elves and demons had actual lore. Real history within the world. All that was known of the fae was mostly guesswork, hinting that they had vastly disparate classifications among their own kind, from ruling classes whose positions were based on pure, inherent power, to lesser fae who were subservient to the fae in each rank above them.

I'd only ever read about three actual fae incursions. Three thwarted attempts to breach the boundary between dimensions and the guardian dragons' defenses. But none of those attempts had occurred in the last thousand years or involved any of my relatives. At least none of the relatives whose journals resided in my mother's library.

A glimmer of frustration, or maybe even anger, flitted over Prince's face. He covered it with a thin-lipped smile and a dip of his chin. But having finished scanning the first couple of pages of his book, I was now looking for something else under the smooth exterior that Brendan Prince presented. Because even with just a quick glance, my practically eidetic memory had kicked in.

The first section of Prince's book was an echo of the tome I'd discovered along with the piece of the crown, both claimed from the estate of a Byrne witch in Galway. Similar word for word in some places. To the point that Prince's work might well have been paraphrased—if not outright copied—from the older text.

That text was currently tucked into the middle of the pile on the corner of my desk, its spine unmarked. Without having the time to verify its origins and authenticity, I had chosen to not display it alongside the crown-piece relic for the gala. I would have to double-check, of course. The volume the Byrne witch had collected was handwritten, but based on the date on the illustrated title page, it most definitely predated the book currently splayed open on my desk by at least two hundred years. Sorcerers could live well into their first century, but not beyond.

I would also need to compare the unusual runes twined throughout the illustrated title page to the sketches contained within the earlier work. But the question of whether Brendan Prince was a plagiarizer was suddenly intriguing. And definitely not in the way I was fairly certain the historian wanted to be intriguing, if I was reading his oddly uncomfortable attempts at flirting correctly.

Well, uncomfortable for me.

Tension ran through Prince's jaw in response to my steady regard. But his tone was perfectly pleasant. "You were saying?"

"I'm just wondering how devoted this fae lord could have been to his so-called fated mate. If she was the one who died so he could flee."

"That is certainly one perspective," Prince said, smiling tightly.

Of course, the older handwritten account could simply be a copy of an even older work that Prince had used as a source. But that only exemplified my disdain for what passed for research among some historians. Copying old tales out again and again, freshening them up, then selling them to the modern Adept as if they were actual history.

Still, that line of thought made me wonder what Brendan Prince might do with any earlier accountings he copied. Did he collect them and hide them away? Or would he go so far as to destroy them?

And if that was the case, rather than the appearance of the magically insignificant crown piece, was it the idea of the journal accompanying the piece coming to light that had drawn him to the gala? Concern for his livelihood, perhaps?

I closed the book, trying to appear thoughtful. "And what do you think they were doing? The two fae? Having crossed into our dimension to build themselves a new life?"

"What do any lovers do under that circumstance?" Prince's tone was stiff. But his violet eyes were still fixed on me intently.

"Well...something that resulted in them being hunted and decapitated couldn't have been all that...peaceful."

"You are very sheltered, Dusk Godfrey." Prince's lips thinned, whitening with rage. He didn't enjoy having his theories of fairy tales questioned. "To think that there aren't monsters in your world as well."

"I know there are. It's my job to know all the creatures that walk this earth."

He smiled again, but still tightly.

I set his book off to the side of my desk. "Thank you. I look forward to reading it." And comparing it to the handwritten version. If it turned out to be true that Prince was less than forthcoming as to the sources of his work, James would be exceedingly pleased. "The illustrations are...detailed. Your designs?"

"Indeed. I'm not a skilled artist, but the renderings just flowed through me when I touched pen to paper."

It was my turn to grin sharply. "Magic does as it wills."

"That it does." Prince shifted out of his chair, grabbing his satchel by the handle instead of the cross-body strap. "I'd love to take you to lunch."

"I'm afraid I'm—"

"I'll check back in," he interrupted before I could refuse, "after I see what your librarian has unearthed for me."

I hummed in response, already itching to snatch the Galway text out of the pile of acquisitions on my desk. It was possible that the older version of the text might lend credence to Prince's book if both were interpretations of an even older source. But apparently the idea of unmasking a shoddy historian was enough to get me out of my snit.

I skipped coffee break to deal with a bunch of memos and requests that had piled up on my desk over the last week. That process mostly involved sorting through each one, then shunting the approved tasks back to James or Crystal. I also still needed to approve the budget for the following year, meaning I needed to schedule a meeting with James to go over it line by line.

On top of operating expenses, I had reduced my employees' six-month probation to three months. Probation that had been imposed because of their knowledge of Ayre Byrne's plan to murder a rare tooth fairy, and that they hadn't stopped her. They also all needed an increase in their salaries, which had been frozen for six years, since Celeste Cameron had been killed.

Words, magical creatures, and items of power were very much my thing. But math and accounting most certainly weren't.

So, forced to focus on my actual job, I tucked Prince's autographed book and the handwritten Galway text into the warded drawer that also held my backpack, leaving Infinity locked away as well. Normally I worked in tandem with my personal archive, but having Brendan Prince invade the office had made me protective.

Okay, 'invade' might have been a little melodramatic.

Over the course of two months, all my other employees had laid eyes on Infinity, and not one of them had questioned me. Granted, I usually didn't do more than simply write in my personal archive when anyone else was in view. But Crystal, James, and Brady wouldn't be working in an archive if their magical sensitivity wasn't acute, so they were all certain to recognize Infinity as a powerful magical object.

Brendan Prince didn't need any more reasons to be interested in me, as Crystal had indicated.

Energy shifted in the front office, heralding the entrance of another Adept. A witch. I could sense her magic even through the wards and had no doubt she'd spotted Prince as she entered. I practically felt the hitch in her usually confident gait.

Her teasing laughter cut through the wards easily enough as well.

Ravine Byrne.

I glanced at the clock on my shelf. It was almost lunchtime, but Ravine and I usually met for lunch at Cove Cafe on Tuesdays, not Mondays. I hadn't even brought the items I'd borrowed from the metal mage with me to work so I could return them.

Ravine appeared in my office doorway, still smiling over her shoulder. Tucked behind her ears, her sleek brown hair was slightly shorter and a shade darker than it had been at the Gala. She must have cut and dyed it over the weekend. Swathed in shades of black and charcoal, including a soft-looking leather jacket, a huge knit cowl, and knee-high laced boots, she stepped through the wards, then turned her blue-green gaze my way, smirking.

"Well…I was going to ask you to grab lunch with me…"

I laughed quietly. "And now?"

She flung herself into the chair before my desk, crossing her legs with a flourish and exposing a lot of skin between her short skirt and her high boots. Anyone else would have been freezing without tights, but presumably the metal mage had heating spells or charms on her jacket and cowl.

"Now…" She flicked a sly gaze my way. "Now I'm slightly concerned that you have other plans."

"I don't. Just a slight backlog."

Ravine raised her perfectly sculpted eyebrows, both the same shade as her hair. Since everyone else in her familial line was a redhead, she must have dyed them as well. "Um, what about the hot male camped out in the main office?" The smattering of freckles across her cheeks and nose that she covered with a complexion charm made an appearance, then faded.

It actually took me a moment to figure out what she was implying. Apparently my scale of 'hot' was not the same as Ravine's. "Brendan Prince?"

She laughed sharply. "You don't have to sound insulted."

"I'm not…I'm just…"

She snorted and waved her hand offishly. "It's fine. I was interested. I am interested. He was…satisfying, bordering on truly skilled. But afterward, the conversation turned to you, and the archive. Three times. Thus freeing up my weekend for other pursuits."

I just stared at the dark-haired witch, slightly thrown that a stranger had been questioning her about me. Three times. And after sex, if I was interpreting correctly. I was also slightly thrown thinking about what Ravine might have told Prince after such an intimate moment…or, rather, moments.

She straightened, everything playful and fun fading from her expression as she uncrossed her legs and leaned toward me earnestly. She lowered her voice. "Hey, none of that. You're a beautiful woman in a position of power over items that interest Prince. Any out-of-town Adept who's also a collector is going to take one look at you, and…want to know how to get in your good graces."

I nodded, but my wariness must have still lingered in my expression, because Ravine scooted forward until she was perched on the edge of the chair and could flatten both of her hands on my desk. Magic twined lazily around the intricate gold cuffs mostly hidden under her sweater.

She smiled toothily, drawling playfully, "Just keep dancing with Kellan Conall exclusively, and everyone will know exactly where you stand."

I blinked.

She elaborated. "No one in their right mind would try to go through Kellan."

I frowned, not liking the inference.

Ravine laughed, falling back in the chair again. "Yeah, yeah, you can take care of yourself. Still…" She shrugged. "It's nicer when you don't get bothered in the first place. If that's what you want. Me? I like being bothered." She grinned saucily.

I smiled back. Being Ravine's friend often meant letting her talk out whatever point she was trying to make. Not that I minded, she was a valuable source of information. And fun.

And yes, I was fairly certain we were friends. We'd gone bowling two weeks ago, just her and me. I'd never played before and had been afraid of breaking things that weren't supposed to be broken, like the pins. Or the floor, for that matter. And even after I understood how the game worked, I made certain to play terribly. The food had been horrid, but Ravine had explained it was part of the experience.

"So...lunch?" she asked. "I have an odd request—"

Brendan Prince appeared in the doorway with a couple of books propped open in his hand. The wards rippled slightly, as if he'd been moving quickly when he brushed up against them. He wandered into my office uninvited, his gaze riveted to the well-worn brown leather tome on the top of his pile. "This is intriguing..."

"Do tell," Ravine drawled, partly twisting in her chair to eye him.

Prince blinked as if he hadn't realized Ravine was in my office. "Oh, excuse me. I didn't mean to interrupt."

"The first one is free," Ravine said, grinning. "But trust me, you don't want to build up a tab."

He laughed quietly, flicking his gaze between me and her, then settling it on the metal mage. "I thank you for the fair warning."

She shrugged one shoulder prettily, flirting and completely in command.

I should have been taking notes. Because I was a blithering idiot around Kellan.

Not that I should be flirting with Kellan.

I would just keep telling myself that.

"You were saying?" Ravine prompted. "Something intriguing?"

"Oh, just…something about doorways…" Prince glanced at the book in his hand, then at me. "Rumors most likely, but always worth investigating."

I had no idea what conversation he was trying to incite. Dimensional doorways were real, of course. But investigating such things—and most often shutting them down—fell under the guardian dragons' purview. And I certainly wasn't interested in chatting about any of that with Prince.

"Doorways to the fae realm?" Ravine asked. "That's your area of expertise, isn't it?"

"Yes." Prince settled his attention on Ravine, snapping the book shut as if he'd come to some sort of decision. A slow smile sharpened his features. "Yes, indeed. But I'd hate to figure out what sort of tab you keep when you're being bored."

Ravine laughed, the sound lilting and warm.

Prince's grin grew, but then he turned to me. "So? If I'm not interrupting…lunch?"

I glanced at Ravine. I really, really didn't want to go for lunch with Brendan Prince and listen to him yammer on about the fae and fated mates for an hour.

She winked at me, then rose from her chair to loop her hand around Prince's elbow. "Dusk was just telling me how swamped she is. Too much time spent on the gala."

Prince nodded sagely. "And you only took over the archive a few months ago, yes? After the position hung open for over six years? I imagine you must be overwhelmed."

I wasn't. And I actually had to stop myself from outwardly bristling at the suggestion that I was that incapable.

"There's a great pub a couple of blocks over," Ravine said, once again saving me from my own inability to be at all diplomatic. Or at least gracious. "Shall we be bad and grab a midday pint of Guinness?"

"Yes, let's," Prince said, his smile firmly in place and directed at Ravine. "Lead on."

Ravine spun herself and Prince toward the door, glancing back over her shoulder to mouth words at me: 'Lunch tomorrow at the cafe?'

I nodded, smiling at her in relief. But I was forced to check my expression when Prince glanced back as they cleared the doorway and the wards.

"I look forward to chatting this afternoon," he said. "I think you will be intrigued."

My smile stiffened, and I didn't respond. Then the two stepped away and out of my sight, quickly departing the main offices.

I immediately pulled Infinity from the warded desk drawer, then wandered into the kitchen to grab my packed lunch.

Despite his earlier threat to do so, Prince didn't bother me for the rest of the day. Instead, he came back from lunch without Ravine, then tucked in behind his pile of books on Ayre's vacated desk. Brady sat sentry at his own desk, firmly situated between the interloper and the stairs to the archive. That also put him between Prince and the bathroom. Which, unfortunately for the sorcerer, meant that he got escorted anytime he used the facilities. Werewolves were highly territorial.

In addition, Crystal kept checking on Prince every forty-five minutes, not so much to make sure he had everything he needed, but to snatch back any book he'd finished reading. The sorcerer historian bore all the hovering and glowering with polite smiles and no sudden moves. But given that he worked in an archive himself, he presumably understood such protective impulses.

The budget meeting with James took far too many hours that I could have been using to dig into my own research, or to work my way through the pile of new acquisitions on my desk. But I got through it, signing off with only minimal changes.

I was glancing at the clock and trying to figure out what I could fit into the last hour of my day when the outer wards shifted, announcing Ravine's return. She crossed through the office without pausing. As she stepped into my office, she shucked off her coat and cowl and flung them over the chair set before my desk without speaking. Then she paced.

"Um, hello again?" I settled back in my chair with Infinity tucked in my lap. Yes, I'd thought about closing my door, forcing Prince to knock, but I didn't like being cut off from the rest of the office. So I'd had my personal archive tucked under the desk and out of sight for most of the afternoon.

"I'm going to ask you a weird favor," the metal mage said, still pacing.

"All right."

"I don't like asking for favors. And I certainly don't like asking them of you."

That was oddly upsetting. "Why not?"

Ravine stopped pacing, spinning to look at me. "Not like that, Dusk. It's just I've been thinking about it since the gala, and trying to justify asking, except I'd totally be trading on our friendship. And you are very clear that there's work Dusk, and then there's friend Dusk."

I blinked, not really following her.

She sighed, settling back against the empty bookshelves midway along on my right. Her gaze shifted out the door. It was likely that she had a clear view of Brendan Prince at that angle. "I'd like to make a copy of the piece of the fae crown. I feel like…it's caught in my brain, and I'd love to replicate it. Maybe even create a new line of jewelry based on it."

"Caught in your brain…?" I echoed with concern.

Ravine snorted, shaking her head. "Nothing like that." She pushed up her sweater sleeves, displaying the intricate gold cuffs that coiled up her forearms. "Metal thwarts most enchantments. My metal, at least. It's not that sort of compulsion."

I tried to not stare at Ravine's armbands, no matter how many pages I was itching to fill in Infinity with the exacting detail of their construction and use, of course and always. But I caught sight of the metal mage's personal artifacts often enough that I knew they changed subtly, like a constant work in progress. Or perhaps depending on whatever spells Ravine had layered into them.

"It's just…" She wafted her hands toward herself dramatically. "It's inspiration, you know? Probably similar to how you feel when you sneak into some creepy tomb, shoo spiders away from desiccated corpses, and find a tiny piece of magical treasure. You want more, right?" She pinned her bright blue-green eyes on me expectantly.

"Sure," I said. "Though your idea of what an archivist does is oddly interesting."

She snorted. "Maybe it's Owen Brady's pillow talk that's…oddly interesting."

Well, that was surprising.

"Not lately," she said quickly. "I don't cheat. I'm not opposed to threesomes, of course. Just…you know. At the same time, not sneaking around." She shook her head with a huff. "We were barely together. Brady had just gotten back from whatever training he had to do to get that dangerous digs certification."

Ah, that made more sense. "I've never gotten a chance to uncover an undiscovered treasure in a tomb," I said.

"You don't have to sound so mournful about it," Ravine teased. "I'm sure we could find some corpse-filled cavern for you to crawl around in."

I grinned at her. "You think?"

She laughed, leaning against the unwarded section of shelves again. The tension she'd carried with her into the office eased. I could actually sense her magic settle back into her cuffs as she glanced out into the main office.

"Why do I get the feeling the crown piece isn't all that has inspired you?" I asked, teasing. "Lunch was…invigorating?"

Ravine smirked. "He is rather dreamy, isn't he?" She sighed, without even a hint of sarcasm.

"Pretty," I said noncommittally. Brendan Prince wasn't even remotely my type.

And yes, apparently I had a type now. Or at least my hormones did.

Though I actually wasn't certain that Kellan even fell into any archetypal romantic constructs. He was utterly unique. Though how unique, I had yet to determine.

And that was most certainly part of the intrigue.

Ravine snorted. "And what puzzle are you rolling around in your constantly working brain? Nothing to do with Prince, I hope?"

I'd completely let the conversation drop. "Sorry."

"He's interested in you." Her tone was flat, and for a moment, I thought she was talking about Kellan.

I almost opened my mouth and confessed.

Everything.

Specifically, how I was totally beguiled by Kellan Conall, and all the reasons I couldn't actually be with him. Assuming he even wanted to be with me. Wanted an actual relationship. If I wasn't just some hard-won conquest.

I still remembered Ravine's warning the first evening I'd met the shifter. *'Everyone has tangled tongues with Kellan Conall at least once,'* she'd said—and it was still haunting me. Just a little.

The metal mage was watching me, one brow raised expectantly. "Prince, I meant. He's interested. And you?"

I shut my mouth, then shrugged, trying for a nonchalance I didn't feel. "He's interested in my archive. And an archivist wants to be wanted for more than simply her archive."

"Like Kellan?"

"Like Kellan what?"

She grinned unabashedly. "You danced once at the gala. With Kellan." Repeating herself from earlier, but now speaking slowly, as if I were an idiot.

An answering grin that I couldn't seem to quash spread across my face. "We've had this conversation."

"Have we?" she purred.

I snorted. "I thought you thought Kellan wasn't a good choice."

It was her turn to shrug. "It's possible I'm biased. Just don't expect…much."

I nodded, trying to ignore the way my heart had suddenly grown heavy in my chest. "I'm a little busy myself."

"That you are. So? Feel like bending the rules for me with the crown piece?"

I pulled my backpack out of the drawer, slipping Infinity into its depths. "Anyone can request access to the archives."

"Really?" she drawled doubtfully. "My mother will be pleased. Your predecessor had a tighter grip."

"She really didn't," I said sourly, standing to step around the desk, then instantly regretting my statement. I hadn't even known Celeste Cameron. I shouldn't have been—

Ravine patted my arm with feigned sympathy. "I won't tattle, Dusk. You're allowed to have a contrary opinion."

"I have contrary opinions all the time."

She laughed, threading her arm through mine. "Out loud or just in your head?"

Well, I had to give her that. "It's a security issue, keeping everything tightly locked down. But the crown piece is an insignificant relic."

"Don't let Prince hear you say that," she muttered. "He's acting like it's the linchpin to some great discovery."

"It helps that he believes in the fae," I said, casting my voice low as I stepped toward the door. "And fated mates."

"You don't?"

I stopped as I glanced toward Prince, wanting to keep the conversation inside the wards. "It's like calling any creature that has black scales, jagged teeth, and acidic blood a demon. Actually, it's even worse, because the dimension that most demons are summoned from is only thinly separated from the world. Near our own dimension, for lack of a better way to explain it. And its denizens are fairly well catalogued."

"But fae aren't?"

"Going back millennia, only a handful of different creatures have been classified as fae by real historians trying to piece together a common mythology. The sightings are exceedingly rare and not well documented." I knew that last part for a fact, given that any such documentation would be well known among archivists with connections to the guardian dragons. I had wondered more than once—with just a twinge of jealousy—how many stories my mother might have coaxed out of Jiaotu during 'pillow talk,' as Ravine had phrased it. Not that I wanted to be intimate with any guardian. I honestly couldn't even wrap my head around the idea. And definitely not Jiaotu. Seriously, ick.

"So it isn't that the fae don't exist," Ravine mused, "but that they might not all be from the same dimension? There isn't enough data to draw that conclusion?"

I grinned at her. "Exactly!"

She rolled her eyes at me, but her tone was still playful. "I'm not an idiot, you know. You don't have to go all proud schoolteacher on me."

I stepped into the main office, Ravine behind me. Brady stood up at his desk as we approached. He had to force his gaze away from Brendan Prince, who was still riveted to the book he held open before him on Ayre's old desk.

"All right then, Dusk?" the dark-haired werewolf murmured. "Can we kick him out now?"

"Down boy," Ravine teased.

He ignored her, cocking his head in my direction hopefully.

"Has Crystal brought the crown piece up yet?" I asked, noting out of the corner of my eye the slight tensing of Prince's shoulders.

The sorcerer had good hearing, not that the office was overly large. His senses were presumably as strong as the spells and artifacts he collected. Enhanced. And given his location and the wealth of information surrounding him, I wouldn't have faulted Brendan Prince for using any and all enhancements he had access to.

"Crystal brought it up already." Brady's gaze flicked to the studious sorcerer, then back to me. "While you were in your budget meeting."

"I'm just going to grab it again."

Brady frowned.

"For me," Ravine interjected.

Brady's frown deepened. "Since when are you interested in fae artifacts?"

"Since I decided to be, asshole," she snapped.

I sighed. "Ravine finds the piece inspiring. She's going to make a copy."

Brady stiffened. "The runes are unique…"

"The piece is broken," I said patiently. Ravine was gripping my arm rather firmly, the witch power writhing around her cuff tickling me. "Even if the runes on it could be used in a malicious fashion, they're incomplete." I leaned closer to lower my voice. "And probably complete nonsense."

Brady matched my tone. "You've said that before, Dusk."

Ravine thrust her face between us. "Why are you being a complete jerk?"

"Because you only think with your hormones," he snarled back quietly. "And now you're compromising Dusk, which compromises my security."

I laid my hand on Brady's arm.

The werewolf started, then met my gaze. He inhaled, visibly calming himself.

"What's going on?" I asked in a whisper.

He flicked his gaze in Prince's direction, then shook his head. "Nothing. Just...triggered instincts." He met my gaze a second time, then nodded. "On overdrive."

I nodded. I'd felt odd all day as well. Since the gala, actually—and even more so since picking up the unknown presence on the bench that morning...as though someone had been waiting to speak with me, but then had left when they saw Brady. So now I was reading way too much into...well, everything.

Granted, I did love to read.

I rested my hand on Brady's forearm a moment longer, letting the quiet of the archive offices settle around us. Only the scratch of Prince's pen across the page of a notebook and James shifting in his chair broke the silence. Both Brady's and Ravine's heart rates settled. I slipped on my backpack. The soft steady hum of Infinity's magic was warm against my spine, aware but not engaged.

There was nothing else.

Nothing nefarious.

Nothing out of the ordinary.

Brady flared his nostrils, breathing deeply. Then he nodded once more. "Crystal is in the basement."

I offered him a slight smile. "I'll be right back."

He sat as I stepped away, crossing into the back hall.

Ravine perched on Brady's otherwise empty desk, swinging one leg. Her back was to Prince. "If I didn't know better, I'd think you were jealous," she murmured to Brady, unaware that I could listen in—as could

Prince, if his hearing was enhanced as I suspected. "And not of me."

"Just leave it alone, Ravine," Brady said caustically as I headed downstairs.

Ravine's magic spilled across Brady's desk, emanating from the Celtic-inspired bands around her forearms. Cupping her hands to manipulate it, she pooled that unleashed energy around the crown piece that she'd set in the center of the otherwise empty desk.

Brady and I stood opposite the metal mage, the width of the desk between us. Brendan Prince was tucked up beside Ravine, so close that he was practically glued to her side. Though his gaze was riveted to the gentle magic slowly encasing the rune-scribed, rough-edged golden relic.

James and Crystal were standing at the end of the desk. Crystal had her phone out, raised toward the spell Ravine was weaving.

"It's not going to record," James muttered to the librarian for the third time.

"It's recording," she insisted.

"It's not going to stick," he said doubtfully.

"This is so fascinating," the metal mage murmured, ignoring everyone. "I've never touched gold that felt like this..." She hadn't laid even a single digit on the relic yet, so she could feel the metal through her magic. Which was seriously cool.

"Because of its age?" I asked. Even though I'd been dismissing the significance of the relic ever since Brady and I found it, I was easily intrigued.

Ravine bit her lower lip and narrowed her eyes. The crown piece lifted under a gentle coaxing of her power, rising until it hovered at the metal mage's eye level.

Brady grumbled under his breath, still not at all pleased.

"No..." Ravine finally murmured. "I've touched older relics, including the Asian gold bracelet you traded with me, Dusk."

Brendan Prince tore his gaze from Ravine's manipulation of the crown piece for long enough to look at me questioningly.

I, in turn, ignored him.

"Have you ever touched a fae artifact before, Ravine?" Prince asked, still looking at me pointedly. "Metal mined and refined from another dimension?"

"Not that I know of." Ravine flicked a questioning gaze at me.

When she'd selected the bracelet from the literal treasure chest that had come with my inheritance, Ravine had helped me inventory a dozen other artifacts at the same time. I'd sold those items to Doran last month. But, as with the crown piece, none of those pieces had felt unusual.

That had been the only time I'd seen the illegal antiquities dealer since he'd been tossed off the Conall estate the night I'd forced him to escort me to the cairn that had housed Morgan's amulet. The vampire had acted like nothing at all had occurred. But he had also thwarted my attempt to buy the jewelry box that had been part of his original clandestine retrieval with Celeste Cameron, making it exceedingly clear that while Doran was still willing to buy anything I brought him, he wouldn't share his own inventory.

I didn't particularly like playing into Brendan Prince's pop mythology, but I also couldn't claim to be an expert when it came to artifacts crafted from other dimensional materials.

I shook my head in answer to Ravine's unvoiced question.

Prince smirked, tucking his hands in the pockets of his pants, though doing so wrinkled the sides of his unbuttoned suit jacket.

With the crown piece still hovering above the desk, Ravine grabbed the tightly rolled object she'd tucked under her sweater collar before casting. I was fairly certain she was actually using her bra strap to hold it in place so that she could have it near even as she kept her hands free. That was rather ingenious.

She hadn't bothered to anchor her casting in a chalked or salted circle. Nor was she pulling from any of the magic embedded into the floor or walls of the archive. The power she wielded was all pulled from her own reserves, in addition to whatever energy she'd stored within her magnificent cuffs.

Ravine Byrne was not even remotely an insignificant spellcaster.

Her eyes blazing witch blue, the metal mage unrolled the cylindrical object in both hands, revealing a thin rectangle of flexible gold, slightly thicker than gold leaf. Her gaze was still riveted to the relic.

The magic she'd called forth twisted and twined around her hands in a blue-tinted haze that quickly surrounded the crown piece. Holding the gold foil spread between her hands, she shifted it toward the relic.

"Ravine," Brady said warningly.

"I'm not going to damage it, asshole."

"You're touching it with your magic right now."

"Dusk is standing right beside you," she snapped. "You think she'd let me do any permanent damage to a relic?"

Brady glanced at me. I was watching every little minutia of Ravine's spell work—every ebb and flow, how the color and density of her power shifted and intensified—while desperately wishing I were transcribing the casting directly into Infinity. If Prince hadn't been standing right next to the metal mage, I would have been feverishly jotting notes into my personal archive.

"Dusk is a little distracted," Brady said sourly.

Ravine huffed, releasing the gold foil rectangle so it hovered directly over the crown piece. With a flick of her fingers to either side, she coaxed the magic she'd coated the relic in upward until it pressed underneath the gold foil.

"Ready." The metal mage was slightly breathless, though with delight, not exhaustion.

"Pay attention to the details of the runes," Prince coached, once more pressing himself as close as he could get without actually touching Ravine and risking compromising her casting. "Hold those in your head...the intricate curls, the sharp edges..."

Ravine quirked an eyebrow in my direction.

I quashed a smile.

She flattened her hands, then pressed them to either side, not touching the relic but directing her blue-tinted magic around it. That energy coalesced, compacting between the relic and the gold foil, then pressing upward. An image began to appear on the upper side of the foil.

Prince hissed in excitement.

Crystal squealed quietly, stepping closer. James checked her with a hand on her shoulder. She nodded, stepping back again.

Magic and technology didn't mix.

Brady's glower deepened.

Ravine's brow was furrowed in concentration. She sharpened the imprint, folding the edges of the metal until it resembled the crown piece in every way except for the burnish of the gold.

"The power wielded by the Adept..." Prince said, gaze fixed to the casting even as he adopted an affected scholarly tone. "As impressive as it is, none of it would be possible without the fae crossing through to this dimension millennia ago. We are all descendants of those first travelers." He flicked his attention to me, his dark hair falling artfully over his brow, and a slight smile revealing the tips of his teeth.

He was just spinning myths out of thin air now, with less than no historical backing. "I suppose that perspective depends," I said coolly. Did he truly believe the nonsense he was shilling? Or was he just attempting to get a rise out of me now? If so, why? "One would have to know how deeply you've been able to delve. What sources you've uncovered. Legitimate sources. Historical and magical."

Prince chuckled. "You have written accounts beyond the creation of this dimension, do you?"

"You don't?"

James snorted.

A smug expression overtook the frown that Brady had been sporting since we'd arrived to find Prince at the archive that morning. But seemingly undeterred, Prince's grin only widened. As if I'd somehow just confirmed instead of refuted his suppositions.

Continuing to ignore all of us, Ravine sighed, quietly delighted. She plucked the impression she'd made of the crown piece from her still-active casting. As she did so, the relic settled on the desk, and the duplication spell faded, though I could still feel the residual coating the now-empty space over Brady's desk.

Ravine peered down at the copy of the crown piece she'd made, a smile swamping her face.

"It's perfect," Brendan Prince breathed, standing at her shoulder. "May I?" He held out his hand.

But Ravine looked up, still grinning, and handed the copy to me.

I took it, noting the anger that flickered over Prince's face, then disappeared. The thin rectangle of gold hummed with Ravine's magic. Two of its edges were stretched to mimic the damage of the original. I leaned over the desk, comparing it to the relic. As far as I could see from a quick perusal, it was a perfect copy. And as far as I knew, the ability to make a perfect facsimile with a purely magical impression was so rare as to be practically unique among Adepts. No wonder Ravine called herself a metal mage.

"Ravine!" Crystal gushed. "I had no idea!"

Ravine shrugged off the praise, grinning but exhausted. "I haven't cast that level of detail before, but I often take impressions of...inspiration. So I can manipulate it and create a line of jewelry or whatnot."

Crystal was undeterred. "Do you know how useful that would be for the archive?"

James nodded in agreement. "We could lend copies instead of originals."

"Yes," Brady said, glancing at me.

I frowned. "Laying hands on the original item is paramount when it comes to delving into magical origins and properties, though." And other than Ravine's magic, I sensed nothing from the copy I held. No flash of the relic's history, nor any understanding of the magic that had originally crafted it, or why it had been created in the first place.

"I agree," Prince said.

The others all ignored him, still looking at me expectantly.

"But archivists, historians, could still visit and request to see the original items," Crystal said earnestly. "They could then take the copy with them to study further. And," she gushed, "they could be safely loaned out to nonmagicals, strictly for their historical or cultural value!"

Well, that was an intriguing idea. I was the Archivist of the Modern World, after all.

"We could find some room in the budget for next year," James added. "The gala was very successful. And you've authorized the sale of the duplicate spellbooks and artwork we've been storing."

"Is this something that would interest you, Ravine?" Crystal asked eagerly.

"The gold is expensive..." Ravine said, sucking on her bottom lip.

"But any metal would work, yes?" Crystal asked.

"Maybe..." Ravine looked at me questioningly. "I could figure out a tiered quote, based on the metal and the size of the artifact. I'm not going to say no to the extra income..."

"Or the inspiration?" I said, smiling as I handed her the duplicate back.

She laughed. "Right."

"It's fine with me," I said, convinced mostly by the others' enthusiasm. "I could see making that work for anyone who doesn't need actual contact with the original."

"We don't all have your fine senses, Dusk," James said. It was meant to be teasing, I thought, but it came out a bit sharp.

Prince reached for the duplicate of the crown piece a second time, murmuring, "If I may?"

Ravine gave it to him.

He spun away to cross toward Ayre's old desk, where a few books and his notebook were still strewn.

Crystal scooped up the original relic from the desk with a black velvet cloth, swaddling it in the fabric. "I'll lock up," she said with a pointed glance at Prince's back. Then she spun on her heel and took off for the archive.

At Ayre's desk, the sorcerer historian appeared enraptured, comparing the duplicate copy to a sketch of a crown in his notebook. Though I had to narrow my eyes to see at that distance.

"I need to get home to Sisu," I said. "And do some grocery shopping before dinner."

A sharp, pleased grin spread over Brady's face. "Closing time," he crowed. Loudly.

Prince flinched, glancing at us, then back at the books still on the desk. "Yes...ah. Thank you for accommodating me."

I retreated to my office before he could make any further requests. Ravine sauntered over to join him.

"Can I buy you another pint?" I heard Prince ask Ravine.

"I thought you'd never ask, sorcerer," she purred.

Brady scoffed. Loudly.

CHAPTER FOUR

EVENING HAD ENCROACHED ON THE MISTY CITY streets as I neared the gate to the estate. Brady slipped away from escorting me with a smile and a wave, heading to wherever he parked his truck every workday. Wilding Manor didn't exactly have a driveway or a garage. Gitta needed to pull sidewalk permits for any large material deliveries.

I shifted the grocery bags I carried into my left hand, and was reaching for the gate latch when I felt that so-familiar glimmer of magic again. The same hint that I'd felt on the bench outside the archive earlier.

I turned slowly, scanning the alcove, then all the way up to the eaves of the brick Georgian buildings that swelled to either side. If I reached for his magical signature, I could still feel Brady nearby. The potent wards that cloaked the estate and sealed the gate simmered behind me.

I took a step, the whisper of cloaked power drawing me back toward the sidewalk. A couple of pedestrians hustled past, heading to the Indian restaurant on the corner. It was almost dinnertime.

The power signature was familiar...and comforting, rather than malicious.

"Hello?" I whispered into the misty air. "Did you need to speak to me?"

I waited, listening to the noises of the city. Heavier traffic a block over. Footsteps on the wet sidewalk up the road. Murmured conversation.

Brady's magical signature slowly faded, then almost disappeared—presumably he'd climbed into his truck—before I decided that I was either picking up residual, or whoever had been waiting for me had left.

I turned for the gate again.

Something shifted behind me. I glanced over my shoulder.

A tiny figure flickered into view, standing across the street under the same lamppost where Kellan had once stood sentry, making certain that Sisu and I were okay after the incident with Rook.

The figure was less than a meter tall, with large, sparkling eyes. Light-brown hair, tangled by the rain and wind. A head that was slightly too large for her far-too-thin frame. Barefoot, she wore a faded, tattered dress that looked store bought.

A brownie.

She disappeared as quickly as she'd shown herself to me.

My heart was suddenly pounding in my chest, but not out of fear. I was overwhelmed. Utterly dismayed. Almost irrationally upset. I breathed deeply to steady myself.

There was something wrong with the brownie. Her magic was dim, faded. And I'd never, ever seen a brownie affected by the weather before. Or wearing store-bought clothing.

And she was so tiny. Too tiny…

Struggling to keep myself in check when all I wanted to do was lunge across the street, snatch her up, and bring her to the manor, I reminded myself that I would never catch her that way. I'd felt her magic only because she'd allowed me to do so. Twice now.

I plastered on what I hoped was a welcoming smile, then rooted through the grocery bag and pulled out a mango. It was completely out of season—as was probably always the case in Dublin, actually—but I'd bought two as a treat for Sisu. The gnome didn't have a mango tree in the greenhouse, as far as I knew.

I set the mango down next to the gate. Then I straightened and set my hand on the latch again, speaking quietly though I wasn't even sure the brownie was still in the vicinity. "If you are lost or need to be found, you're always welcome at Wilding Manor."

The boundary magic stirred at my command, absorbing the implications of my directive. Brownies had always been welcomed at Wilding Manor, but the one haunting my footsteps might not have been able to gain entry if she wasn't related to the brownies who had once claimed the estate for their own.

It was possible that claim still held, even though it had been a couple of centuries at least since the brownies had made their home in the manor. My supposition was that they'd abandoned the house and property after Jiaotu-who-was passed on her mantle. That the grief of losing their guardian had caused them to move on.

Standing in the chilly evening, I reflected on just how little I knew of brownies in general. Not only were they rare, but for a race that enjoyed working alongside other Adepts, they were exceedingly private. Their use of glamour was masterful, cloaking their magic so thoroughly that even someone with my level of sensitivity couldn't pick up their movements if they chose to hide from me.

The brownie didn't show herself or approach.

With my heart feeling leaden in my chest, I opened the gate and stepped through onto the stone path that led to the manor. Lights winked on as I allowed the gate to fall shut behind me, hoping that the brownie would follow.

She didn't.

I stepped through into the great room, the heavy carved door quickly closing behind me, unbidden as usual. A soft touch of magic from the manor flitted over me, drying my coat and boots. I'd turned toward the cloakroom before realizing that the door had been removed. Plastic sheathing hung in its place.

Kellan had started installing the custom built-ins, working from designs Ridge had drawn. As with the kitchen and bathroom cabinets, he'd constructed most of the woodwork at a workshop off-site. I had to quash a sharp spike of disappointment that he'd already left for the day, since I couldn't feel anyone in the house except for Sisu, Bethany, and Morgan. The twins were gone, so perhaps Kellan had taken them home early.

The quiet simmer of Bethany's werewolf magic and the bright steady pulse of Sisu's power beckoned from the direction of the library. Morgan was still tucked in her tower, as expected. But I still found myself checking every time I came and went—and multiple times while I was at home—that the death goddess was exactly where she should be. I knew that was silly, though, because there was no way I'd miss it if she ever went wandering.

I set the grocery bags down to shuck off my backpack and wool coat, only to have the manor greedily claim the bags. And then my coat. It teleported them away just as effortlessly as it had dropped the furniture in Morgan's tower.

I shook my head, laughing as I unlaced my boots. "Are you going to put those away? The milk and cheese need to go in the fridge."

My boots were snatched away the moment I toed them off. Apparently, the house was acting as butler while the cloakroom was under construction, though that made me wonder how I was supposed to get my boots back. They were my favorite.

I joined Bethany and Sisu in the library. In his typical combo of hoodie, shorts, and large wool socks, my little brother was sprawled on the hardwood floor in front of a small fire in one of the two fireplaces. His white-blond head was bowed intently over his iPad, writing on the screen with a Bluetooth pencil. So far, the electronics had held up, which was a sign that Sisu was getting better at keeping a tighter hold on his power. I'd managed to not short out my phone yet, but I still rarely used it.

Tucked into one of the two recently recovered high-back brown-leather chairs set before the fireplace, Bethany looked up from the book she was reading as I entered. She had her golden blond hair in a long loose braid curled over one shoulder, and was wearing a deep-green mohair sweater and pristinely black jeans. "Good evening, Dusk."

"Bethany." I smiled. "Sisu."

Preoccupied, my brother only grunted in response.

I opened my mouth to tell him about the brownie I'd spotted. Then I realized that I wasn't certain how to explain that...in any way, really.

I didn't want to get Sisu's hopes up. He missed the brownies from my mother's estate—Missy in particular—and from the guardian nexus. But he was settling in at the manor. The friendship with Lile and Neve helped ground him. Even Jiaotu seemed to sense it. When the guardian of Northern Europe had visited the previous week, he'd stayed for almost three days instead of whisking Sisu away to the nexus or elsewhere.

I had interacted with Jiaotu more in the last months than I had in the first five years of Sisu's life. Though if I dug into the circumstances of that a little further, I was fairly certain I would discover that my mother hadn't welcomed the guardian into her home since Jiaotu had given her Infinity—then had insisted that she give the personal archive to me. I hadn't been aware of that until Sisu told me, and according to him, my mother and Jiaotu had fought at the time. From that point on, Jiaotu's visits with Sisu hadn't involved any overnight stays, not until after my mother had gone on the collection that had now kept her away from home for fourteen months.

The heavy feeling in my chest that hadn't completely eased since spotting the brownie deepened again. I missed my mother desperately. So much so that since we'd arrived in Dublin, I'd been actively trying to just not think about her, as terrible as that was.

"Do you have a moment, Dusk?" Bethany asked.

I nodded, happy to be distracted. "Of course. Let me just check for messages."

"Got it," Sisu said, scrambling to his feet and holding the iPad out to Bethany. A map of Europe was displayed on the screen, with the countries and major cities labeled in Sisu's block printing.

Bethany changed the color of the Bluetooth pencil to red, then began to make corrections with Sisu hanging off the arm of her chair. My little brother grunted, acknowledging each one.

Shoving thoughts of my mother out of my mind, I crossed deeper into the library. Setting my backpack on the desk, I checked the noticeboard for notes, finding nothing. I owed Zeke a letter and still hadn't heard back from Aunt Josephine in Crete since our arrival in Dublin. Though that wasn't unusual.

I thought of writing Mistress Brightshire about the unfamiliar brownie. I knew that at least one of the Brightshire brownies from my mother's estate had been checking on us—and had been doing some cleaning, even though this wasn't their estate. Even if Mistress Brightshire didn't know the brownie, she might at least know if she needed help.

I was missing something. And maybe that was part of the same disconcertion that had been tickling my senses since the gala. Thankfully, it wasn't that same feeling of foreboding that had haunted me when Ayre was racing around the city trying to unleash Morgan. Or rather, trying to leash the death goddess, then harness her power.

Was it the presence of the brownie that was unsettling me?

If she was descended from the brownies who had previously claimed the estate, back when Jiaotu-who-was was still in residence, then she should have been able to return without invitation. There would have been no reason to even ask permission or to wait for me at the museum or on the sidewalk. That was how brownie magic worked. They tied themselves to estates or occasionally to a particular bloodline, anchoring their power with that claim. No permission needed.

The brownie's magic was unfamiliar, though. At least what little I could pick up of it. So I was fairly certain she wasn't related to the Brightshire family who oversaw my mother's estate, or the Winterbloom, Winterblossom, and Wintersprout families who oversaw the nexus and attended the guardian dragons.

A delicate honeyed scent drew my attention away from my cascading thoughts. A brand-new beeswax candle was sitting on a brown tile on the corner of my desk. It was embossed with ferns, their delicate, spiked fronds curling up to the top of the round pillar.

We didn't have bees on the estate. Not yet, anyway. I had found a hive that allowed the keeper to extract honey without disturbing the bees, but it was on back-order. My plan was to gift it to the gnome, who I still knew only by the initial G—though Sisu had turned that into a name, "Gee." It also wasn't the right time of year to source a nucleus colony, aka a 'nuc,' a small honeybee colony meant to be set up in a new location.

I picked up the candle, sensing a touch of witch magic. Then I got a better look at the tile it had been sitting on—brown with an iridescent sheen. The tile from my bathroom. I touched it, immediately picking up Kellan's magic, faded but unmistakable.

The candle was a...gift?

Grinning to myself, I pressed it to my nose and inhaled deeply. The scent was decadent and somehow soothing in a way that had nothing to do with any magic.

The candle definitely belonged in my bathroom, and Kellan had presumably thought so too, given the choice of tile. But he hadn't wanted to invade my space.

Sisu's tone shifted, becoming argumentative. I set the candle down, tuning into what was presently happening around me instead of entertaining thoughts of candlelit baths and wondering if my tub was big enough to comfortably hold a certain shapeshifter. Still, I couldn't seem to stop myself from grinning like an idiot.

Bethany quelled Sisu easily, sending him back to work on the iPad without raising her voice. From my backpack, I grabbed Infinity and the handwritten tome that Brady and I had uncovered at the Byrne witch's estate in Galway—the book I thought Brendan Prince had used as source material, or perhaps even directly plagiarized. Then I crossed to the second chair before the fireplace.

"I've been meaning to talk to you," Bethany said quietly, glancing at Sisu's bowed head, then back to me.

A fission of stark anxiety flushed through me. "Tell me you're not quitting," I blurted, sitting down abruptly. Infinity vibrated in my hand, echoing my spike of concern.

"No!" Bethany waved her hands. "Sorry. No, not that."

"Do you need a raise? I know Sisu can be…ah…" I glanced at my baby brother, who hadn't bothered to look up from his map. "Exuberant…"

She laughed quietly. "It's not that either. But…I don't want to interrupt your dinner."

"Dusk is making us pierogies for the first time." Sisu rolled over on his side, tugging a gold antique pocket watch strung on a long gold chain from his pocket. "I've asked Uncle Beckett's watch to tell us when we need to start."

There was also a clock and timer on his iPad, but I hadn't been able to coerce Sisu to give up possession of Uncle Beckett's watch. That wasn't surprising, though, given that the watch had warned Sisu, the twins, Len, and Bethany of Ayre Byrne's attack almost two months before. Actually, it was the presence of Morgan, who Ayre had been trying to pull power from, that had triggered the magic embedded into the watch, not the black witch herself. Either way, though, that previously unknown function of the watch was over and above its ability to spout questionable weather predictions and unerringly track the present date even through dimensions and inadvertent time travel, as it had been created to do.

I'd had no idea that the watch could be programmed, verbally or otherwise, as an alarm. But Sisu's abundant magic was currently very...responsive. Malleable. For lack of a better way to put it.

Bethany raised one eyebrow questioningly at Sisu's pierogies comment.

"You were studying Poland last week?" I said, clarifying. "I bought some premade pierogies. And onions and sour cream."

"Right." The werewolf tried to smother a smirk, unsuccessfully. "We didn't discuss food, though. Just magical creatures and some mythology."

Sisu shrugged. "I did extra reading."

I placed Infinity on my lap along with the handwritten tome, settling my hand on my archive. "You wanted to discuss something?"

Bethany nodded, glancing briefly at Sisu again.

"I didn't do anything," he protested, looking over his shoulder at me. "Well, not anything that was all that bad."

"I try to not keep much from Sisu," I said gently, understanding Bethany's hesitation. "It just raises more questions."

"It's not..." she started to say, then shook her head. "Sorry, this is awkward. And it's none of my business..." She leaned back in her seat with a huff. "I'm a rather private person, for a werewolf. I'd...you seem the same..." She flicked her gaze to me for confirmation.

I certainly couldn't deny that now. Though before being tasked with an undercover mission from the guardian dragons, I wouldn't have thought I was an overly private person.

"Everyone has secrets," Sisu said.

"Of course," Bethany said smoothly.

"Some things shouldn't be talked about," he added. "Not unless you want to draw attention."

Bethany frowned.

"We're reading a new book at bedtime," I said, for clarification. Then I looked pointedly at Sisu. "It's fictional. Not real."

Sisu shrugged belligerently. "So you say." He returned his attention to his iPad, swapping the map he was supposed to be filling out for a game of some sort.

Bethany laughed quietly under her breath, her gaze on the fire. "Werewolves…" She corrected herself. "Shapeshifters form packs to help them maintain control and focus. Occasionally, though, a pack can get so insular that it causes other sorts of dominance problems. Infighting."

"For the leadership positions?" I asked, slightly concerned about interrupting, but of course, always wanting to gain as much insight as possible on the rare occasion that another Adept was willing to share a life experience with me.

She nodded. "The Conall pack is large. And exceedingly established. There's room within it to grow, to change. No one challenges the leadership because…well, it would be idiotic. The Conalls have held the alpha, beta, and most of the enforcer positions for generations. But also, no one is forced to be something they aren't here." She shifted in her chair, tucking one leg underneath her, her gaze still on the fire. "I'm sure you've noticed that it's the Conall pack, not the Dublin pack or the Ireland pack."

I had, and it was unusual. Most packs were identified by geographical location.

"I'm not sure exactly when that changed," Bethany mused. "Gitta would know. But I believe there was a

Dubhlinn pack for a couple of centuries, then the Co-nalls rose in power and unified more than just the city and surrounding areas. There's a smaller northern pack as well." She shook her head. "I'm off topic."

"I don't think you are," I said, grinning.

She laughed quietly. A warm, pleasant sound. "I'm sure you don't. You're an archivist, after all. Brady is also really, really nosy. And opinionated. About everything."

"Nice," I said, laughing at the implied insult.

She just grinned at me.

"But you weren't born into the Conall pack, right?" Bethany's accent hinted at a British heritage. And she'd gotten two degrees from Cambridge.

"No. I've been a member of two other packs." She frowned thoughtfully. "I'm not sure this subject requires such a deep background."

Sisu curled his legs underneath him, attention still on his game. Then he scooted back until he was resting against the corner of my chair, tucked between Bethany and me. He liked a good story almost as much as I did.

Bethany's gaze fell on his bowed head for a moment, then she nodded to herself. "My first pack was small, from Finland. I was three years old when another pack tried to…" She cleared her throat, correcting herself again. "When they tried to absorb our pack. My parents, who were the alphas, didn't…survive this…transition."

I nodded, understanding. A larger pack had attacked and slaughtered Bethany's pack.

"My youngest aunt managed to get away, with me and five other children. She found refuge with the Manchester pack, where I was raised. Manchester welcomed us with open arms, especially because four of the six of us were female."

"Children are important," Sisu interjected, just to prove he understood what we were talking about. "To pass on magic. And traditions."

That was something Mom would have said. Something she had said, to both of us.

"Yes," Bethany said.

"But you moved to Dublin." Sisu glanced up at his tutor with a grin. "Like Dusk and me."

"Yes." Bethany smiled. "After I got my degrees. But I originally met Aisling Conall through the Academy, and she...offered me an enforcer position with her pack based on..." She glanced over at the fire, then looked at me. "I mean, ultimately it's all about injecting new blood, isn't it? No matter how valuable my skills are. Murder and kidnapping of women and children wouldn't go over well if practiced by a pack as prominent as the Conalls. Or Manchester, for that matter."

"I know you're highly valued by—"

She waved me off. "I'm happy here. And...if it wasn't right with Kellan..." She shrugged. "Aisling has had her fair share of lovers herself, though she only married Odane."

It clicked then. What she was trying to tell me.

Aisling Conall had recruited Bethany for many reasons—but one of those reasons was as a possible mate for Kellan.

"I'm slightly surprised..." I said carefully. "I mean, you're very beautiful..."

She barked a laugh. "Kellan might not like being under anyone's thumb. But...he is a man, and that was almost seven years ago now. And why wouldn't I test it out? He holds a powerful position in the pack. I was new. It takes years to carve out a secure spot in an established pack."

"But...it didn't work."

"It didn't work. We went back and forth on it for almost three years. Out of boredom, I think." She laughed. "Ultimately, we weren't compatible. I always felt like…" Her gaze settled on the fire again. "He was worried about…breaking me. Um, I don't mean…he's not…" She flushed. "Not physically…"

"I know you're talking about sex," Sisu said huffily. "I'm not stupid."

I touched the top of my little brother's head, pulling his attention to me. He glowered but set his iPad down. "Bethany doesn't mean sex. You know that relationships are complicated. Not everyone gets married or stays with the same partner. For many different reasons. Like Mom."

He crossed his arms, his glower deepening. "I know."

"Should we start dinner?" I asked.

He tugged the watch out of his pocket, opening it gently. "Yes," he said, still mostly belligerent. Then, abandoning his iPad, he hopped to his feet and took off out of the library.

I looked at Bethany. "Did Kellan ask you to speak to me?"

She shook her head. "God, no. We're friends, of course. But I wouldn't imagine he'd be happy about me bringing it up with you. But, ah, I've never seen him…he's different around you. It's…whatever is going on with you two, it isn't casual."

"Nothing is going on."

She looked surprised. "Oh, okay…I thought…you danced together." She glanced over at my desk, presumably at the candle.

"You danced the entire night," I said, smiling.

"Of course I did." She hit the 'I' hard. "I'm also always very careful to select amenable partners who won't read much into their selection."

"But Kellan doesn't dance?"

"Not in public."

Footsteps pounded back through the great room, then Sisu burst into the library. "Hey, Bethany? You want to stay for dinner?"

Bethany glanced at me.

"That would be lovely," I said.

She grinned and looked at Sisu. "Yes, please."

"How many pierogies do you want?"

She levered herself out of her chair. "I'll come help."

"Cool." Sisu spun away and took off toward the kitchen a second time.

Bethany paused, looking back at me. "I didn't want to make you uncomfortable, Dusk."

"You didn't."

She nodded doubtfully. "I just wanted you to know I'm not an obstacle. No matter what outcome Aisling is hoping for. She knows better than anyone that were-wolves don't mate for life just because they think they should."

Ah, there it was. Kellan's mother still hoped Kellan would choose Bethany as his mate.

"I'm not the right candidate for that position either," I said a little stiffly.

"Right. Well, that's between you and Kellan." She crossed toward the open doorway.

I rose as well, holding on to Infinity because apparently I needed a constant security blanket these days. I set aside the Galway book, though.

Bethany paused a couple of steps beyond the door-way, looking back at me. "You'd be hard-pressed to find anyone as loyal, Dusk. As fiercely protective and loyal as Kellan Conall."

I already knew that about Kellan. I also knew—and had known even before understanding Aisling's hopes and dreams for her son—that I wasn't pack. And I could never be pack.

Witches might be able to breed with shapeshifters. But dragons couldn't. And that was only one of the reasons there wasn't a future for me with Kellan.

Bethany raised her hands. "I won't mention it again. Shall we flash boil the pierogies, then fry them with the onion?"

"Sounds good to me."

After dinner, Bethany helped clean up the kitchen, then took off. Left alone, I spent some time getting Infinity to absorb the handwritten book from Galway, realizing belatedly that I'd forgotten to bring Brendan Prince's autographed edition of his book home with me for comparison purposes.

Perhaps I unconsciously didn't want it shelved in my library?

The Galway tome had gotten off to an underwhelming start right from the introduction, expositing a theory that the significance of fated mates among the fae had been usurped by the desire to accumulate power through arranged or even forced matches. With no references or citations of evidence, naturally. So even though I studied the symbols and the handwritten text until it was time for Sisu's bedtime stories, I didn't make any significant discoveries. Then, slightly peeved that I'd wasted a couple of hours on it, I decided to just hand the tome over to James in the morning and leave the matter of source materials and possible plagiarism to the historians.

I would be more than pleased to not have any more contact with Brendan Prince. I could dig into my to-do pile and my personal research for the rest of the week.

After getting Sisu settled into bed, I climbed into a hot bubble bath. With my new candle.

I had meant to soak only for a few minutes, then meditate for just long enough to get my brain unwound enough to sleep. But I ended up staying until the water had cooled enough to drive me out of the tub—thinking of Kellan the whole time. Wondering if he believed in fated mates, or that werewolves should mate for life.

CHAPTER FIVE

RUNNING LATE TO MEET RAVINE FOR OUR REGULAR Tuesday lunch, I got all the way through the front door of Cove Cafe before I realized that two other people were already seated with the metal mage in a booth against the back wall.

Brendan Prince.

And Kellan Conall.

I stumbled.

Over nothing.

Despite having been trained in various martial arts since I could walk. Despite having unrivaled senses among my peers. Despite having a brother with a propensity for leaping from dark corners with the implicit demand that I catch him in midair an instant later.

I stumbled over nothing.

"Dusk!" a cheerful woman called, yanking my attention away from the unexpected group seemingly waiting for me, and toward the glassed counter that ran the entire length of the wall to my left.

Cove Byrne grinned at me, her hands on her hips with a sandwich in the making spread out before her on the counter. Pots of soup simmered behind her, the salad station standing to her right. "First time you've been late."

I glanced back at the booth holding Ravine, Prince, and Kellan. They were all looking at me expectantly, presumably having seen me hustle past the front windows and enter. Now that I was in the cafe, I could pick up Kellan's and Ravine's distinctive magical signatures, but outside, those had just mingled with the numerous other residual trails coming and going from Cove's popular lunch spot.

Kellan frowned, then turned to ask Ravine something. His voice was pitched low enough that I would have had to strain to eavesdrop over the general chatter of the full seating area.

The metal mage shrugged, seemingly brushing Kellan off. Then she waved me over, as if I hadn't seen them.

Cove lowered her voice, now glancing between me and the corner booth. "Something wrong, Dusk?"

I shook my head, unwinding my scarf. "No...thanks. I just thought..." I trailed off. I'd thought I was having lunch with Ravine, and Ravine alone.

I offered Cove a smile. She was in her late thirties, and unlike most of the other Byrne witches I'd met so far, had light-brown hair and the more typical witch blue eyes. She was tall, and for a maker of such tasty treats, seriously ripped. There were very few things I coveted beyond books and magical artifacts, but I would have loved to have Cove Byrne's upper arms.

Maybe it was all that kneading dough for her bread making.

Speaking of which...

Cove beckoned me toward the counter with a plate of 'palette cleansers,' as she called them. The plate was light blue, matching all the other ceramics in the cafe. Everything else—walls, counters, tabletops—was white. The treat was some sort of soft cheese on a square of bread.

"Brie," Cove said. "On my whole-wheat-and-cranberry bread."

My stomach actually rumbled, and I barely stopped myself from simply snatching up the offering at lightning speed, knowing that the cafe customers were always a mixture of the magically and nonmagically inclined. And witches weren't supposed to be able to move as fast as dragons anyway.

I popped a single so-called palate cleanser in my mouth and groaned as the first flavors exploded over my tongue. The brie was creamy, almost buttery, with a slightly earthy finish. The cheese paired perfectly with the slightly sour bread and slightly sweet cranberries, complimented by what I thought might have been a hint of citrus.

"Orange peel?" I asked.

Cove pinched her forefinger and middle finger to her thumb, ran those fingers across her lips, then twisted her hand at the corner.

I'd never seen the gesture before. So I just stood there blinking at her uncomfortably for a moment. This was one of the reasons I didn't much like leaving the archive—I routinely ran into references, mannerisms, and colloquialisms that I didn't have any personal experience with or context for.

I hazarded a guess. "It's a secret ingredient?"

Cove flashed me a grin. Then she glanced toward the trio at the booth and beckoned me forward again.

I was pretty much as close as I could get to the glass panel that shielded her workspace without leaning against it. Once more, I assumed this was just a gesture meant to imply something…another secret perhaps?

I leaned forward slightly. Cove did the same. So I'd guessed right. Thankfully.

"I assume I have you to thank for Kellan Conall gracing the cafe with his presence?"

"Um…"

Cove didn't wait for me to actually articulate an answer. Which was good, because I was still seriously confused. "With the way Ravine is practically hanging off that sorcerer," she continued.

She grimaced. It was a subtle expression, but I caught it.

"You don't like him?" I asked quietly, genuinely curious. Because everyone else, other than James and me, seemed to find Brendan Prince charming. Well, except for Brady, but that was just a territorial response.

Cove shrugged. "I'm sure he's fine. Just not for our Ravine."

"Because…he's a sorcerer."

She waved me off. "No, no. The Byrne magic is powerful enough to withstand the addition of sorcerer blood. But Ravine needs someone who can handle her." Cove flashed me a wide grin. "And before you danced with Kellan at the gala, a few of us were hoping that person was you."

I flushed.

Flushed. Like a child caught stealing a treat before dinner.

Was Kellan getting the same fallout from that one dance?

Cove clucked her tongue at me. "Go, go." She glanced at the clock behind her. "Knowing you, you'll be leaving promptly…that only gives you half an hour. I'll bring you soup and your regular sandwich right away. The others have already ordered."

That regular sandwich would be the chicken and roasted vegetables. "On the cranberry bread?"

"You bet."

I stepped away, still a little bit thrown that my comings and goings—that my life in general—had become a topic of such interest. But speaking of the gala…

I spun back. "Cove! The catering for the gala was excellent. Thank you so much." Cove hadn't been in the kitchen, but she'd premade most of the food her Adept staff had prepared and served.

Her smile was genuine. "I'm glad."

I crossed toward the booth. Kellan slid out of his seat at my approach, offering me the side next to the wall across from Ravine. Prince stood up as well, reaching for me.

"You're late," Ravine said bluntly, watching the sorcerer historian instead of addressing me. "And you seemed to have a lot to say to Cove."

Completely thrown by her tone—on top of the general oddness of the unexpected gathering—I blinked at Ravine, coming to a stop beside Kellan but not sitting.

Silence fell between us all for long enough that the other sounds of the cafe filtered in. Quiet chatter from other customers. The sound of one of the servers steaming milk. The ping of the old-fashioned cash register.

Prince dropped his hand when I ignored it. He turned to look at Ravine with a frown.

The dark-haired witch finally glanced my way, opening and closing her mouth. Then she flushed and looked down. She relaxed her clenched hand, flattening it on the white laminate tabletop. "Sorry," she mumbled. "I just know your lunch break isn't very long."

"I texted," I finally said, filling the awkward space with an even more awkward apology. One I hadn't realized I needed to offer. "There was…something that needed my attention at the archive." James had been going through a new batch of acquisitions right before lunch and had inadvertently set off some sort of replicating spell that had buried him in rapidly duplicating books. Brady had dug him out while I found the original spelled tome and neutralized it.

Naturally, I set the offending book aside to study—having to pull rank over both Brady and Crystal to do so. It was a brilliant, nonlethal distraction.

Ravine flushed deeper. "I didn't think to check. You...you don't usually text."

"I understand the etiquette," I said stiffly.

Ravine whipped her head up. "I'm not..." She glanced at Prince, then back at me. "Sorry, this is awkward. I thought it would be fun, but I should have..." She flicked a guilty gaze at Kellan, then pressed her lips together.

Prince clapped his hands once. "Well, I'm glad you joined us, Dusk." He gestured toward the booth. "Shall we?"

Kellan touched the small of my back lightly, pitching his voice low. "You should at least eat something, Dusk."

I nodded, still feeling completely out of place. I shucked off my backpack and slid into the booth, unbuttoning my wool coat but not removing it.

Prince sat beside Ravine, and Kellan slid in beside me. The booth seat wasn't really wide enough, so his thigh pressed against mine. I had the weird impulse to spread my hand over his leg, to seek grounding in his presence. That might have been an effect of his shapeshifter magic. It might also just have been part of whatever drew me to Kellan in the first place.

Prince murmured something to Ravine as I tucked my backpack, Infinity stowed within it, between myself and the wall. Then I dug through the pack to retrieve the boxed items I'd brought to return to Ravine. The hairpins and the mask she'd loaned me, the folded rain-coat, and a thank-you gift from my treasure chest.

Kellan leaned in, whispering, "You didn't know I was coming?"

I shook my head, glancing at Ravine across from me as I set the folded coat and the boxes on the table.

Kellan curled his fingers into a fist. "Do you want me to leave?"

I gave in and settled my hand on Kellan's thigh, as close to his knee as I could reach without making it obvious that I was touching him under the table. I really wasn't interested in discussing anything remotely personal in front of Prince.

He brushed his fingers over the back of my hand in acknowledgement, then shifted so his left arm settled across the back of the booth behind me, his right hand still fisted on the table. His gaze flicked between Ravine and Prince. His magic was churning slightly.

Kellan was pissed.

And honestly, so was I. I felt like I'd been ambushed.

Ravine was watching me, smiling tentatively and obviously picking up on how uncomfortable I was. "I...um, I thought a double lunch date would be fun. But I probably shouldn't have sprung it on you, Dusk."

I nodded, silently pushing the coat and boxes across the table toward her.

Kellan didn't have the same polite compunction. "Probably," he drawled sarcastically.

"You don't have to be an ass about it," Ravine snapped, sounding more like herself as she reached for the fabric-wrapped package on top of the boxes.

"Apparently I do," Kellan shot back.

Prince raised his hands, chuckling. "Now, now, children—"

Both Ravine and Kellan shot him equal looks of disgust.

Prince laughed louder, settling his gaze on me as if expecting me to join in. "I'm just glad for the opportunity to meet Dusk outside of a...formal setting."

Kellan turned his glower on Ravine. "So you already said, sorcerer."

Ravine dropped her gaze from Kellan once more, but then shrugged affectedly as she freed the ribbon from the bit of brown-velvet fabric I'd used to wrap her thank-you gift. "Silly me, thinking you'd like to see Dusk away from the manor."

"I very much like to see Dusk, in any venue, at any time." Kellan's tone could have ground glass into a fine powder. "But I'm not interested in being used as..." He glanced between Ravine and Prince, then just settled back in his seat.

Ravine glared at him.

Prince cleared his throat, looking pointedly at the velvet-swaddled gift. "What have you there?"

Ravine sighed, flipping open the corners of the fabric. Then she just blinked down at the rose-gold hairpin I'd dug through the treasure chest to find. It glistened with residual magic that hinted at more than just a simple spell meant to help keep it in place, akin to the spells that Ravine had used on the pins she'd tamed my hair with. A tapered U shape about ten centimeters long, the pin was sharply spiked on both points, as though it might have had a secondary use as a close-contact weapon.

Ravine's lips parted as she whispered, "Dusk..."

"A thank-you," I said stiffly. "For your help with making certain I was ready for the gala."

"In case she needs to gouge out the eyes of her next dance partner?" Prince said, clearly amused.

No one answered him.

Ravine ran her fingers over the pin, presumably picking up the glimmer of residual. "This is too much," she said.

"You don't want it?" I asked.

She blinked at me, then laughed. The sound was a little edged, still a little off. "Of course I want it. But..." She cleared her throat. "Even if it weren't ancient—"

"Late eighteenth century," I said. "Not that old."

"The magic coating it, adding to the value of the solid rose gold..." Her tone firmed. "Doran would pay dearly."

"It's a gift," I said, forcing myself to hold still, though I really just wanted to get up and leave.

Ravine met my gaze. And for the briefest moment, I could see she was going to refuse the hairpin.

I'd miscalculated something with the gift. Or maybe it was just the wrong timing...or the public venue...

That ache made itself known in my chest again.

Kellan pressed his leg against mine. A subtle move of comfort, the rest of him so still that he could have been carved out of granite.

Prince tapped a finger on the table. "Do tell us what was so intriguing to hold your attention at work, Dusk?"

I found a polite smile from somewhere in the depths of my being, though my instincts were still all over the place.

Ravine tossed her head, plucking up the hairpin. She smoothed her hair back into a messy twist, pinning it into place with my gift. Shorter tendrils fell around her face prettily. "Thank you, Dusk."

Before I could answer Prince or Ravine, the metal mage deliberately ran her hand down Prince's arm, settling it somewhere in his lap.

"Let's not talk about work," she pouted playfully.

Annoyance flickered over Prince's face, but he nodded.

Cove and one of her servers appeared at the edge of the booth, laden with plates. Everyone else had apparently also ordered sandwiches, which were tucked next to steaming cups of soup. As they deposited the plates on the table, I leaned into Kellan slightly. "Thank you for the candle."

He smiled, the expression reserved but warm. "How did you know it was from me?"

I just grinned at him, accepting my plate from Cove.

He laughed quietly, nodding thanks for his food. "Robin Cameron makes them, and I thought of you when I saw her newest—"

"Oh," Ravine said sharply. "You keep in touch with Robin, do you, Kell? Well, I guess you always like to keep your options open."

Kellan stiffened.

Cove paused partway through setting the final plate in front of Prince, but staring at Ravine. Aghast.

I glanced down at my own meal. "Cove," I said, my voice remote but weirdly bright, "can you wrap the sandwich for me to take with me? I've got to get back."

"Really?" Prince said. "I was hoping—"

I set the soup to the side of my plate. "Yes."

"Of course," Cove said, throwing a look at Ravine, setting down Prince's plate, and retrieving my own.

"Mine too," Kellan rumbled, pulling his arm from the back of the booth and also setting his soup to the side.

Nodding as she grabbed his plate as well, Cove stepped away from the booth.

Ravine pressed her hands to her cheeks, flushed and holding herself almost uncomfortably away from Prince. "I'm...sorry..."

I picked up my spoon and dipped it in the soup, remembering to allow it to cool slightly before eating. It was butternut squash with a hint of nutmeg, but I barely tasted it.

"Dusk..." Ravine said.

"I really am busy," I said.

Kellan dug into his soup.

Prince cleared his throat, looking between me and Ravine. "But you'll still make it to the solstice celebration tonight, yes? I understand it's not to be missed. Ravine and I were going to pick you up. You and your brother?"

I looked up and locked eyes with Ravine, suddenly and utterly incensed that she'd mentioned Sisu to Prince. That she would mention him to anyone, no matter how irrational that was.

Under the table, Kellan settled his hand on my knee. "Brady and Erin are picking Dusk up."

"What?" Ravine cried.

"Protocol," Kellan said rather nastily. Then he looked at Prince steadily. "As a most honored guest of the Conall pack."

Prince responded to whatever threat was implied by Kellan's statement with a smirk and a slight nod of his head.

"I'd pick you up myself," Kellan said, turning to me slightly. "But that same protocol demands that Gitta and I be there ahead of time."

He hit the word protocol hard. Again.

Ravine flinched.

Aware there were undercurrents of tension unfolding around me—multiple threads of them, none of which I understood—I just ate a few more spoonfuls of soup, then pushed the bowl away and grabbed my backpack and my scarf.

Kellan immediately slid out from the booth.

I followed.

"Dusk...please," Ravine said. "I'm sorry."

"No," I said stiffly. "I shouldn't have come once I knew I was going to be late."

"I'll drive you," Kellan said, touching the small of my back again.

"I'm fine. I can walk faster." I managed to pull out another polite smile for Prince. "Enjoy the rest of your lunch." Then I turned away, catching the look Kellan threw at Ravine as I crossed toward the counter to grab my sandwich from Cove.

The brown-haired witch passed me a paper bag. "I added a couple of almond cookies for dessert."

"Thank you." I pulled my wallet out of my backpack.

She waved a hand at me. "It's covered."

I should have argued with her, but I really, really just wanted to get back to the archive. "Thank you."

Cove glanced between the trio at the booth and me, opened her mouth, and then closed it with a shake of her head. "Hopefully I'll see you tonight."

I nodded, turning toward the exit. Already trying to figure out how to get out of going to the pack celebration. Except I knew Sisu would be upset over missing his first 'grown-up' party. An expression he'd learned from the twins.

I pushed through the door, catching Kellan's raised voice behind me.

"What the hell was that shit, Vinnie?"

"I thought she'd find it...fun," Ravine said.

"Fun?" he growled. "You've known Dusk for how long? And you thought she'd enjoy being surprised like...this?"

There was something implied in that pause. A gesture perhaps, but I didn't catch it. Instead, I walked swiftly away, tugging on my backpack and scarf.

Maybe there was something wrong with me. My social ineptitude and discomfort was becoming rather obvious, yes. But something beyond even that. I couldn't figure out what had just happened with Ravine. If I'd done or said something wrong, I had no idea what it could have been.

Mesa Byrne was waiting for me in my office.

I almost fled.

I had no idea why she was there, and I was still feeling rattled. Much more so than I preferred to be when facing a conversation with the head of the Byrne coven—especially if that conversation was going to be...difficult.

I wanted to flee from my own archive.

I quashed the impulse before it had barely formed in my mind.

I was a dragon. Dragons didn't run from any situation. Not even a dragon disguised as a witch.

Well…at least not from any situation that involved the archive or my duty, because apparently I fled before anything even remotely personal. Including surprise double dates.

I tugged off my scarf and coat, hanging both on my coatrack to dry. Mesa's long wool coat was already there. It had been raining for the walk back from the cafe, and I'd found myself regretting not taking up Kellan's offer of a drive.

For more than one reason.

The other reasons weren't things I could follow through on though, so getting damp was the better choice.

"Sorry," I said, crossing to and around my desk. "I didn't know we had an appointment."

"We don't," Mesa said breezily, closing the book she'd been reading and setting it on her crossed knee.

It was the handwritten red-fabric tome from Galway—claimed from the house of Mesa's aunt. She must have plucked it off the pile on my desk where I'd set it that morning. I was still planning to hand it and Prince's book over to James, mentioning my suspicions about the books having a common source or that Prince had directly plagiarized it, unattributed and unacknowledged. I just hadn't had time for that particular conversation yet.

"I knew you were having lunch with Ravine," Mesa continued. "So I thought being here when you got back wouldn't be too much of a disturbance."

Pale-skinned and red-haired, the head of the Byrne coven looked to be in her midforties. But since that would have placed her just a decade ahead of River, her eldest, I knew she was much older. She was dressed in pristinely pressed navy-blue wool slacks, heeled boots, and a black V-neck lightweight merino wool sweater.

The beads speckling her hand-knit black lace scarf caught the light as she leaned forward and set the book, open to a sketch of the crown piece, on her side of the desk.

I tugged Infinity out of my backpack and placed it on my side.

Mesa's attention flicked to my personal archive, then back to me, the slightest of smirks quirking her lightly glossed lips. As I sat across from the elder witch, I tilted my head toward the sketch that she obviously wanted to discuss.

But instead, she said, "You danced with Kellan Conall at the gala."

I blinked, momentarily thrown by the abrupt change of conversation.

Mesa waved her hand. "I've already apologized for my earlier…assumptions."

I assumed she was referring to the time she'd verbally attacked Kellan about making a quick conquest of me. The first time she and I had met—over Rook's unconscious body. And she hadn't actually apologized for that at all.

Her smirk turned almost self-deprecating, as if she were reading my mind and partly agreeing with me. I found myself smirking back.

"I've never seen Aisling's boy court someone so openly," Mesa said, drumming her fingers against her knee thoughtfully. "But we don't grow and prosper without the addition of new strength, new ideas. And you aren't an average witch, not even for an archivist."

Mesa Byrne paused, looking at me steadily as if expecting me to fill in the space in the conversation.

I didn't. Because I honestly wasn't completely certain what we were talking about. And if the topic was

Kellan, that was far too personal to address with the head of the coven.

"For a Godfrey, you are very...contained. Even for a newly adopted Godfrey." She hit the word 'adopted' hard. Oh yes, Mesa Byrne had figured out much, much more about me than I'd hoped, despite our limited interactions.

Again, she left a space for me to fill. Again, I didn't.

Her smirk grew into a grin. "Power, charisma, even an...occasionally misplaced sense of duty. You have that in abundance, like all the Godfreys. But to this date, I've never met a Godfrey who understands the value of quiet observation. Of considering all the options..." Her gaze fell to Infinity on my desk. "Of gathering all the information before making decisions."

"You're saying the Godfreys are rash?"

"Impulsive."

"I'm not sure that Auntie Pearl would agree."

Mesa laughed. "Then she has a selective memory."

I still had no idea where the conversation was going. But oddly, I felt more at ease with Mesa than I had at lunch. An unexpected double date, a type of social interaction I'd only read about, was overwhelming. But the conversation with Mesa wasn't intimidating in the slightest. I knew how to talk to powerful people with hidden or secret agendas.

After all, I'd been doing that for most of my life.

That said, the way she was seemingly tying Kellan's supposed interest in me with my not acting like a Godfrey remained a mystery.

Mesa settled back in her chair, still smiling to herself. She flicked her fingers toward the red book and the sketch of the crown piece relic. "You've read it?"

"I've done a first pass."

"It's all total conjecture."

So Mesa Byrne knew something about the actual origins of the crown piece. "Was that why you sent me to collect the items from your aunt's house?"

She sniffed. "Requested. Not sent."

"The magic of the relic is practically mundane."

"It's not the single piece that presents the problem."

"What problem?"

Mesa shrugged. "That isn't always for the coven to know."

I flipped open Infinity to the first blank page, uncapping my fountain pen. Then I scrawled across the paper:

Personal notes—Mesa Byrne: The origin of the crown piece.

Mesa laughed quietly. But then she paused thoughtfully, looking off to the side.

"You're thinking it's coven business," I said, a little disappointed.

Mesa shook her head. "Just attempting to figure out how to formulate my thoughts in a way that will sound...believable to an archivist. To someone who practically demands empirical evidence for every thought."

I almost bristled at that. But then I had to acknowledge, if only to myself, that Mesa Byrne had me pretty well figured out.

"You know that there are beings who...watch over our world." Mesa's gaze was fixed to me. "Beings who step in when they deem it necessary. Or who task certain covens with the protection of certain secrets."

A twist of energy ran down my spine. She was talking about dragons...maybe even guardian dragons specifically. I tried to keep my expression neutral. "Of course. I assume the Adept who stepped in after Ayre set the soul sucker loose in the archive six years ago would have been one of them."

Mesa grimaced at the reminder of her sister's misdeeds. For lack of a better way to phrase it. Ayre might not have intended to do any harm six years ago. But she'd gone black not even two months past in an attempt to…actually, I still wasn't certain what Ayre's ultimate goal had been. Seeking power, clearly. Though whether over the archive or over the coven, I didn't know.

"I didn't meet that individual," Mesa said. "The only person who made it out alive was Owen Brady, and his memories are practically nonexistent. Or so he claims…"

She left that statement hanging between us, once more giving me space to fill. Apparently, that was a conversational technique of hers. I didn't doubt she was exceedingly successful with it, but I was pleased over not having fallen for it myself.

"You were saying?"

The elder witch huffed. "A number of noses were put out of joint when I took over the coven. Ayre's and my aunt's, specifically."

"Which was why your aunt moved to Galway. Into Murphy coven territory."

Mesa nodded. "I wasn't aware of it at the time, but she'd been tasked with watching over this." She leaned forward and tapped the sketch of the crown piece. "Having had the obligation passed down to her from my paternal grandmother, her mother."

I tugged the book forward, narrowing my eyes at the sketch. The original crown piece, still tucked away in the archive, was practically inert. Seemingly completely benign. Having the guardians task a coven with watching over it seemed…unusual.

"Are you saying you want it back?"

"Yes."

"You don't think that it's safer in the archive?"

Mesa waved her hand. "I'm sure it's perfectly safe. But this is a duty that falls to the Byrne coven. To me."

I leaned slightly forward, grinning with what I hoped was some of that Godfrey charm I didn't actually have a biological claim to. "And what other objects of power does the coven watch over at the behest of these...beings?"

Mesa laughed, the sound as soft and as friendly as anything I'd ever heard from her. "Become my witch, Dusk Godfrey, and perhaps you'll find out when those tasks one day fall to you."

I pouted, feeling playful. "I doubt it. Not with your three in line ahead of me." Since meeting the Byrne siblings, I'd become fairly certain that one of the coven's not-so-well-concealed secrets was that they bred for and practiced the power of three at least once in a generation. Individually, River, Ridge, and Ravine were powerful. But with their complimentary powers, and bound together by blood and magic, they'd be formidable when all three focused on a single task. Possibly unstoppable.

"I'm sure the Godfreys have more than enough secrets to keep you occupied," Mesa said, still fishing.

Well, there was Sisu and me to start. And a portal in a bakery, apparently. And Warner Jiaotuson somehow being Pearl's grandson-in-law, even though dragons didn't go with witches any more than they went with shapeshifters.

I just smiled at Mesa.

"And of course, there have been recent issues with the Myers coven," Mesa mused, her magic sparking in her eyes. "And the Dunkirks...well, the Dunkirks..." She shook her head, deliberately trailing off.

"Are you trying to woo me, Mesa Byrne?"

She shrugged playfully. "I don't think I need to woo you, Dusk. I think your inheritance, the archive, and Kellan Conall will keep you here in Ireland for many, many years."

I stiffened slightly at the mention of Kellan, and Mesa's eyes narrowed, noting my reaction. Her tone hardened, all playfulness gone. "He isn't a problem, is he?"

"Absolutely not," I cried, possibly too quickly.

Mesa's gaze remained fixed on me.

And this time, I fell for it, awkwardly filling the space. "The Conalls are...allies and have been amazing with helping Sisu and me get settled. As have your three."

"That estate is a lot for a twenty-five-year-old witch to inherit. At the same time as taking over the head curator position here."

"I'm up for it."

"I know you are."

Slightly desperate to change the subject, I slid the handwritten book back toward Mesa. "Can you tell me who wrote this accounting? Are the dates accurate at least?" Mesa might not have been able to spill coven secrets to a Godfrey witch, but if the dates in the hand-written accounting were accurate, they would at least give me a place to start. "And why do you think it's conjecture?"

"The fae?" Mesa scoffed. "I have no doubt that the crown once belonged to someone powerful. Maybe it's even a source of power when not in pieces. But this fated mates story?" She snorted delicately. "Magical bonds can be forged, of course. But not by destiny. Or fate, if you will. And love is the most disruptive, destructive force in the world. Perhaps in every dimension."

I blinked. I'd never heard that particular take before.

"No, I don't know the author. But I assume that my aunt, Corrie, found the text when researching the origins of the crown piece." Mesa stabbed a finger at the book. "Which was not her place. Not her task."

"Because it might have drawn attention to something the coven was meant to conceal," I murmured.

"Yes." Mesa sighed. "I do wish you'd spoken to me before including it among the gala displays."

I opened my mouth, but she raised a hand, cutting me off. "I'm not telling you what to do in your own archive. You've made your boundaries very clear. It's just..." She sniffed. "You've given Brendan Prince and people like him more fodder for their ridiculousness."

"There is an interesting connection between this text and Prince's newest work," I said thoughtfully.

Mesa leaned forward. "Is there now?"

"I can't prove it yet. I haven't had the time."

Mesa tapped her fingers on her knee. "The sooner the better. Ravine is oddly infatuated with him. I, of course, am not allowed an opinion when it comes to her...flings." She held her hand up, forestalling any comment from me. "I know, I know that's as it should be. He just...bothers me. Yet all my single witches absolutely flock to him whenever he blesses Dublin with his presence, Crystal included."

"He bothers me too," I said, admitting it out loud. "And I have no idea why."

Mesa raised an eyebrow at me. "I suspect any suspicion that his book plagiarizes my aunt's research would be enough for you."

Mesa Byrne was a wily witch. "The feeling predates that possible discovery."

Mesa nodded thoughtfully. "You'll do as I ask?"

"Return the crown piece to the coven?"

She nodded.

"I see no reason to keep it in the archive," I admitted. "But I'd love to spend some more time with a couple of your aunt's spellbooks."

"Corrie was very skilled. I'd love to discuss your notes about the collection and the books whenever you have a moment."

"I'd like that too," I said. Utterly truthfully, to my own surprise.

Mesa rose without further comment, crossing to retrieve her coat from the coatrack and sliding it on. "Enjoy the pack solstice celebration tonight."

"Will you be there?"

She laughed knowingly. "Oh, no. I wouldn't fit in. Not now. But it was the highlight of my year, many a time, in my twenties."

She swept out of my office without another word.

So…watching over the crown piece was a task set by a dragon—or even a guardian dragon—for the Byrne coven. In Suanmi's territory.

That was surprising, given the minimal residual power the relic still held, but more than intriguing enough to follow up on. Though there was no way I was going to approach the guardian herself on the topic. Even I wasn't foolish enough to want to subject myself or the coven to the fire breather's…disapproval. At least not without understanding the full history of the crown piece first.

Knowledge was the ultimate weapon, after all. Especially against a guardian dragon. Though, holding that guardian's attention for long enough to state my case and get any lingering questions answered would be tricky.

Bethany had already left for the day by the time I got home from work. I found Sisu, Neve, and Lile in the kitchen with Len. Flour and other ingredients appeared to have exploded all over the kitchen island and the surrounding floor.

Len was standing sentry over the oven, with the trio all lined up at the island. All had been assigned different tasks and were wearing smocks that I was fairly certain were just large T-shirts with the arms and necks cut off. Sisu, Neve, and Lile looked up at me as I entered, grinning in perfect synchrony. And for the first time in my life, I pulled out my phone and used it to take a picture.

"We're making cookies!" Sisu said. Icing sugar dusted his cheek.

"I'm in charge of the sprinkles!" Neve cried gleefully. Her lips, teeth, and tongue were oddly bright pink.

"No," Len said, barely containing his amusement. "You *were* in charge of sprinkles."

Neve snickered. The red tin of sprinkles looked suspiciously emptier than the other colors, which made sense given the state of the six-year-old.

The island was divided into two sections—a space to roll out the cookie dough, cut it, and place it on a baking sheet. Then a space to decorate the cooled cookies. Len had an uncooked sheet of cookies waiting to the left of the oven and about two dozen cookies cooling on wire racks to the right.

Lile and Sisu were currently cutting out dough while Neve frosted a cooled batch of cookies with white icing. As she finished each one, she set it onto parchment paper laid down across the far end of the counter.

"What are you making?" I asked.

"Cream-cheese cutouts," Lile said, her tone and expression serious as she focused on cutting out a cookie in the shape of an evergreen tree.

When she was satisfied, she nodded at Sisu. My brother carefully peeled the raw tree from the heavily floured marble counter and placed it on a waiting cookie sheet, already half full.

"Two inches apart," Sisu said. "Len says that's the best spacing."

I glanced over the trio's heads at Len.

He grimaced. "Sorry about the mess. Bethany left early to help with the setup at the Conall house. It's a family recipe. My family. From California."

"We're making gifts," Neve said brightly, gesturing toward a half-dozen Christmas-themed boxes on a side counter that I hadn't noticed in all the chaos.

The timer on the oven went off. "I'll check," Sisu announced, jumping back off his stool.

Len opened the oven as he and Sisu both peered into its depths. Sisu cocked his head to one side. "Just starting to brown on the edges. Two more minutes?"

"I concur," Len said, closing the oven and setting the timer.

My chest constricted. With happiness, I thought—but I wasn't certain I'd ever felt that specific sensation before. I'd been so worried about dragging Sisu with me, away from everything he'd ever known. And he was okay. He was—

Sisu took the opportunity to dash around the island—moving far too quickly for a witch—and wrapped his arms around my hips.

I settled my hand on his head, grinning down at him as he grinned up at me.

"Want a taste?" he asked. "Len says we're allowed to have three each. Too many more and we'll ruin our dinner at the solstice celebration. I've never had smoked lamb or soda bread, have you?"

"No, I haven't."

"You're falling behind," Lile said to Sisu.

Neve huffed, climbing from her stool onto Sisu's abandoned perch. "I'll help."

"Not without washing your hands!" Lile cried. "You'll ruin them!"

"Calm down!" Neve snarled back. "You don't have to be so bossy about everything, like all of the time."

Len settled his hands on his daughters' shoulders. They visibly relaxed under his touch. He met my gaze over their heads, the green of his shapeshifter magic glinting in his eyes, then fading.

I had noticed more than once that all the Conalls had been very careful to immediately deescalate even minor outbursts from the twins since Ayre Byrne's ritual had forced them into wolf form—a form their magic should have been too immature for them to achieve. Or to achieve safely, at least.

I ran my fingers through Sisu's hair, which was in rather desperate need of a cut. Even after nearly two months in Dublin, I still hadn't gotten him to a barber. Then we all just took a quiet moment.

Sisu disengaged from my waist, heading to the iced pile of cookies on the far corner of the island.

Neve climbed off the stool, then dragged it over to the sink to wash her hands.

After eyeing the selection critically, Sisu chose a cookie and brought it to me—an angel covered in clear sugar sprinkles. Then he went back and selected a red-sprinkled sled, offering it to Lile. "It's okay to take a break," he said solemnly.

She wiped her hands on her T-shirt smock and took the offering.

The timer went off. Len pulled the cookies from the oven, exchanged the baked cookies for one of the unbaked sheets, and set the timer again.

Sisu selected two more of the iced cookies—a green-sprinkled tree and a red-and-green-sprinkled holly branch—offering one to Neve and one to Len. Then my brother returned to the tray of iced cookies and took one more for himself, a star with multicolored sprinkles.

Once we each had a cookie in hand, Sisu looked us over, grinning. "Happy solstice!"

We all chimed in to respond in kind, then ate our cookies. They had a hint of lemon zest, which was nice. Though the icing and the sugar sprinkles were too sweet for me.

"We're still going? Right, Dusk?" Sisu asked quietly. For once in his life, he appeared to be savoring a treat. Just taking little nibbles. Len had simply popped his holly cookie in his mouth whole.

Despite still feeling uncomfortable over the odd lunch with Ravine, and not at all certain what was going on with Kellan, I wasn't going to miss the opportunity. Or to deny Sisu the experience of a pack celebration. "Of course."

"Yay!" Neve and Lile crowed.

"Kellan mentioned you needed a ride," Len said, glancing at the clock on the stove. "But we'll need to be quick if we don't want to miss all the best food. Maybe only time enough for one last tray."

Lile opened her mouth to protest, but her father interrupted her. "The rest of the dough can go in the fridge, for tomorrow." She snapped her mouth shut, grinning. Neve and Sisu returned to their assigned workstations.

"I'd better get changed," I said, still really having no idea what to wear to a pack solstice celebration.

Len glanced at the bowed heads of the trio, then indicated that he'd follow me out. I paused in the doorway, but he stepped past me, farther into the great room.

Ah, he wanted to be out of hearing range. Though we'd probably have to be upstairs for Sisu not to hear whatever Len wanted to discuss.

"Dusk." Len cleared his throat, then bowed his head toward me, practically whispering, "Would it be all right for the girls to come back and sleep over tonight? Normally, they could just stay at the house with Bethany, but…" He grinned at me, a slightly wicked glint in his gaze.

"But Bethany might not be home herself tonight."

"Always best to give her that option." A quick frown replaced the grin. "Um, unless you…had other plans…yourself…" He glanced around the great room.

I interjected quickly, not wanting to address whatever he was implying. "I don't."

"The Conall house will be full. Most of the wolves will sleep there. I just…ah, I mean, so could Neve and Lile…"

"I'm happy to have them here, Len," I said, letting him off whatever hook he was currently swinging on. Presumably with Bethany also otherwise occupied, he wanted some alone time with Gitta. "I'm taking the morning off myself." I wasn't, in fact, but I could work from home.

"Perfect." He grinned, sweeping his gaze over me, then winking. "Don't wear anything you don't want to get covered in sand."

He headed back into the kitchen before I could interrogate him further. That was a rather specific but obscure wardrobe suggestion.

CHAPTER SIX

DOZENS OF VEHICLES LINED THE NARROW ROAD LEADing to the pack manor house and the circular drive, leaving just enough space for Len to roll up to the entrance and drop us at the front door. As we'd driven in, I'd gotten a better look than I had on my first visit. The main house was surrounded by sprawling lawns with minimal greenery—likely so that any intruders would be completely exposed when approaching. The rest of the property was heavily forested.

"It's taken almost a century," Len said, noting the direction of my gaze. "To buy all the adjacent properties and regrow the forests."

"But the house is older," I said. The main section of the house was of Georgian construction, but it had numerous additions that weren't encompassed by that architectural influence.

"Yep. The Conalls have held this part of Ireland for a long time."

Bethany had mentioned that finding a secure place in a pack as established as the Conalls, with most of the roles traditionally occupied by the main branch of the family, was difficult. Len was also technically a newcomer. 'New blood,' as Bethany had called it.

"You go ahead." Len nodded toward the house as he slowed the SUV to a stop. "I'll find parking. You'll find the younger kids gathered in the media room. And the older kids on the beach." He laughed, amusing himself. "But you should say hi to Aisling before you head there."

"Thank you."

In the back seat, Neve, Lile, and Sisu were already unbuckling their seat belts and trying to open doors that had the child locks engaged.

"Just let me know when you want to head home with this crew, and I'll drive you back."

It was a long trip back to the city, especially if Len actually intended to stay overnight at the pack house with Gitta. "We might be able to find someone else headed that way," I said.

Len grinned. "Yeah, you might."

Slightly unsure of what he was implying, I climbed out of the SUV, aware that we were causing traffic to back up in the drive. Magic thrummed through the ground, including the thickly graveled driveway. A wild energy, far more intense than anything I'd felt the first time I'd been on the property. It made me want to twirl around in it, just for the moment it took for my own power to adapt to it and ease its touch. I slung my backpack over my shoulder, Infinity within it as always. Then, balancing the oranges that we'd assembled in one of the gnome's woven-leaf baskets in one hand, I opened the back door for the kids.

They tumbled out in a mess of limbs and giggles, somehow managing to not crack their heads at the same time.

"Dusk!" a voice called from my left.

I looked over, spotting Crystal along with another witch I vaguely recognized from the gala. Both were in dresses that seemed far too lightweight for the end of December. Taking Len literally about not wearing anything I didn't mind getting dirty, I had worn a brown sweater dress over tights, along with my favorite brown boots.

"Hi, Crystal!" Sisu shouted gleefully.

"Who's that?" Neve muttered, her shoulder tight against my brother's.

"Yeah," Lile added. "You know you're supposed to introduce us properly."

Sisu huffed. "Come on, then."

He took off toward the librarian with the twins at his heels as I shut the back door and waved to Len. He pulled away, followed by three other cars that had already disgorged additional guests—including Ridge, River, and Rook.

Ridge was wearing a printed dress shirt over jeans. Rook wore a blue shirt-dress over tights, and River looked supremely elegant in a V-neck black cashmere sweater, black satin pants, and spiked heels. Her red hair and pale skin gleamed, as did the gold necklace she wore.

Feeling seriously underdressed, I crossed toward the wide-open heavy oak doors of the front entrance. Ahead, Crystal grinned at Sisu, Neve, and Lile while she introduced her companion as Beryl Dunkirk.

As the Byrnes stepped past her, Neve made a lunge for Rook, grabbing the ten-year-old's hand and hauling her toward the house. Lile did the same with Sisu. Laughter from all the adults followed in their wake.

"We have to greet Grandmama properly too," Neve cried as she hustled away. "Come, Dusk. I'll introduce you." Apparently, Bethany had been teaching the kids some etiquette leading up to the solstice celebration.

I smiled at Ridge, who grinned back at me easily. Then I glanced at River, who returned my reserved nod. We followed the kids inside.

The entrance hall of the pack manor house was large, dominated by smooth granite floors and thick wooden posts and railings, with a grand staircase sweeping up to a second-floor walkway from either side of the front door. Aisling was situated practically at the center of the room, flanked by Odane and Gitta.

Odane, the pack beta, was tall and broad-shouldered; his skin, eyes, and hair were all shades of dark brown. Standing next to the slim, pale-skinned, green-eyed, and red-haired Aisling, it was easy to see that Gitta and her twin brother, Kellan, were a perfect blend of their parents' genetic traits. All three were dressed semi-formally, with Aisling in a flowing scoop-necked gown that was cinched simply at the waist, Odane in jeans and a tunic that carried hints of what might have been a traditional Caribbean design, and Gitta in a dress with a plunging neckline that fluttered prettily just below her knees when she moved.

Neve and Lile shot forward, dragging Sisu between them until they were perfectly arrayed in front of the alpha, beta, and scion of the Conall pack.

Kellan wasn't in the vicinity, presumably because he wasn't part of this apex of the pack's hierarchy. But that didn't stop me from reaching for his magic and instantly sensing him nearby.

Neve, Lile, and Sisu each pressed a fisted hand to their chests, then bowed formally. They were so perfectly in sync that I had no doubt they'd practiced the move.

Rook shot the trio a withering look that suggested they hadn't included her in that practice. Then she bobbed her head and shoulders in a brief curtsy.

I paused a few steps away, Ridge and River directly behind me. Crystal and her friend were hovering just inside the door.

Both Odane and Gitta struggled to suppress delighted smiles, but Aisling maintained her typical cool reserve. She flicked her fingers to indicate the trio could straighten.

"Granddaughters," Aisling said, her voice melodious in the high-ceilinged room. "Introduce us."

Neve and Lile each turned toward Sisu.

Neve swept her hand outward formally. "Sisu Godfrey…"

"…brother of Dusk, archivist," Lile finished.

I kept an eye on Sisu, but he just nodded, thankfully content with having his introduction truncated to not include our mother. Or his demigod father.

"You know Rook," Neve said with a shrug.

Gitta covered her mouth with her hand, coughing delicately. Stifling her laughter.

Aisling shot her eldest a look.

"It is a pleasure to be invited to your solstice celebration, Alpha Conall," Sisu said, grinning madly.

"It's good to meet you, Sisu," Aisling said. "So now I can put a face to all your…exploits."

Sisu bobbed his head, utterly serious. "Education is very important."

It was Aisling's turn to quash her reaction, which she did by turning to Gitta and gesturing to the kids.

Gitta clapped her hands. "Let's get some food and then meet up with everyone else for the movie." She spun toward an open door under the sweep of the staircase. The twins and Rook immediately followed.

Sisu glanced back at me, tugging at the straps of his secondary backpack. We had engaged in a rather extensive discussion about how it would be inappropriate for Sisu to bring his sword to a pack solstice celebration. And since it seemed impossible for Sisu to resist pulling that weapon from the spelled backpack given to him by his father—or, more specifically, from the invisible sheath that had been added to that pack—I'd persuaded him to leave the pack at home.

I nodded to my brother as I stepped forward.

He met me halfway, relieving me of the gift basket. It was filled with winter oranges, including navel and blood oranges, kumquats, mandarins, and clementines. The gnome grew many citrus varieties no matter the season and had also crafted the basket—a delicate weave of citrus leaves that had so far showed no sign of fading or withering.

Sisu pivoted, offering the fruit to Aisling.

"It's tradition to bring a gift, right?" Sisu asked her, still slightly nervous that our research was flawed. "And Dusk says it should have a significance to the occasion, so…like…oranges at Christmas. Though in the original story, St. Nicholas gives away gold coins."

Aisling surveyed the basket. "From your gnome?"

Sisu grinned. "Yes, alpha. But I picked the fruit myself, from the greenhouse. Well, Dusk and me. With permission."

Aisling selected a large navel orange from the basket, carefully inspecting it. "They look…delicious."

Sisu bounced on his heels, grinning. "We have cookies too. But those are for our party."

Um, our party?

"Afternoon tea and a gift exchange on the twenty-fourth," Sisu added. "We're still working on the invitations. But Neve and Lile added you to the guest list."

Aisling's gaze flicked to me questioningly.

"This is the first I'm hearing of it," I said.

Sisu knocked his shoulder into my hip. "It's a surprise!"

I looked down at him. "A surprise?"

"Yes! We…" His face crumpled. "Oh no. I wasn't supposed to say anything."

I touched him lightly on the head. "We'll talk about it. Will you take the basket into the kitchen for Alpha Conall? She needs her hands free to greet her guests."

Aisling set the orange back in the basket. "Yes, thank you, Sisu."

Sisu shuffled his feet, nodding miserably.

I brushed his too-long hair away from his eyes. "Go enjoy your first barbecue. I'll come say hello in a little while."

"I'm not a baby," he said, his misery over revealing the secret Christmas party abruptly forgotten. "I don't need to be checked up on."

"Fine. Go then," I said. "Have fun. Be gentle."

He practically snatched the basket from Aisling, then took off in the direction Gitta had gone with Neve, Lile, and Rook.

I turned my attention to Aisling, who wasn't bothering to hide her amusement from me.

"A delightful age," she drawled.

"Yes, every year seems to be so."

She hummed, eyes narrowing on me. "Do consider dancing, archivist. Many of my guests would love to join you."

I caught Odane's frown out of the corner of my eye, which let me know that Aisling's comment didn't feel odd only to me. I smiled stiffly. Then, taking the alpha's words as a dismissal, I started to turn away.

"Kellan is pit master for the next hour or so," Odane said, his voice a low, deep rumble. His accent carried a pronounced French inflection.

I had no idea what that meant either, though now it was Aisling's turn to throw a look at her beta.

"River!" Aisling cried, dismissing me utterly. "Ridge!"

Okay, then.

I turned my attention toward the far door—and spotted Ravine just a few steps beyond. The dark-haired witch was wearing her typical ensemble, featuring a boyfriend sweater, a short lacy skirt, and knee-high boots. The skirt was dressier than normal though, intricately woven lace over a black underskirt.

As I approached, a massive kitchen opened up behind Ravine. She cast an anxious look at me, pushing up her sleeves to reveal her Celtic-inspired armbands—in what I was now starting to understand was a nervous gesture. "I saw Sisu, so I guessed you'd arrived," she said.

I smiled at her, but was still feeling thrown by Aisling's odd dismissal. And by my interaction with the metal mage earlier that day.

"I'm sorry," she said, sounding just as miserable as Sisu. "I don't…I don't know what…no, I do know. I was just being a bitch, pure and simple. A jealous, conniving bitch."

I blinked at her, rather dumbly.

She barked a laugh. "Please. I…should have…Brendan heard that you and I normally have lunch on Tuesdays and practically invited himself. And then that seemed…unbalanced, so I invited Kellan. God, he even asked if I'd told you, and...I mean, I didn't lie outright. More by omission. Jesus, he chewed my fecking ear off about it. I didn't realize that you two..." She waved her hand and shook her head at the same time. "That's not the point."

"What is the point?"

She laughed again. Sadly. "Right. I'm trying to apologize and not doing a very good job of it." She tamped her mouth shut, lips whitening as she shifted her gaze over my shoulder.

Ridge stepped by us, grinning at her as he headed into the kitchen. "Little sister."

"Brother."

"Ravine," River said coolly as she followed Ridge toward what appeared to be a buffet. "I had no idea you'd be here, since you were supposed to come with us." She sniffed, not bothering to wait for Ravine to respond.

Enough food to feed an army—or an entire pack of shapeshifters—was arrayed across a large trestle table in the dining area adjacent to the kitchen, including cold salads, various types of smoked fish, chilled shellfish, cheeses, and what I was fairly certain was the smoked lamb that Sisu wanted to try. A literal mountain of breads and buns flanked it all, with a wide array of desserts occupying a separate table.

More pack members bustled around in the kitchen proper, including Bethany and Brady. Ridge and River picked up plates from the corner of the table and started filling them. Behind everyone, doubled glass doors stood open to the back patio despite the chilly evening.

"Apparently, I'm pissing everyone off today," Ravine muttered.

"You came alone?" I said.

She flushed. "Brendan drove. I'd been working on refining the copy of the crown piece all afternoon, and he was kind enough to offer." She grasped my arms earnestly. "Forgive me. I really, really like him, and I'm making an ass of myself."

"I still don't understand—"

She growled under her breath, frustrated. But at herself, not me. "He finds you 'utterly compelling.' All right?"

Her accent had shifted, as though she had directly quoted Prince.

I grimaced. "Because I'm the head curator—"

"Ugh, yes, I know. That's why I'm the bitch." She leaned in, wagging her eyebrows. "We worked it out, if you know what I mean."

Though I still wasn't entirely comfortable with what had happened at lunch—or feeling like I fully understood it yet—it was hard not to grin back at Ravine when she was grinning at me. So I did. She laughed, pleased, and slung her arm through mine, dragging me toward the buffet.

Ravine pushed a plate into my hands. "Kellan is manning the barbecue. Literally." She smirked suggestively. "Cooking steak and smoked bangers perfectly, wearing an apron, and exposing those...forearms. You might want to take a picture."

I blinked, once again rendered mute by her teasing. Okay, fine, my brain had just gone blank as it thrust the image she'd described to the forefront.

Would taking a picture be rude? Or...I mean, people did take pictures to commemorate celebrations, right?

Ravine giggled gleefully, grabbing the salad tongs. "Eat, Dusk. You'll need the energy."

After dinner, with Sisu ensconced in the main house along with the other younger pack members and guests, a large portion of the celebration relocated to the beach. Drawn in that direction myself, I followed the path that had been carved through a wide stand of trees running along the shoreline, feeling the thrum of power saturating the estate increase with every step.

I wasn't at all surprised that the pack had so carefully reclaimed and cultivated the land. And with power thrumming from every section of the property, warming my skin and filtering in to gently vibrate through my bones, I also understood why they gathered on the longest night of the year, and why they invited other Adepts to join them. Shifters fed their power into their land in small amounts continually and evidently could do so at even greater levels during their gatherings.

That was utterly intriguing.

The wooded area gave way to a rocky shoreline. The tide was low enough to expose a beach tucked at the apex of a cove. A bonfire had been built on the damp sand, surrounded by carved log benches set well back. Just beyond the fire, well within the reach of its blazing warmth, over a dozen shapeshifters in human form danced, even though no music played. Not in the traditional sense, at least.

Instead, the shifters whirled and twirled to the undulating natural power they'd called forth under the solstice moon.

The full moon was two days past, but the waning gibbous was still a bright orb in the darkened sky. Even

173

the nearly constant misty rain had seemingly given way under the pull and sway of the pack's magic.

Ahead of me, Ravine threw her head back and laughed. She wrapped one arm around Brady's, with Erin already doing the same on his other side. They darted toward the throng of dancers together. Everyone was already barefoot, though I wasn't certain where they'd all left their shoes.

Other shifters and their guests were milling about, chatting with drinks in hand or lounging on the log benches. Even from the base of the path, the fire was almost too warm, though the evening was chilly. Those milling guests included Brendan Prince. The sorcerer historian had indeed arrived with Ravine, but after returning from parking the car, he'd thankfully been occupied throughout dinner, mostly talking with James and Crystal.

Other shifters and Adepts brushed past me. I'd paused a couple of steps off the path. But before I could decide if I was going to strip off my boots and tights and join either of the groups, laughter drew my attention back to the dancers.

Bethany. She and two other female werewolves, all of them various shades of blond, were in the process of tugging a sweater over the head of a tall, exceedingly well-muscled male with light-brown skin—

My stomach dipped.

No, not just any male.

Kellan.

Well…it was clearly hot for those dancing so near the bonfire…but no one had warned me that clothing was optional on the beach.

Kellan put up what appeared to be a token protest. Then, grinning, he finally tossed his thin sweater to the side and allowed himself to be pulled into the throng of dancers. Barefoot in the sand, he was now clad only in low-slung jeans.

Bethany shimmied off her dress, leaving on a slip that barely covered her ass. The other two women with her stripped down to tank tops and underwear. The trio who'd coaxed Kellan to dance were breathtakingly beautiful in the light of the fire and the moon. Their eyes blazed with the green of their shifter magic.

The energy thrumming from the thick, damp sand under my booted feet increased, deepening in tone and tenor when Kellan and the female shifters joined the dance.

Gitta was just off to one side, dancing with Len and the Nordic shifter, Thurston. She was wearing a lacy bra and just the flared skirt of what I'd assumed was a dress. The men were shirtless.

They were all beautiful. Sleek, lithe, powerful. The dancing was a tribute, I realized. To their land, to their territory. No formal ceremony necessary. Just the fire, the moonlight, and the power rolling off the shifters.

I'd never seen so much raw magic and gorgeous flesh in one place at one time. Dragons weren't prudes, certainly. But we were solitary creatures. Perhaps because there weren't that many of us, and we were spread out all over the world.

Ravine threw her head back and laughed. She'd lost a few layers of clothing as well, stripped down to a lacy slip that skimmed the tops of her thighs. The metal mage threw her arms up into the air, writhing and bouncing next to Erin. Magic glinted from the cuffs that covered her forearms.

With a massive grin plastered across his face, Brady, also shirtless, threw his head back and howled. The noise was completely inhuman, though it emanated from a human throat.

The other shifters howled in unison in response, and the thrum of the magic responded in turn as the pace of the dance increased.

I was still staring at Kellan, having stopped only a meter or so onto the beach, and forcing others wandering along the path to step around me.

Bethany had said he didn't dance.

At least not in public.

And though it was utterly ridiculous, some part of me, some tiny kernel of…something within me…just withered, watching him surrounded by other shifters, by his people. With all their exposed skin beginning to glisten, magic roiling and writhing between them, connecting them.

Because why shouldn't Kellan be participating? Why shouldn't he touch Bethany lightly on the hip, or another of his partners on the shoulder, as they swirled around him?

It was just…my chest ached in a completely different way than it ever had before at the sight. And even I had to admit, it had nothing to do with how unsettled I'd been since the gala, or how much I hated all the many lies I'd been forced to spin since arriving in Dublin.

I'd been starting to think, just a little part of me, that maybe…maybe it didn't matter, wouldn't matter, that I wasn't actually a witch. That maybe Kellan—

"You don't dance?" a voice murmured to my right.

Surrounded by so much compelling magic, I hadn't felt the shifter approach from only a couple of steps away. I barely stopped myself from flinching.

A small smile curled Odane's lips, the firelight reflecting from his dark skin. His gaze was fixed on the ever-growing throng of dancers. Up close, the Conall beta was intimidatingly broad through the shoulders, though shorter than Kellan. It was obvious that all three of his children had inherited his physical strength.

"The magic is intoxicating," I said, avoiding answering his question directly.

He chuckled. "Many would agree."

I smiled, nodding. But when Odane gestured, inviting me to sit with him on the nearest of the log benches ahead of us, I noticed Brendan Prince watching. His back was to the water, the bonfire before him.

I didn't want to invite a stilted conversation—or any conversation, really—with the arrogant historian. I also didn't know anyone else on the beach, outside of those who were dancing.

"I was actually just going to check on Sisu," I said to Odane.

He met my gaze. "Your brother, Neve, and Lile are eating three different kinds of popcorn in the media room, watching something animated. The older children will keep an eye on the younger."

I laughed quietly. "Getting the younger to listen is the true test." Especially with Sisu.

Odane nodded almost absentmindedly. His attention returned to the dancers.

As had mine. To Kellan, surrounded by women. Three more shifters had joined his tight-knit group, slightly off to the side of the main group.

"You've already rescued our youngest generation, Dusk," Odane said quietly. "As well as myself." The beta had been another of the Adepts taken by Ayre Byrne, their power fueling the dark ritual that had brought Morgan into the world. "An act that places the pack forever in your debt."

"That's not—"

He held up his hand, cocking his head toward me. "No one could or would ask you for more. But I will say that you joining the dance, lending your power to the pack on this solstice, and hopefully many more solstices to come, would be a great gift."

Not sure how to respond to that, I simply nodded. "Thank you."

Odane side-eyed me for a moment, his green shapeshifter magic flaring in his eyes. Then he grinned. His teeth were almost shockingly white against his dark skin. "After you check on your brother, perhaps."

"Perhaps."

He snorted, amused. "Power is such an interesting phenomenon. Everyone wants it. Everyone wants to be the best, the biggest, strongest, brightest." Odane's gaze shifted to the dancers again. To Kellan. "But the most powerful often find that they have no equals. No one to either hold their hand or keep them in check."

The beta of the Conall pack looked back at me pointedly. Steadily.

And I actually struggled to not squirm under that gaze. I couldn't relate to his musings. I had lots of equals and wasn't even remotely the most powerful among the dragons. Except…that wasn't true in Dublin. Not unless one of the guardians dropped by for a visit. Or Drake. Or even Zeke, for that matter.

Okay, I was just proving my own point.

And Odane was still looking at me, as if he expected an answer.

"The…the balance of power is usually…kept in check," I said, stumbling to formulate some sort of intelligent response. "It ebbs and flows…" I reached out to the energy thrumming under our feet, rising and flowing around our ankles and calves as more and more dancers filtered down to the beach. "You, the pack, feed the land tonight. And the land holds that power in turn until the pack needs it again."

Odane nodded. "Yes. But I wasn't speaking of the balance of energy in the earth. I was talking of natural pairings." He cleared his throat. "Mates, if you will."

"Mates?" I echoed doubtfully. How was it that every conversation I stumbled into in the last few days ended up circling around the same theme?

I blamed Crystal.

"Partners." He nodded toward the dancers. "Take Brady and Erin, for example. The rest of the pack knew that they'd find their way to each other eventually. They are well matched in strength, with both of them pack enforcers. And also, they offset each other's weakness. But the same isn't necessarily true for Gitta and Len..." He trailed off thoughtfully, but didn't elaborate.

"I'm not following you," I said, hating to admit it. "I mean, my parents weren't...there are lots of different types of relationships throughout our lives, yes? Is that what you mean by balance?"

"Of course..." Odane trailed off. Then he shook his head as if begrudgingly letting the subject go. "Have a good evening, Dusk." He touched my elbow lightly, then crossed toward the bonfire, already waving to other guests.

Just as he turned away, I heard him murmur something more. Something like, "I learned a long time ago to let the boy fight his own battles..."

Brendan Prince was making a move in my direction, grinning and trying to catch my eye. Ravine's assessment of his interest—that he found me utterly compelling—echoed through my mind. I didn't want to compel him. Or anyone else.

Or, rather, anyone other than...

I glanced over at Kellan, startled to find that he was looking my way. He'd stopped dancing, though those surrounding him hadn't. He raised his hand as if about to call me over.

I shook my head, tilting it slightly in Prince's direction.

Kellan shifted his gaze.

I turned on my heel, swiftly crossing back to the path that would take me to the main house. I wanted to avoid Prince, certainly. But mostly, I was back to feeling unsettled in my own skin. Again.

It was possible that I just had an allergy to crowds. A crowd being two or more people I didn't know, apparently.

I sighed at my own idiocy, stopping and trying to talk myself into going back, into joining the dance. If only for the experience. A good archivist would never pass up such a chance.

But then I heard Prince's muted voice behind me, questioning Odane, I thought. And I picked up my pace.

Who knew that dragons fled before sorcerer historians?

No, not a dragon. A head curator. And any legitimate head curator would do just about anything to avoid someone like Brendan Prince.

There. Now I didn't feel like so much of a coward.

I was halfway back to the house when a massive pulse of magic tugged me off the path and into the woods.

Literally.

One moment, I was cresting a slight rise and the main house was coming into view. The next, I was dashing off through the moonlit evergreens. My heart was racing even before I'd identified the abrupt swell of power I could suddenly feel on the edges of my senses.

Because just under that unknown manifestation, I swore, just for a moment, that I'd felt a whisper of Sisu's magic.

In my backpack, pressed between my shoulder blades, Infinity vibrated. Not in warning, but in acknowledgement.

I ran. I could feel the shoreline drop off to my far right but not see it. The taste and scent of saltwater, churned dirt, and the broken branches and crushed underbrush I was leaving in my wake filled my nonmagical senses. The forest had been allowed to grow wild. I was heedless of everything except the swell of power dead ahead, still with its trace of fledgling dragon...and now...baby shifter beneath it.

The twins.

I leaped over fallen trees and plowed through thorny, tangled vines. With each footfall, the thrum called forth by the shapeshifters' solstice celebration faded behind me, letting me focus on what was ahead. I could feel it...a wrongness...a miasma of dark energy—

No.

Not wrong. Not even dark.

More like an otherness. A pocket of otherworldly energy. Then the hum of Sisu's bright magic. Then, even quieter, Neve and Lile.

Having never been in this section of the pack property, I had no idea where I was or where I needed to go. So I ran flat out. A broken branch scraped my cheek hard enough to draw blood. The wound was given barely enough time to heal before I got sliced again, propelled forward by a sharp, almost senseless need to get to my brother—

The power suddenly compressed, halving.

Or...diminished?

As if it was moving...

No. As if its source had been...cut off?

I stopped. Barely any moonlight filtered through the magic-imbued woods. I listened, straining, all my senses thrown open.

I could still feel Sisu ahead of me. Moving, I thought. Drawn in the same direction? So he'd sensed the magic as well, but hadn't found the source. Not yet.

I pivoted once more, just in case I was missing some detail. Conscious of the unknown something that I'd felt like I'd been missing for a few days now.

I felt the thrumming power evoked by the shifters on the beach clearly. Farther away and on the other side of me, I felt another pocket of condensed magic. Multiple mixed Adepts at the manor house.

The diminished pulse of power was expanding again, but it still felt condensed compared to when it had first pulled me into the woods. As if it was an unknown Adept. Or...a magical creature? Not a power source or spell.

I spun to take off after Sisu and the twins again. As far as I could tell, they were still heading for the unknown entity.

A tickle of energy nearby brought me to a stilled readiness. My bone blade was in my hand, though I didn't remember pulling it from the sheath strapped to my thigh under the sweater dress.

Infinity vibrated, warmth radiating down my spine, then easing.

Still not a warning. Simply an awareness? I was still working out how my personal archive communicated.

The brownie I'd spotted outside Wilding Manor revealed herself, half hidden behind a wide tree trunk. She pinned her too-large eyes to me, magic sparkling within their dark depths.

My chest suddenly felt weighted with...sadness?

Was that my own emotion? Or a projection of the brownie's emotional state?

She was holding something in her large hands—a piece of metal, stained with a dark patina of oxide or grime, jagged edged along one side. I couldn't pick up any magic from the object—but I could barely feel the brownie herself, even with all my senses wide open.

We stared at each other for what felt like minutes. Her gaze dropped to the bone blade in my hand, and I would have sworn her face crumpled.

She wasn't the source of the otherness I could still feel. That entity or manifestation was farther away, as were Sisu, Neve, and Lile.

The brownie bowed her head, twisting her hands around the object she held. She had revealed herself to me deliberately. My heart pounded, aching, as I waited to see why.

She raised her deep-set eyes to meet mine. Her frame was almost skeletal. I would have sworn she was even slighter than she had been when I'd first seen her, if that was even possible.

When I was very, very young—younger even than Sisu was now—I'd gotten a glimpse of Mistress Bright-shire's father, Abe, only a couple of weeks before he'd passed away. He'd been in the kitchen pantry at my mother's estate, appearing out of nowhere to thwart my attempt to sample a dessert that had been tucked away for after dinner.

Abe and I had stared at each other. I'd startled him as much as he had me. Even living in the same home, it was rare to see a brownie who didn't want to be seen. We hadn't spoken, but he'd given me a cookie and grinned at me. Indulgently. However, the terror of seeing him so frail had sent me running to my mother, the cookie forgotten in my hand.

She had sat me down on the settee in the library with a book in hand and told me that Abe's tie to the estate was no longer enough to sustain him. That he had decided it was his time to fade.

The brownie standing in the shadowed forest was far younger than Abe Brightshire, but she was half faded from the world already. It hurt to look at her.

But I didn't look away.

"Are you…are you all right?" I asked, lowering my blade.

She blinked, shakily tucking away the grimy object she was holding in a pocket of her ragged store-bought dress. Then she pressed her hands to her chest, dipping her chin mournfully. "I cannot say no."

She whispered so quietly that I barely caught the words. She had an accent that reminded me of Welsh, but wasn't. Or perhaps it was some regional variant I hadn't heard before.

I opened my mouth to speak—

Neve shrieked from ahead of me, though I still couldn't see her.

Then Lile screamed.

The brownie disappeared with barely a whisper of power.

I was running again, hearing Sisu shouting something. And as I ran, I realized that the brownie had deliberately shown herself to me for the second time, and I still had no idea why.

A giant octopus was attempting to climb over the edge of a craggy cliff that appeared to drop off into nothing. From my vantage point at the edge of the forest, at least. I could barely hear the crashing surf under the shrieking emanating from the three tiny figures darting around and underneath the octopus's long limbs, each of those limbs thicker than the trees at my back.

The creature appeared to be seeking purchase on the rocky outcropping, its passage slowed by the afore-mentioned shrieking trio. Shrieking in delight, not terror.

Though with a massive otherworldly octopus in the mix, it was hard to be certain in a single glance.

And I had a feeling that calling it an octopus was just my mind's attempt to make sense of what I was see-ing. The cephalopod was an iridescent turquoise, energy shifting around it, pulsing from underneath its thick skin. Its black, perfectly round eyes were front facing, with silvered crescent moons for irises. It opened its oval maw to display a multitude of jagged teeth, including doubled fangs.

It huffed at Sisu, Neve, and Lile.

Yes, huffed. As if peeved.

The smell of pungent seawater wafted across the outcropping, carrying the reek of fermentation.

Perhaps the children's shrieking was hurting its ears? Not that I could see any obvious ears, or nose, even though the creature's bulbous head made up more than half its total bulk. It was roughly the size of a double-decker bus. Perhaps two? And I could see only a portion of its body and six of its limbs, the undersides of which were lined with long runs of doubled, hooked claws rather than suckers.

The cephalopod was the source of the otherworldly power. Not the pulse that had initially drawn me from the path, but the more diminished sense of power I'd felt as I was running. Which made much, much more sense than whatever was going on having something to do with the brownie.

And yes, I was standing stock-still, just a step beyond the tree line. Staring as the creature kept clawing its way forward, rising over the outcropping, blocking the entire edge of the cliff.

Infinity hummed rhythmically against my back. It took me a moment to realize my personal archive was keeping time with Sisu's, Neve's, and Lile's delighted shrieks as they attempted to leap over one of the cephalopod's thick limbs. Or were they trying to leap onto it?

Energy pulsed from the massive creature, knocking Neve and Lile tumbling. It made use of the cleared space to pull more of its bulk up onto the outcropping.

With a shout, Sisu dashed to the side, launching himself at another of the creature's long tentacle limbs—one that was currently clawed into the rock, anchoring the cephalopod. My brother sprawled across the limb, which was thicker than he was tall, struggling to find purchase. He actually managed to get his legs underneath him. Feet slipping, arms out for balance, my baby brother then raced along the limb and attempted to scale the main body of the turquoise cephalopod.

The gigantic creature paused, turning its blackened gaze on my brother with...

Well, with a look of utter disbelief.

I knew that feeling intimately.

Another long limb flicked overhead, its tip narrowed to a fine point. It snagged Sisu by the backpack, picking him up, then holding him hanging in midair before the cephalopod's eyes.

It stared at him. Like it might have been contemplating eating him.

I surged forward, vaguely aware of the twins coming to their feet as I did so.

Only seconds had passed.

The cephalopod brought Sisu closer. The crescent moons in its eyes widened, then narrowed, as if trying to focus on the tiny figure it had captured.

Getting to within a few meters, I was still unable to see how far the cliff dropped off behind the otherworldly being, but I could hear the surf more clearly. The creature utterly dwarfed me, easily as tall as a two-storey building. As tall as Wilding Manor, not including the central tower.

"Stop!" I cried, throwing my arms to the sides and letting my hold on my magic completely drop. My power crackled around me for a heartbeat—letting me know that I'd just shredded Jiaotu's glamour. Again. Then that magic punched outward, flooding the rocky outcropping and radiating into the forest behind me.

Lile and Neve grabbed for my legs, as if I'd unintentionally knocked them off balance.

The cephalopod swiveled its gaze from Sisu, still dangling in midair, to me. Two of its limbs shot past me, finding purchase on the rock. It shifted the bulk of its body farther onto the outcropping, then stilled.

The creature returned its intent regard back to my brother.

"Let your magic out, Sisu," Lile cried, still wrapped around one of my legs. "Like Drake taught us."

On my other side, Neve climbed my leg to fist her hands in my sweater dress, and added, "Form a shield!"

The twins' own magic hummed against me—a delicate melody compared to the creature we were facing, but power that I hadn't been able to feel so acutely before they'd been forced into their wolf forms by Ayre Byrne.

"It just wants to play!" Sisu cried. But he loosened his hold on his own power, as commanded.

Right. Because what else would a massive other-worldly creature cross into our dimension to do? Other than play with fledglings?

The cephalopod pulled Sisu closer. The crescent-moon iris of its left eye narrowed to a mere slit as it tried to focus on the baby dragon dangling from the tip of its tentacle.

Panic swamped me. My bone blade, no matter how powerful it was, suddenly felt like a toothpick in my hand. I needed something longer, something I could throw...

The blade began shifting in my hand before I'd even articulated that thought, that need, in my own head. It lengthened, the hilt rounding and thickening.

Until I was holding a long, sharp-bladed staff.

Without thinking too much about it, I hit the rock under my feet with the end of the staff, bellowing, "Enough!"

My power boomed across the outcropping, back through into the forest, and over the water beyond and below the cliff.

The cephalopod's gaze shifted to me. And stayed.

"Dusk!" Sisu cried delightedly, straining to see over his shoulder. "Look at your blade!"

Ignoring him, I shouted, "Release my brother, or I will make you do so!"

The cephalopod lowered Sisu, then released him with a lazy flick. Not as gently as I would have liked, but it was a huge creature, and my brother was minuscule in comparison. Sisu rolled, tumbling into the forest. Lile and Neve released their holds on me to dash after him.

And yes, my baby brother was giggling like mad the entire time.

Jiaotu was going to have my head.

"It was just supposed to be a barbecue. And a dance," I mumbled, not quite certain who the hell I was preemptively justifying my actions to.

The cephalopod reached for me with one of its limbs, first curling, then coiling it around me. Its sickled claws, each the width of my hand, were only a breath away from brushing my arms, forming a cage up to my waist.

Then it leaned forward, its huge bulk instantly obscuring my sight of the starlit sky. All I could really see were the crescent moons that swam in its black eyes, each of which was almost as tall as I was.

"Dusk?" Sisu called out from behind me. For the first time since I'd laid eyes on the creature and the trio, my brother sounded scared. "What if it doesn't want to play?"

Magic from the otherworldly creature rolled and roiled around me. But none of it touched me or invaded my space.

Then I felt a brush of power against my mind.

A psychic knock.

Creatures who were about to tear you limb from limb rarely asked permission first.

I wasn't terribly experienced with telepathic communication. All right, I was practically the opposite of telepathic. But I formed a thought in my mind, layered it with a welcoming intention, and visualized projecting it outside my body. *Yes?*

"It's okay, Sisu," I said out loud. "Just keep a step back with Lile and Neve, okay?"

Power washed over me, almost overwhelming my every sense in a single blink. I gripped the bone staff tighter, allowing its connection to the earth to ground me, and gave my mind a moment to sort out the feelings and images the cephalopod was projecting.

First, a sense of understanding…

Then an image of me, glowing with intense golden-tinged power.

Then an image of Sisu, glowing as well. Just not quite as brightly.

So the creature recognized our magic, recognized my…

An image of the white-bone staff I still held flashed through my mind, then another image I didn't quite catch.

I shook my head, trying to focus. *I don't understand.*

The cephalopod pushed the unseen image again. A golden object with jagged edges flashed through my mind. I tried to hold onto it. To really see it, take it in.

The brownie had been holding the same object, its gleaming surface obscured by a dark patina, only minutes before.

Yes! I responded. *I've seen that. Does it belong to you?*

Another brush of power touched me, but slightly less intense, as if the creature was sorting out how to communicate with me as well. More images flickered through my mind.

I took a deep breath, forcing myself to be patient, to give my natural talent for translation time to kick in, as I waited for the images to align themselves.

A doorway in a rocky cliff.

An outline of magic-bright symbols.

Then a woman who glowed with power, holding that same relic. The one I'd seen in the brownie's hands.

The woman's dark hair was pulled back into a severe bun, her face younger than I'd ever seen her. Not that she looked particularly old in the present. But it was the extra-long katana slung across her back that was unmistakable. I'd seen that blade—had seen her—at the base of my bed not two months ago.

I had briefly wondered in that moment if she would be the last thing I ever saw.

Suanmi.

The fire breather.

The guardian of Western Europe.

In a rush, the full implication of all the images came together in my mind, mixing in a bit of creative guesswork.

The cephalopod was a sentinel, entrusted with the relic—the image of which was now seared into my brain—by Suanmi. It must have been centuries ago, perhaps soon after Suanmi had taken on the mantle of guardian.

And the doorway?

An opening to another dimension.

Oh, shit.

A tight tsunami of power poured out of the forest behind me. The cephalopod unwound its tentacle limb from around me as I spun to face the new arrival, realizing I knew the feel of his magic only after the octopus had withdrawn the bulk of its own power.

Kellan.

In his warrior form.

A wickedly clawed, impossibly broad-shouldered, dark-gray monster prowled out from the deep shadows of the tree line. His eyes glowed with the golden-green of his unique shapeshifter magic, and he lifted his lip in a vicious snarl, sizing up the cephalopod.

Kellan's claws lengthened. He lowered his head, ears pinned back, readying a charge.

"It's under control," I snapped.

Then Sisu, Neve, and Lile were dancing around Kellan, speaking all at once, regaling him with everything that had happened in the last few minutes. From what I could make out, they had bravely held the creature at bay until I arrived.

Kellan attempted to shove the trio behind him, snarling at the cephalopod again. "This is pack land!" His accent was a deeper-than-usual Irish lilt, his words perfectly articulated even though most shapeshifters couldn't speak at all while in their warrior forms. "Trespassing will not be—"

The octopus flicked one tentacle wickedly fast, trying to knock Kellan back with the tip of that limb. Kellan took the blow to the chest with a pained grunt. He was driven back a half-dozen paces, feet gouging through dirt and rock as he fought to maintain his balance. But he somehow held against the blow, upright and firmly planted.

Oh, wow.

The trio cheered, thrusting tiny fists in the air.

"Kellan!" I shouted, dashing between the cephalopod and the shapeshifter. I hammered the end of the staff on the rocky ground again. Then once more for emphasis.

Kellan lowered his head, narrowing his eyes at me and glowering balefully.

"I'm taking care of it! Not every situation requires tooth and claw!" And I definitely didn't need the cephalopod projecting images of Suanmi into Kellan's head, forcing me to explain who she was or how I was connected to her.

Kellan made a show of smelling the bone staff, curling his lip in displeasure. Apparently, he'd forgotten he could speak in warrior form. Either that or he was so angry he couldn't form words, let alone full sentences.

Granted, the scene before him didn't look good. What with me telepathically communing with a gigantic, eight-legged, clawed-and-fanged creature from another dimension while the children gamboled about.

"I didn't even need my sword," Sisu said brightly, wrapping his hand around Kellan's massive, clawed forefinger.

Using their uncle's ruined clothing as handholds, Neve and Lile literally scaled Kellan, then wrapped their arms around his neck, feet braced on his hips.

"Dusk…" Kellan growled. "Step out of the way."

I placed one hand on my hip. "Are you going to fight an unknown being with children hanging off your neck?"

In a show of support, a long turquoise tentacle curled around my lower legs, shimmering with power and followed by another telepathic tap. No images this time. Just a sense of understanding…and trust?

Kellan was trying to untangle Lile and Neve from his neck. But obviously not wanting to inadvertently hurt or scratch them, he was having a hard time of it. Even more so because Sisu was still holding his forefinger and grinning at me madly.

The power emanating from the cephalopod began condensing behind me. More clawed limbs wrapped around me.

Then, its tentacle limbs undulating, the octopus began to shrink.

It kept shrinking. Its limbs tangled in my unbound hair. Its power continued to abate, or perhaps simply tighten behind me.

Kellan's eyes narrowed, still glaring at me.

I glared back.

Claws catching in my sweater dress, the cephalopod settled on my shoulder. Heavy but bearable.

Neve burst out laughing, pointing and then slapping her uncle's chest. Lile giggled.

"What? What?" Sisu cried.

"The octopus!" Neve gasped. "It looks like...like...it's wearing Dusk's hair...like...like a wig!"

Sisu blinked at me. Then he began laughing, clutching his stomach with one hand.

Lovely.

A brownie had just shown me a relic that Suanmi had deemed important enough to hide in another dimension, protected by a powerful sentinel. Anger and frustration were rolling off Kellan in waves I could practically feel. But at least the kids were amused.

The octopus began touching me, light little taps on my cheeks, chin, neck, and collarbone, projecting amusement and satisfaction. I caught a projected image of Kellan coming out of the forest, all magnificently wild, then an image of me radiating power and tamping down with my staff.

Shaking my head with another huff, I projected back the image of the doorway. Finding that doorway and returning the cephalopod to its own dimension through it was my first priority. And not just because I knew that Sisu and the twins would be out here the very next chance they got.

The octopus tugged at my hair.

"Are you communicating with it?" Kellan grumbled with utter disbelief.

"Of course," Sisu piped up. "Feel its magic?"

"I feel its magic, all right," the shapeshifter snarled.

That elicited another round of giggles from Neve.

I turned in the direction that the cephalopod was tugging, pausing when the creature pressed my right cheek firmly. I was now gazing out over the cliff.

"Dusk!" Kellan snarled.

"I'm just figuring it out, Kellan," I snarled back, crossing toward the cliff edge with an otherworldly turquoise octopus perched on my shoulder. The staff shrank in my hand as I did so, returning to its regular bone-blade form. I sheathed it.

I paused a few steps from the sheer drop down to the open ocean below. Far, far below. Waves crashed onto a rocky shoreline jutting out over deep water. I could see the bonfire blazing in the cove to my far right. The dancers were tiny at this distance.

Kellan joined me, the children finally detached from him and now lined up around our legs. I reached out with my senses. We stood there for a moment, shoulder to shoulder as the chilled breeze slowly seeped past the fading adrenaline to cool my skin.

I could feel a glimmer of power. Directly below me.

Of course the dimensional doorway was carved into a sheer cliff. Why the hell not?

"Can I dive off here?" I asked Kellan, hearing the reluctance in my voice. On top of not having a great sense of exactly how far that jump might be, I'd never dived off any cliff. And certainly not in the dark, no matter how bright the moon was overhead.

"Do you really need to?"

"Can I walk around and reach the base from the beach?"

"Not really. Not without swimming through the rocks and against the incoming tide."

"Do you want me to leave a dimensional doorway wide open?"

He huffed an exasperated breath.

Sisu made a break for the cliff edge. I grabbed him by the backpack. Thankfully, he hadn't gotten up enough speed to tear the straps off.

"I can help!" he cried.

"You three are going back to the house with Kellan," I said. "And you aren't going to mention the gigantic octopus to—"

"What?!" Neve cried.

Lile howled, "No!" at the same time.

"But I'm good with doorways!" Sisu cried. He grinned up at me. "They open for me all the time."

I narrowed my eyes at him, seriously hoping he was talking about locked doorways in the house and not other doorways—such as those found in the nexus.

His grin widened, magic dancing in his eyes.

"You will not mention the octopus to anyone," I said again, "until I figure out what's going on."

The cephalopod reached down to tickle Sisu's ear. My brother giggled encouragingly.

I sighed. I would circle back to the opening-random-doorways issue just as soon as I got a moment.

"And I need to seal this door," I said. "Not open it."

"We're quick learners," Neve said earnestly. "Drake said so!"

"Yeah." Lile bobbed her head. "And the werewolves jump off the cliffs here all the time."

"Adult werewolves," Kellan interjected. "In the summer."

Neve placed her hands on her hips. "Well, Drake says we're just as powerful as—"

"Who the fuck is Drake?" Kellan growled, rounding on me.

"Bad word, Uncle!" Neve cried.

Lile giggled.

The cephalopod, still simmering with power, took the opportunity to crawl across my shoulders, completely tangled in my hair now. It gazed down at the twins, then looked up at Kellan, amusement rolling off it.

So wonderful that we were deemed entertaining by powerful magical beings from other dimensions. That was exactly the reputation I was striving so hard to build.

I crouched to unlace my boots. "Kellan?"

"I'll get them back to the house."

"You're no fun," Sisu said, stamping his foot. "And I was good. I didn't even pull my sword."

I pinned my brother with a look.

Neve and Lile went still.

Sisu ducked his head, but his hands were still fisted at his sides.

"Good?" I echoed softly. "Where are you supposed to be right now?"

Sisu tightened his shoulders. "Exploring is a valuable—"

"Where are you supposed to be?"

He mumbled under his breath. I caught it but waited for him to repeat it.

His bright-blue gaze flicked to me, then down to my feet. "Watching the movie." His tone strengthened. "But it was boring."

"We'd seen it five times already," Neve interjected.

Kellan snarled, a short but sharp rebuke.

Neve clamped her mouth shut.

"What promises did you make me?" I asked quietly.

Sisu shuffled his feet.

I was worried that he wasn't going to answer, and my heart was aching for taking him to task in front of his friends. I was loath to push him. But then Sisu stepped forward and threaded his arm around my neck on the opposite side from the octopus.

He pressed his lips to my ear. "But, Dusk," he whispered, "there's a magical octopus on your shoulder."

I laughed before I could stop myself. Kellan's amused snort confirmed just how sensitive his hearing was as well.

Sisu pulled back a bit, looking at me earnestly. "And we'll write all about it? Right? When we get home? To Mom?"

My stomach soured, and I struggled to maintain the smile that had been effortless a moment before. "Yes, of course. To Zeke as well if you like."

Sisu scrunched up his nose. "I don't need the lecture."

Kellan barked a laugh that he then tried to cover with a cough. Unsuccessfully.

"Are we going to be punished, then?" Lile asked seriously.

"Did you run toward the danger instead of away like you're supposed to?" Kellan asked.

"No," Sisu said earnestly. "We knew the octopus was friendly!"

The twins backed up this statement with a chorus of agreement.

Kellan pinned me with a look. "This is your influence."

"Really?" I said archly, pulling off my boots. "I've only known the twins for two months. Maybe take a good look at yourself."

He shook his massive head at me, but his ears were no longer pinned back. He grabbed Neve, placing her on his shoulders, then snagged Lile around the waist.

"You'll be right back?" Sisu asked me.

My heart did that squelching thing it so often did, and I touched him lightly on the head. "I'm just going to get the octopus home and seal the doorway. Then we'll go home ourselves and have some ice cream and some of the cookies you baked."

"Yes!" Neve said.

"That's some harsh punishment, Dusk," Kellan grumbled.

I threw him a look. "Your family might not miss you, Kellan. But Sisu really only has me right now. He's mine—" My throat closed, choking off the rest of my words.

My mother had been gone for over a year. And Sisu's father was one of the most powerful beings in the world. His schedule wasn't conducive to rearing a child.

Kellan actually dropped his gaze and grimaced. At least I thought it was a grimace. His beastly visage lent itself more to snarling and growling than contrition, so it was hard to tell.

Sisu tugged Uncle Beckett's watch out of the pocket of his shorts. "How long do you need?" he asked. "I'll time you, and we'll come back to help if you take too long."

I smiled at him, desperately trying to look confident. "Enjoy the rest of the movie. And you know what to do if for some reason I don't return in a couple of hours."

He bobbed his head. "Call Papa. But...I...I don't know the way home."

"There are phones in the house," Kellan said, trying to be gentle, but his beast form just made everything coming out of his mouth sound like death and destruction.

"Those phones won't work!" Sisu cried, abruptly on the edge of panic.

I touched his cheek lightly, pulling his attention to me before he could spiral. "Kellan will drive you home, okay?"

Sisu looked up at Kellan questioningly. Kellan nodded, carefully threading a clawed finger through the loop on the top of Sisu's backpack.

"Okay," Sisu whispered. "But you'll tell me everything when you get back."

"I'm not going anywhere. I know better than to step through doorways."

Sisu patted my cheek. "You're always good, Dusk. That's why I'm allowed to be…less than good."

I snorted doubtfully. "That's not how it works."

"It totally is," Neve chimed in from Kellan's shoulders. She patted her uncle on the head, then added, "Just like Mom and Uncle Kellan."

"Mom is the good one," Lile added, just in case I couldn't figure that out for myself.

Kellan growled. I stifled a smile.

"See?" Sisu said.

"Right…" I said, looking up at Kellan. "And I'm the bad influence."

Sisu threw up his hands, then executed a flawless pirouette, somehow managing to slip out of Kellan's grasp without damaging the backpack.

"Ta-da!" he cried, golden sparkles shooting from his fingertips. "Race you back!"

He took off toward the woods.

Neve and Lile cried out, wiggling and protesting until Kellan set both of them on their feet. They took off after Sisu.

Kellan tried to glower at me again. "I blame you."

I shrugged, hiking up my dress to undo the sheath on my thigh.

"I'll be right back," Kellan said, eyeing me like maybe he wanted to wait around to see what else I was going to strip off. "Wait for me."

"Nope," I said, setting the sheathed bone blade to the side just for a moment.

He snarled under his breath—an interesting mixture of curse words in Irish and older Gaelic—but then he loped off after the kids.

The cephalopod climbed off my shoulder, slowly undulating toward the cliff edge as I stripped off my backpack and then as much as my clothing as I could bear to be parted with—so not my bra or underwear.

This was going to be really, really cold. Even for a dragon.

Ironically, if I actually were a witch, I probably could have conjured a heating spell or two.

I strapped the bone blade on my now-bare thigh.

The octopus had grown again, now the size of a bear. I was painfully aware that I was leaving Infinity behind, knowing that my archive's hatred of water made swimming with it not an option. I stepped up, curling my bare toes over the rocky cliff edge. A stiff breeze rose, blowing all my hair from my shoulders and chilling me thoroughly.

The bear-sized octopus rolled off the edge of the cliff, disappearing from sight.

I jumped into the dark surf after it, forcing myself to not think about the fall.

CHAPTER SEVEN

CHILLED AIR FLASHED OVER ME, THEN A FRIGID DARK-ness swallowed me, overwhelming all my senses. I hit rock bottom—literally—and sprang off, ignoring the crushing cold as I stretched my arms upward toward the moonlit surface.

I picked up the muted tenor of the guardian magic sealing the doorway the moment I swam to shore and found the first handholds to haul myself out of the water. Still, I had to scale about a quarter of the cliffside—the octopus at my side and climbing with ease—to reach a narrow shelf and the rune-marked archway that the other-dimensional cephalopod had telepathically projected to me.

The brownie, presumably, had unsealed a doorway to another dimension. A doorway that Suanmi herself had sealed long ago. The brownie had then stolen the relic from under the watch of its sentinel, forcing the cephalopod to chase her into our dimension.

The only problem was that, even though brownies were exceedingly skilled magic users, I'd never heard of them doing anything of that sort. Not opening doorways, not thwarting guardian magic. And certainly not sneaking up on gigantic cephalopods. As far as I was aware, thievery of any kind was strictly against their personal and communal codes.

Outlined in dim symbols, the doorway was closed but not sealed. I was shivering, my thick mane of hair still streaming water down my back and legs as I pressed my hands against the rough rock of the cliff, listening to the power etched into it.

Perched next to me, the octopus—now the size of a large dog—curled a limb around my ankle, then gently pressed me to the side. I obeyed, stepping as far out of the way as the narrow ledge would allow.

Stretching upward on six of its eight limbs, the cephalopod brushed the tips of its other two limbs against the symbols outlining the door in a complicated sequence of movements that I didn't quite catch—which was fine by me. I wasn't interested in opening the door once I was done sealing it again.

Power pulsed through and from the creature's turquoise limbs, and the golden magic residing in the runes flared brighter. Among those runes, I noted a carved symbol that looked similar to a fleur-de-lis at four points around the door—the bottom corners and where the top began to curve into an arch. Anchor points etched into the stone by Suanmi?

Magical energy churned within the craggy rock, though it had no discernible color, at least not in the moonlight. Then the cliff face abruptly faded away to reveal a darkened landscape beyond, with a purple horizon that gradually darkened to near-black overhead. That sky backlit what appeared to be a number of stone monoliths of various heights, some sharply pointed, some large enough to be speckled with shapes that might possibly be trees. The rock formations jutted out of deep pools of still water that were streaked with silver. Light from a moon I couldn't see from my vantage point?

I was gazing into another dimension.

Despite being soaking wet and crazy cold—and with yet another mystery involving a stolen artifact on my hands—a thrill ran through me. My heart was racing as I greedily tried to see…well, everything. To lock it all into my brain so I could attempt to describe it, even sketch it, for Infinity later.

For what I was fairly certain was the first time, I bemoaned the fact that I wasn't more skilled with a pencil.

The cephalopod ran a tentacle up my lower leg, its sickled claws scraping my bare skin harmlessly. Its power brushed my mind again, questioningly.

I tore my gaze from the dimension beyond the doorway, then hunched down so I could meet the octopus's black-eyed gaze.

"Thank you," I said, not certain that the creature could translate English, but hoping my intention was obvious.

With another gentle push of its power, the cephalopod projected the image of the relic that the brownie had stolen into my mind again.

I nodded, once again trying to memorize the piece so I could sketch it later. It looked oddly familiar, yet I knew I'd never seen it before. Perhaps it related to something else I'd once studied.

"I will retrieve the relic and ask the guardian Suanmi if she would like me to return it to you."

I got blasted with a sense of amusement, then a tumble of images of Sisu, Neve, and Lile.

I laughed. "They'll never forget you either."

The cephalopod let go of my calf, undulating across the rocky shelf toward the open doorway. Energy shifted within the rock and the rune-delineated archway.

Then the creature was on the other side, gazing back at me.

For one completely overwhelming moment, I almost followed.

I almost stepped through after the octopus. I could feel the power of the purple-kissed dimension even from the other side of the doorway. It beckoned. It made silent promises—wicked promises to the power so tightly contained underneath my skin. Though I was clad only in a soaking-wet bra and panties, with my bone blade sheathed along my right thigh, the urge to explore was…intense. And utterly irrational.

I raised my hand in a silent goodbye.

The cephalopod stretched up on two of its tentacle limbs, dancing the other six in another complicated pattern to close the doorway from the other side. Energy shifted in the archway, which shimmered and then solidified into solid rock again.

Ignoring a spike of bereavement—honestly, I really had no business punishing Sisu for following through on the same sorts of urges—I pressed my hand to the cliff face, closing my eyes and listening to the remnants of the magic that Suanmi had originally used to seal it.

Though apparently, the original seal hadn't been brownie-proof. A mystery that was almost as intriguing as whatever the relic might represent.

I breathed deeply, allowing my magic to stretch out from my hand as I would when taking impressions from an artifact. Thankfully, sealing a dimensional doorway would take a whack of power, so I didn't have to worry about my inability to be delicate with such things.

Energy churned around me, warm enough to dry my skin, though it didn't lift my soaking-wet hair. I was still figuring out this particular aspect of my personal magic, so I kept my eyes closed and simply projected pure intention.

I needed to seal the doorway, working with the magic already embedded into the stone.

I needed to seal the doorway...

To protect the pack...

To protect Dublin...

To protect the world, really. Because the next gigantic cephalopod—or whatever other even-more-frightening creatures might call that particular dimension home—might not be quite so friendly.

They also might not recognize the authority of a dragon, which I was fairly certain was the reason that the cephalopod hadn't pursued the brownie itself.

Energy—a manifestation of my magic—settled around my ankles. It spread to the side. Then, oddly, it went upward and overhead. Hints of honey and citrus scented the air.

I opened my eyes to see that a completely out-of-season wildflower had sprung forth around the doorway, seemingly growing out of bare rock. Compact, cup-shaped, bright-pink flowers with needlelike leaves on long stems had erupted from the stone, interspersed among the faded runes that outlined the doorway.

Well, that was new.

Grinning madly, I brushed my fingers through the blossoms, bottom to top, then over my head. Adding more and more of my magic to the flowers with each touch, imagining filling each petal one by one.

After three passes, I settled my fingertips among the blossoms around shoulder height and pushed pure intention through them into the cliff face. Just as I had when I secured the wards on the central tower and in my library and office.

Energy rustled through the blossoms once again, pouring from me shockingly fast and taking my breath with it. Then the flowers, the faded runes, and the rock combined, leaving behind an etched archway that connected all the symbols that had previously sealed the doorway.

Momentarily faint, I stepped back to survey my work. The magic of the dimensional doorway was...contained. Muted. That was ideal. It would take someone with a high sensitivity to magic to even notice any hint of it now.

Only the fact that I was going to have to eventually report to Suanmi—and possibly have her double-check my work—dulled my self-congratulatory triumph. Actually, making me a little ill. Enough that it was easy to convince myself that conversation could wait until I'd retrieved the relic from the brownie.

A shiver ran through me, reminding me that I was now slowly freezing to death. Which would be a ridiculous way for a dragon to die. Figuring out how to track down the brownie was a problem best considered when I was on dry land and warm again.

I peered up, considering scaling the sheer face of the cliff. But just in case there was another option—I did like to be thorough—I scanned the area around me.

A small fire drew my attention to a tiny cove off to the right, much closer than the distant beach. A large figure stood on the shore, looking my way.

Kellan. In his human form, though still half naked.

Well, he had said he'd return.

I would have to swim to reach him. But the fire was rather enticing, and scaling a wet cliff while freezing to death definitely didn't appeal. Also, I was a little drained. Not physically, and not enough to be detrimental. But more than I'd really ever been before. I had channeled a lot of energy into the doorway seal.

Before I could think through my options any further, I dove off the narrow shelf into the deep open water. Then, fighting the current that rather gleefully tried to smash me back against the sheer cliff, I swam toward the cove. To the promised warmth of the fire.

To Kellan.

I waded out of the water onto the rocky beach, straight into Kellan Conall's open arms.

It was the huge, toasty-warm towel he was holding out that drew me. Obviously. Though I wasn't about to deny that I enjoyed the way his eyes had brightened as I'd cleared the water and strode toward him, trying not to shiver.

"Nice dive," he said huskily, wrapping me in the towel and holding me to him.

And yes, I pressed my forehead against his bare chest and let him hold me. Indulging just for a moment in the strength of his arms, the warmth of his body. He had opted for black sweatpants after changing back from his warrior form, and nothing else. He rubbed his hands along the plush towel, up and down my back, over my arms. His touch was firm and sure.

"Doorway is sealed," I mumbled, not raising my head.

He grunted in acknowledgement, continuing to dry me off without unwrapping me from the towel.

We stood like that for longer than I should have allowed, until I started shivering, and Kellan pulled me closer to the small fire he'd built on the rocky beach. If there were any sandy patches in this tiny cove, they were underwater.

Even then, I actually had to step away from Kellan before he allowed his arms to drop.

He bent down, grabbed a second towel from a log situated near the fire, then handed it to me. I wrapped the first towel around me, it hung past my knees, then grabbed the second to dry my hair.

Kellan watched me.

And I couldn't help smiling at him, just a little.

I'd never had anyone watch me like Kellan did. And in that moment, I knew that it was because he thought I was worth watching. Not because he was worried about me, or my secrets.

He grinned, chuckling quietly, then gestured toward another of the logs. My backpack, my clothes, and an additional pile of clothing were all sitting next to it. "I thought you might need new underthings."

"Thank you," I murmured, crossing to the pile. I hunkered down and unzipped the backpack. I reached in to press my hand against Infinity. My personal archive hummed under my touch, as if welcoming me back.

Kellan, still gloriously shirtless, sat down across from the fire, leaning against a log with one knee folded up. His gaze remained on me. "Explain, please."

I nodded as I sorted through the clothing he'd brought, but focused on getting dressed before answering. New cotton underwear and a tank top, with the tags still on. As well as sweatpants. All in shades of gray. Which was good, because without a bra, my nipples were dark enough to show through anything lighter in color.

Now why did that thought shove itself to the forefront of my mind?

Coiling my hair in the second towel, I held onto the first as I worked out how to get my sheath off my thigh and shimmy out of my own soaking wet underwear and bra while still under cover. I was mostly successful. Kellan's grin indicated he liked the show.

"Apparently, you have a dimensional doorway on your family's land," I said.

"Pack land," Kellan corrected me quietly, as if the distinction was important. "This section was acquired about fifteen years ago."

I blinked, glancing over at the tall trees that edged the shoreline. "The forest was here then?"

He shook his head. "Regrown. Helped along by the Byrne witches, River specifically. She's worth the money. Though we also trade services."

I nodded, setting my still-sheathed blade slightly closer to the fire. The leather of the sheath was soaked through. "Best I can piece together, the other-dimensional cephalopod was guarding something. It was a sentinel for a relic of some kind. I need to sketch it."

"And the relic was stolen tonight?"

"Apparently." I snapped the tags off the new underwear, tugging on the panties under the towel.

Kellan's heated gaze was doing wonders to warm me from within. As was the sight of him with the fire highlighting his rather breathtaking chest and ridiculous abs.

I was suddenly peeved that abs like that didn't automatically come with dragon genes. Even a warrior would have to work for that level of muscle definition.

"So whoever stole the relic used the solstice celebration as cover," he mused.

I snapped my head up, not having put that together yet. "Yes. The power in the land would have obscured any flare-up of magic at the doorway."

"That's why it took me so long to feel it."

"Well, you were rather occupied," I said before I could stop myself from sounding just a little jealous.

Kellan flashed a knowing grin at me.

I shook my head, pulling my hair out of the second towel to get the gray tank top situated around my neck. Then I turned my back to Kellan, allowing the body towel to drop around my hips as I pulled the tank top on. I did so successfully, but lost the towel. It pooled around my ankles.

A soft, almost inaudible rush of breath emanated from the shifter sprawled out on the beach behind me.

Ignoring both him and the flush of desire that heated my own skin, I tugged on the sweatpants before I turned back to meet his gaze.

"Not at all how I wanted to be occupied tonight," he murmured.

For a moment, I couldn't remember what we'd been talking about. I had a practically eidetic memory, but Kellan Conall scrambled my brains.

"You left the beach," he said, as if offering clarification as to how he would have preferred the night to progress. "Because you felt the doorway open?"

I shook my head, grabbing my backpack and joining him by the fire, leaning back against the log with a bit of space between us. "No. I wanted to check on Sisu…" That sounded like a lie, or at least not the complete truth. "I was uncomfortable," I blurted.

Kellan just nodded. "Brendan Prince."

Relief flooded through me. That was a perfectly believable excuse for what had been a much more complicated emotional response to the bonfire and the dancing. "Yes. I mean, I guess it's obvious that I don't do well in crowds. Though, honestly, it's never been a problem before…"

"Magical sensitivity," he said with a slight shrug.

I stared at Kellan blankly, absorbing the truth of his statement. I'd thought I was just socially inept all of a sudden but—

"Have you ever been continually surrounded by so much magic that wasn't your own...or of a similar type?"

Oh, yes. Kellan Conall knew I wasn't just a witch.

He shifted his gaze to the fire. "It happened to me when I...came into my full potential."

"I'm not there yet," I said honestly. "And I'm sure it will get easier. Lots of new...relationships..."

He grunted quietly, then let me off the hook. "So we hunt down the stolen object?"

"I retrieve the relic, yes." Just as soon as I figured out how to find a brownie, one of the only beings who might actually be capable of true invisibility. Or they were so skilled at cloaking and illusion that they seemed to move invisibly, similar to Jiaotu. And either way, brownies could teleport at will.

Kellan smirked knowingly. "The relic was housed on pack land. That makes it my responsibility."

"This is only pack land now. It wasn't when the..." I caught my slip right before I mentioned the guardians and Suanmi. "When the doorway was created."

Kellan's eyes narrowed. "I'm not going to debate with you, Dusk. I trusted you to secure the octopus creature, and you will trust me to back you in your hunt."

I blinked, partly bristling at his insistent tone and partly recognizing the undeniable truth of his statement. Thinking rapidly through everything I knew about the situation—which wasn't much—I leaned closer to the fire, finger-combing my hair in the hopes that the heat would finish drying it.

Kellan seemed content to wait, possibly thinking through something himself. His gaze was steady on the fire.

"I have to do some research," I murmured. "We're tracking a brownie, and I'm actually not sure exactly how to do that."

"A brownie." Kellan's tone was abruptly flat, as it had been when confronted with the reality of the gnome. For someone keeping secrets that I had to assume were almost as significant as mine, he hated not knowing…well, everything.

Just like me. We just had different reactions to the accumulation of knowledge. I enjoyed the process, while he was—

"Dusk," he growled, "a brownie?"

Yeah, impatient.

I flashed a grin at him.

"You do that on purpose," he muttered.

"Do what?"

"That thoughtful pausing thing."

"It's not on—"

He reached for me, sliding his hand around to cup the back of my neck. And suddenly he was way too close. His fingers and palm were warm and slightly rough. Callused. His grip was firm.

My breath caught, and all thought tumbled right out of my head.

I met his fierce, determined gaze, only realizing after I'd done so that I'd also lifted my chin. Closer to him. His lips parted. He angled his head, shifting his big body toward me.

I wanted him.

I wasn't certain I'd ever wanted anyone as much as I wanted Kellan Conall. I wanted the strength that was barely contained under his touch. I wanted to luxuriate in his—

I slammed my hand against his chest, halting his forward movement.

He frowned, pausing but not withdrawing.

My heart was beating rapidly.

He hadn't even kissed me, yet I could feel warmth pooling in my belly, seeping lower. His skin was hot. Granted, I was still cool despite the fire, but he was so…so warm and…solid.

I clenched my hand, pressing my fist against his chest instead of trailing my fingers down the hard line of his body. Oh gods, I wanted to trail my fingers…

"Dusk?" he asked huskily.

Another jolt of desire shot through me, settling in the apex of my legs. That was fast. So, so quick to ignite. Too quick. "No."

"No?"

"No," I said, speaking carefully, though my body had a completely different answer.

"No…" he murmured, easing back but not dropping his hand from my neck, clearly confused.

I cleared my throat, shoving all the desire down deep, smothering it in logic. He was a shapeshifter. I was a dragon disguised as a witch. I had a job to do. Desire, want, need weren't the sorts of arguments I could take to the guardians after I wound up blowing my cover. After ruining…well, everything.

I twisted out of Kellan's hold, though he didn't really try to stop me. Straightening, I pulled on my sweater dress over the tank top and the sweatpants, tucking my wet undergarments and my bone blade in my backpack. I halfheartedly brushed off my feet, then pulled on and laced my boots.

Kellan watched me the entire time, not moving a muscle.

The silence stretched tautly between us.

I slung the backpack over my shoulders, then folded the towels he'd brought with him. I would return them to the house when I retrieved Sisu.

"Thank you," I said stiffly, not quite meeting his steady gaze.

He raised an eyebrow. His expression was otherwise inscrutable.

"For the...fire, the towels." I shook my head, feeling flushed in a way that had nothing to do with the fire and everything to do with the fact that I knew I was acting like an idiot. I knew I was mishandling...everything.

I had to move.

I had to keep moving.

I pivoted toward the tree line, aware that I wasn't completely certain how to get back to the manor house. So much pack magic still flooded the area that pinpointing the main—

Kellan broke his silence before I'd put more than two steps of distance between us. "I got it, Dusk. That you wanted to keep your distance. That Sisu and your job are your priorities, so I backed off..."

It was rude to keep my back to him, so I forced myself to meet his gaze. Because I wasn't a coward, no matter how I'd been acting.

"At least as far as I was able." Kellan's expression was half smile, half grimace. "I gave you time to settle. But...you want me. You want me as much as I want you."

I didn't say anything. Because a denial would mean outright lying, and I was so tired of lying. Desperately tired of it.

But an admission would push us places where I couldn't go.

No…where I shouldn't go.

"You're not afraid of me, are you, Dusk?" he asked quietly.

"Afraid?" I frowned. Was that what he was picking up from me? Fear?

"Of the monster within?"

Monster? Not wolf?

"You think of yourself as a monster, Kellan?"

He shrugged as if he didn't care one way or the other, but his hand was fisted on his knee, his shoulders tight. "You watch me."

"You watch me."

"I most certainly do. Yet you never close the space between us, you never take the last step. Or any step for that matter."

I didn't have an answer for him, not without just lamely repeating what I'd already said. My 'no' was as clear as I could possibly be. More words would muddy the situation even further.

"Do you wait for everything to be handed to you, Dusk?" His tone was edged with frustration.

"I can fight for what I want," I said stiffly. But I realized even as I said the words that it was possible I'd never actually fought for anything in my life. Not for myself, not that way. I would fight to preserve what I already had, of course. But I wasn't certain I'd ever wanted something that it was necessary to fight for.

Kellan was smirking at me again, like he could read my thoughts. Lying there, sprawled out against the log, firelight dancing across his skin, defining every muscle. "Me, Dusk. You want me. Your heart rate increases. Your breathing slows, your pupils dilate just a bit. I know you want me. I can smell it on you, under all that honey you use to mask your scent."

I had no idea what he meant—though I most definitely smelled right now, of seaweed, saltwater, and damp cotton, and I had most definitely compromised Jiaotu's glamour—but a flush of anger rose at the ridiculousness of his statement.

I narrowed my eyes.

He gazed back at me with eyes bright with laughter, still lounging back on the damn log.

"It doesn't even remotely matter what you claim to smell on me, Kellan Conall," I said, quietly livid.

The laughter died in his eyes—or perhaps that was his magic I was seeing. He finally straightened, then stood. "Why is that, Dusk Godfrey?"

"Because I don't choose partners with my body. I do so with my brain."

"And I'm not good enough to fuck?"

"I'm sure you are. I'm sure you have plenty of partners waiting for your return to the party. But I'm not interested in being your plaything. I love my job. I love my house. And I have Sisu to look after."

"I don't play," he said stiffly.

"All evidence to the contrary."

"Gossip and hearsay..." he snapped, warming up to the argument.

I cut him off. "I make my own choices based on my own gathered evidence. It's insulting that you think otherwise."

"Dusk," he purred, clearly changing tactics, "I'm not interested in being a plaything either."

"Then I suggest you start acting accordingly."

He laughed, low and warm.

Heat flooded through me, settling in my nether regions. Again. Damn it. Thankfully, the slight breeze was blowing against me. Not that I believed that Kellan Conall could smell my desire, but…just in case.

And double damn it. I'd just made it sound like I was interested in being pursued.

"Your suggestions have been noted," he said. He leaned down to grab a bucket I hadn't seen from behind the log. From it, he dumped wet sand onto the fire to snuff it out. "I'll modify my approach."

Modify his approach? "I'm not a conquest."

Kellan didn't answer, reaching in and separating chunks of what had to be blisteringly hot firewood with his bare hands, making certain it wouldn't catch again.

I contemplated walking off without him, but I didn't want to be accused of playing games myself. Of forcing him to pursue me.

Leaving the empty bucket upside down, he plucked up a long-sleeved T-shirt also tucked behind the log, tugging it on as he prowled toward me.

I both mourned and celebrated the loss of the view. Kellan had the most amazing chest I'd ever laid eyes on—and I'd trained with many a warrior dragon. And there was also the mystery of those runes that had appeared when he'd transformed, which I found entrancing—

I shook my head, trying to clear it.

He closed the distance between us. "Again. We are in agreement."

I blinked. I'd lost track of the conversation.

He stood, staring down at me for a moment, then quirked an eyebrow. "I'll walk you back."

"Apparently I haven't been clear, Kellan." A tiny fissure of pain opened in my chest, derailing me.

He stepped closer, crowding me just a little. The proximity forced me to crank my head back to continue meeting his gaze. "Dusk," he murmured gently. Patiently. "We have time to dig into each other's secrets."

His mention of secret sharing derailed me even further. I wanted to know what actually lay underneath Kellan Conall's skin. What power ran through his veins.

He leaned into me, not touching but more than close enough to do so. He tilted his head slightly, breathing me in. And no doubt getting a wash of seaweed and stale saltwater for his trouble.

We just stayed like that, hovering in the moment. The breeze stirring my partly dry hair, warmth radiating from Kellan.

"I'm not interested in sharing," I blurted.

What a stupid thing to say. I wasn't interested, period. This wasn't some negotiation.

He leaned back slightly, frowning. "Neither am I."

"I know you are...still interested in Bethany." And perhaps the two other gorgeous werewolves he'd been dancing with next to the bonfire?

"And I told you that your information is outdated."

"I have eyes, Kellan," I snapped.

He smirked. "If you weren't interested in me, you wouldn't interpret affection between friends as—"

"Your definitions of affection and friend are very different from mine."

"I believe we've already established that we work from different dictionaries." He leaned slightly closer. "And that being pack is different than being a coven witch, though not by much. Except you aren't comparing the Conalls to the Byrnes, or even to the Godfreys. Are you, Dusk?"

I didn't answer. I didn't know how to answer. Damn him.

Kellan Conall tied me up, twisted me around. Why was I still standing in the middle of the woods? All flushed and utterly frustrated? Wanting—

I spun on my heel, striding off along what might have been a narrow deer path cutting through the undergrowth and steadily climbing upward through the forest. But I had no idea if I was headed in the right direction.

Kellan swore under his breath in a mixture of Irish, English, and Gaelic. Then he caught up to me, swerving around the tightly spaced trees to stay at my side. "Have you been talking to my mother again? Bethany was her...hope for my future." I could hear, more than see, him sneer the words.

"A hope you didn't mind at least toying with." Where was I going with this?

Kellan snorted. "Bethany is beautiful. Strong. Intelligent. We're a good fit. In theory. And we were both single at the time. Why wouldn't we?"

I didn't answer. Honestly, I wasn't quite in control of what I was saying. And I was more than a little swayed by the confirmation that Kellan wasn't actually with Bethany.

Except I couldn't be swayed. There was no 'me' to be swayed. Because I was in Dublin, in Kellan's life, under false pretenses.

"Why?" he drawled. "Isn't that who Zeke is to you? Your uncle, not yet fiance?"

He had me there. Utterly.

"We're not blood related," I snapped lamely. "And Zeke isn't the reason that..."

Nope. I wasn't having that conversation either.

"The reason that...?"

I shook my head, clutching the towels to my chest as I continued to climb through the dark woods. I stumbled at one point, turning my ankle on a root, and Kellan snagged my elbow.

Warmth and a lick of magic practically exploded between us, even through the barrier of my clothing. I gasped, yanking away from him and stumbling even more.

"Fine." Kellan's tone was suddenly hard. "You want me, Dusk, you let me know. I get that you have secrets, but I'm not running after you." He cleared his throat. "Any more than I already have."

He stepped ahead of me, striding away. The ground leveled out just ahead of us.

"And I already told you that I'm not playing games."

"I'm not accusing you of doing anything but...being cautious. Because of Sisu?" Tossed over his shoulder, his words turned into a question.

I huffed. The two of us barely managed to converse at all, and when we did, we apparently just talked in circles. "I already told you that Sisu is my brother."

Kellan rounded on me, halting our forward progress. "And I told you..." He stifled his rebuke, running a hand through his hair.

I watched him in the filtered moonlight. And I realized that we'd made it to the edge of the woods, the brightly lit pack manor house visible in the distance.

"I don't want just a couple of kisses," Kellan abruptly snarled. "Or just a moment of your time."

"And announcing that angrily is supposed to...what? Sway me?"

"I'm not angry. I'm frustrated at our inability to have a simple conversation."

Gods, so was I.

I sighed, swaying unsteadily on my feet. And then the truth just tumbled out of my mouth.

"We're tripping over our secrets."

Kellan went completely still. His green-gold eyes glinted with his unique magic.

I opened my mouth.

Nothing came out.

I tried a second time.

Still nothing.

"How dangerous is it, Dusk?" he asked quietly. "For you to be truthful?"

I shook my head. "Danger doesn't factor into it. Just...duty. And you?"

He cast his gaze to the side, then nodded slightly to himself. "I'd say...lives depend on it. On me."

My stomach hollowed as I abruptly realized that this conversation was an ending of some sort. An up-front acknowledgement of the impassable barriers between us.

Kellan waited for my response, holding on to his power tightly.

I could suddenly feel Sisu's energy nearby and then the twins'.

I had to make a choice.

I couldn't keep coming back to this point with Kellan, then only halfheartedly walking away.

"I...I..." From the depths of my backpack, Infinity hummed encouragingly, further grounding me in the moment.

I needed to settle on something. Something actionable.

Kellan wanted to help retrieve the artifact. That was...perfectly understandable. That wasn't about mixed-up emotions or secrets. That was my actual job. And Kellan's actual duty.

So I would ask him to meet me tomorrow, midday, after I'd had a chance to do some research.

I lifted my gaze to articulate that request.

He was looking at me…just looking at me. And even deeply shadowed, I saw…I saw want in that gaze. Need.

And patience.

That moment we'd shared when we'd been tracking Ayre Byrne back to the city, a reflection of…self, stretched between us again. Not sexual, but something…deeper?

"The plan was for the twins to sleep over tonight," I blurted, completely changing the subject. "At the manor."

"Who asked?" Kellan's voice was a quiet rumble. "Gitta or Len?"

"Len."

He nodded. "He wants a moment alone with Gitta."

I thought about Gitta dancing at the bonfire, even more involved with her two partners—Thurston and Len—than Kellan had been with his pack mates. And I suddenly saw the difference between those two observed interactions.

I also realized that Kellan must have left the dance to follow me. Because he'd said he hadn't felt the octopus creature until he was near.

"Do you think he's going to get it? Time alone?"

Kellan looked at me pointedly. "I think he's gotten a lot of chances already."

He meant Ayre kidnapping the twins. "Kellan, Ayre Byrne was unusually powerful—"

"I know. And so does Gitta. We both heard your conversation with Sisu, Dusk. And that idiot still stepped outside despite your warnings."

"Ayre was going to be able to breach the wards whether or not Len was inside."

He shrugged, muted anger rolling off him. "Let's just say it wasn't the first time."

I blinked, juxtaposing Kellan's anger with what Len had said over breakfast. About not being able to prove himself. "So that wasn't the first time Neve and Lile have been taken," I said, "when Len was watching over them."

"No." Kellan folded his arms, glowering down at me. "You changed the subject. Again."

I laughed. "I can juggle a variety of topics at one time."

"Multitasking is overrated," he murmured, his gaze caught on my mouth. "I prefer pure focus on a single task."

Desire curled in my belly. "Do you...do you...would you drive us home?" I asked. "I...could make us hot chocolate. If it's okay for you to leave the party." Gods, I sounded utterly lame. And I had no idea what I was really offering. No idea what I could offer. Kellan had drawn his line in the sand clearly.

Not just a couple of kisses.

Not just a moment of my time.

"Yes. I'll take you all home. But first, so we know we're both...contemplating...the same thing..." He gently feathered his fingers across my cheek, starting to lean into me.

I rose on my toes and met him halfway, brushing my lips across his. Flickers of restoked desire shivered through me.

He grinned, brushing my lips with his in return.

That was our only point of contact, the two of us trading the lightest of kisses back and forth a few more times. I felt like I was on fire, yet didn't ever want to be cool again.

"Dusk!" Sisu cried from my far left.

Kellan groaned, pressing his forehead to mine for a brief moment, then turning slightly away.

Our shoulders brushing, we stepped out of the woods. Sisu was barreling across the grass with the twins losing ground in his wake. As was becoming too common, he was moving too fast for a five-year-old witch. Way too fast.

But Kellan knew that already. As did the twins, no doubt. And they were the only ones with eyes on us.

I dropped the towels and spread my arms wide, bending slightly at the knees to take the hit.

Sisu sprang forward into my arms, and I swung him around and around. He giggled with mad glee.

Neve and Lile practically tackled Kellan. He slung Neve over his shoulder, grabbing Lile under the arms and tossing her overhead.

Sisu wrapped his arms around my neck, pressing his lips to my ear. "You came back," he whispered.

My heart was in my throat. "I'll never leave you if I can help it."

Kellan stepped closer, pressing his shoulder against mine. Neve was cradled across his chest, Lile riding his shoulders now. He wrapped a hand around the back of Sisu's head but met my gaze, his expression a mixture of emotions I couldn't interpret. But steady and intent.

That, I understood.

"Let's head home," I said, speaking to Kellan even though he and I weren't…well, we shouldn't—

"For cookies and ice cream," Sisu said, wiggling to get down.

"Yes," I said, setting him on his feet.

Kellan did the same with Neve and Lile. The trio took off toward the house.

"Have you packed an overnight bag?" Kellan called after them.

"Yes!" Neve and Lile shouted in a chorus.

Kellan turned to me, magic glinting in his eyes. His voice was husky when he finally spoke. "Lead the way, Dusk."

There was a lot of implication in that simple statement. But I just nodded, retrieved the towels, and followed the twins back to the manor.

Infinity hummed against my back. It felt like a gentle encouragement, but I might have been reading too much into it.

I allowed my fingers to brush against Kellan's as we walked. Closer to the manor house, the moonlit night, filled with the energy called forth by the werewolves' celebration, didn't feel as chilled as the temperature would have suggested. Kellan's slightly rough fingertips brushed across my wrist, and I smiled because it was the best thing I'd ever felt. Against my skin, through my nerves.

I was in so, so much trouble.

He laughed huskily.

"Don't pretend you can read my thoughts, Kellan Conall," I said tartly.

"While being in your head would be...exhilarating, Dusk Godfrey," he murmured, "I'm just happy to be in this moment. With you."

Shouts preceded Sisu, Neve, and Lile barreling back toward us. We'd meandered long enough that they'd managed to grab their overnight bags and say their goodbyes.

Kellan grumbled playfully.

I laughed, drawing a look from him that I couldn't interpret. Surprise? But tinted with a softness, a gentleness. An openness.

Like...like he adored me.

I didn't look away. Not even when Sisu caught my hand and started pulling me around the house, chattering away about the movie. Managing to keep pace even with the girls tucked around his legs, Kellan reached for me, threading his fingers through my hair and pulling me close enough to brush his lips across mine in another of those almost-kisses.

Then he was flipping the girls over his shoulders and striding off toward the cars lining the drive while they squealed. While I was still savoring the echo of his lips against mine.

Oh yeah, I was in trouble.

But I knew...I knew already, even having no idea of Kellan's secrets or how he'd react to mine—

I knew that I'd fight to hold onto that trouble. If it meant I got to experience Kellan Conall.

We rounded the house to find fewer vehicles parked along the circular drive than when we'd arrived. Kellan paused next to the back passenger door of a hulking green SUV, his attention trained to his right as he set Lile and Neve down. Sisu released his grip on my hand, jogging the last few steps to join the twins.

It took me two more steps to see why Kellan was glowering again.

Ravine and Brendan Prince were strolling, hand in hand, toward Ravine's tiny electric car. Their pace was unhurried, her shoulder pressed against his, her enchanted gaze fixed on his face.

They reached the car at the same time as I reached Kellan's side. Prince held open the passenger door, and Ravine slid into the seat, trailing her hand down Prince's arm, hand, and fingers as if she didn't want to lose contact.

"Vinnie's going to get an earful about that," Kellan rumbled, holding the back door of the SUV open for the kids to climb in.

A muted but furious debate ignited among the trio over who should take the middle seat.

"She can date who she wants," I said, trying to be supportive.

"But she can't just invite whoever she wishes onto pack land." Kellan's gaze was riveted to the couple as Prince circled the car and opened the driver's-side door. Was it odd that he was driving Ravine's car? I didn't know the proper protocol for people who'd just started a romantic relationship. "An invitation that will be rescinded as soon as he leaves."

I glanced up at Kellan. His magic rolled over his eyes, and he flared his nostrils.

"Why?" I asked, genuinely curious. I couldn't even figure out why Prince bothered me—his magic was so benign he barely registered to my senses—so it had to be a personal, emotional reaction.

Kellan locked his golden-green gaze on me, lowering his head slightly to force eye contact as if he was about to impart something of great importance. "Because you don't like him, Dusk. That's a good enough reason for the pack."

Something warmed in my chest, and I smiled up at him, even though I knew I shouldn't encourage…well, anything.

He touched my cheek again lightly, his own expression softening.

"Fine!" Sisu huffed loudly. He followed Neve into the back seat, having apparently lost the argument about who was supposed to sit in the middle.

Kellan, chuckling quietly, dropped his hand and took a step back to open the front passenger door. I had to drag my gaze away from his in order to climb into the vehicle.

So apparently I did understand some of what Ravine was feeling with her new paramour.

Kellan shut both doors. The kids were now quietly haggling over what to watch on their iPad for the trip back to the city.

I glanced toward the metal mage's car. Prince had paused before climbing in, looking back at me. He offered me one of his sharp smiles, raising his hand.

Kellan crossed around the front of the SUV, his shoulders stiff and his glare firmly in place.

Prince's smile widened.

I turned back to address the kids. Sisu was holding the iPad in his lap. "You could try to nap. You must be exhausted."

My statement was met with three identically incredulous, unwavering stares.

I huffed. They would fall asleep as soon as the vehicle started moving.

Kellan slid into the driver's seat. As he closed his door, I heard the quiet crunch of gravel under tires as Ravine's car pulled away ahead of us.

Kellan started the SUV, his attention out the front window. "Seat belts?"

"Done," the twins and Sisu sang in chorus.

Kellan allowed the SUV to roll forward slowly, as if wanting to leave some space between us and Ravine's car. We'd be heading back into the city practically on top of each other.

"So aside from me not liking him," I asked quietly, "what are you picking up from Prince that you don't like?"

Kellan grunted. Enough time passed before he answered that we'd pulled out of the long drive onto the narrow street. "He's using Ravine."

"For her magic?" That was a possibility I hadn't thought about. But given how impressive her ability to make a copy of the crown piece relic had been—impressive enough that Crystal and James were already preparing to rewrite next year's budget based on one demonstration—it made sense.

"He's using her to stay close to you. Because he's obsessed with you."

I frowned doubtfully. Kellan threw me a look, his hands tightening on the steering wheel.

Aware of the kids murmuring quietly in the back seat, I whispered, "I think I'd know, Kellan, if someone was obsessed with me."

He snorted. "Would you? Took me nearly two months to get your attention."

I almost snapped back at him, but then he flashed a playful grin, and I realized he was flirting. So instead, I said, "You had my attention from the first moment I laid eyes on you, Kellan Conall."

"Yeah?" he teased, flicking his gaze up to the rearview mirror. It was difficult to flirt openly with three sets of ears in the back seat. "We'll have to compare our first…impressions somewhere more private."

I just grinned at him, not committing to anything. Then I settled into my seat and pulled Infinity out of my backpack. I still had a job to do.

CHAPTER EIGHT

AS WE HEADED BACK ALONG THE DARKENED HIGHWAY into the city, I jotted pages of notes into Infinity, asking my personal archive to not absorb the ink before I had a chance to review my reckoning. I outlined the incident with the octopus sentinel, making detailed summaries of each of the telepathic images the other-dimensional creature had sent me, and hoping I wasn't missing any of the finer details. Almost-eidetic memory or otherwise, I'd never actually tried to absorb a projected telepathic communication before.

That done, I then focused on sketching the octopus's memory-image of the relic the brownie had stolen. A soft murmur of the movie the kids were watching filled the darkened interior. Kellan seemed even bigger than usual, silent and steady, filling the driver's seat.

If I allowed myself to think about it, I could still feel Kellan's lips brushing across mine—along with a flush of residual thrill that I'd been the one to close our first kiss. It had been my choice. Apparently, my tendency to barrel into situations without knowing all the facts ahead of time was becoming a habit. First, the incident with connecting Infinity to the internet, causing a blackout in Oslo. Then accepting the position in Dublin with only the barest of inklings of what it entailed. And now kissing Kellan Conall.

It didn't help that I could feel a touch of Kellan's energy every time he stole a look at me, almost as if he was checking that I was still actually in the vehicle with him.

"The brownie..." I murmured, speaking out loud in an attempt to settle my thoughts. And then instantly realized that was a bad idea.

"Brownie!" Sisu cried. He turned to Lile and Neve. "You have a brownie?! And you didn't tell me?"

"What?!" Neve cried. "We wouldn't—"

"We don't keep secrets," Lile spat, sounding actually angry.

I spun around, settling my hand on Sisu's knee. He quieted under my touch, blinking at me. Neve tapped her finger on the iPad, muting or pausing the movie. Then she and Lile gazed at me just as attentively.

And in that moment, with their expectant faces lit by the light of the iPad, their bright eyes on me, the soft hum of their magic brushing against me, I realized that as fiercely as I loved Sisu and the life we were building together, I adored the twins. That my little brother was more...that Sisu had a bigger capacity than I did for—

My brother grasped my wrist. "Is it bad? With the brownie? Is it bad?"

I was scaring him with my silence.

"No." I choked out the word. "Well, I mean, I'm not certain yet what's going on with the brownie, but I'll explain."

Sisu grinned brightly. Neve and Lile leaned a little closer.

For some reason, I set my pen down, lifting my right hand off Infinity and settling it on Kellan's arm. He kept his hand resting on the gearshift while he drove.

"I just realized," I said, struggling to simplify every emotion that had just rushed over me. "That I'm very...happy."

"Sleepovers are fun," Neve said enthusiastically.

"Especially at Wilding Manor," Lile added. "Lots of places to explore."

Kellan chuckled quietly.

I turned back in my seat, sliding my hand off his arm. He twined his fingers with mine as he'd done on the dance floor, prolonging our contact.

I picked up my pen and focused on my notes in Infinity. "I've sensed the same brownie three times now. She's deliberately revealed herself to me twice, the first time Monday morning when Brady and I arrived at work."

"And that's unusual?" Kellan asked.

"Oh, yes," Sisu said. "If brownies don't want you to see them, you just don't. And I have very good eyes. Papa said so."

Sisu was referencing Jiaotu's comment about the time he'd fought a multidimensional being and had needed to keep Sisu with him. "It's a talent that runs in our family," I said quickly, before my brother could elaborate. "Seeing magic." I wasn't ready to just blurt everything out to Kellan—we both had to figure a lot of things out. But I was really tired of lying to people I cared for.

"Uncle Kellan says we might be able to see magic too," Neve said helpfully.

"But not until after puberty," Lile added, sounding a little disgusted.

"Puberty..." Neve growled. "Yuck."

"We're going to delay that as long as possible," Lile said matter-of-factly.

"Have a plan, do you?" Kellan asked, quietly amused.

"Dusk," Sisu said a little impatiently, "the brownie wanted to talk with you? Did you ask her to come to Wilding Manor?"

"I gave her the option, yes."

"Yay!" Sisu cried.

Neve and Lile started peppering him with hushed questions about brownies. They practically had their foreheads pressed together.

"That's not..." Kellan hesitated, softening his tone as if he needed to remind himself—almost a moment too late—that I wasn't his to command. "An open invitation seems unwise."

I nodded. "For any being other than a brownie, perhaps. But..." I recalled the way the brownie had looked. Already half-faded. Dying, perhaps. "She might need our help. And the only way I can help her is with the estate."

"Dusk," Kellan said, still trying to be reasonable, "she just unlocked a doorway to another dimension and stole a relic from a gigantic octopus."

"Well, the sentinel might not have been quite so big at the time of the theft."

He threw a look at me.

I smiled.

Kellan blinked, frowned for a moment, and then returned my smile. As if it had taken him a moment to realize that I was teasing him. And that he liked being teased by me.

"But you're right." I returned my attention to Infinity, flipping a half-dozen pages back to review my notes from the beginning. "She's acting completely out of character for a brownie. Brownies aren't expert thieves as far as I know, despite having the perfect skill set for it."

Silence settled around us. The kids didn't turn their movie back on, choosing instead to curl up together as much as their seat belts would allow.

Kellan hadn't asked me if I needed more light to work by. The moon was still bright overhead, and of course, I could see the gold glint of my favorite ink easily enough. But running into the woods without him leading had no doubt given that little secret away. Assuming he hadn't already figured it out the night we raced across Dublin after Ayre Byrne.

I was partway through a more detailed sketch of the relic that the octopus sentinel had drilled into my mind, trying to figure out whether the edge that had appeared jagged was actually intentionally cast in that shape, when I finally connected...well, something.

I snapped my head up, noting that we were driving through the city now.

"The archive," I whispered. "Kellan, I know it's late, but I need to stop at the archive."

He nodded, slowing, then taking the next left instead of continuing straight. Then he said, "Tell me."

I raised Infinity into his line of sight, open to the sketch I'd just completed. Then before I could obsess about revealing too much, I brushed my finger across the page, silently asking Infinity to recall the sketch I'd done of the crown piece Brady and I had collected in Galway. The crown piece that had so interested Brendan Prince and inspired Ravine.

Kellan grunted thoughtfully as the second sketch appeared under the first.

"Line them up, please," I murmured, speaking to Infinity. "Second sketch on the right."

The two sketches shifted, blurring and then re-setting on the page, slightly smaller. They didn't match exactly. Infinity could only work with what I fed into it, and I wasn't an artist. But the pieces definitely went together.

Displayed with the first piece, aligning the sides that might have been torn asunder, and disregarding the patina that it must have picked up when stored underwater while the octopus watched over it, the second piece formed another side of the same crown. The upper edge wasn't randomly jagged at all, but was intentionally peaked.

I hadn't gotten a clear enough sense of the second piece to see if it bore the same symbols as the first, though. Or perhaps the octopus saw things on a different level of detail than I did, so it couldn't telepathically project those symbols into my mind in a way I could properly perceive them.

"What does that mean?" A quiet growl underlaid Kellan's question.

"I have no idea." I settled Infinity on my lap, staring out at the bright city instead of down at the sketches. The images were already burned into my mind's eye. "Not yet."

The crown piece was sitting on its assigned shelf in the basement archives, safe and sound. The magic sealing the entire underground level, thickly coating the rock walls and floors as well as the secondary warding on all the shelves, was undisturbed.

"That?" Kellan snorted. "It's a hunk of metal. Not enough residual magic to see, even through the wards on the shelves."

I couldn't disagree.

I hadn't disagreed.

I glanced down the aisle. Sisu, Neve, and Lile were tucked against the nearest wooden filing cabinets, staring at the iPad again. Though as I watched, Neve's head lolled for a moment before she snapped herself awake.

Kellan followed my gaze. "Might have to carry them back to the SUV."

It was almost midnight. Kellan had insisted on accompanying me into the archive, which had meant we couldn't leave the trio in the car.

My mind clicked back to the decision I was trying to make. "Mesa Byrne indicated that this object was entrusted to the coven for safekeeping."

"Then what the hell was it doing in Galway for you and Brady to collect?"

I smiled, amused and oddly pleased. Kellan had a delightful way of cutting through bullshit. Or maybe just not taking any bullshit from anyone.

He also didn't like rules being broken...

"What's that look, Dusk?" he murmured. "You were smiling, you looked at me, and now you aren't. We're past the keeping-new-secrets phase."

"It's not anything...new. I'm just...you like things that are well defined. You might not like my...definition?" I grimaced, but I couldn't think of any better way to put it.

He grunted. "Let's assume that we're both worried about revealing certain things about ourselves, and set it aside until we can deal with it properly."

I nodded, turning my attention back to the crown piece. "Obviously the individual pieces aren't the issue."

"But combining them might be."

I nodded, thoughtful. "All myths are based in some reality."

"That's a rapid change of subject," he drawled, not disagreeing.

I flashed him a grin. "I'll get there."

"I'll enjoy the process."

A fissure of something warm and almost needy cracked open in my chest. I cleared my throat, ignoring it. "Brendan Prince has this theory of fated mates. He's classified them as fae and claims that the crown was destroyed when the female of the pairing was murdered."

"And what really happened?"

I tilted my head thoughtfully, allowing my fingers to play with the invisible ward sealing the shelving unit. "Best guess…?"

"You know how I feel about your supposed guesses, Dusk."

Kellan thought my guesses were better than most people's facts. The warmth in my chest was spreading rather distractingly.

I refocused again. Two crown pieces. Each given to different sentinels, for lack of a more specific way to describe the pieces' protectors. And at least one of those pieces—the one that had been stolen by the brownie—had been tasked to the other-dimensional cephalopod by a guardian, Suanmi.

"Piecing together the little bit we know, and assuming that the story Prince is peddling isn't completely fabricated, I'd say that hundreds of years ago, two Adepts proclaimed themselves to be royalty of some sort and tried to take over territory that wasn't theirs to take. They were thwarted by another Adept of power. And the crown was confiscated."

"And cut into pieces," Kellan said, nodding. "But why?"

"I'm not sure. But again, as a best guess..." I flashed a grin at Kellan. He grinned back. "Perhaps the crown ties into how they planned to hold the territory they invaded. A tool of some sort. Perhaps for...mind control? Or something subtler, to make others amenable to following them? Or it could be an amplification device."

"I meant, if it was too powerful, then why not destroy it?"

"That's not the way of..." Guardians, dragons, preserved magic as much as possible.

Kellan raised an eyebrow at me teasingly. "The way of...archivists?"

"Yes," I snapped playfully, quashing my own grin.

"But as far as we know, there could be any number of more pieces?"

I hummed, opening Infinity to the two side-by-side sketches. "One more, at least. If it was a full circle, rather than a headpiece or a coronet. And possibly a top piece, or a gemstone. Even multiple gemstones." I gestured toward the relic on the shelf. "See the divots across the top edge? Or what I'm assuming is the top edge."

Kellan leaned in, narrowing his eyes. "Could just be a design detail."

"Agreed. But my question is...do we leave it here or take it with us to the manor?"

Kellan stuffed his hands in the pockets of his sweatpants, tipping back on his heels thoughtfully. Then he deliberately looked down the aisle at the sleepy pile of kids.

I followed his gaze, understanding his concern.

"Right," I said. "Leave it here."

"Brady says the archive wards are impenetrable now."

"Nothing is impenetrable. Especially if the brownie makes an attempt to gain access. But without kidnapping one of the staff and forcing us to allow them entry, it'll take time for someone to breach the archive wards. Time that would alert me."

"And Brady."

"Crystal too, for that matter. She's tied herself so tightly here that..." I hesitated. I'd never had a reason to think about it before, but Crystal might come to serious harm if the archive wards were ever torn asunder.

"That what?" Kellan prompted.

"She could get hurt. But it would take someone exceedingly powerful to simply tear through these protections. And anyone that powerful..." I paused, realizing I was about to make an outright declaration that I couldn't support. Or explain.

Kellan let me off the hook I was dangling on, verbally at least. "Anyone that powerful would tweak those fine senses of yours the moment they set foot in Dublin."

I flushed. "Near the archive, at least. Or Wilding Manor." Unless, of course, they could mask their power as well as the guardians could. Another thought occurred to me. "Plus, I gave the brownie permission to enter the grounds of the estate..."

Kellan grimaced, still pissed.

"You didn't see her, Kellan," I whispered defensively. "She...she's..." My voice cracked, and I pressed my hand to my chest. "She's fading."

I met his intense gaze, running my hand through my hair to try to settle myself, and realized it had dried in a crazy, tangled mess. "Something is very wrong with this entire situation. Actually, something has been bothering me since the gala. Like I'm missing something. But it's just...hanging there, just out of my grasp."

He touched my shoulder lightly. "Like...with the immediacy you felt the night we chased Ayre Byrne across the city? And you bottled a death goddess?"

"I didn't bottle..."

Kellan smirked at me.

"No," I said, answering his actual question. "It's not that...nowhere near that intensity."

"Okay, then. We'll gather more facts. Get the kids to bed, and you'll send your letters or make some calls. And by morning, you'll feel more settled." He took off down the aisle.

I hesitated a moment, staring down at the relic. Again. Second-guessing myself.

But I'd touched it. Had traced it. It wasn't an item of power in any way.

I pressed Infinity to my chest, then headed down the aisle to scoop up Sisu. Kellan was rousing the girls, just enough to get them into his arms and back out to the SUV.

Having somehow already kicked off the top sheet and duvet in the time it had taken me to step out into the hall and reach back to turn off the overhead light, Sisu was sprawled out across his bed, snoring quietly. Exhausted. Not surprising, given the adrenaline jolt of discovering the other-dimensional octopus, then staying up into the early-morning hours.

Kellan had settled Neve and Lile in the room across the hall. Five of the bedrooms as well as the main upstairs bathroom had now been basically renovated with fresh paint and sanded floors, but were still lacking in furnishings. That included the room that overlooked the rose garden, which Suanmi had laid claim to.

Sisu had selected the room across from his for 'his guests.' Mattresses, pillows, and bedding had been easy to order, for that room and the one Zeke had claimed as well. But the attics hadn't yielded any more furniture, and apparently, I was a bit picky when it came to buying. Or possibly just a little too busy?

Okay, I was actually hoping to negotiate with the brownies who ran my mother's estate to let me have access to the plentiful attics and old family furniture under their charge. But it would take me months to gain Mistress Brightshire's permission, assuming I even could.

Stepping into the hall behind me, Kellan left the twins' bedroom door partially open. I did the same with Sisu's.

"You know, they're just going to crawl into Sisu's bed the moment they wake," he whispered to me, grinning.

"Or the other way around."

"Nah. Sisu's got more interesting things in his room."

I laughed, my shoulder brushing Kellan's as we headed along the hall and down the stairs into the great room. "Do you still want the hot chocolate I promised?"

"I'll make the hot chocolate. You go do what you need to do."

I took off for the library without further prompting. I needed all the books Zeke could send me on brownies, and should probably ask Mistress Brightshire too. But I wasn't actually certain whether Mom's estate library or the Giza archive that Zeke was overseeing in Mom's absence would have anything that could help me call or track a brownie who didn't want to be found.

What I should do was pick up the phone on the desk that was connected to the guardian nexus, and just call Suanmi. But I didn't, because I...well, I hadn't solved anything, had I? And doing so was my job now. In Dublin, at least.

And also, yes—I was terrified of looking incompetent in the eyes of the guardian.

I had my face buried in Infinity even as I stepped into the darkened library. "Please scan Grandfather George's journals for any and all references to—"

Energy flickered around me. The house was...doing something.

I spun slowly in place, taking in the still mostly empty dark-wood shelves, the heavy gold brocade curtains, the wooden shutters open wide on either side of the large, night-darkened windows. My walnut desk sat close to the far left corner. The runes that were set into the desk under the old-fashioned rotary phone hadn't triggered. Nor had the portal drop point on the opposite corner of the desk. The noticeboard was empty.

I stretched my senses up toward the central tower. But the wards I'd set in place and bolstered during my daily visits with the death goddess held firm.

No. The house itself was reacting to something.

The flickering energy turned into ripples, as if the estate were a pond and something had just dropped into it. Though they were domed, the boundary wards were actually somewhat comparable to a large body of water. But piercing the surface tension wasn't as easy as simply skipping a rock.

Kellan appeared in the library doorway, his magic an intense golden green in his wide and wary eyes.

"It's not Morgan..." I whispered, turning slowly in a circle again.

Magic shifted up and down the walls, then undulated across my feet. Not aggressively, though. Not defensively.

"The wards?" Kellan asked, picking up one foot, then the other.

"It doesn't feel like anyone's trying to breach them with force…" I murmured.

Infinity began humming, almost purring. Encouragingly. Loudly, to my ears at least.

Kellan's gaze dropped to the archive I was clutching in my left hand. Well, that answered any lingering questions about his magical sensitivity. It was acute.

The energy that always underpinned the house continued to fluctuate. It danced over my skin almost…

…almost questioningly?

"Yes," I said, realizing as I voiced my consent what was happening, even though I'd never felt it before.

"Dusk?" Kellan growled, disconcerted and therefore instantly pissed. His default when confronted with any new situation.

"Yes," I said again, firming my tone. Then I added for Kellan's benefit, "Any brownie or other magical creature in need of sanctuary, who has no intent to harm the residents, is welcome at Wilding Manor."

Sisu, quickly followed by Neve and Lile, dashed into the library. All their eyes were wide in wonder, rather than fear.

Sisu grabbed my free hand. "It's the brownie!"

"Yes," I said. "I think it is."

The house groaned. Its energy flexed around us once more, then settled back into the floors and walls.

Nothing else happened.

"Dusk?" Kellan snarled questioningly.

I shook my head. "I'm not sure, but I think this…this estate was once the territory of a family of brownies, though not necessarily of the same bloodline as the brownie who revealed herself to me. My initial permission to enter might not have been enough—"

A small figure appeared, directly between Sisu and me, and Kellan and the twins. Her skin was ashen. Her large hands were pressed to her chest as if in pain. Her head was bowed, her stringy, light-brown hair hanging forward. She was still wearing the store-bought dress, but it was even more dirty and ragged than before.

Sisu cried out, lunging forward. I caught him by the shoulder before he could reach the brownie.

The brownie looked up, scanning each of us. Her eyes were sunken, her cheekbones harshly prominent.

Kellan stifled a pained moan.

The brownie was dying, not just fading now.

"My…" Her gaze settled on me. Her voice was full of gravel, each word scraping across her vocal cords. "My master…my master intends to retrieve—" With a strangled cry, the brownie collapsed onto one hand and knee, gasping for breath yet still trying to speak. "He will…harness the power of the—"

Fine chains suddenly appeared, twisting around the brownie. Strung between a choker on her neck and manacles on her wrists and ankles.

Kellan flinched, starting forward even as I struggled to keep my emotions under control.

The brownie cried out, raising a hand to him.

He swore quietly, backing off a step. "I'm sorry. I would never hurt you."

"Dusk! Dusk!" Sisu cried.

"I see. I see, Sisu," I said soothingly, far calmer than I felt.

Because I'd never seen a brownie chained before. Had never seen a brownie held against her will before. Brownies followed a different set of magical rules than other Adepts—so much so that I wouldn't have thought such a thing even possible.

I slowly lowered myself to my knees before the brownie. Now that she wasn't trying to speak around the geas that the master she'd mentioned had obviously forced upon her, her breathing slowly evened out.

Sisu pressed against me. His hands were fisted in my sweater as he too held himself back. Kellan was practically a statue across from us, Neve and Lile clinging to him. The muscles on his neck strained by the effort it took to hold himself in place.

"Did you know, my brother, that brownies are not originally of this dimension?" I spoke conversationally, wrapping my arm around Sisu and tucking him next to me.

"They fled," Sisu said hesitantly, looking at me and then the brownie, gaining confidence. "They left their other home before the guardians sealed all the doorways."

The brownie's eyes grew wide. She settled into a crouch, seemingly too tired to stand. Her magic was so dim even I could barely feel it.

"And what did brownies do to sustain their magic in this dimension?" I asked, prompting Sisu.

He bit his lip, shaking his head.

"They tied themselves to magic," I said. "Land or estates or occasionally an Adept family. And by caring for that land, that house, or that family, brownies would pull life-sustaining magic from that mutual agreement."

The brownie's chin started quivering. She twisted her fingers together.

The chains had disappeared. For now, at least.

She had no idea what we were talking about. That was how someone had been able to chain her, perhaps even force her to do things. Draining her inherent magic. Slowly killing her in the process.

"The Brightshire family chose Mom's family estate," I said, still speaking as if I were just chatting with my brother, understanding that directly addressing the brownie might trigger the geas again. "Centuries ago. Not all their blood relatives need to live at the estate, but as long as a single Brightshire descendent claims the estate, the others of her bloodline are sustained."

My brother loosened his hold on my sweater. A wide grin swamped his face. "Some places have so much magic that a whole bunch of different brownie families live there!"

I grinned, nodding. He meant the nexus, where the Winterbloom, Winterblossom, and Wintersprout brownies had claimed their territories and anchored their familial lines.

Kellan, Neve, and Lile were so still I thought they might not be breathing.

I looked at the brownie crouched before me, then at Sisu again. "This brownie is chained."

The chains were still invisible. Hidden, once again, by the brownie's own glamour. Her cheeks flushed, and she dropped her gaze to the floor.

"No brownie can be chained," Sisu said gently. Then he added indignantly, "Though they're more than capable of locking someone else up."

"Generally only when that person is having a temper tantrum and needs a time-out," I said wryly.

Sisu huffed, shrugging.

"It's the ties to their territory, to their Adept family, that sustain brownies," I said as gently as possible. Still pretending that I was talking to my brother. "A bond that is chosen by that brownie. It can only be by choice. Do you understand?"

Sisu nodded.

The brownie nodded too, but the gesture was shallow. Tentative. Still uncertain.

But before I could offer further clarification, she spoke. "I am the last…the last of the Eventide."

"Eventide?" Sisu asked. "Is that what we should call you?"

The brownie shifted her sad, wide-eyed gaze from me to Sisu, wringing her hands together. "I am no one," she said roughly. "I'm only my master's."

I nodded, worried about how far I could push her without triggering the geas again. "Your master…" I hesitated. Speaking directly against a person she'd been involuntarily bound to wasn't a good idea. But she'd said she was the last of the Eventide, and all I could think was that her entire familial line might have died off while tied to the same so-called master.

And I couldn't…I couldn't allow that to happen to her.

I unsheathed my bone blade slowly, then held it in my open palm. Showing it to the brownie as passively as possible, so she could feel its power but not be threatened by it. "If you do not wish to be chained, I could remove those bindings."

She shook her head vehemently. "No, no. He would get very angry."

"Those chains are bad," Sisu said gently. "And anyone who would chain you is bad."

Her chin quivered again. "Brownies serve their masters. That is their sole purpose."

"By choice," I said. "But you're not bound to your master. If you were, he would have no need to chain you. You can choose. You've always been able to choose. You could join another brownie family. Or an established estate—"

"Dusk," Sisu whispered, "she can come here to Wilding Manor. The house wants her."

A gentle simmer of energy under our feet punctuated Sisu's statement. The house agreed.

The brownie slowly curled her hands around the invisible chains that bound her wrists. She was listening. Understanding.

"You could break the chains, Dusk," Sisu said, becoming insistent. "Miss Eventide could stay with us. With Gee, and Morgan, and the imps when they hatch!"

"Yes," I said, keeping my gaze on the brownie. She was looking overwhelmed. Like she might disappear at any moment. "But it's up to Miss Eventide to choose. She could choose to reach out to the power in the house, in the estate, and she could step out of her own chains."

Sisu glanced between me and the brownie, then back at me. "Because you breaking the chains might be bad?"

I nodded. I had no idea what countermeasures were built into those bindings. I might kill the brownie in the process of removing them, trying to free her.

"Choose…" the brownie murmured. "The house…"

The energy that underpinned the manor took that as an opening, pressing around us warmly, welcoming.

"And you wouldn't have to stay," I said. "If you decided you didn't like it here, you could find another family or estate. We could introduce you to other brownies—"

"I am the last…" she said. But there was a note of hope in her raspy tone.

The energy of the manor pressed around the brownie again. She spread her fingers with a sigh, closing her eyes. Perhaps communicating with that energy on a level I couldn't feel or hear.

"There used to be brownies here," she whispered. "With the guardian."

I was hyperaware of Kellan listening in, absorbing everything, but I still answered truthfully. The brownie's life was literally in the balance. "Yes. I believe so."

"And the gnome?" she asked.

"Gee," Sisu supplied helpfully. "The gnome is Gee. Or some name that starts with G."

"The gnome cares for the greenhouse and the gardens," I said. "That is Gee's choice."

"And the dark creature who occupies the tower above us?" The brownie opened her sunken eyes, pinning her gaze on me. They sparkled with magic now.

"Morgan," Sisu offered.

Kellan shifted, as if to speak, then stopped himself.

Well, the secrets were all tumbling out now, weren't they?

"Morgan is bound to me," I said, for everyone's benefit. "By me."

Miss Eventide tilted her head thoughtfully, her voice firmer. "The house holds her as well."

"Yes. As directed by me. But if you choose to stay with us, for however long, you will not be bound to any other creature here. Not me or Sisu or Gee or Morgan. You can choose to bind yourself to the estate. To the house. With no need to serve anyone else. The estate and I will protect you."

She stared at me, dumbfounded. Her grip on the invisible chains intensified. "My choice."

"Yes."

"And there are others like me."

"Yes."

Her eyes welled with tears. "He cannot hold me without the chains. He cannot force me to...he cannot take my life energy without permission. I can choose. I...I can live."

A pain born of pure emotion shot through my chest. I struggled to ignore it, to keep my face and voice calm. I'd never heard of an Adept leeching life from a brownie. I had no idea such a thing was possible. Brownies weren't from our dimension. Their power was completely different from that of other Adepts and should therefore be incompatible. "Yes."

She straightened, deliberately fisting her hands before her. The thin chains, the collar, and the manacles appeared again.

"A house...land..."

"We welcome you, Eventide," I said formally. Setting down my bone blade, I reached out my right hand, still clutching Infinity in my left. "You can stay as long as you want. There is magic enough to sustain us all at Wilding Manor."

Sisu reached out his hand as well. "Do you know your magic sparkles?" he asked, hushed. "That's a good name for your new life. Sparkle."

"Sparkle..." The brownie nodded. "Yes."

Then she dropped the chains, stumbled forward, and grasped our hands.

Energy shifted around us, emanating from the house.

The brownie's power poured out of her in a rush, coating the chains that bound her, flowing into the hardwood, and spreading through the room and up the walls. Then that energy pushed farther, farther, through the house and out into the estate.

The brownie gasped, shuddering. The power kept flowing out of her until she was swaying on her feet, held aloft only by Sisu and me.

"Dusk..." Kellan said, concerned. "The chains?"

He was worried she was being hurt by the bindings. "They're inconsequential to the power a brownie wields," I said.

"Inconsequential," the brownie murmured. Sparkle.

All the energy she'd fed into the house, the estate, came rushing back into her—but even stronger. It held what felt like pure unfettered joy from the house, along with a lick of magic from Sisu and me as well.

Sparkle gasped, her eyes flying open. Then the manacles and collar clicked and fell away, clanking against the hardwood floor.

The power—the bond between the estate and the brownie—faded into a low simmer. Soon, Sparkle would be able to move through the manor and the property without even me knowing it.

I released her hand, as did Sisu. He was grinning madly.

Sparkle surveyed the chains at her feet. Then, with a dismissive snap of her fingers, she caused them to vanish. With another snap of her fingers, she was suddenly swathed in a simple gold brocade dress with a ruffled hem—which looked suspiciously like the curtains.

Some color had eased back to her sallow complexion, but she would need time to truly heal.

Neve snuffled, crying and smiling. Lile gripped her twin's hand, pressing her face against her uncle's leg as if doing so might hold back the emotions overwhelming her.

"I am Dusk Zhi Godfrey," I said formally, on the edge of joyful tears myself. "Archivist. Head curator of magical antiquities at the National Museum of Ireland. Sister of Sisu. Daughter of Trissa. Wilding Manor is my estate, bequeathed to me for the duration of my lifetime."

Sparkle nodded, then looked to Sisu.

"Sisu Jiaotuson Godfrey of Wilding Manor," he said, barely containing his excitement. "Son of Jiaotu and Trissa. Brother of Dusk. I don't have any titles yet because I'm only five. But I have a sharp blade and a golden egg."

The brownie's gaze shifted to Kellan.

He cleared his throat. "Kellan Conall. Shapeshifter. Son of the alpha. Pack enforcer. I'm in and out of Wilding Manor because I'm a contractor hired by Dusk to renovate the estate." He touched Neve and then Lile's shoulders. "My nieces, Neve and Lile, daughters of Gitta."

"Sparkle Eventide," the brownie said, smoothing a hand down her dress. "Of Wilding Manor."

"There will be others to meet," I said, "if you wish."

"I will...I wonder...what are my duties?"

"We may discuss that when you know you wish to stay," I said. "But for now, I think you should tell us of your concerns, and why you stole the crown piece. Afterward, you should do whatever you feel will aid in your healing."

"The house is in a dreadful state," she said. "There is much to be done. I will have to discuss the separation of duties with the gnome."

I quashed a smile. "As you wish."

She nodded, placated. "The witch you claim as friend is in jeopardy. My master...my former master plans to use her to once again harness the power of the crowns."

Crowns? Plural? All the hair on the back of my neck stood up.

"Ravine?" I asked, clarifying.

She nodded.

"And your former master..."

Oh, shit.

It all clicked together finally. The thing I'd been feeling since the gala.

Since meeting him.

"Brendan Prince," I said. It wasn't a question.

"His true name is Cadfael. A high lord of Evenfall."

My stomach soured as I understood the thing I'd been missing. The thing I'd overlooked because his magic was so weak, and he was so exceedingly annoying.

Brendan Prince wasn't a sorcerer. He wasn't a historian. He wasn't just sensationalizing fairy tales for profit.

And what were the so-called fae famous for wielding? Glamour. The magic of illusion and enchantment. To my senses, Prince's appropriated sorcerer magic felt inconsequential because it actually was. Because he was a fae. Or at least he had claimed that designation for himself.

And I was an idiot. For dismissing him, for sneering at his book that I'd hoped was plagiarized. For not seeing...

Not seeing what?

"Prince...was trapped in this dimension when an attempted incursion was thwarted?" I asked Sparkle, feeling my way through all the seemingly unrelated bits of information I'd accumulated. The crown piece, and the tale of fated mates that Prince had been gushing about at the gala. "And...his mate was killed?"

Killed by Suanmi. The guardian of Western Europe had entrusted one piece of the crown to the octopus, another to the Byrne coven, making certain each was sealed in separate dimensions. Clever. Or, at least, it should have been supremely clever.

"Dusk..." Kellan grumbled warningly. He hated being the last to know. Anything.

I shook my head at him, focusing on Sparkle. "And the significance of the crown?"

"I do not know, mistress. Only that he wears one himself."

Two crowns...dual crowns. With only one of them hewn to pieces by a guardian. Which would mean...

"Does he have the third piece?"

"He knows where it is, mistress."

"Sparkle," I said, trying to keep my tone even, "you don't need to call me mistress. I am Dusk."

Sparkle just lowered her eyes and nodded.

"And Ravine..." I looked at Kellan, my mind whirling with all the implications. "Ravine is a metal mage. She can make the crown whole again. Prince doesn't need to steal the first piece from the archive. He had Ravine make a copy, right in front of me...which means the magic, whatever power Prince is trying to access, it isn't embedded into the metal."

Kellan grimaced, his cellphone already at his ear.

"It might be the combination of symbols," I said. "Or maybe if he has the second and third pieces plus Ravine, Prince thinks that'll let him harness enough power."

"What power?" Sisu asked quietly.

"I'm not certain yet, my brother. Crowns...coronets, any sort of magic worn on the head often means mind-control spells, or the amplification of mind control. But I'm just guessing."

Kellan grunted, then tried calling a second number.

"Do you know where the third crown piece is, Sparkle?" I asked.

"In the catacombs."

"Are they in the city?"

"Under a church in the middle of the city. With a large tower and arched stone supports."

"Christ Church Cathedral," Kellan said, his fingers flying over his phone now, texting. Apparently, whoever he'd called hadn't answered. Granted, it was exceedingly early in the morning, and most of the Adepts he would want to call had been up all night.

I shot to my feet, laying my hand over his firmly enough to hold him back as I furiously thought through the ramifications of Prince using Ravine to piece together a crown of unknown power. "Wait."

"Dusk," Kellan growled, "there's a reason we're a pack. There's a reason for covens. We have the numbers."

"Numbers that could get swept up in this...whatever this is. This so-called high lord of Evenfall might simply be attempting to return home..."

Except I'd already closed a doorway that night. I looked at Sparkle, who flinched as if expecting me to hurt her.

"Sparkle," I said gently, "you stole the artifact that the octopus was guarding. Did that doorway lead to the Evenfall dimension?"

"Octopus," Kellan snorted derisively.

"Cephalopod," Sisu chimed in helpfully. "A predatory mollusk."

"Yes, Mis...Dusk." Sparkle nodded, twisting her fingers together again. "The second piece of the crown."

So if he had simply wanted to return to his own dimension, Prince could have just had Sparkle open that doorway, then walked through. But that thought brought something else to mind.

"Are you from Evenfall, Sparkle?"

She nodded, her gaze wide. And still deeply, deeply wounded.

So that was how she'd been able to override Suanmi's seal. Or at least part of the how.

"I could lead you, Mistress Dusk." Sparkle's voice wavered with fear. She squeezed her hands to fists, determined. "To my former master."

Shaking my head, I changed the subject slightly. "Do you wish to return...home?"

The brownie jutted out her chin. "To be hunted by more of them?" she said, defiant now.

That pleased me more than it probably should have, because staying was and should be Sparkle's own choice. But I'd missed having a brownie in the house. "We can find our way. You never have to leave the estate unless you want to. You never need to see your former master again."

Relief softened her expression, and she bobbed her head.

"We need someone to stay with the kids," Kellan said, tugging his phone out from under my hand.

"Like you?"

He laughed humorlessly. "I go where you go."

"I'm coming with you," Sisu declared, arms folded and brow furrowed in a direct mimicry of Kellan's typical expression. Well, typical around me, perhaps.

"Us too!" Lile and Neve cried in unison.

"I'll look after the young ones," Sparkle said. "If you trust me."

"It's not a matter of trust," Kellan said kindly. "It's a matter of power in numbers. Brady can be here in fifteen minutes. It will take you longer to change, Dusk."

I narrowed my eyes at him.

He flashed me a grin.

"Text Brady," I said.

He did.

I kneeled before Sisu. My brother made a half-hearted attempt to twist away, avoiding my eyes. I lowered my voice. "I need you to make sure Sparkle is okay."

Sisu met my gaze, worrying his bottom lip. Lile and Neve pressed up at his sides.

"And if...if something happens?" Sisu whispered.

"Try...try sending a note to Mistress Brightshire."

He nodded solemnly.

"With the noticeboard, Dusk?" Neve asked.

"Yes. That's not how brownies usually communicate, but it might work."

"And if not?" Lile asked.

I looked at Sisu. "Then use the phone." Call the nexus, I meant. To ask for help. "Be specific."

My little brother squared his shoulders. "I understand. I will look after the manor and everyone else."

A flutter of emotion flitted through my belly. Pride riding a wave of pure adoration. I grinned through it. "I'll be right back."

Sisu nodded, throwing his arms around my neck. He released me only a beat after, then held his hand out to Sparkle. "I'll show you everything."

The brownie blinked at me.

I nodded, softening my smile. "The house is yours now. But we'll wait until morning to meet the gnome, Gee." And Morgan, though I didn't say that out loud. I definitely needed to reinforce the rules with the death goddess, to include a brownie who was not to be bound to her every whim.

Sparkle slipped her hand into Sisu's.

"Okay, this is Dusk's desk..." Sisu said, tugging the brownie with him as he stepped farther into the room. Neve and Lile were on their heels.

I straightened, pinning my gaze to Kellan and offering him a toothy smile. "Don't slow me down."

He grinned back at me, his teeth suddenly far, far sharper than mine. "Give me something to chase, Dusk darling, and I'll never stop."

I lowered my voice. "Aren't you all full of promises, shifter."

"I'm just getting started."

I laughed, surprised by the huskiness of my own voice.

Forcing myself to leave Kellan to coordinate his people, I headed upstairs to change. I needed to text Ravine. Something that wouldn't make it obvious to Prince that his brownie had defected, and that we were on our way to quash any attempt of his to use Ravine to reforge the crown.

I was still far too unclear on what the crown did. But the fact that Prince was a self-proclaimed fae high lord in hiding was enough to amp up my sense of urgency.

Just checking in, I texted Ravine. *I had fun tonight. Would love to chat about it. Are you still awake?*

Lame. And stilted. But since it was fairly obvious to everyone at this point that I was inept when it came to any sort of social interaction, it would do. The chances that the metal mage would answer at this late hour were effectively nil—whether she was asleep, and Sparkle was wrong about the pressing timeline, or whether she was deeply enthralled and getting ready to reassemble a fae artifact from its shattered pieces.

As I slid the bone blade into the built-in sheath on the right thigh of my dragon leathers, I realized something rather ruefully. Two things, in fact. First, I had been blatantly wrong about classifying beings from a certain dimension as fae—if the high lord of Evenfall claimed that designation for himself. And second, I was about to make an enemy of the only fae I might ever come into contact with, other than the octopus sentinel and any of the brownies I'd known. Unlike with Morgan, there would be no chats over tea and cookies, no notebooks to be filled and verified.

Still…maybe I could salvage the situation?

I quashed that misplaced hope quickly. A mythical fae or not, Prince had made his choices a long time ago. And like Brady had said not even three days before, not every situation was an anthropological event.

Sometimes I could look at life through the supremely focused lens of an archivist. And sometimes…I had to fulfill the dragons' duty. To protect the world and all the magic in it, above everything else.

But just to be clear, even if only to myself, I might be willing to admit that fae wasn't just a generic classification, but I still wasn't remotely sold on the fated mates concept.

CHAPTER NINE

I WOULDN'T HAVE FOUND THE SECONDARY ENTRANCE TO the catacombs underneath Christ Church Cathedral without Kellan. At least not so quickly. Because there was nothing magical about the structure itself. But we'd found Ravine's tiny car abandoned—parked illegally on the far side of the property with the doors thrown open. And that had let Kellan pick up Ravine's scent and follow it around the back of the church and down a cleverly hidden staircase.

A door at the bottom of the stairs had been closed, but the tarnished latch and the newer padlock had been sheared through cleanly—by Ravine's magic. Other than that residual, though, I couldn't sense even a hint of other magic nearby. Only Kellan.

Beyond the door, we crossed through a series of long, narrow stone halls. Kellan, at the lead, was so large that he blocked my view. If not for Ravine's car and Sparkle's insistence, I would have thought we were sneaking into a purely nonmagical site. Still, the muted industrial lights, sporadically strung along the low stone ceiling on long runs of electrical wire, were already on. Indicating that someone had passed through recently and not left yet.

We had run all the way from the manor, rather than grabbing Kellan's SUV and worrying about traffic and parking, taking off the moment Brady and Erin stepped through the gate of the estate. I hadn't even managed an apology for ruining their night. Or rather, their early morning. I also knew that Brady had argued with Kellan, via text, over accompanying the two of us rather than babysitting, and I didn't want to waste time getting into that again.

Christ Church Cathedral was one of the oldest human-built structures I'd ever walked through, with its origins traced back to 1038. Sisu and I had taken the tour last month. While the site had undergone numerous restorations over many centuries, the crypt was the oldest surviving part, dating from 1188, and was one of the largest medieval crypts in Ireland or Britain. The space was a maze of stone columns supporting the entire footprint of the cathedral, and was used to store numerous historic stone pieces and statues. But the section that Kellan and I now slipped through hadn't been part of the public tour. I wasn't entirely sure yet whether it was even connected to the main crypt.

Finally sensing a residual touch of magic ahead, I settled my hand on Kellan's shoulder. He paused at my touch, and we stood tucked within a dark pocket between a broken light and the grimy, muted bulb we'd just passed. The silence felt like it had substance.

I listened for any hint of what might be ahead of us, but only picked up our quiet breathing.

Slipping my hand from Kellan's shoulder, I slid around him. The narrowness of the passageway caused all sorts of interesting bits of our bodies to brush against each other. But I was more sharply aware of the low level of terror simmering just under my skin.

Fear for Ravine.

Because although I was trying not to, I could think of only one plausible reason I wouldn't be able to sense her magic even though Kellan could still pick up her scent.

She was dead.

I was holding out for some other reason, of course, however implausible. And quietly praying for that implausibility, to whatever gods might have been listening to a dragon archivist skulking through the catacombs of a Christian church in the early-morning hours.

I stretched my senses out before us. The hint of magic I'd previously picked up felt like it was ahead but slightly to our right. Except there was a stone wall there that appeared completely solid.

I turned my head so Kellan could see me, tapping my nose and pointing up ahead, then to the right.

He nodded in agreement.

Trailing my fingers along the cold stone wall as we continued traversing the hall, I reached for the power I could feel, assessing it with all my senses. I was only a few steps away from what I thought might have been the source of the magic when my hand fell into an empty space.

Kellan grabbed my arm with a suddenness that made me flinch, drawing me back. Holding me tucked against his chest, he leaned around me, practically pressing his face against the wall that wasn't a wall at all.

He sniffed the air repeatedly. A low, darkly tinted growl rumbled through his chest, then he shook his head. He couldn't scent anything from the wall that had given way to nothing, and it was pissing him off.

There was something utterly pleasing in starting to know someone well enough that I could pick up on his moods and thoughts—and instead of that making me wary, I simply accepted it.

Unfortunately, I couldn't communicate my own assessment nonverbally, so I whispered against his ear, so quietly that I could barely hear myself, "Glamour."

Kellan looked at me sharply, questioningly.

Guessing at what he was asking, I shook my head, leaning closer again to whisper, "Unknown magic user. But I know the magic we can feel beyond." Because now that I was closer, I recognized the guardian magic. Suanmi's power, specifically. "I felt it used to seal the doorway in the cliff."

The presence of the guardian's power at a second site wasn't particularly comforting. Though if Suanmi had assigned a sentinel to watch over the second crown piece, then perhaps Prince was preparing to get the final piece from another sentinel.

Kellan shifted, glancing between the wall that wasn't a wall and me. Then he rolled his shoulders and pressed his hand against my hip.

I took a step to the side. Then, at his steady look, I took another step, giving him space.

He closed his eyes, hands clenched at his sides, head bowed. Then an intense wash of power rolled over him. That magic brightened, so much so that I had to look away or risk compromising my eyesight.

When I looked back, Kellan had taken on his warrior form—an unusually seamless mixture of his werewolf and human forms, including an elongated snout and sharp upper canines. He was now so tall that he was forced to hunch down in the narrow corridor, his pointed ears flattened to his broad head.

He stripped off the remnants of his ruined long-sleeved T-shirt with quick flicks of wickedly sharp claws that were longer than my fingers. But the black sweat-pants he'd swapped for his previously ruined jeans had mostly survived the transformation, around the slight narrow of his waist and hips, at least. He was sleek yet somehow bulky. Covered in a dense dark-gray fur, he blended into our badly lit surroundings so well that I had to focus on his glowing golden-green eyes to truly see him. Though that sense could also have been an aspect of his magic.

Intriguing.

Or it would have been if I hadn't been so worried about Ravine that I felt like my skin was on the verge of unraveling.

That thought helped me ignore a completely inappropriate impulse to step forward and run my hands across Kellan's chest in the hopes of triggering the runes I sworn I'd seen on him in his warrior form two months before.

Shrugging off the last vestiges of his transformation, Kellan bared his teeth, chuckling quietly.

All the hair rose on my arms. I had to fight through a momentary need to flee.

Though I'd seen the transformation multiple times now, apparently I wasn't yet accustomed to the dark menace that radiated from Kellan in this form.

I grinned at him, though, drawing my blade from its built-in sheath. Kellan dipped his head even farther to sweep his glowing eyes over me. It was the same look he'd given me back at the manor, when I'd come downstairs in my dragon leathers.

My grin widened, and I let my magic loose. Having already shredded Jiaotu's glamour, there was no point in hiding the extents of my power now.

I was quite certain that playing games with a being as potentially powerful as a high lord of Evenfall wasn't going to get me terribly far. In fact, I had no doubt now that Brendan Prince had known exactly what I was the moment he met me. Especially if I was correct about him abandoning his high lady to die under Suanmi's blade.

Kellan glanced toward the glamoured wall, then over at me, indicating he wanted me behind him. Except there really was no room behind him. He was that big. But just to be obliging, I stepped up beside him, keeping my bone blade lowered. Infinity's warm hum between my shoulder blades spiked in anticipation.

I settled my hand on Kellan's back so he'd know I was with him. He stepped through the glamour without further prompting.

Closing my eyes, I did the same.

The stone floor remained solid under my feet. I opened my eyes, taking in what appeared to be a broad antechamber filled with crates and dusty furniture...folding chairs and tables? Was the church using a possible entrance to another dimension for storage?

The thick layer of dust coating the floor and everything else spoke volumes, though. No one had used this room in years. Or at least no one nonmagical.

Kellan loomed slightly ahead of me, having taken only two steps into the room. His head slowly swiveled to take in the entire stone chamber a second time.

"How disappointing," a familiar voice drawled, the accent thicker and more lyrical than before. No longer the hint of what I'd thought was Welsh. "Hiding behind your brute. I expected more from a...from an archivist. But then, hiding is your thing. Isn't it, Dusk?"

I stepped up beside Kellan, carefully and deliberately scanning the room to take in everything I could absorb before turning my attention to the figure who'd suddenly appeared, lounging casually against the far wall to my right.

His height, his slim physique, and the dark hair swept back from his high brow were the same. But everything else about him was…more. Other. His eyes were now undeniably purple, his dusky skin radiant. His ears curved up to a point at the top. And his features were sharper, more inhuman.

He had called himself fae when peddling his own story. A story he hadn't plagiarized or lifted from older sources after all. Corrie Byrne had somehow gotten her hands on an early handwritten accounting of the story of Brendan Prince's own life—aka Cadfael, a high lord of Evenfall.

But why write anything down at all? Why expose himself that much?

The glamour hiding a second person in the antechamber fell.

Ravine. The metal mage stood before a rune-marked arched doorway that was three times the width of the arch that had been etched into the cliff.

Damn it twice over.

Either Prince was teasing me by revealing Ravine and the sealed doorway, or he was worried about expending too much energy holding the glamour in place. I hoped it was the former, but was fairly certain it was the latter.

Prince had been waiting for an audience. Or specifically for me? But again, why? Why risk exposure before completing his plan? Why risk me being as powerful as Suanmi? The guardian had already thwarted him once and had killed his so-called fated mate while doing so.

Ravine's back was to us, her arms spread to the sides and her dark-haired head thrown back. She held the two crown-piece relics cradled in each upturned palm. Her eyes blazed with a bright-blue power that I couldn't otherwise feel or taste. She was dressed in the same sweater, skirt, and boots she'd been wearing at the pack celebration.

I narrowed my eyes, feeling slightly blind with my magical senses so expertly blunted. But I was almost certain that the third part of the crown was embedded at the top of the sealed dimensional doorway's arch.

The final pieces of the so-called high lord's plan clicked into place.

"And what did you just put together, clever girl?" Prince asked, amused.

"You've been using your work, peddling your tale, to find the two missing pieces of the crown."

Prince flashed me a wicked grin.

"But you always knew the third piece and the doorway was in Dublin."

He shrugged affectedly. "I carved the doorway from the other side, didn't I?"

I touched Kellan's arm, stepping away as he took my cue to search the area. My being able to see Ravine's power but not feel it—as with Prince—meant that the room was sealed, even if I couldn't sense a boundary line. But I had no idea what would happen if I tried to cross that line and simply grab the metal mage.

"Did you, though?" I said dismissively, deliberately not looking at Prince as I scanned the floor and the walls more thoroughly. "Or was it your more-powerful mate who broke through to our dimension? The one who sacrificed herself so you could flee..." I met his gaze. "Like a coward."

Anger flickered briefly behind Prince's purple eyes. Then he chuckled. "Oh, I knew I liked you the moment I set eyes on you. And of course I mean the actual you that you keep tucked behind that shoddy glamour. The you that's on full display tonight."

Ravine still hadn't even acknowledged our presence, as if Prince was somehow holding her. Forcing her to do whatever she was doing.

Kellan crouched to look closer at something on the ground—a small area that had been wiped clear of dust and dirt.

Prince followed my gaze, lowering his voice. "Does your brute know about your double life, Dusk? Ravine certainly doesn't. But don't worry your pretty, powerful head. I kept your secret."

"Can you feel the loss yet?" I asked, following Kellan's lead to scan for other recently cleaned sections of the floor and walls.

"The loss?" Prince snapped, growing testy.

"Of your brownie. The last of the Eventides." I pinned my gaze to his, shifting closer. Only a meter and a half between us now. Yet I knew he wouldn't have been acting so casually if he thought I could easily close that space.

His eyes narrowed.

"Or can't you feel the severed connection?" I raised my hand, lining myself up to the mark that Kellan had uncovered, then pressing my palm forward until I felt the slightest bit of resistance.

An invisible barrier. As I'd suspected. But the fact that I couldn't sense the energy fueling it concerned me, especially if that meant I was going to have to break my way through with more force than finesse.

Because without knowing what was going on with Ravine, I had no way to know that Prince's barrier wasn't being fueled by her life.

Confusion flickered over the self-proclaimed high lord's face. Then he smiled, fully revealing his teeth. They all ended in sharp points.

Power stirred in his eyes.

Finally.

"You killed my brownie. I'm impressed."

"I freed her," I said.

"Ah." He laughed mockingly. "That's more like it. Never mind. I'll recall her before we cross through."

"You've been sustaining yourself by pulling power from the Eventides. How many of her family have you killed to keep yourself hidden?"

"To bide my time? Time that my love bequeathed to me? Every single one. But no worries. Once the doorway has been reopened, I shall no longer have need of such…lesser beings."

I was going to run him through with my bone blade.

Oh, yes. I knew it.

I could feel it.

I had never killed a sentient being before, but I was going to end Brendan Prince. I had no idea what he planned, though the size of the door he'd claimed to have carved indicated something on a large scale. But it wasn't going to come to that.

I wasn't certain what was reflected in my face, but that something quashed the high lord of Evenfall's smile. He straightened away from the wall, his hand falling to his side as if he carried an invisible weapon.

I tightened my grip on my bone blade, sliding one foot back for leverage, readying to—

With her arms still outstretched, Ravine snapped her head up. The runes outlining the doorway shifted, drawing my attention.

No, not shifted. The symbols had somehow lifted away from the stone, leaving indentations behind. As did the hunk of metal that I had guessed was the third piece of the fae crown Brendan Prince had spent centuries trying to collect.

My heart rate ratcheted up.

The runes on the door weren't just painted symbols. They were metal. Each one was a sliver of gold that most likely matched the metal of the crown pieces Ravine still held. Though as Ravine had already felt when copying the first crown piece—the copy in her right hand now—it wasn't gold. Not the precious metal mined from our earthly dimension, at least.

The metal runes, freed from the stone at Ravine's behest, liquefied in the air, streaming toward her. She brought her hands together, cupping them. She coaxed the streams of metal to twine around the two pieces she already held—the relic stolen from the octopus sentinel and the copy of the Galway relic.

The third crown piece hovered just above. As if waiting to be utilized.

"Ravine!" I shouted.

The metal mage didn't turn, didn't acknowledge me.

I pressed my hand against the barrier between myself and the witch. It had very little give. Which meant it might be brittle.

"Show us, my darling one," Prince crooned, speaking to Ravine. "Your friends are here to witness your magnificence."

Still wielding power I couldn't feel, Ravine slowly pivoted, the blue of her magic so bright in her eyes that it obscured the upper half of her face. Her attention was riveted to the metal slowly settling in her hands. It twined around the relic pieces. Then those pieces rose into the air to hover next to the third piece.

I tore my attention away, uncomfortably aware that I had to ignore my own fascination with new magic to do so. I frantically looked around for more markings on the floor. To my left, Kellan was doing the same.

I spotted a partly cleared spot on the wall, where a symbol was scored into the stone. I didn't recognize it, but it felt familiar. Like the runes on the title page of Prince's book. The handwritten one, not the one he peddled to undiscerning Adepts.

Under the press of Ravine's power, the molten fae gold she'd pulled from the doorway melded with the crown pieces, first shifting, then flowing, then smoothing. The third piece of the crown settled over top of it all, forming front-facing peaks.

A perfectly reconstructed crown hovered in the air before Ravine's outstretched hands.

Prince clapped, glancing between me and the metal mage. "Come now, Dusk. That's a beautiful display of power for a mere witch."

Ravine stood completely motionless, fingers still outstretched. Her blue eyes were wide and unseeing.

"You're compelling her," I said coldly.

"Just little touches. At least until tonight, which required more focus. Coming home with me after the gala, the lunch. Copying the crown piece because I knew I wasn't going to be able to get it from you. Inviting me to the pack celebration—"

"Which got you access to their land."

"Indeed. Pack boundaries are primitive, but annoyingly resilient. I'd been working on getting that piece for years. The witch was surprisingly resistant. But sex has a way of breaking down those sorts of boundaries."

Kellan, crouched by another symbol etched into the stone floor, snarled viciously.

Prince chuckled, delighted. "Tasted her, have you, brute? Do you share, Dusk? I hadn't gotten that sense from you. And you know I'm not going to let you keep him."

I had no idea what Prince was talking about. But his game had gone on long enough. I now had all the information I needed to finish it before it fully began.

I tugged off my backpack, pulling out Infinity.

Prince's eyes widened. He took an anticipatory step in my direction. "Ah, here we go."

Ignoring him, I flipped Infinity open, recalling the inner title page of Brendan Prince's handwritten book with a silent push of intent. The book that Corrie Byrne had collected while guarding the first crown piece for the coven, as tasked by Suanmi.

"I'm surprised you've stayed so well hidden, Prince," I said. "Since you've already handed me the key to your undoing. Perhaps it's your underwhelming magic in this dimension."

"My power is holding you at bay, isn't it? It has me a mere moment away from unleashing an army of Evenfall on this realm."

My stomach soured at the confirmation that Prince was planning on following through with his long-ago attempted invasion of our dimension. Though how he was going to implement that plan after so many centuries away, I had no idea.

Forcing myself to focus, I scanned the sketch of the doorway in Infinity, mentally comparing it with the symbol on the wall to my right. I found the match quickly—the symbol on the bottom corner of the sketch.

I swiftly crossed to Kellan, locating the symbols he'd found on the floor and on the left-side wall. They matched two more of the runes on the door in Infinity's sketch.

"The symbols mean nothing in your hands," Prince snarled, seemingly guessing at my intent. "They cannot simply be erased or rearranged—"

"How about unlocked?" I said. I turned Infinity so he could see the illustration, tapping a finger to the symbol sketched in the middle of the upper archway. A symbol that I was now certain was also mirrored on the center section of the crown—the section that Ravine herself had copied—though I wasn't quite close enough to compare it to the reconstructed crown still hovering before the metal mage's outstretched hands.

Prince's nostrils flared. "Ridiculous."

"I just have to triangulate," I said, speaking to Kellan. Based on how the symbols on the floor and walls were positioned, it was going to be an educated guess as to where the unlock symbol should be triggered. I was also guessing that the crown had something to do with unlocking the catacomb doorway. Because why else had Prince come here with Ravine, rather than simply forcing Sparkle to do his bidding as he had at the Conall estate?

The only thing I could rely on alongside all the guesswork was that magic, at least in our dimension, was heavily based on intent.

Especially my magic.

Prince snapped his fingers.

Ravine blinked. As she came to awareness, the crown settled into her hands. She met my gaze.

"Dusk! I wanted to call you and—"

"Enough," Prince commanded. "Give me the crown." He held his hand out to her.

Sheathing my blade, I grabbed my pen from my backpack, sketching the symbol that I hoped would unlock Prince's invisible barrier on a blank page in Infinity. I checked it for accuracy three times.

"The scrambling around is just so cute, Dusk," Prince said. "But I'm going to require you to be more regal in bearing."

Ravine's brow furrowed. She cocked her head oddly, first in Prince's direction, then following his gaze to me. Her frown deepened.

Kellan's lips pulled back in a snarl, revealing wickedly long and sharp teeth. All the hair rose on the back of my neck in response. He raised his clawed hands, poised as if ready to try to rip the invisible barrier asunder.

"I knew it," Ravine hissed. "I knew you wanted him."

"I'm sorry," I whispered to my personal archive. Then I ripped the sketch of the symbol I'd drawn from Infinity. "I'm so sorry."

Infinity shuddered. Energy expanded outward from, then contracted back into my wounded archive. Fighting the urge to soothe that wound, I shoved the archive and pen back into my pack, then joined Kellan at the edge of the barrier. With the sketch in one hand, I struggled to get the pack secured on my shoulders.

Ravine's bright-blue gaze was riveted to me. Then she smirked. "I can be powerful too, Dusk." She tightened her grip on the crown.

I caught Prince's frown from the corner of my eye.

The metal mage raised the crown, deliberately holding it over her head.

"No!" Prince shouted. "You aren't powerful enough."

He lunged for her, though I was already certain he couldn't actually take the crown from Ravine without permission. That was why he'd released her from his beguilement. Magic had rules, in all dimensions.

Ravine placed the crown on her head.

I pressed the sketch of the rune against the barrier. Kellan was close enough to brush against my shoulder, ready to charge forward when I broke through—

Power exploded around Ravine. Magic I could see but also feel and taste now, tangy and cloying.

Prince threw his arms up to shield his face.

The page from Infinity stuck to the invisible barrier. But the barrier didn't fall.

Fear gripped my heart.

Ravine laughed, low and throaty. Power blazed from her eyes and her Celtic-inspired cuffs.

"The symbol needs a command…" I muttered, talking through my instincts, my intent, even as my throat threatened to close up. "Unlock…" I whispered, tearing my gaze away from the power undulating around Ravine to stare fixedly at the rune. Willing my magic to translate the symbol for me. And hoping desperately that it was a word in the first place.

I flicked my gaze to Ravine.

The energy streaming from the crown settled around her. Literally. A cloak of blue witch magic draped around her shoulders, then flowed smoothly down her back.

Prince was staring at her, mouth agape.

Stepping behind me, Kellan wrapped his hands around either side of my face, sharp claws caressing my cheeks. "Focus…" he whispered as he directed my attention back to the rune adhered to the invisible barrier.

I pressed my fingers against the paper, against the inked symbol, trying to relax.

Ravine moaned. In pain? In pleasure?

Triggered by the inherent magic that allowed me to translate any writing, the hastily copied rune shifted under my gaze, re-forming.

"Oh…" Ravine gasped again. She moaned breathily, her face flushed with pleasure.

Then she started panting. Chest heaving. Her expression tightened, lips pulling back from her teeth.

Pained.

Then panicked.

The word 'unlock' appeared on the page.

"Unlock!" I shouted, stabbing my magic through the word, through the torn page, like a blade.

The barrier barring Kellan and me from the rest of the room cracked.

The shifter stepped to the side and punched it, the blow backed by a wallop of his magic. Adaptable, changeable magic that was already naturally resistant to being contained or held.

The invisible wall shattered.

Ravine started screaming. Her hands were grasping, grabbing at the crown, trying to remove it. Her expression was tortured.

Then she fell, convulsing.

Prince lunged for her.

I got to the metal mage first, grabbing her around the arm and carefully lowering her to the ground. Kellan slammed his open palm against Prince's chest. The so-called fae never saw it coming. He flew back, slammed into the stone wall, and tumbled to the ground unconscious.

"Dusk!" Ravine cried. Then she screamed. "Dusk!"

Her face was thinning, graying.

"The crown is pulling too much," I whispered. "Too much magic."

"We need the witches," Kellan snarled. Energy churned around him as he started to transform into his human visage.

Ravine was still trying to remove the crown, but I settled my hands over hers. She writhed against me, half slung over my lap. Infinity was sending out warning blasts against my back. But I wasn't certain if that was a reaction to what was happening with Ravine or what I was about to do.

"Give it to me," I said. "Ravine, give me the crown. That will get it off you."

Her eyes widened in comprehension, but she sobbed. "No, Dusk. It will take you…"

Kellan crouched beside me, human again and half naked with his phone in hand. "I don't have a fucking signal down here."

"It's okay." I tried to project utter calm, though the strain of doing so was intense. "Ravine is going to willingly bequeath the crown to me. And everything will be okay. Ravine?"

She shook her head again. Blood vessels had burst in her eyes. She was bleeding from her ears.

I pressed my hands to her cheeks. "You're dying, my friend. Let me help you."

Finally, she nodded shakily.

I threaded my fingers through hers, so that I touched the crown and her skin at the same time. Energy streaked through my skin, running down the bones of my hands, wrists, and forearms.

I glanced over at Prince. He was still out.

Casting my voice low, I spoke to Kellan. "This…there's a lot of power here. Don't…don't let me open the doorway."

He snarled. "Dusk, don't make me stop you—"

I lifted the crown free from Ravine's head.

Her eyes rolled up, and she slumped across my lap.

I held the crown aloft, keeping it as far from my head as possible. I just had to get Infinity from my pack and get the crown contained within my archive's pages.

Kellan gently pulled Ravine into his arms, leaning in and listening. "Breathing. Her heart rate is quiet, though. Unsteady."

"Text Mesa," I said, my voice sounding as shaky as I suddenly felt.

The crown was…so powerful. So…pervasive. It wanted…me…

"Dusk?" Kellan asked warily. "Remember, you wanted to put that down."

"I do." My voice steadied. "I just need to get into my backpack. I need Infinity. But you need to get Ravine away. I…it might try to grab her again." Perspiration beaded my forehead. My arms began quivering. "Quickly…"

Kellan straightened, lifting Ravine and gently propping her next to the door to the hall. It didn't appear cloaked from this side. "I'll grab your book—"

"No," I cried. My arms were shaking from holding the crown, though it felt almost weightless. "Don't try to touch it. You'll have to cut the straps…"

Kellan straightened, stepping toward me.

Power sliced through the antechamber, stirring dust and dirt. The shifter slammed against an invisible barrier, stumbling back.

"Now," a cool voice said from behind me. "Where were we?"

Brendan Prince straightened, dusting himself off. Then he paced around me, his purple gaze gleaming with delight. "Oh, yes. My high lady. You've found me at last."

Kellan hit the barrier with a roar.

It held.

Prince kneeled before me. "Now…" He smoothed his hands up over his brow and across his head. A golden crown—a perfect duplicate of the one I held—settled on his forehead. "Let's get you crowned and finish what we started."

"Don't be an idiot," I snapped.

He chuckled, threading his fingers through and under my hair, then grasping the back of my neck firmly.

He wrapped his other hand around my right wrist, to stop me from drawing my bone blade.

The crown was between us, practically pressing against both our chests now.

"I knew who you were the moment I saw you. My love reincarnated."

All right. That was a piece of the puzzle I hadn't been expecting.

"Put on the crown," Prince said. "And I'll prove it to you."

Kellan hit the barrier again. Prince looked over at him, his expression sly.

I followed his gaze. Kellan was pacing, systematically testing the barrier with his fists and claws. Ravine was still slumped against the wall, head lolling.

"I could kill her with a whisper," Prince breathed. "It's a talent of mine, once I've taken a mind. Which is why the brownie isn't as free as you believe."

Prince needed to be dealt with. The door needed to be permanently sealed. And whatever was waiting on the other side of that door needed to be resolved as well. Because I had no doubt that Brendan Prince needed more than whatever power the dual crowns held to invade our dimension.

And the longer I held it, the less sway the reconstructed crown had over me. My dragon magic was rising to counter its influence.

"This isn't going to go the way you wish," I whispered to Prince.

He flashed me a wicked grin. "Show me, my high lady."

I put the crown on my head.

I lost a few moments.

My mind was overwhelmed, blanked by power.

My hearing came back first. Kellan was snarling viciously, pounding over and over again on Prince's barrier.

I forced myself to breathe, realizing that I might not have been doing so for those uncounted moments. I became aware that I was still on my knees, with Prince holding both my wrists.

I could feel the so-called high lord of Evenfall's magic now. A deep thrumming energy. His grip was firm, proprietary.

I could also feel the energy that coated the dimensional doorway, and how that energy connected to Prince. But also to me.

I blinked, my sight returning.

Cinched at my neck, a golden cloak of power had settled over my shoulders, pooling all around me. Undulating so prettily that Morgan would have been utterly jealous, the cloak was weighty, thick with magic.

My magic, unleashed.

The weight of the crown pressed against my forehead was almost insubstantial in comparison.

Prince, similarly cloaked but in a deep, velvety purple, touched my face with the very tips of his fingers. His magic tickled my skin as he raised my head. His purple eyes were full of power now, making it that much more impressive that he'd kept that power so well hidden behind his glamour. His intense gaze searched mine, as if trying to see who I really was now that I'd claimed the crown.

I smiled at him, summoning every good memory I had within me to sell the expression. Then I breathed, "Cadfael?"

His real name, according to Sparkle.

Something shifted behind his eyes, and he moaned. A terrible, broken sound.

I pressed my hand against his chest. "I'm...confused..."

Somewhere to my left, Kellan fell silent.

Prince laughed, breathy and thrilled.

A little part of me died inside at my deception, at using his love against him.

Transferring his hold from my wrist to my shoulders, he pulled me forward into a kiss that I didn't see coming and had a hard time accepting. His lips were cool and hard, his sharp teeth pressing, grinding against my own lips until I softened my mouth.

He threaded his fingers through the hair at my temples, partly touching my crown.

And in doing so, he angled my head just enough that I could see Kellan.

Still in his human form, he was standing stock-still. His expression was terrible...harsh with disbelief.

On the pretense of raising my hand to Prince's shoulder, I flicked my fingers at Kellan, hoping he'd understand.

I was still me.

Still on mission.

He clenched his jaw, nodding.

Prince abruptly pulled me to my feet, releasing my mouth to glance over at Kellan. His eyes narrowed for a moment. Then he looked at me, confirming I was still gazing up at him as if enchanted. Befuddled, but enchanted.

He smirked.

I wasn't going to keep up the pretense for long. I'd never actually been intimate with anyone I didn't want to be touching. Though I knew that made me unusual even in this supposedly enlightened day and age.

My gaze flicked to Ravine, who was still unconscious and propped against the wall...

Had...had Prince...raped her? Or had she invited him to her bed willingly the first time, letting his ability to beguile her slip through her shields? She'd mentioned that her cuffs thwarted most compulsion enchantments.

But wasn't beguilement, or any sort of mind control, rape in and of itself?

Prince caught my shift in focus, pressing his hand against my cheek to coax me to meet his gaze again. "Shh, shh..." he breathed, trying to calm me.

I slammed my hands against his chest with just about all the force I could muster at close range.

He stumbled back, rubbing his chest with one hand and holding up the other palm toward me.

Kellan grunted in approval.

"It was nothing." Prince grinned widely. "A distraction. A means to an end."

I glared at him.

He chuckled. "So jealous. Shall I kill her? Prove she means nothing, to soothe you?"

I spun away from him, turning my attention to the dimensional doorway in the stone wall. Ravine had stripped its protections away when she reclaimed the pieces of the crown that Suanmi had sealed it with. Which likely meant it was a permanent bridge to our dimension. Otherwise, the guardian would have collapsed it.

Or it couldn't be collapsed from this side.

The first licks of fear squirmed through me. I glanced back at Kellan. He was running his hand along the barrier between us, testing its strength in a subtler way. Looking for any weakness to exploit.

I swallowed, then risked speaking to Kellan directly. "Sisu…"

Something cracked in my chest.

My brother was too young to lose me when Mom was already gone.

"Tell Sisu that I will always love him, whether I'm by his side or not."

That was what Mom said to us every time she went on a collection.

Kellan's hand dropped limply to his side. His expression was grim. "You promised him, Dusk."

"I know," I whispered.

Prince crowded against me angrily. "What's this?"

"My brother," I said, allowing my fear to reflect in my face, in my voice. Honestly, I wasn't certain I could suppress it. "We're going through, aren't we? To your dimension?"

"Our dimension," Prince said. "We will reestablish our rule, then we'll be back."

"Back?" I echoed as if confused, overwhelmed. I didn't really have to act very hard, but the more info I could pull out of Prince for Kellan to hear, the better.

Prince grinned nastily. "Oh, yes. We're going to finish what we started. And then two worlds will bow to us."

He grabbed my hand, threading his fingers through mine and turning me away from Kellan. I risked one more glance back, hoping, praying that Kellan could read my expression. Trying to tell him that while I could kill Prince on this side of the doorway, I wasn't certain that doing so would stop whatever was happening on the other side.

Whatever might have been triggered when the doorway was unsealed by Ravine.

And yes, Suanmi would come if I failed. The guardian would thwart any invasion. But there would be casualties.

I swallowed, offering Kellan a smile.

Kellan Conall would be one of the first to die. He was standing right by the bloody doorway. And I knew he'd stand sentry until it was obvious I'd sealed it.

Prince pressed his hand to the stone wall. "Come, my darling high lady."

I lined my own hand up with his.

He grunted, satisfied.

Energy shifted from the wall, cracks appearing in the stone, running the width and height of the archway.

Prince whispered in a language I'd never heard spoken out loud before. But I now knew that I'd seen it written in the book from Galway. He repeated the phrase two more times. Power erupted in a halo around the crown on his head, then bloomed under the palm he'd pressed to the stone.

Prince glanced at me. "Take us home, beloved."

And there was the last piece of the puzzle. It took two people, both wearing the twinned crowns, to open the doorway to the Evenfall realm. Which was why Prince hadn't done it before or used Sparkle to collect the third crown piece.

I repeated the same phrase he'd spoken, having memorized it simply by hearing it. But in vocalizing it, I translated it to English in my mind.

No one world.
No prison.
Can hold those fated to walk the earth together.

I spoke the phrase twice more. Power churned around my crown, pooling under my palm and undulating down and across my manifested golden cloak.

The stone wall disintegrated.

The wide archway opened to reveal the purple-hued world I'd gotten a glimpse of through the cliffside doorway.

But this time, I stepped through, my fingers twined with Prince's.

Even if it meant leaving Kellan, Ravine, and Sisu behind.

Because it was my duty to do so.

I felt the magic of the barrier holding Kellan at bay fade as Prince crossed the threshold of power shimmering between one dimension and another. I followed at his side.

I didn't risk glancing back a third time.

I knew what I had to do. And I needed to move quickly, without regrets.

Because I was a dragon, not a witch.

And it was a dragon's duty to protect the world and all the magic within it.

CHAPTER TEN

THE SKY BEHIND THE SPAN OF CRAGGY MOUNTAINS was various shades of purple, lightening to a whited-out lavender overhead instead of the black I'd seen before. Apparently, perpetual twilight still shifted from evening to morning in the Evenfall realm. Twin charcoal moons, one smaller than the other, were pinned in that expansive sky, about midway up. The larger of the two was ringed with a brighter glow, as if it blocked a hidden sun.

Prince and I stood with our fingers still entwined on a rocky outcropping, gazing into a large valley that sloped away from us. The landscape was punctuated by the deep pools of water and stone formations that I'd glimpsed through the doorway I'd sealed behind the other-dimensional octopus.

No. The fae octopus.

Even I could admit when I'd been wrong.

I was *more* in the Evenfall realm. Even though I couldn't immediately sense what that *more* meant to me, for me.

Any remnants of Jiaotu's glamour that had clung to me had been stripped entirely away between one step and the next. Or perhaps I'd never fully been myself, even before the glamour...

Perhaps something had unlocked in me...and I was now fully realized.

That thought was still nebulous, though. A feeling, a sense of self, not a fact. Revolving around me, in me, settling over me. Burrowing deeper and deeper...

Evenfall was only a shade away from dusk. And even on Earth, I was always the strongest during the hour of my birth. So perhaps the *more* I felt was due to that same as-yet-unexplained phenomena of my power?

Strength flooded through me. I knew I could crush Prince's hand with a mere twist of my fingers. I could have him on his knees, head bowed to my superiority, with a flick of those same fingers.

My senses sharpened. The air was delicately fragrant. Soothing, yet invigorating. I could see individual branches on the craggy trees speckling the far-off foothills. And I could hear...

Everything.

The shift of Prince's clothing as he turned to look at me. The gentle rush of the underground rivers that fed the shimmering pools. The sharp call of a creature in the distance, and the answer it provoked.

Energy flowed down the golden cloak that trailed along the rocky ground behind me, even as I absorbed energy from that same ground with every step I took.

Dragons perpetually pulled power from the world, immediately feeding it back. But I had never felt that process so acutely before.

All that extra power, that extra strength, even before unsheathing the bone blade that writhed with magic against my thigh, as if it too had become more aware in this dimension.

With that blade in hand, I could rampage across this world, carving through anyone who stood in my way, and leaving behind bodies on which to build—

Heat seared through me, through my back.

I absorbed it as I would a blow, thinking I'd been attacked. But before I could spin around to see who had crossed through the open doorway behind us, another pulse hit me, and I recognized the power.

Infinity.

I was still wearing my backpack.

I was a dragon, yes. But also an archivist.

I was Dusk.

Prince was watching me. Closely.

I met his gaze steadily.

He smiled, wickedly satisfied. "I knew you were meant to be mine. All that power tied up inside you."

I wasn't certain what he meant by that. My power had been hidden, but not tied. Not bound.

He scanned the horizon. "The others will feel your arrival. So let's make it official and wake our host. No need to get bloody ourselves, not before we need to." He flashed another smile at me. "Unless you want to, my darling high lady."

I glared at him, no need to keep up the pretense now that he'd shown me how the doorway operated. I just had to reverse the incantation and seal it with the crown.

From this side.

My stomach soured. I ignored it.

Prince chuckled, leaning into me. "How long are you going to hold a grudge about the witch?" he asked, completely misinterpreting my silence. "If you had been agreeable and not so well-shielded, you could have been by my side from the start. Then I would have had no use for the witch. Or needed her to copy the crown piece."

"Ravine," I snapped. "If you're going to beguile someone, use her...rape her...then you should know her name."

"Rape," Prince scoffed. "That implies unwillingness—"

My blade was in my hand and pressed under his chin before he could complete the sentence.

He tightened his grip on my other hand. But other than tilting his chin up slightly, he didn't react otherwise. "So bloody. So violent," he purred, leaning into the blade. "So delectably...eager."

The blade sliced into his dusky skin easily. And yes, eagerly. His blood was shockingly dark against the white bone. The golden runes that decorated the blade writhed, churning with—

Moving faster than even I could react, Prince grabbed my wrist, twisting away from the blade. Then, overpowering me—though again he had surprised me—he managed to slice my own blade across the back of my other hand. My fingers were still entangled with his own.

Blood bloomed across the back of my hand—a deep red coating and mixing with his own blood on the blade.

Prince laughed, excited. The shallow slice across his neck had healed, leaving only a smudge of dark blood across his smooth skin. His power flooded from him, feeding back from the ground. Just as mine did.

He was also more powerful in the Evenfall dimension. As I'd expected.

Prince brought the back of my hand to his mouth.

Realizing his intent, I started to twist away, but the wound thankfully sealed over before he could taste my blood. Our mixed blood.

He gnashed his sharp teeth at me playfully. "Later, then. But first…"

Releasing my hand, he spun me by the wrist he still held, bringing the bone blade between us. Then he flicked it up and out with a deliberate motion.

The droplets of blood that still coated the blade splattered on the ground in front of us. I could feel the power combined in those tiny drops. Too much power to be used so frivolously—

A boom punched through our immediate surroundings, as if something had exploded beneath us, though the ground didn't move. It boxed my ears with invisible energy. Then that energy blasted through the wide valley before us. Somehow filling it, like a gigantic wave of sound and energy.

No.

A tsunami of power.

In the valley, the rocks…cracked. The ground heaved upward between the pools of rippling water, then crumbled.

I gasped.

I had assumed that the valley was filled with craggy rock formations of various sizes, just as I'd seen through the first doorway. But those weren't natural formations…

Energy writhed under my feet…under our feet. Denser and…wilder than before. Power awakened from just a few drops of our combined blood.

Prince could never have done this without another Adept strong enough, powerful enough to wear the reconstructed crown.

Without me.

I'd made a terrible mistake. Not in rescuing Ravine, but—

Prince, still holding me fast by my wrist, pulled me forward to the edge of the outcropping. Laughing, he thrust our linked hands over our heads.

Creatures were clawing their way free from the stone formations...hundreds of creatures of all shapes and sizes, filling the wide valley spread out before us. The closest were less than a dozen meters away. They'd been released from some sort of massive stasis spell, not rock or stone as I'd assumed.

The fae creatures were deadly. There was no other way to absorb their aspects quickly enough to assess the situation more accurately. All of them were armed, whether with claws and sharp teeth, or massive blades and axes primed with the energy that underpinned the dimension around me. To my far left, a mass of tiny winged creatures rose in a pretty spiral, glittering with magic that I didn't need to touch to know was poisonous. The pixie-like creatures then combined into three humanoid forms—white-haired, white-skinned, legs and arms far longer than their torsos. Beside them, six other creatures as large as oxen rose on thick legs, settling clubs the width of trees over their shoulders. Their mouths were tusked, their armored skin a deep charcoal.

Where the base of the outcropping met the valley floor, standing four rows deep and easily a dozen per row, armored soldiers gazed up at us. The stasis spell that had held them, had cloaked them, was reduced now to a fine gravel around their booted feet. Their skin color ranged from pale to dusky to charcoal, their eyes gleaming with magic in various hues of purple, from near-black violet to a lighter purple-gray. A few wore cloaks as Prince and I did, though nowhere near as long. They carried a range of weapons—broadswords, staffs, dual blades, axes. But I could feel the power that told me the bladed weapons were secondary to their magical abilities.

Mages.

Fae mages.

One figure, slightly taller than the others, stood at dead center, directly across from us. Dark hair flowed over his massive shoulders. Square jaw, piercing eyes. Black armor. He wielded a mace, but carried what I assumed were spells or potions attached to a bandolier across his chest.

A warlord, perhaps.

Prince's warlord.

Prince roared something in that other language, speaking too quickly for me to even attempt to translate it. Then he repeated himself in English, for my benefit. "Welcome your new high lady, Dusk! We have returned to you!"

The farthest reaches of the army looked as though they were still just breaking free of the stasis spell. But as one, every single creature before us thrust a limb or a weapon in the air and roared their response.

I had to stop this.

I had to stop this now.

The bone blade lengthened in my hand, thickening.

Prince released my wrist, settling his hand on my shoulder and smiling at me with utter satisfaction, with wicked glee.

Slowly, unobtrusively, I lowered the blade—more like a sword now—to my side.

Prince's gaze dropped to my mouth. He yanked me forward into his arms, his intent clear. To claim me in front of his army, his generals, his warlord.

No.

My army.

I twisted out of his hold, spinning around and back in the very same motion. Bending my knees slightly and angling my back foot for more leverage, I swung the sword forward, not even knowing what shape the bone blade had taken. Just knowing that it had responded to my need. That I'd run out of time to assess the situation.

There was no going back.

I brought the katana of white bone around with all my strength, all my power, and I sliced off Prince's head in a single blow.

The army filling the valley went utterly silent.

Contrary to the laws of physics, Prince's decapitated head spun upward even as blood spurted from his neck, splattering my face, neck, and chest.

His body fell.

I stepped to the side, katana held ready.

Stretching my free hand up, I watched his head spin. Just as every fae in the valley was watching.

The crown freed itself of his flesh.

The twin to the crown I still wore.

Then it fell, landing in my waiting hand.

Power boomed through the valley again, washing over the awaiting army, reverberating, then flooding back to me.

And I was once again *more*. More me.

Not wholly in my own skin...not wholly in control of my actions...

Or perhaps in complete control, as I'd never been before.

I placed Prince's crown on my own head, over the crown I already wore.

Energy writhed around me, searing my skin, taking sight and sound with it. That power melded the crowns into something new. Then all the power Prince had wielded in the Evenfall realm settled over me, layer after layer of *more*.

More of me.

More of who I was supposed to be. More, more…

My sight cleared, my gaze settling on the impossibly silent army stretched out across the valley before me. My golden cloak undulated around me as pure power. The crown had burrowed into my skin, anchoring itself into my skull.

I raised my white-bone katana over my head. The golden runes etched across the blade were still stained with the blood of the former high lord of Evenfall.

I roared. A dragon battle cry.

The fae army roared back in kind.

They stomped. They chanted. My name.

Over and over again.

Dusk! Dusk! Dusk!

I wasn't just a high lady, or even a princess or queen.

I was the Empress of the Evenfall realm.

Directed by the fae I'd dubbed the warlord, my army gathered itself into what I took to be specific legions, perhaps readying themselves for inspection. I still stood on the outcropping, perched above the valley with the open doorway at my back. Adjusting to the sheer weight of the power I now wore.

I wasn't certain if time ran at the same rate in the Evenfall realm, but being in stasis for centuries as they were reckoned on Earth had to come with a certain amount of toll.

Magenta flowers bloomed from Prince's body and his decapitated head. They bore spiked petals of deep pink streaked with gold, the blooms resembling one of the rare orchids that Morgan had somehow charmed from the gnome…

Morgan.

Oh, gods. The death goddess was only bound to the tower for the duration of my life. And…and was I actually living if I wasn't in the same dimension?

Would she know?

Would I have severed that binding, that connection, just by crossing through into Evenfall? Or even when I'd taken on the mantle of—

"A mantle…" I whispered.

Dragons took on mantles of power when they became guardians. Was that why this me, this *more*, felt so right? Except I wasn't that kind of dragon…

I gathered my golden cloak in one hand, realizing for the first time that I was now wearing a hard leather vest and bracers. Bronzed armor.

My backpack was gone.

I pressed my hand to my stomach, feeling an answering pulse of power.

Infinity.

I had…I'd absorbed…I'd somehow inadvertently transformed my personal archive into armor. To protect myself.

Something cracked in my chest under an onslaught of horrifying, hate-filled, knee-weakening grief.

I had destroyed Infinity. And possibly loosed a death goddess on the children. On Brady and Erin. On Sparkle and the gnome.

On Dublin.

Prince's body suddenly crumpled under the weight of the alien orchids, disappearing under that onslaught of nature.

No. Not nature.

My magic.

That was how my magic manifested in the Evenfall dimension. At least one particular aspect of my power. I could feel its ongoing connection to me.

I took a steadying breath, noting that a number of the mages had gathered into a tight knot. Generals perhaps? Or whatever the fae equivalent was? They were deep in conversation around the black-armored warlord, who was watching me closely. Assessing me, while the others murmured in venomous undertones in a language I still hadn't had the time to grasp.

They were urging the warlord to challenge me.

It only made sense.

And, compelled to keep my crown, I would kill him. I would kill them all. Just as I'd killed Prince and stolen his power. To protect my loved ones on Earth.

Even from myself.

I was that sort of being now.

A murderer.

And I would do it again. I would still do my duty.

I pinned my gaze to the black-armored warlord, and he stilled. The katana shifted in my hand, widening slightly even as the tip elongated and sharpened along one edge. The blood-smeared golden runes that decorated white bone pulsed with power. My power.

I tapped the butt end of what was now a bladed staff to the rocky ground, just once. A brisk breeze flooded the valley in response, sweeping away all that remained of Brendan Prince. The magenta orchids spun outward off the outcropping, raining all over the tightly grouped armored mages.

A single orchid settled on the warlord's shoulder. The half-dozen generals who'd gathered around him stepped away.

He grinned up at me, his expression feral and admiring.

I had an inkling that I could have simply ordered the entire army to disband. But that they might also have been under my protection...from those 'others' who Prince had mentioned might feel my arrival in Evenfall.

I needed to gather more information. But before I could focus myself, energy shifted behind me.

I had left the doorway open.

I spun to confront whatever threat was coming my way.

Kellan stood framed within the doorway between the world and Evenfall.

With Sisu perched on his shoulder.

The shapeshifter, in human form and fully clothed, stepped over the threshold. The energy underpinning Evenfall rose to meet his first footfall. It grabbed hold, streaking up his leg and into his torso. His own magic responded. Expanding, flourishing, shredding through his sweatpants and T-shirt, writhing and roiling over him.

He transformed under the onslaught.

And not into a wolf.

Not even into his warrior form.

No.

Kellan Conall wasn't a werewolf.

He wasn't even a shapeshifter who could assume another animal form.

At least not in the Evenfall realm.

He broadened, stretched. Claws sprouted from his now-massive feet and hands as bulky gray armor replaced his human skin. Horns had sprung forward from his temples, thick, wickedly pointed, and curled forward to protect the sides of his head. His visage remained almost human in his new form. He was simply twice as large as any human, Adept or otherwise, I'd ever seen.

Under a thick, wide brow, the golden-green of Kellan's magic shone from his wide-set eyes.

Sisu shrieked. In utter delight.

Shining like the bright star he always was to my eyes, my baby brother wrapped a hand around one of Kellan's horns, unable to actually close his fingers around it.

And he laughed. "Dusk! Look at Kellan!"

"I see," I murmured. My face flushed, my heart pounding. But not with fear.

Kellan chuckled, striding toward me. Every aspect of him was now a deep, dark promise of utter annihilation.

But not for Sisu.

Not for me.

Magic glinted along two thin lines stretching out behind Kellan and Sisu. Those threads ran through the darkness that shrouded the open dimensional doorway.

I traced the glimmer back, realizing that Kellan and Sisu had thin golden ropes tied around their wrists, anchoring them to their dimension.

Our dimension.

Because Kellan Conall wouldn't have brought my brother through without giving him a way back.

Power shifted around me as Kellan scanned the immediate area, then the valley behind me. His lip pulled back in a dark snarl. Sisu, still perched on his massive shoulder, grinned down at me.

Then Sisu's backpack tore open, and a winged creature climbed from it to perch on his shoulder. It stretched its long neck, sniffing the air. Flexible crystalline scales lined its body, refracting the light of the purple sky.

"Oh, hello!" Sisu said happily.

Surrounded by the magic of Evenfall, the golden egg so casually given to Sisu by his demigod father had hatched.

The creature might have been a wyvern in our world. A being of myth and legend. But as with Kellan, its form was different in Evenfall. It began to bulk up, spreading wings out behind Sisu's head. In mere moments, it was too large to perch even a single three-clawed foot on Sisu's shoulder, so it took to the air.

The crystal-scaled wyvern swooped overhead, scanning the valley just as Kellan had. Then, tucking in its thickly veined wings, it shot down, slamming into the ground to perch at the edge of the outcropping.

Its body was now the size of Kellan's SUV, its tail twice that long and lined with crystalline spikes.

The wyvern looked back at us and barked. Twice. A sharp question both times. Its blackened, front-facing eyes were iridescent. Flicking just the tip of its massive tail like a cat, it swung its sleek head back to survey the valley, standing guard.

I threw my head back and laughed. Kellan and Sisu joined me. The dark promise of Kellan's tone intertwined with the light sweetness of my brother's voice.

The army and its warlord stood ready in the valley. Wary. Watching us.

More exotic blossoms shifted around me in response to my laughter. They swirled gently in the sweetened air.

Yes. This was what I wanted.

This was who I wanted with me. By my side.

The bladed staff in one hand, I reached for Kellan, for Sisu, beckoning them forward. In response to my unvoiced intention, dark-brown roots to my immediate left sprang forth from the otherwise barren ground, twisting, twining around themselves.

"We came to get you," Sisu said. He was hanging forward off Kellan's horn with one hand, feet planted on his chest.

Kellan, glorious, intimidating, and huge, towered over me, bearing the weight of Sisu's magic without effort. He bared his teeth, snarling in agreement.

The flowers called forth by my laughter adhered to the thickening roots, slowly building, twining upward to form a column beside me, then flattening at around the height of my elbow.

"Come back with us, Dusk," Kellan rumbled, eyeing the roots and blossoms darkly. His Irish accent was thick and lyrical in his Evenfall beast form.

"Back?" I echoed, shivering as the magic radiating from Kellan kissed my face, neck, and collarbone. My golden cloak undulated around me, reaching around Kellan's legs and hips as I pulled more and more power to me, feeding whatever my magic was building. Whatever my power had heard in my unvoiced intention.

My intent to stay.

"Home," Kellan said, leaning forward so he could meet my gaze as he did. To impress upon me how serious he was. "Where you belong."

I laughed, breathy and light-headed from all the magic I held, all the power I could wield in Evenfall.

Because now that Kellan had come, had brought Sisu with him, why would I go back? If they were with me, why would I give up everything else?

The roots began to snap and curl on the top of the column, weaving and folding—until they formed what appeared to be a crown of jagged wood and dark blossoms.

A crown for my chosen one.

I looked from that crown to Kellan. "We could be…wild here. Unfettered. Ourselves."

"Yes," he said, acknowledging and echoing the ache in my chest. The need.

I waited. The moment stretching between us was dark and sweet, thick with power and tingling with energy. With anticipation and desire, and an expanded sense of that rightness, of that reflection of self, that had passed between Kellan and me twice before.

Kellan knelt down, bringing Sisu with him so that their heads were almost even with mine.

A thrill ran through me. I reached for the dark crown, intending to set it on Kellan's head. But Sisu touched my cheek, pulling my attention to him.

He was so golden. A breathtaking beacon of lightness. "Dusk," he said, "you promised to come home. Always."

I had promised, but…

"We could make a new home here," I said earnestly. "You, me, and Kellan. And the wyvern!" I laughed again, releasing more and more power only to have it cycle right back into me. I swayed, momentarily heady with it.

Kellan set a huge hand on my hip, steadying me. His touch was grounding.

I cupped his enormous face in my hands. His skin was searingly hot. "No one could tell us what to do," I whispered. "There would be no lies. No…"

My voice trailed off.

There would be no duty.

Except…

I didn't shirk my duty.

And I loved my work…my house…my life.

I glanced at the crown of roots and flowers, then back at Kellan. "Would you stay?" I whispered, already knowing I couldn't, I shouldn't, ask it of him, of Sisu. "If I asked?"

"Always," he said, his voice a deep rumble full of every promise we wanted to make to each other.

I looked to Sisu. He reached up and placed his fingertips on my crown. I threaded my fingers through his and lifted the crown from my head. It came easily, effortlessly, though I knew that anyone else, anyone but Sisu, would have had to kill me to remove it.

Kellan's crown crumbled.

He sighed. A deep, melancholy sound that echoed the confusing, roiling emotion in my own chest.

In the valley, the mages began to attack one another.

In an instant.

They turned against each other, fighting for dominance. Then one of them would eventually win—the warlord, no doubt—and the violence would spill into our dimension.

The wyvern surveyed it all, head lowered and bright eyes gleaming with satisfaction.

"I have to seal the doorway from this side," I said, looking back at the darkened archway.

"No," Kellan growled. "You'll seal it from the side on which you belong."

"But—"

"No," Kellan snarled. His hot breath and a punch of his magic danced across my skin. "I'll carry you out if I have to."

My lip curled. My hand tightened on the crown. He thought he could move me against my will, did he? Well, I would—

Sisu climbed off Kellan's shoulder. And the moment his feet touched the ground and all the power that underpinned it, fear streaked through me so intensely that my knees weakened.

Sisu shouldn't have been in Evenfall. I could barely handle the onslaught of power, meaning my baby brother might well get swallowed up. He could become lost, and—

I snarled right in Kellan's face. Well, the middle of his chest. He was annoyingly tall in his current form.

"Yeah, yeah," he grumbled. "I knew what I was doing."

Sisu curled his hand around mine, then grabbed Kellan's forefinger with the other. Tugging on us firmly, he turned us back toward the doorway to our dimension.

With a sharp bark, the wyvern awkwardly tumbled after us. Unwieldy running on two legs, it shrank until it was small enough to alight on Sisu's shoulder again, claws digging into my brother's torn backpack.

Hand in hand, Kellan, Sisu, and I crossed through the dimensional doorway.

Because Kellan was right.

No other person could have called me back. No other bond was strong enough.

But for Sisu, I would set a crown aside. For Sisu, I would walk away from more power than I would ever wield again. For Sisu, I would abandon an entire dimension.

For Sisu, I would be just a sister.

Just Dusk.

CHAPTER ELEVEN

As I CROSSED THROUGH THE DOORWAY BACK INTO THE catacombs under Christ Church Cathedral, a cascade of power fell away behind me, leeched from me into Evenfall. For a moment, the golden cloak stretched between me and the open archway. Then it tugged free from my shoulders, dissipating.

The armor I'd subconsciously somehow formed out of Infinity constricted across my chest, then abruptly released.

Glass tinkling against stone drew my attention to my left. Sisu, still holding my hand, was gazing up at me sadly. The wyvern was gone, having shed a few crystalline scales.

But before I could speak, Kellan inhaled sharply, stumbling a step. He'd transformed back into his human form, somehow managing to not drop Sisu's hand in the process. Chest heaving—and completely naked—he met my gaze over Sisu's head.

I smiled shakily.

"Thank the fuck," Ravine groaned. Looking completely drained, the dark-haired witch was kneeling on the stone floor across from the dimensional doorway. The thin threads of gold secured to Sisu's and Kellan's wrists stretched back to her. The slack had coiled on the stone and across her knees, but ultimately led to her intricate Celtic-inspired cuffs—which had been reduced to a single thin bracelet on each wrist.

Her magic was so drained that I could barely pick up even a hint of it, including the power she must have channeled through those golden threads.

Sisu released my hand and Kellan's, skipping forward and flinging his arms around Ravine's neck. "I got them both," he whispered loudly. "Like you told me."

Kellan and I exchanged another glance. He grimaced ruefully.

He had been a moment away from accepting that crown.

A moment away from staying with me in Evenfall.

Poor Sisu.

Only five years old and having to drag his elders back from…from…

I closed my eyes, swaying, exhausted from having all that power stripped away. But also…also from having that life ripped away. A life with Kellan, unfettered and—

"Put on some fecking clothes, Kell," Ravine groused. She was holding onto Sisu like he might have been the only thing holding her upright. "You know I don't love visiting what I can't have."

Chuckling tiredly, Kellan crossed to a pile of clothing in the corner. Sweats. He must have grabbed an extra set from his SUV when he'd collected Sisu.

Suddenly remembering, I pressed my hand to my chest. I was wearing my dragon leathers again. With my backpack secure on my back. Relief flooded through me as Infinity hummed gently in response to my spike in anxiety. My bone blade was back in my leathers' built-in sheath, though I didn't remember putting it there.

I still clutched the now-doubled crown in my hand.

The doubled crown.

I spun to the still-open doorway.

Two crowns had to be better than one, right?

"Yes." Ravine sighed. "Let's close that." Then she abruptly burst into tears. Violent, ragged, heart-wrenching tears.

I reached for her, but she waved me off. "The creepy open doorway, Dusk. Then me."

My heart constricted in my chest as Ravine continued sobbing, holding onto Sisu as he tried to soothe her. Kellan finished tugging on a T-shirt, then stepped closer to press his hand to the metal mage's head. She hooked an arm around his leg but continued to cry.

I kneeled before the doorway, unable to see anything through it, but knowing that a battle to command an army was still unfolding on the other side. Crystal scales the size of my thumbnail were scattered on the stone floor.

Following some instinct to do so, I carefully brushed the sharp-edged scales into a ragged line. Then I set the crown down on the stone floor at what I roughly deemed the center point of the archway. Nine scales made for an odd number, so I carefully plucked one from the right side of the crown, tucking it into my pocket. For Sisu.

That left four on either side. Eight total. A lucky number. Or Infinity. Depending on interpretation.

Then I contemplated cutting the combined crown into pieces, as Suanmi had done centuries ago.

But I thought about the flowers that had manifested in Evenfall, and the flora that my magic brought me to construct wards, and I decided I didn't want to dilute the power contained in the doubled crown. Suanmi had had only one crown when she sealed the doorway the first time, but with two—

I could still feel Brendan Prince's blood cooling on my skin.

I swallowed, swaying before I caught myself.

I wiped my hand across my forehead. It came away clean.

"Dusk?" Kellan asked softly over Ravine's shaky breaths.

I stiffened my shoulders, forcing myself to close my eyes and focus on nothing but the task before me. I pressed all ten of my fingertips to the points of the crown, which were actually sharp enough to break through my skin. It was my blood that had roused Prince's army. Well, mine and his combined. And since I would always have his blood on my hands, and I needed all the power I could muster, I allowed those tiny wounds to well, adding a thick drop to each point of the crown.

Then I shoved all other thoughts, all self-recrimination, away.

And I just settled.

I let my power pour into the crown, visualizing that magic spreading out from the relic and across the stone threshold to pick up the crystalline scales. Then I coaxed those ropes of energy to twist and twine up the sides of the doorway, as the roots had in Evenfall. Tightening intricate knots around the eight wyvern scales at even intervals, the ropes of power met overhead at the highest point of the archway. I knotted them over and over, picturing Ravine's ever-changing Celtic-inspired cuffs in my mind. Recalling all the times I'd tried to sketch them from memory.

I poured more and more of my magic into the working, allowing pure intent to filter through me now—the intent to close, to seal, to protect.

The crown melded with the stone floor under the pressure of my fingers, flattening and smoothing until my palms were pressed to the floor.

I pulled back on my magic. And found that there was hardly anything left.

I had drained myself.

For the first time in my life.

My transformation in Evenfall, having that power stripped away, and then channeling the last of my reserves into sealing the dimensional doorway had taken almost everything from me.

And I still wasn't certain it was going to be enough.

I opened my eyes.

A radiant golden design—a series of interlocking knots with a glimmering wyvern scale in the center of each—stretched across the stone floor, arcing up and across the wall without a single break. The outline of the double crown was etched into the stone in one misshapen, but still continuous ring.

As I watched, the golden glow faded from the archway until the pattern was barely discernible from the stone itself.

The doorway to the Evenfall realm had been sealed.

"Impressive," Ravine murmured.

"Dusk is powerful," Sisu said brightly. "Mom and Papa both say so."

Kellan stepped up beside me, pressing his hand against the wall and tilting his head as if listening. "You closed it permanently?" he asked in a whisper.

"I doubt it." I sighed, pivoting to look at Ravine and Sisu. Because honestly, I wasn't quite ready to try standing up.

Ravine's eyes were red, her face puffy. "I'm so sorry," she whispered. "I...I thought I knew what I was doing."

"His enchantment was subtle."

She fisted her hands around the remains of her Celtic-inspired bands. She was partway through winding the threads she'd used to anchor Sisu and Kellan into balls. "He couldn't grab hold of you."

"Our magic is different," I said gently.

She shook her head. "Yes, I know. I'm just being...stupid."

Sisu stepped up to me, taking my face in his hands. His magic was still robust, warm and comforting. Stepping into Evenfall had completely stripped away Jiaotu's glamour.

"I would have missed you," he said far too seriously. But before I could answer, he asked tentatively, "Will you check my backpack?"

I nodded, and he spun around. The top of the pack was still torn open from when the wyvern had escaped from it in Evenfall. So not everything that underwent a transformation in that realm automatically reversed itself.

Me, for example.

I was a murderer now. I had judged Brendan Prince and factored his life against all the lives he would destroy if he unleashed his army.

"Dusk?" Sisu's voice was strained. He was taking my silence badly.

I thrust my arm into his pack and wrapped my fingers around the golden egg, still intact. Plastering on a smile, I held the egg out to Sisu.

A wide grin swamped his face. He cupped the egg in both hands, practically pressing his nose to it. "You are so beautiful," he whispered to it. "And so fierce!"

I pulled the crystalline scale out of my pocket, placed it in my palm, and showed it to my brother. "I used the other scales to seal the doorway. Careful, it's sharp."

He blinked at the scale, then nodded as if I'd bequeathed him something epically profound. A holy relic. "Maybe Gee would like it?"

I laughed quietly. "It's not an egg to hatch."

No. My baby brother was already cradling and petting a golden egg that contained a potentially vicious creature. A creature that I would have thought was extinct had I not seen it with my own eyes.

"Oh!" Sisu cried. "For Sparkle. Like a housewarming gift."

"Okay." I slid the scale back in my pocket.

Sisu passed me the wyvern egg, and I tucked it into his backpack for him. He spun around, grinning at an exhausted-looking Kellan and a puffy-eyed, drained Ravine. "Think of the story we have to tell now!"

"That's what I'm worried about," Ravine muttered.

Sisu frowned at her. "You don't like being a hero?" He crouched down, hands on his knees, his gaze on the thin golden thread that Ravine was finishing up winding into tight balls. "Dusk will have a lot of questions about what spells you used to anchor us." He pointed, grinning madly at the metal mage's all-but-ruined bracelets. "And Kellan said you were hurt!"

Ravine offered him a shaky grin, then looked at me.

I nodded. "Evenfall could have swallowed all three of us. Once he got wind of the crown piece resurfacing, Prince was going to get that door open. No matter what he had to do, or who he had to use."

Ravine sighed raggedly, swallowing harshly. "It's just...I took him home, Dusk. And I...I know that..."

She flicked her gaze to Sisu, editing herself. "Being…intimate can make you more susceptible to—"

"Enough," Kellan said abruptly. Stepping closer, he swept Ravine up in his arms in the same motion.

She squeaked, grabbing hold of his neck.

He turned to look at me. "To Wilding Manor?"

Sisu reached for me. I actually needed his help to get to my feet. "Yes. All of us."

"We're going to run out of mattresses," Sisu said. "I told you we needed at least one for each room. That's fifteen, not five. Just counting upstairs."

Kellan flashed me a grin.

I laughed quietly, my legs starting to feel stronger as we traversed the narrow, badly lit corridors and found our way out of the catacombs.

The sky was in the process of lightening with the first hints of dawn as we shut the door at the bottom of the hidden staircase behind us. More time had passed in Evenfall than I'd realized.

Terror suddenly streaked through me—completely appropriate but utterly mistimed—as I thought about what I'd almost done. What I'd almost sacrificed. I tightened my hold on Sisu's hand, then immediately softened my grip.

I would never again question how easily an archivist could slip away through dimensions or time. It was like the pure need to do so was wired into my genetics.

Sisu bumped his shoulder against my thigh, grinning up at me.

"My car…" Ravine murmured from behind us, still nestled in Kellan's arms.

"I had Gitta pick it up," Kellan said.

Ravine sighed. "Well, that ruined her night."

Kellan's tone flattened. "It was over long before. She was actually at Wilding Manor when I picked up Sisu, sleeping with the twins." He flicked his gaze to meet mine. "I didn't mention the doorway or why I'd come back for Sisu. To anyone."

I nodded, having already known that Kellan could keep secrets. But pleased that he was willing to protect mine.

Ravine sighed, still upset but seemingly not surprised. "It doesn't get any easier, does it?" she whispered. "Relationships..."

"I don't know," Kellan murmured. "Sometimes it might be exactly what you need it to be."

I could feel his gaze on me as we rounded the corner, and I smiled even though I wasn't completely certain I understood the undertones of their conversation—

Two dragons in full armor were blocking the side alley that led to the street beyond.

Suanmi. The fire breather. Guardian of Western Europe.

And a younger dark-haired dragon. Her ward, Drake.

Not a hint of magic emanated from either of them, but they didn't need it. Arrayed in skintight black dragon leathers and inscrutable expressions, they were intimidating enough.

A long katana was sheathed across Suanmi's back, her dark-brown hair cinched in a tight, sleek bun. A golden broadsword peeked over Drake's shoulder. A light breeze came out of nowhere to feather his nearly black hair away from his wide brow.

The doorway had drawn the guardian's attention.

I stumbled to a stop, feeling Kellan set Ravine on her feet behind me.

"Hey, Drake!" Sisu cried gleefully, cutting through all the layers of tension.

Drake offered my little brother a wide grin. "Sisu!"

Suanmi flicked a disapproving look at her ward. He lost the grin, but not the glint in his eye.

Silence stretched as Suanmi's dark-hazel gaze swept over us all. Her expression was remote. "You seem a little worse for wear, Dusk." Her smooth French accent was more pronounced. Deliberately, perhaps?

"Yes, guardian. I just spent some time in the Evenfall realm."

She sniffed. "How antiquated of you to call it that."

"Not I. Cadfael. The self-proclaimed High Lord of Evenfall. Also known as Brendan Prince."

Ravine stiffened. More accurately, what remained of her magic constricted around her.

Suanmi's eyes narrowed thoughtfully, then her lip curled. "There were two of them."

"Yes."

"How utterly despicable of him to sacrifice his mate to me," she snarled. "Then to run. To hide. The coward."

A shiver of dread ran up my spine, triggered by the guardian's blazing condemnation. My own reaction, not Infinity's. I swallowed. "Yes."

Tucked behind me, Ravine's magic relaxed, as if she'd been comforted by Suanmi's assessment of Prince.

Tension still radiated from Kellan.

"Explain." Suanmi sniffed offishly, her spike of ire as easily snuffed as it had been ignited.

"Prince pieced the broken crown back together and opened the doorway. I crossed through, killed him, took both crowns, and sealed the doorway with them."

Suanmi smirked, possibly a little pleased. "Permanently?"

"I'm not sure. I'm rather drained."

"Drake," Suanmi commanded.

The younger dragon immediately stepped forward, striding past us.

"Don't wander," Suanmi added.

He offered her a wink over his shoulder. She sniffed, tilting her chin dismissively.

He took off in a jog, disappearing almost instantly. I still couldn't track his magic.

"Shapeshifter," the fire breather purred, shifting her focus.

I swore, just for a heartbeat, that I saw licks of fire in her fixed gaze. Before I could check myself, I angled one shoulder just in front of Kellan, drawing Suanmi's attention.

She raised an eyebrow. "Introduce us, then."

I hesitated for long enough that I felt Sisu glance up at me. I rested my hand on his head and stepped to the side. "Kellan Conall, enforcer of the Conall pack, son of the alpha." I looked toward the fire breather. "Suanmi, guardian of Western Europe."

Suanmi's lip quirked. "He's with you, is he?"

"Yes."

"And me!" Sisu declared, grinning.

Suanmi laughed.

And just for a moment, the predawn world rumbled with her mirth.

Kellan pressed against me, as if fighting the instinct to grab me and run.

Then Sisu's bright laughter joined the guardian's, once again soothing the almost-smothering tension. The heightened awareness that the situation might tip over into unsalvageable before I could draw my next breath.

Suanmi smiled at my brother, the expression as warm as I'd ever seen on her. She beckoned to him. "Come, littlest one of us all. We have not properly met."

Littlest one of us all.

Did that mean that my brother was…?

Sisu stepped forward obligingly. Kellan tensed.

Suanmi's suddenly hard gaze settled on the shapeshifter pressed against my shoulder, not a hint of mirth in her expression. "I was acquainted with one of your ancestors, shifter." She curled her lip derisively. "But not for long."

Kellan went completely and utterly still.

The fire breather's cold gaze flicked to Ravine, and she added, "I'm not at all surprised to find you absconding with witches."

I deliberately shifted my feet, forcing Suanmi to acknowledge me. "Ravine Byrne, metal mage. Youngest child of Mesa Byrne, head of the coven and one of the Convocation."

Dismissing Ravine and me both, Suanmi's expression shifted from utterly detached to warm and welcoming again as she returned her attention to Sisu. "You look just like your grandfather Tien did when he was your age."

"Do I?" Sisu grinned up at her.

Kellan glanced at me, disconcerted.

Oh, yes. Lots of secrets were getting cracked wide open today. On top of the secrets already revealed.

Though Suanmi appeared to be in her midforties—younger even in the predawn light—she was actually over six hundred years old. Which made her knowing Sisu's grandfather at age five rather questionable.

"Grandpa Etienne," Sisu said excitedly, either ignoring all the tension in the alley or completely oblivious. "You know the rug in the nexus library, Dusk? Grandpa Tien collected dangerous objects for the treasure keeper, including the rug! Papa says it has a habit of getting out every fifty years or so. I was thinking that...maybe the rug would like to visit Wilding Manor next?"

That last bit came out in an explosive rush.

I shook my head at my baby brother—I really didn't need him freeing a magic carpet from the nexus library—but couldn't help but grin. And apparently, Jiaotu had been sharing stories with his son. I would need to ask for more details later. I was trying to piece Sisu's family tree together for him as an upcoming birthday present.

"Yes." Suanmi smiled gleefully. "A delightfully vicious thing, isn't it? It has a habit of getting bored and aligning itself to the most powerful Adepts it can find, who in turn grow rather possessive." Her gaze turned thoughtful. "That particular incident left a rather delectable scar on Tien's inner right—"

Drake appeared beside me.

Kellan flinched, then grabbed Ravine when she stumbled back.

"Sealed," Drake said. "I could sense a stroke of Dusk's potent power. And I saw the muted remains of a...spell?" He glanced at me questioningly.

I shrugged. Call it a spell or a casting or whatever, I worked my magic the way it worked.

Drake grinned at me. "I'm pretty certain the connection has been severed."

"Lovely," Suanmi said, holding her hand out to Sisu. "Come, escort me to Wilding Manor. Do you think it's too early to pick up croissants on the way?"

Ravine cleared her throat. "I can text my cousin. She owns Cove Cafe, and I'm sure she'd let us sneak a dozen before opening."

"Perfect," Suanmi purred. Golden shards of magic glinted in her eyes, highlighted by the rosy-hued light dawning over the city. "And some chocolate."

"For breakfast?" Sisu asked doubtfully.

Suanmi laughed, bright and chiming. More magic reverberated through the alley. "Of course, my littlest one."

Sisu grasped Suanmi's offered hand, and they headed toward the street. As the fire breather's front foot fell on the sidewalk, the muffled sounds of the slowly waking city filtered through the surrounding buildings. As though the guardian's mere presence muted the nonmagical world around us, with no obvious or overt magic needed.

Drake leaned over, trying to see the screen of Ravine's phone as she texted. She pressed it to her chest, then glared at him playfully.

He hit her with a high-wattage grin. She actually stumbled under this onslaught of charm and affability.

"You think your cousin has any cupcakes?" Drake asked.

Ravine blinked at him. "For breakfast?"

"Oh, yeah," he said. "Best time to eat cupcakes."

She swallowed, tearing her gaze away. "I'll ask."

"Perfect."

I darted after Suanmi and Sisu before they stepped completely out of sight. The others picked up their pace behind me.

"Now…" Suanmi said. "Tell me everything you and Dusk have been up to since coming to my city."

"We have a brownie now," Sisu said enthusiastically. "Her name is Sparkle Eventide."

"Well, it's about time." The guardian sniffed. "And my bedroom renovations?"

Sisu glanced over his shoulder, grinning back at us. "Kellan is overseeing that. He is brilliant with woodwork. And he has the coolest horns!"

"Oh," Suanmi said, not bothering to look back. "That's just fine, then."

"Horns?" Ravine murmured, darkly delighted but not bothering to look up from texting Cove.

Kellan's power tightened around him, his shoulders stiffening. Protectively, I thought. But, walking close enough that his shoulder occasionally brushed mine, he kept his gaze intently fixed ahead, on Suanmi and Sisu.

"The experience was rather transformational," I said, not looking at Kellan. "For all of us."

Ravine sighed sadly. "I'm so sorry."

"You said," Kellan rumbled. "We don't need to hear it again."

"How is it that you're an asshole even when you're trying to be nice?" Ravine snapped.

"I'm not trying to be nice," Kellan growled.

Drake chuckled.

I quashed an exhausted smile.

And then, with a quick detour to the cafe, we all went home to Wilding Manor.

CHAPTER TWELVE

I FOUND MYSELF AT THE BASE OF THE CENTRAL TOWER steps even before forming the intention of checking on Morgan. I was halfway up before I thought of a justification for my visit. It was the twenty-fourth—the day of Sisu's party, the afternoon tea and gift exchange he'd sprung on me the night of the solstice celebration. I had all but forgotten, but he hadn't.

We had people coming over for tea and cookies and to open presents. So I needed to double-check that my crossing through into Evenfall hadn't weakened the wards.

But that wasn't why I stepped inside the room at the top of the tower. The wards were perfectly fine. I'd been able to feel that they were as solid as always the moment I'd stepped onto the property that morning, with Suanmi, Drake, and everyone else following in my wake. That wasn't why I pressed against the heavy wooden door, allowing my head to fall back and my eyes to close under the alert gaze of the death goddess lounging in her chair—her throne, so cloaked in power that the wood and brocade had blackened.

She withstood the silence for the space of only three full, deep breaths. "What? No tea and cookies?"

I was worrying Morgan.

She hid it well, but I could hear it in her clipped words. With an internal sigh—at myself—I pushed away from the door and wandered over to the north-facing window she favored. For the orchids, but also for its view of the forest and the open lawn where Sisu, Neve, and Lile often played or trained.

"Did you…" I hesitated. I wasn't friends with the death goddess. I couldn't be. That wasn't my role in our relationship. I leaned over, smelling the vanilla-scented orchid and allowing it to steady me.

"If you're here to kill me," Morgan said stiffly, "just do it."

I whirled around, blinking at her.

She sniffed, tossing the well-worn paperback she'd been reading to the floor. It was a space opera judging by the image of a moon, a spaceship, and the figure of a weapon-toting woman on the cover.

"You think I would install you in this tower, at great risk to myself and my brother, just to kill you?" A sudden, completely irrational anger flashed through me, conveniently distracting me from all the other irrational emotions I'd been wallowing in since returning from the cathedral.

We'd lost all of Wednesday to the Evenfall realm, stepping out into the Thursday dawn. After an impromptu breakfast with the guardian and Drake, after which both departed, Ravine and I had pretty much slept through the entire day. Gitta and Kellan had taken the twins home by the time I woke in the late afternoon. Ravine stayed for dinner, then slipped away afterward, pale and quiet, though her magic was slowly reasserting itself. We hadn't talked about what had happened.

Morgan gazed at me steadily. The silver of the power that marked her as some sort of divinity was still just a thin ring around her black irises. "You've removed your glamour," she said, as if that was an answer to my question. "You have all your delightfully pungent power tucked away this afternoon, but early yesterday…"

"…you felt something different through the bond?"

She arched a thin black eyebrow. "The tie that binds my will to yours, you mean?"

"Please," I scoffed. "Would you rather I stuffed you back in your amulet?"

Her nostrils flared. "A cage is a cage."

Shaking my head, I crossed to the door. I had no idea why I'd come up in the first place. Seeking to…what? Commiserate? Soothe my ruffled feathers? I had done what I needed to do.

I should have known what Prince was the moment I shook his hand. He shouldn't have gotten the other two crown pieces.

But I hadn't really believed in the fae, had I?

Just like I hadn't really believed in the death goddess now installed in my central tower. Until it was almost too late.

I was arrogant. Blinded by my own preconceived notions. And because of that, I'd almost…

I'd almost stayed in Evenfall. Abandoning Sisu, and triggering a cascade of—

"So…not an execution," Morgan said.

I shook my head to clear it, keeping my back to the death goddess. "What will you do? When I die and the binding ceases to be?" I turned to look at her. "Would you have slaughtered the children yesterday morning?"

The muscles in her face jerked. She slammed her hands against the arms of her chair and shoved herself to her feet. "Because that is all I am? Death?"

She gathered herself, perhaps realizing how very human she was acting. Then, with her red dress once again undulating prettily around her ankles, she crossed to the north-facing window.

I leaned back against the door again. But I was watching the death goddess this time.

Morgan tucked the tips of her blackened fingers into the nearest pot. The gesture was seemingly unconscious, as her attention remained fixed out the deep-sill window.

"Do you think it will snow?" I asked, echoing her question from before...before I'd almost abandoned everything. Including myself.

Her eyes flicked to me, though she didn't turn her head. She didn't answer. Which was fine, because I was just trying to get us back to wherever we had been...before.

"I killed a high lord of the Evenfall realm last night," I murmured.

"Did he give you another option?" the death goddess asked.

"Such as?"

She shrugged. "Worshipping your every footstep."

A joke.

I was fairly certain.

"He gave me a massive army and an entire realm to rule. Though it was possible I would have needed to conquer it first. There was some talk of 'others.' "

That got Morgan's attention. She eyed me for a moment, then snorted. "But your duty won out."

"Yes."

"And what did the high lord plan to do with the army?"

"Invade our dimension."

"Which the guardians would never have allowed."

"No."

"So...no loss, then."

It was just that simple for her.

"I could have stayed," I whispered, revealing the dark dream I'd been harboring in my heart. "I was incredibly powerful there. More so after taking on the high lord's mantle. And it was...wild and free..."

"No rules. No duties tying you to little brothers or death goddesses."

"Yes."

"You would have been bored out of your mind within days."

I laughed involuntarily. The sound harsh but true. And then I realized how right she was.

How sad was that? That in this moment, Morgan knew me better than I did myself?

"I can still feel his blood splattered across my face...my neck..." I said, speaking mostly to myself.

"Your first kill?"

"You know it was."

Morgan sniffed. "I am proof that if there was another way, you would have taken it."

I blinked at her. Was that why I'd been drawn to the tower? To remind myself of—

"Revel in that feeling, my golden jailer." She flashed a disturbingly gleeful smile at me. "It's your power to absorb, to harness now. Take it as your due."

I shook my head at her.

She chuckled darkly, swinging her attention back to the window. "If it snows..." Her tone was oddly muted, vulnerable. "I'd like to go for a walk on the grounds." She set her silver-ringed, black-eyed gaze on me. "I've never felt snow on my skin." She sniffed dismissively, as if it really meant nothing to her. "I presume I will loathe the experience."

"And how will we walk without you attempting to subvert the situation?"

"You will wear the amulet." Her tone was detached, as if handing the amulet over to me—the means with which to control her—meant nothing.

That gave me pause. I watched her for a moment, then changed the subject. "Have you met Sparkle?"

"Sparkle? What a dreadful name."

"Sisu picked it."

"Oh, well. I'm sure it's…fine, then."

I smirked. Morgan the death goddess had a soft spot for Sisu. That didn't mean I even remotely trusted her around him. But it was oddly sweet.

"Sparkle?" she prompted, regaining her imperious tone. "Another bedraggled creature you've doomed to a life in chains under the pretense of rescuing them?"

Oh, yes. Morgan didn't like appearing at all softhearted.

"Sparkle Eventide," I said.

The brownie, still bedecked in gold brocade, appeared at the utterance of her full name. She stood to the side of the room's second chair, her large hands folded neatly and her head tilted toward me. Her dark eyes were pinned on Morgan, though.

"This is Morgan," I said.

"Yes, mistress." Sparkle wore a brooch fashioned from the crystalline wyvern scale that Sisu had given to her. It glistened with magic.

"Dusk," I reminded Sparkle gently.

She didn't respond or look away from Morgan, whose own gaze was locked to the brownie's. I ignored the staring contest.

"Sparkle understands that she doesn't answer to you, Morgan. She doesn't serve you."

Morgan sniffed. "I have the house." She flicked her fingers toward Sparkle. "What need have I of another servant?"

"Sparkle is a brownie. She has claimed Wilding Manor as her territory."

Morgan narrowed her eyes.

My lip twitched. The death goddess couldn't feel Sparkle's magic. She'd had no idea that the brownie had even been in the house.

Well, this was going to be interesting.

"I must return to the kitchens, Mistress Dusk," Sparkle said. "Master Sisu is expecting guests at any moment."

"Thank you." I didn't correct her again on the titles. If she needed to define Sisu and me in a certain way for her own comfort, it wouldn't be fair to force her to stop.

Sparkle disappeared without even a whisper of magic.

"You get used to it," I said.

Morgan pinned me with an utterly disinterested gaze—an expression that I was coming to understand meant she was anything but disinterested.

Was it odd that I was beginning to be able to read her?

"You are more than simply death," I said quietly.

Morgan turned away. "Your beautiful brute is here."

I'd felt Kellan cross through the gate minutes earlier, but she must have picked up the warm greeting the house had given him when he crossed the threshold.

"When it snows, we will go for a walk."

Morgan's back stiffened. "That will do."

Kellan was perched in the deep stone sill of a window halfway down the tower stairs. His head resting back, eyes closed. He was wearing dress pants and a teal-blue cabled sweater that clung to his upper body as if were sentient enough to adore him. The color was striking against his light-brown skin.

But that wasn't what stopped me in my tracks. That wasn't what stopped my heart, then caused it to beat erratically.

Kellan was holding Infinity on his bent knee. His hand spanned the entire front cover.

"I couldn't find you," he murmured without opening his eyes. "Your scent just stopped."

I didn't answer. I couldn't answer. My voice and everything I wanted to blurt, to shout, was literally clogging up my throat.

He was touching Infinity.

No one could touch my personal archive. Not Sisu, not my mother. Jiaotu was the only other person who I'd ever seen do so, either because he was a guardian dragon or because he'd given me Infinity in the first place. Not that I'd known that at the time.

Kellan's eyes cracked open slightly, gazing up to where I'd paused just above him along the twist of the stairs. His golden-green magic gleamed from his eyes for a moment as he triggered some aspect of it. "Dusk?"

I opened my mouth, then closed it.

He frowned, straightening but not standing.

"Should I...should I not have looked for you?"

I managed to shake my head. To raise my hand and point. At Infinity.

Kellan's expression grew concerned, confused. He glanced down at my personal archive. "Yeah, I thought that odd. It was here." He stood, gesturing to the stairs in the same motion. "Like you dropped it on your way up. I didn't think...I thought you wouldn't want its pages to get..." He trailed off. "I've done something wrong."

I managed to make it down a couple more steps until I was standing only one step up from the small landing before the window. I'd left Infinity in my room. On my bedside table. So had my personal archive tried to follow me and not been able to get through the tower wards?

I resisted the urge to snatch it from Kellan. Because even if Infinity had somehow been trying to join me, he still shouldn't have been able to pick the archive up.

"Dusk," he grumbled gruffly, covering his confusion, "you're worrying me now."

I shook my head, running through everything he'd said. He'd been looking for me...unable to follow my scent...then had spotted Infinity on the stairs...

"The house must mask my scent," I said, my voice a little thin. "When I visit Morgan..." But then what? Infinity had decided to show Kellan where I was?

"The death goddess."

I huffed. "She's not a goddess, Kellan."

I closed the space between us, touching the corner of Infinity but not trying to take it. My personal archive hummed under my caress.

Kellan stiffened, loosening his hold.

I took Infinity from him, brushing my fingers over the cover. "What does it look like to you?"

"Infinity?" he asked, obviously having picked up the fact that I'd named what likely appeared to simply be a magical book to his eyes. "Bronzed, aged leather.

Metal corners. Gold runes of some sort in a vaguely oval shape, but pointed at the top and bottom."

The power contained in Infinity shifted. A single golden eye with a vertical pupil opened, then winked. At Kellan, not me.

He grumbled, slightly disconcerted.

"Did you feel compelled to pick Infinity up?" I asked, trying to sound casual.

"I just didn't think you'd want it lying there," Kellan said stiffly.

My bloody archive was... flirting?

I looked up at Kellan, finally meeting his gaze.

And, of course, we stared at each other for a bit. Just breathing, with the silent but warm press of the house around us.

Kellan smiled. Then he held up a folded piece of paper between his first two fingers. "Found this," he said quietly. "Almost put it through the wash."

The paper was the same color and thickness as Infinity's pages, specifically the page I'd torn from my archive to use the unlock rune.

"I grabbed it before I came through to get you with Sisu. Tucked it in the pocket of my backup sweats just in case you..." He trailed off, swallowing. "Are you okay, Dusk?"

"Did you feel compelled to do that as well?"

"I can do things just because I want to do them, Dusk."

I allowed Infinity to unfold in my hand. It opened to reveal the ragged edge of a torn page as my personal archive anticipated my unvoiced request.

Kellan unfolded the page he held. The word 'Unlock' was still printed across it. He set the page within Infinity, roughly lining up the torn edges.

Energy shifted the moment he let go. Infinity's power unfurled from the binding to reclaim the page I'd ripped from it. To heal the wound I'd knowingly inflicted.

Because I'd needed to. Because I really hadn't had any other choice. Just as I hadn't with Prince.

The reattached page looked perfect. The word 'unlock' slowly faded, absorbed into Infinity.

"You would have snapped Brendan Prince's neck," I murmured, not looking at Kellan. "Without any hesitation."

Kellan shifted thoughtfully. "After seeing that fucking army? Yeah, I would have. I'm sorry it fell to you."

I met his intense green-gold gaze. "I think that...magic was different in Evenfall."

He cleared his throat, obviously not ready to broach just one of the many conversations we needed to have. But I wasn't interested in secrets. Not yet, at least.

"Do you believe in fated mates?" I blurted.

Kellan raised his eyebrows, clearly confused by the change of subject.

I pushed forward before he could respond. "I think...in Evenfall...in that magic...fated mates might not just be a story."

He nodded. "I agree."

I laughed, feeling a little breathless as I dropped my gaze to Infinity. Closing it, I tucked it next to my chest.

Kellan tilted his head, lowering his voice though no one else was nearby. "Is the book one of your secrets?"

"No...I mean..."

He held up his hand. "I'm not prying. Not pushing."

I shook my head. "You shouldn't be able to touch it. That's all. But personal archives are...adaptable. Changeable. I have no idea what bringing Infinity into

Evenfall might have done to it." I flushed. "I, um...I think it might be trying to woo you. To flirt."

Kellan's eyebrows shot up.

"It's tied to me," I added hurriedly. "It's an archivist thing."

Kellan's magic sparked in his eyes, and a slight smile curled his lips. "Woo me. Because it's tied to you?"

"Maybe." I shrugged, feigning indifference. "Maybe Infinity knew you had the torn page and was encouraging you to give it back."

Kellan flashed an amused grin that didn't stick. His expression became serious. Almost unyielding. He brushed his fingers over the back of the hand I had curled around Infinity. My personal archive hummed again, exceedingly satisfied. The sensation was strong enough that I wondered if it was actually audible.

"I would have you know me," Kellan said gruffly. "I would know you."

My heart rate ramped up. Again.

Kellan had brought me back from Evenfall, though I knew that he would have stayed in that wild world with me. And with Sisu. The shifter would have stood at my side, accepting a crown and commanding an army. And we would have fit. We would have been wild, unhindered, unfettered, together. Free to indulge that part of our natures.

Kellan rubbed his thumb across the back of my hand. "And not because of some amped-up magical connection we felt in the Evenfall dimension," he said, as if heading off an argument I hadn't even thought to make. Well, not yet.

Clever shapeshifter.

I opened my mouth, realizing that I wanted to tell him everything. Who I was. What I was. Even though

I already knew that Kellan and I might have lost our chance to be together, to forge our own path.

But instead of sharing the rush of truths tickling my tongue, I leaned forward. Pleased that standing a step up from Kellan evened up our heights, I threaded my fingers through his thick hair, brushing my lips against his.

His eyes closed. A soft sigh exploded against my mouth, breathing a touch of his magic across my skin. He deepened the kiss.

Warmth and energy shifted between us. Then he was pulling me against him until our bodies aligned. I wrapped my arms around him, holding Infinity pressed against his shoulder. He captured the back of my neck, cradling my head.

I flicked my tongue against his lips, and he opened his mouth, inviting me within. I moaned, tangling my tongue with his. His hand on the small of my back tightened, pressing me against him until there was no room between us.

His magic was intoxicating. And I'd destroyed Jiaotu's glamour. Kellan could see all of me now, taste and feel all of me.

And I wanted that.

I wanted him to know me. I wanted to know him.

I slid my hand under Kellan's sweater, seeking skin contact. Then suddenly felt eyes on me, on us. I went still.

Kellan stiffened as well.

Still embraced, we looked over to find my brother perched in the windowsill. Sisu giggled madly, then struck one of his gargoyle poses. But he was so amused that he'd managed to sneak up on us—with the help of the house, no doubt—that he couldn't hold it.

Sighing, I stepped away from Kellan.

My brother launched himself at me without warning. I caught him, as always, but stumbled a little, hitting my back against the wall to do so. Thankfully, I managed to keep hold of Infinity. Sisu wrapped himself around me, pressing his mouth against my cheek and blowing hard.

He dissolved into more giggles, then wiggled out of my hold and took off down the stairs. "You have to come see what Sparkle did for the party."

I wiped my brother's splattered spit off my cheek.

Kellan was desperately trying not to laugh. I narrowed my eyes at him, and he gave in to the impulse, actually laying his hand across his stomach as he guffawed.

I snorted, taking off down the stairs. Still chuckling quietly to himself, Kellan followed me to my bedroom, lingering in the hall as I placed Infinity back on my bedside table.

The house pinged a warning right before it opened the front gate to admit the first of our guests—the twins, Gitta, Len, and Aisling Conall.

I crossed back toward the hall.

At the door, Kellan reached for me, asking for my hand. And I knew that meant more than the simple gesture indicated.

"You already gave me a yes," he murmured. "And you are too brave...too fierce to back away now."

I nodded, repeating his declaration back to him. "I would have you know me. I would know you. Just...maybe somewhere more private?"

He chuckled. "I'm sure we'll figure something out. There are a lot of bedrooms."

I gasped playfully. "The least you could do is woo me a little first, Kellan Conall."

Wrapping his arm around me, he pressed me gently against his chest. "Let's start with your Christmas gift, shall we, Dusk Godfrey?"

I nipped his bottom lip, and he grumbled appreciatively. "Yes, let's start there."

It snowed at dusk.

I bundled up, but couldn't manage to get Sisu to wear a coat over his hoodie. Or a hat.

The barefoot death goddess at my side looked resplendent in her silky red dress. I wore the amulet that housed Morgan's remains—most likely the ashes of her heart, but possibly a mixture of other organs as well. It was next to my skin, tucked under many layers designed to keep out the chill. The amulet was far, far heavier than it should have been. And almost uncomfortably warm.

Sisu raced ahead of us, across the back lawn and toward the greenhouse. We were going to check on the imp eggs and on Gee the gnome.

Morgan raised her face to the tiny snowflakes, then flicked out her blackened tongue to catch one. She glanced at me from the corner of her eye. "This will do."

I grinned at her. Our guests had left an hour before, off to family dinners and other holiday gatherings. The twins had put up a bit of a fuss, but Gitta was strangely quiet. In fact, she hadn't said a word to Len for the entire visit.

In the deepening shadows, the red of Morgan's dress reminded me suddenly of Brendan Prince's lifeblood. I hadn't felt the lingering memory of that blood across my skin for hours. Not since I'd spoken to Morgan and kissed Kellan.

"Yes." I scanned the property. Sisu was all the way to the greenhouse now and tugging on the door, which apparently wouldn't open for him. He was carrying a pineapple. A gift for the gnome. "This will more than do."

ACKNOWLEDGEMENTS

With thanks to:

MY STORY & LINE EDITOR

Scott Fitzgerald Gray

MY PROOFREADER

Pauline Nolet

MY BETA READERS

Anteia Consorto, Terry Daigle, Gael Fleming,
and Megan Gayeski Pirajno.

FOR THEIR CONTINUAL ENCOURAGEMENT, FEEDBACK, & GENERAL ADVICE

Nicole Deal – for the illustration of Kellan
SFWA
The Office
The Retreat

ABOUT THE AUTHOR

MEGHAN CIANA DOIDGE IS AN AWARD-WINNING WRITER based out of Salt Spring Island, British Columbia, Canada. She has a penchant for bloody love stories, superheroes, and the supernatural. She also has a thing for chocolate, potatoes, and cashmere.

For recipes, giveaways, news, and glimpses of upcoming stories, please connect with Meghan on her:

New Release Mailing List: http://eepurl.com/AfFzz
Personal blog, www.madebymeghan.ca
Twitter, @mcdoidge
Facebook, Meghan Ciana Doidge
Email, info@madebymeghan.ca

Please also consider leaving an honest review at your point of sale outlet

ALSO BY MEGHAN CIANA DOIDGE

NOVELS

After the Virus
Spirit Binder
Time Walker
Cupcakes, Trinkets, and Other Deadly Magic (Dowser 1)
Trinkets, Treasures, and Other Bloody Magic (Dowser 2)
Treasures, Demons, and Other Black Magic (Dowser 3)
I See Me (Oracle 1)
Shadows, Maps, and Other Ancient Magic (Dowser 4)
Maps, Artifacts, and Other Arcane Magic (Dowser 5)
I See You (Oracle 2)
Artifacts, Dragons, and Other Lethal Magic (Dowser 6)
I See Us (Oracle 3)
Catching Echoes (Reconstructionist 1)
Tangled Echoes (Reconstructionist 2)
Unleashing Echoes (Reconstructionist 3)
Champagne, Misfits, and Other Shady Magic (Dowser 7)
Misfits, Gemstones, and Other Shattered Magic (Dowser 8)
Gemstones, Elves, and Other Insidious Magic (Dowser 9)
Demons and DNA (Amplifier 1)
Bonds and Broken Dreams (Amplifier 2)
Mystics and Mental Blocks (Amplifier 3)
Idols and Enemies (Amplifier 4)
Misplaced Souls (Misfits 1)
Awakening Infinity (Archivist 0)
Invoking Infinity (Archivist 1)
Compelling Infinity (Archivist 2)

NOVELLAS/SHORTS

Love Lies Bleeding
The Graveyard Kiss (Reconstructionist 0.5)
Dawn Bytes (Reconstructionist 1.5)
An Uncut Key (Reconstructionist 2.5)
Graveyards, Visions, and Other Things that Byte (Dowser 8.5)
The Amplifier Protocol (Amplifier 0)
Close to Home (Amplifier 0.5)
The Music Box (Amplifier 4.5)

DOWSER SERIES ♦ BOOK 1

CUPCAKES, TRINKETS, *and other* **DEADLY MAGIC**

MEGHAN CIANA DOIDGE

DOWSER SERIES ♦ BOOK 2

TRINKETS, TREASURES, *and other* **BLOODY MAGIC**

MEGHAN CIANA DOIDGE

DOWSER SERIES ♦ BOOK 3

TREASURES, DEMONS, *and other* **BLACK MAGIC**

MEGHAN CIANA DOIDGE

ORACLE SERIES ♦ BOOK 1

I SEE ME

MEGHAN CIANA DOIDGE

ORACLE SERIES ♦ BOOK 2

I SEE YOU

MEGHAN CIANA DOIDGE

ORACLE SERIES ♦ BOOK 3

I SEE US

MEGHAN CIANA DOIDGE

RECONSTRUCTIONIST SERIES ♦ BOOK 1

Catching Echoes

MEGHAN CIANA DOIDGE

RECONSTRUCTIONIST SERIES ♦ BOOK 2

Tangled Echoes

MEGHAN CIANA DOIDGE

RECONSTRUCTIONIST SERIES ♦ BOOK 3

Unleashing Echoes

MEGHAN CIANA DOIDGE

THE AMPLIFIER SERIES: BOOK 0

THE AMPLIFIER PROTOCOL

MEGHAN CIANA DOIDGE

THE AMPLIFIER SERIES: BOOK 1

DEMONS & DNA

MEGHAN CIANA DOIDGE

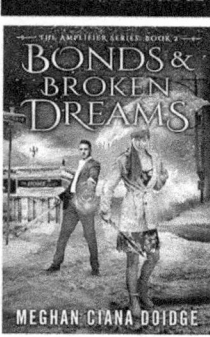

THE AMPLIFIER SERIES: BOOK 2

BONDS & BROKEN DREAMS

MEGHAN CIANA DOIDGE